MAKE THEM PAY

MAKE THEM PAY

MA COMLEY CRAIG MARTELLE
IAN W. SAINSBURY M K FARRAR JEFF SHELBY
G. K. PARKS MICHELE PW JR POMERANTZ
JACK PROBYN JOHN HINDMARSH D.K. GREENE
DREW AVERA DOUGLAS DOROW
STEPHEN COUCH ARLEIGH JACOBS N. GRAY
A.K. HUGHEY FALLON RAYNES TOM FOWLER
JONATHAN SHIPPERLEY STEVE DAVISON
KES MCDANIEL

CRAIG MARTELLE, INC

Cover by Ryan Schwarz, thecoverdesigner.com

Craig Martelle, Inc
PO Box 10235, Fairbanks, AK 99710
USA

First US edition, March 2021
ISBN (Print) ISBN: 978-1-953062-10-9

Created with Vellum

ACKNOWLEDGEMENTS

Curators
Craig Martelle
Robyn Sarty

Beta Readers
James Caplan
John Ashmore
Kelly O'Donnell
Micky Cocker

CONTENTS

FOREWORD

CRAIG MARTELLE

Make Them Pay – when those who think they are beyond the law come up against those who operate outside the law, get ready for fireworks.

I want to highlight the good work of the 20Booksto50k® Facebook group to improve the overall professionalism of authors across the world by helping them to help themselves.

This anthology is a part of that. What does it take to write a story to a professional standard and then work with a publisher to bring it to the reading public? There are some great stories in here.

The benefit of putting these together is in working with the great people out there, authors I would have never otherwise met. Same with you. However you found this volume, you made the right decision in picking it up. You won't be disappointed, and who knows, you may find your next favorite author within.

This volume was about bringing justice for those who couldn't bring it themselves. We want that champion to exist. And we want them to deliver harsh justice to those who deserve it.

And nothing more. Save the day and enjoy well-deserved time on the beach, listening to the waves roll in.

And maybe a live heavy metal band playing at the pool nearby. I digress. Music is a guilty pleasure that I enjoy. I can never do away with a smartphone now since I have a gazillion books downloaded to it and a about twenty Gb of music, painstakingly organized into playlists. And Bluetooth headphones.

In my thriller, music is big in his life, too. Rush. Bring it.

Go have some fun. Disappear into other worlds for a short time and enjoy the ride. I hope you like what you see.

Craig

SYSTEM FAILURE

M K FARRAR

When the system fails, only murder will put it right.

1

"Pull me up!" Terror filled the man's voice. "Please, don't do this!"

It was three a.m., and no one was around to hear his cries.

The man dangled from the bridge, only the rope wrapped around his shins and tied to the metal railings preventing him from falling into the rushing waters of the River Avon below.

In the distance, Bristol's city lights winked in the night sky. Light pollution meant the stars weren't visible, but the moon was almost full, casting the world in a silvery glow.

Tonight, the captor embraced the darkness.

The man writhed and squirmed, reminding his captor of a moth trying to thrash its way out of a chrysalis. If he managed to free himself, however, it wouldn't help him at all. All that would happen was he'd achieve what had already been planned, and he'd fall, headfirst into the river.

Not that it mattered. He was going to fall anyway.

Blood from the gash above the man's eyebrow dribbled into his hairline. Fat droplets plummeted through the air and landed, unseen, into the river, the red vanishing in the gallons of churning water.

Normally, at this time of year, the water would be slower and not so deep, but the previous day one month of rain had fallen in twenty-four hours, so now the possibility of menace filled its black depths.

"Please, you don't have to do this. Let me go!"

The captor leaned over the barrier to watch the struggling bug. "Not going to happen."

He'd considered using tape to cover the man's mouth, preventing this kind of exchange from happening, but if the body was found with residues of glue across his lips, the police would know this hadn't been an accident, or even suicide. It was the same reason he'd snapped on a pair of gloves and had a baseball hat pulled down over his already short hair—though the hat would hide his face should he be caught on CCTV.

Besides, he was enjoying hearing him beg.

The knots in the rope would give out eventually—they'd been tied in exactly the right way so after a certain amount of struggling, they'd finally come unravelled. The man might be begging to be pulled back up, but the captor had no intention of doing so.

There was a chance the rope was going to leave marks around the thighs and ankles, but there wasn't anything he could do about that. He'd hoped the jeans and boots would go some way to protecting the skin, but he couldn't protect it completely. If he got lucky, by the time the body was discovered, it would have been so battered against the rocks and bottom of the river the marks wouldn't be so obvious.

"Help!" the man screamed, bucking and thrashing. "Someone, help me."

The movement only loosened the rope, his body weight working it farther down his shins. If the boots came off, he'd fall.

"Careful," the captor warned in a low growl. "Keep doing that and the knot's going to give."

The man froze, and a whimper drifted up to the captor.

He took cold satisfaction in the sound.

Earlier that day...

Detective Ryan Chase lined up the items on the left side of his desk—pencil pot, calculator, stapler—and then on the right—notepad, personalised mug, screen cleaner. He almost turned away, but the niggling voice in his head insisted something was wrong and needed to be checked again. He scoured the surface to discover his mouse was too far to the right on the mouse mat. With one finger, he nudged it slightly back to the left, allowing the tension to release inside his chest and the insistent voice to quieten, if only for the moment.

"Everything okay, sir?"

He jerked his head up at the sound of his sergeant's voice and gave a curt nod. "Yeah, everything's fine."

His palms itched to check the position of the items again, but he clenched his hands into fists and stuffed them in his pockets. "See you tomorrow."

Detective Sergeant Mallory Lawson picked up her coat and slung her bag over her shoulder. "We're going for a drink down at the Cliff Arms, if you fancy it?"

He shook his head. "Not tonight, Lawson. Thanks anyway."

But she hesitated, clearly not wanting to let it go. "You sure? I figured you might want some company, you know, because..."

Her voice trailed off, but he knew exactly what she'd intended saying.

"Thanks, but that's the exact reason I don't think I'll be good company."

He could have done with having someone who could vouch for his whereabouts tonight, but he was going to have to rely on his neighbour saying he was home. He'd make sure of that. He wasn't naïve enough, especially considering the business he was in, to think he wouldn't be looked at.

In his pocket, his phone vibrated. He sighed. He knew without checking that it was his ex-wife, Donna, but, despite the day, he didn't want to return her call. Maybe it was wrong of him, but she wasn't supposed to be his problem anymore.

He wondered if he should feel guiltier about the way things had gone down with them. Should he check she was all right, or was it just going to end up being yet another conversation about how things should have been different? He couldn't tell her, of course. Couldn't tell her things *would* be different, she just needed to give him a few more hours.

Donna had held him responsible. He'd assured her things would go the right way and they could trust in the system. The law was his thing —he was a part of it—and it had failed her.

It had failed all of them.

That was why he was in this position now.

Mallory threw him an additional smile. "You're always bad company, but we keep inviting you anyway."

"More fool you. But seriously," he faked a yawn and rubbed his hand across his face, "I'm pretty beat. One drink and I'll be asleep on the table. I just want to go home and get my head down."

His sergeant knew what day it was just as much as he did, which was why she was so hesitant to let him go, but she couldn't force him. Besides, the rest of the team had left already, and she was going to miss out on the first round.

"Hope you manage to get some sleep then," she said. "See you tomorrow."

He nodded but stayed in position, waiting for her to leave. There was no chance of him getting any sleep tonight, but not for the reason Lawson assumed.

He waited until she'd vanished out of the door, and then he turned back to his desk and reorganised the contents.

Ryan hadn't been lying when he'd said he was going home. Not that his flat was much of a home these days. It was a place he ate and slept, but he felt more at ease when he was at the office.

Before he did anything else, he knocked on his neighbour's door. She answered almost immediately.

Mrs Furst was in her eighties but remained sharp upstairs and religiously walked three miles every day.

"Hello, Ryan." Her gaze flicked across his face. "You look like shit."

"Thanks, Mrs Furst. I appreciate the compliment."

She sniffed and shrugged. "I say it as I see it. What can I do for you?"

"I'm waiting on a parcel and wondered if anything had been dropped off with you while I was out?"

She frowned. "No, nothing was left with me, sorry."

He already knew that would be the case. He'd made sure to order the parcel with a delivery date estimated to be between today and tomorrow, but that he knew from past experience ran notoriously late.

"Ah, that's a shame. I was hoping to have it for tonight. Guess I'll be spending the evening in front of the television with a cold beer. It's been a long week. Have you got any plans yourself?"

Her eyes narrowed in suspicion at his questions. "I hope you're not thinking of asking me out. You're not really my type."

He chuckled. "That's okay, Mrs Furst. You're not really my type either. I was just being polite."

"That's a relief. Have a good evening. I'll keep an eye out for that package of yours."

"I appreciate that."

She closed the door, and he crossed the hallway to his flat, happy to have planted the seed. Hopefully, should she be asked, she'd say he was home all night.

There was nothing more he could do now except prepare himself. He resisted opening the liquor cabinet and helping himself to a drink, hoping to quiet his own voice in his head. But he needed to stay sharp. He'd been preparing for this day for a long time and he wasn't going to fuck it up now by making a stupid mistake.

Ryan checked his front door, making sure it was locked, and then turned the television up loud enough to be heard through the wall, but not loud enough to warrant any complaints.

The items he needed were already in the boot of the car. He swapped his suit for some black jeans, and an equally black hoodie, and stuffed his feet into a pair of boots that were a size too small. He would pull the hoodie up to hide his face and add extra protection with a baseball cap wedged down on top of that. He made sure none of the items had any defining marks on them. He knew better than anyone that the slightest detail could unravel a case. His final addition was some disposable gloves.

He hesitated.

Had he locked the front door? Was he sure? How did he know he hadn't imagined it?

Knowing he wouldn't be able to silence his brain and focus on anything else, he gave in quicker than normal. *One, two, three, four...* twists of the handle. Yes, the door was definitely locked.

It was time.

Thankful his flat was on the ground floor, Ryan climbed out of the rear window. He made sure it was still unlocked so he could get back in the same way. *One, two, three, four.* Yes, safe. He straightened and glanced around, ensuring he hadn't been seen. He didn't want there to be any reason he'd have to explain himself. He wanted Mrs Furst to be able to say, if asked, that he'd got home at seven p.m. and hadn't left again until morning.

A set of rented garages were positioned at the back of the building. He paid just over fifty quid a week for the privilege of renting one, but in the city, where parking was hard to come by, it was worth every penny. But his car had been parked on the street for the past couple of days, and another vehicle was hidden behind the garage door.

He'd wanted to keep the old Ford Mondeo out of view. He'd bought it from a crooked body shop, paying cash, knowing full well the owner of the garage wouldn't put it through the books. The car was destined for the scrap heap anyway and most likely wouldn't make it through an MOT. Not that Ryan cared about that. He was planning to drive it to the scrapper first thing in the morning.

The number plate was partially obscured with a splatter of mud—something he was taking a gamble on. It increased his likelihood of being pulled over by a uniformed officer, but if that happened, he'd placed his bets on being able to talk his way out of it. Being stopped would screw up the rest of his plans, however, and he'd have to rethink, but he figured that was better than the alternative—having the plate identified via the increasingly large number of CCTV cameras around the city and it being traced back to him.

He rounded the car and clicked open the boot, double-, triple-, and quadruple-checking he had everything he needed, and then climbed behind the wheel.

He drove to the street where the block of council flats was located and parked on an unlit part of the road. Cole Fielding would be getting home within the next thirty minutes.

Ryan yanked the hood up over his head and wedged the baseball cap down to hide his face. From previous surveillance, he'd already pinpointed exactly where the CCTV cameras were on this road, and even which of the flats had their own home security. Luckily, the poverty in this area meant they were few and far between. Anyone who'd dare to place such expensive equipment on the outside of their properties would most likely end up with it nicked anyway.

He'd deliberately left his phone at home, aware it could be tracked, if needed, but right now he wished he'd brought it with him. He needed a distraction. What if the little bastard decided not to come straight back to the flat?

Cole Fielding had only been released from prison first thing this morning and had already been set up with a job. It was only working behind the counter of a local Co-op, but Ryan didn't think the fucker deserved even that. It was some do-gooder, outreach programme, handing ex-convicts a job and a place to live before they even got out in the hope that they wouldn't go on to reoffend. Normally, Ryan would have supported such programmes, but he couldn't in this case. It was bad enough that Cole had only been inside for a handful of years, but then to be handed a brand-new life with no effort on his part, sickened him.

Where was he? Cole should have been here by now.

Maybe he'd stopped by the pub or met up with some old friends, though Ryan wondered how many of them he had left after what had happened. At Cole's age, all his old school buddies would probably have drifted off by now and forgotten about him. Gone on to do bigger and better things and left him behind.

Good, it was the least the bastard deserved.

Movement caught Ryan's eye, and he sat up straighter, trying to get a better look. Sure enough, Cole sauntered down the street, his hands shoved in his pockets, and a 'don't fuck with me' expression on his smug face. He kicked out at a Coke can, which hit a nearby parked car and bounced off again. Cole laughed.

Prick.

Rage filled Ryan, and he did his best to focus his emotions. Losing his shit now wasn't going to help him. He needed to stay calm and in control. Reaching into the footwell of the car, he picked up an item he'd kept there for this moment.

He waited until Cole had walked past—not noticing there was someone in the car—and then Ryan carefully opened the door and climbed out. Cheap earphones plugged Cole's ears—not the wireless expensive brand kids wore these days, but the cheap kind that came free with the purchase of a mobile phone. That he had anything at all in this world only served to increase Ryan's anger.

The stairwell leading to each floor of the high-rise was positioned on the outside, with only cracked and graffitied glass boxing it in. Ryan let Cole pull open the door and go inside, but before the heavy door could swing fully shut, Ryan put out a gloved hand and stopped it. In his other hand, he held a thick coil of rope.

Mercifully, no one else was around, but even if they were, they wouldn't have recognised him. He kept the hoodie up, the baseball cap yanked down over the top of it. At a glance, and from a distance, he guessed an onlooker would put him at a much younger age. Not a man in his forties.

Ryan picked up on the tinny beat of the music from the headphones. Cole literally wouldn't hear him coming.

Gripping the rope in both hands, he took several fast strides up the staircase, behind Cole. When he was close enough, he hooked the rope over the top of the man's head, so it settled around his neck in exactly the right position, and then snapped it tight.

He yanked Cole off his feet, dragging him back down the handful of steps he'd managed to climb. Ryan lost his footing with the weight of the man and slipped down the final two steps but managed to stay upright.

Cole might be young, but he was also only about five foot ten, and had a slender build. Though Ryan had twenty years on him, he was also an inch over six foot and had been preparing for this ever since he'd heard how soon the son of a bitch was getting out. Whatever spare time he had in between the job he spent down the gym, pushing himself harder, lifting heavier, driving himself to exhaustion.

A strangled cry of surprise and anger burst from between the other man's lips. Cole's hands automatically went to the rope around his neck, scraping at it, trying to create space between the coarse fibres and his skin.

Cole was strong, but Ryan couldn't let him get the upper hand. There was too much chance of someone walking down the stairwell or spotting them from the street. He'd been lucky so far, in that things had remained quiet, but that luck was bound to run out eventually.

Cole's feet peddled against the concrete floor. Ryan pulled tighter on the rope. He didn't intend to kill him—not yet anyway—but he needed him unconscious so he could move him.

The younger man's eyes bulged, his face turning puce. He clawed and scrabbled at the rope with his fingers, and strangled whistles escaped his lips. His back arched and bucked, but all his focus was on the rope around his throat.

Ryan felt nothing but cold fury. He yanked the rope tighter. He could kill him right now if he wanted to. He had it in him. But no, he wanted to make sure Cole Fielding knew exactly who was handing him his death and the reason behind it, and he couldn't do that here.

It seemed like eternity, but finally Cole went limp and slumped to the floor.

Ryan hesitated for a moment, wanting to make sure he was definitely unconscious, but not wanting to push his luck so he ended up either killing Cole or being disturbed by someone. He released the tension on the rope.

There was one thing he needed to do before he moved him.

He bent over Cole's motionless form and patted down his pockets. Sure enough, he located the shape of a mobile phone in his pocket. Ryan let out a growl. The phone was brand-new. It must have been one of the first things this fucker had done when he'd been let out. He dropped the phone to the floor and lifted the heel of his boot and stamped on it, releasing another burst of anger that he'd been holding on to for the past four years. The phone was in a dozen pieces, and he spotted the SIM card, picked it up in his gloved fingers, and snapped it in half. It wouldn't be traced any time soon.

He kicked the rest of the phone behind the staircase. No one would pay any attention to a smashed phone around here.

To be fair, they probably wouldn't pay much attention to him hauling an unconscious man around over his shoulder, either.

He bent over Cole again, checking for a wallet or anything else that might help to identify him.

The foot came out of nowhere, striking Ryan across the bridge of his nose. Pain exploded through his skull, and he covered his face with both hands. Fuck! He hadn't wanted to get injured in any way—anything that might get people asking questions wasn't a good thing. He checked his fingers. No blood. That was good.

Perhaps more important was that the shithead had rolled over onto his front and was now trying to crawl. Cole had been weakened by the attack though, and coughed and wheezed as he went, dragging himself elbow after elbow across the concrete floor.

Ryan couldn't let him get away.

"Where do you think you're going?"

He dropped onto Cole's back, slamming him to the floor. He wrapped his hands around his throat from behind and squeezed. Cole bucked and thrashed beneath him, but Ryan's superior weight kept him pinned, and the other man was still weakened from being choked by the rope.

Cole finally fell still once more, and Ryan risked releasing his hand from around his neck. His heart raced, and he raised his head, glancing around, certain someone would have seen him by now. Though he felt as though he'd been in the stairwell forever, in reality, only a matter of minutes had passed.

He was careful not to kill the bastard and pressed his fingers to the side of Cole's neck until the weak but steady tap of his pulse beat beneath his skin. Even dying here, alone, in this piss-stinking stairwell, was too good for him.

Ryan climbed off Cole and then leaned to haul him over his shoulder.

Shit, he was heavy. Heavier than Ryan had anticipated. Even with all the weightlifting in the gym, his back twinged in protest. He didn't care, though. Even if he ended up never being able to stand straight again, he would get this done.

With Cole positioned over his shoulder in a fireman's lift, Ryan checked the floor to make sure he hadn't overlooked something that would point towards him being here, and then pushed his way out the door and into the fresh night air. This was probably the most dangerous part—the part where he was out in the open, with numerous windows of the flats surrounding him. Even with the hoodie and baseball cap keeping his face covered, he preferred it if he went unseen. If someone challenged him now, he'd be screwed.

But his luck was in and, somehow, he made it across the small grassy area between the building and the pavement and reached the car. He hadn't bothered to lock the heap of junk, and he managed to balance Cole at the same time as depressing the button to pop the boot. He lowered his head and shoulders and rolled the younger man into the empty space and carefully lowered the lid.

Finally, he felt like he could breathe.

This was far from done yet.

He drove out of the city, praying his partially obscured number plate wouldn't get him pulled over. Within fifteen minutes, he'd left the bright lights of the city behind and was driving through the surrounding countryside. He knew exactly where he was going. It was far enough away from the city that it would be unlikely he'd be disturbed during the early hours of the morning.

Ryan couldn't stop his thoughts going back to the day it had happened. He'd played it over in his head a million times before, wishing he'd done something differently, wishing he'd picked Hayley up from school just a minute later or earlier. It was supposed to have been a treat, Daddy picking her up. Because of his work, he rarely managed to wrangle it, but he'd been forced to take a couple of days' holiday or he'd lose them, and since they weren't allowed to take children out of school during term time anymore, he'd decided to use the time to catch up on some DIY at home while she was at school.

Hayley had slipped his hand to run across the road where her friend from school had been waving at her. The car had come out of nowhere. It had hit her full-on, sending her flying. The bastard had barely slowed. Ryan hadn't even got a glimpse of the driver, he'd been so filled with horror at the sight of his five-year-old daughter lying bloodied and bent in the road.

She'd died before the ambulance had arrived.

His life had shattered at that moment and never been rebuilt. On top of having to cope with the soul-destroying grief of losing his only child, and trying somehow to stop his wife from falling apart, he'd then had to live with the knowledge the man responsible hadn't even cared enough to stop.

Cole Fielding had been nineteen at the time of the incident. He was twenty-three now and still had his whole life ahead of him.

The police had tracked Cole down eventually, but by that time, hours had passed, and the breathalyser had shown he'd been drinking, but he wasn't over the limit. That didn't mean he hadn't been when it had happened, of course. He hadn't had a full license, and hadn't had any insurance, and claimed that was the reason he'd run, not that he'd known he'd been over the limit.

A later investigation had shown Cole had spent the whole lunchtime in a local pub. Witnesses had said he'd been drinking pints of lager with his mates, but they didn't have any proof of that. Cole had insisted that he'd only had one drink and would have been under the legal limit. When he was asked why he hadn't stopped that day, he'd said he'd panicked and hadn't known what he was doing. He claimed not to remember anything after the accident, but that he'd had a drink afterwards to settle his nerves. The back calculation by the forensic toxicologist hadn't been enough to prove for certain that he would have been over the limit when he'd run over Ryan's daughter. Of course, the prosecution argued that he'd hidden out, knowing he needed to buy himself time for his blood-alcohol levels to decrease. He hadn't been panicked or blacked out. The son of a bitch had known exactly what he was doing.

Cole had laughed in the courtroom. He'd called the family a bunch of wankers for putting him inside for an accident. He hadn't cared that he'd stolen a little girl's life and had destroyed everyone's lives who loved her as well.

That was what made it all so unfair. If he'd stayed and faced up to what he'd done, he'd have been in line for fourteen years inside, but instead he'd got eight and only served four of them.

Ryan had known he would never be able to continue his life knowing Cole was out there, carrying on with his life as though nothing had happened. He'd wanted to kill him then, but he'd needed to wait. He had no intention of losing his job and going to jail. That bastard had taken one thing he loved from him, and Ryan wasn't going to let him take something else.

He had him now, unconscious in the back of his car.

And nothing would stop him from making sure Cole Fielding paid for what he'd done.

By the time he reached his location, he could tell the man in his boot had woken. Steady thumping came from the back, together with muffled shouts. Ryan had anticipated him waking up again. While it was going to make certain aspects of the next part of his plan more difficult, there was also something he needed Cole to be conscious for.

He reached his intended location and pulled to a halt, switching off the engine and killing the lights. He threw open the door, climbed out, and rounded the car to stand at the boot. The thumps and shouts grew louder, and Ryan braced himself. Cole was going to put up a fight, but Ryan had the physical advantage now, in that he wasn't the one confined to a car boot.

Sucking in a breath, he popped the lid open.

Ryan was ready for him.

Instead of trying to throw himself out, Cole kicked, hoping to hit the detective in the face, but Ryan had anticipated the move and reared back, ducking the flying foot. The moment Cole drew back his leg back for a second kick, Ryan leaned over the other man and threw his fist.

A couple of swift punches to the face had Cole dropping back into the boot, groaning in pain.

Ryan checked the gloves to ensure they hadn't split during the punches. Satisfied they were still intact, he fished out the long length of rope he'd thrown in with Cole.

First, there was something else he needed Cole to do.

"You know why you're here?" he said to the partially conscious man.

"'Cause you're a fucking psycho," Cole managed to snap.

"Do you want me to break your nose?"

"Nah, man. Fuck's sake. You don't have to do that."

Ryan kept his voice level. "Then let me ask you again. Do you know why you're here?"

"No, I don't."

"You don't recognise me?"

Cole gave a wet chortle. "In that get-up?"

Fair point. Ryan had done everything he could to hide his face. A part of him wanted to yank off his cap and hood in some kind of big reveal, but the sensible part of him that still existed told him it wasn't worth it. If someone happened to drive past, he could be identified.

"I'm the father of the little girl you murdered four years ago."

Cole groaned and sank back into the boot. "Ah, fuck."

"Yeah, fuck. Now I need you to do something for me."

"What?"

"I want you to write an apology to my wife." It was none of Cole's business that she was now his ex. "You never said sorry for what you did, what you stole from us. Not once."

"I'm not writing no fucking letter."

"It doesn't have to be much. Just a few words admitting what you've done."

"You know what I did. I served time for it."

Nowhere near enough.

Ryan fished out the pen and paper he'd brought for this reason. Just like with all the other items, he'd made sure they were widely available and easily purchased from numerous shops so they couldn't be traced back to him.

He threw the pen and paper at Cole. "Write it."

"Fuck you."

"You want me to put the lid down and shut you back in there? It wouldn't take long for me to find somewhere to take the handbrake off and make sure it isn't in gear and have the car roll off a cliff."

Cole glared at him in the dark.

Ryan jerked his chin. "Just do it."

The younger man's scowl deepened, but he scrabbled around for where the pen and paper had fallen.

"What do you want me to write?"

"Something simple. I'm sorry for what I did. I hope you can forgive me—or something along those lines."

"And then you'll let me go."

"Yes," he lied.

Cole let out a sigh, as though doing this was so much hassle, despite him having robbed them of their child. Ryan's hatred intensified. He'd wondered if Cole's stint in prison might have changed him and made him more remorseful. Maybe, he'd thought, after he'd picked Cole up, if Cole cried and told him how sorry he was and how he regretted not stopping and should never have had a drink and then got behind the wheel, Ryan would have changed his mind. Perhaps he'd even have let Cole go. But this was the same little prick who'd been in court that day, still acting like the tough guy, not caring in the slightest that his actions had killed a child.

He scribbled out the note and shoved it back at Ryan.

I'm sorry for what I did.

"Short but sweet," Ryan commented.

"It's what you wanted, isn't it? Now, let me go."

Ryan cocked an eyebrow. "You can't have actually thought I was going to let you go."

He slammed the lid down again.

Using some rubber tubing he'd prepared earlier, he attached it to the exhaust pipe, then pulled it around to feed through the rear door window and push between the back seats into the boot. Cole hadn't noticed. He was too busy yelling, calling Ryan a cocksucker, among other things. The hollow thuds of his feet hitting the metal shell of the car were painfully loud. Ryan went back around to the driver's side, where he started the engine.

It helped to drown out Cole's panicked shouts. He clearly thought Ryan was going to come good on his threat to let the car roll off a cliff with him inside it.

But Ryan had other plans.

The exhaust filled the car with poisonous carbon monoxide fumes. It would be enough to knock him unconscious once more, but Ryan still didn't want him dead yet. He wanted the bastard to suffer.

The shouts and bangs filtered down to muffled knocking and finally died away altogether. Ryan gave it another few seconds, counting down to ten, and then turned off the engine. He went around to the boot and opened it again.

If it wasn't for the bloodied face and the abrasions around his neck, Cole would have appeared to be asleep. Ryan reached in and felt for a pulse. He was still alive.

He'd been lucky not to have anyone drive past him yet. If someone stopped, thinking, perhaps, that he'd broken down and was in need of help, he'd be in trouble. He was betting on the general public's tendency not to stop for strange men in a remote area in the middle of the night to keep him safe.

Ryan picked up the length of rope and wrapped it around Cole's ankles and calves, so the bottoms of his legs looked like a bound piece of pork belly. As was his safe number, he knotted it four times—a loop of the rope, followed by a knot, and repeat.

He checked on Cole's breathing—shallow but steady—and then worked to lift him out of the boot. He strained hard, hauling him over his shoulder, carrying him over to the metal railings of the bridge. He looked down into the rushing water below. The drop was a good one hundred feet, and if Cole hit headfirst, which he hoped he would, the impact should break his neck, and he'd drown.

Keeping Cole balanced over one shoulder, he tied the other end of the rope to the metal struts of the bridge. He knotted it one, two, three, four times, and gave it a few extra tugs, just to make sure. He didn't want it coming unravelled—not yet anyway.

With a grunt, he hoisted Cole from his shoulder and onto the railings. He stared down at the water again. The same water that would become the man's grave.

The man teetered for a moment, hinged over the metal rail. Ryan grabbed him by the thighs and, without a second thought, pushed.

Cole fell through the air but was brought to a sudden halt by the tension of the rope. He hung there, swinging back and forth, upside down.

Ryan waited.

He inhaled a deep lungful of the cool night air. An owl hooted somewhere in the distance. The water churned beneath.

Then the screaming started.

How must it feel to wake up like that, to come round only to find all the blood had gone to your head and a river rushed beneath you? He hoped Cole was terrified. He hoped he was so scared he had pissed himself, so urine was running down the inside of his clothes and dripping down his face. Hatred filled him, swelling inside him, making him feel more powerful than he should.

"Oh, good," Ryan called over the railing. "You're awake."

"Pull me up! Please, don't do this!"

Ryan gave him a moment to swing and consider his life choices.

Cole continued to beg. "Please, you don't have to do this. Let me go!"

"Not going to happen," Ryan growled.

Cole bucked and thrashed in the air. "Help! Someone, help me."

"Careful. Keep doing that and the knot's going to give."

Cole gave a thin whine of fear.

Ryan went back to the car, and he picked up the item from the back seat. He returned to the railings and Cole, leaning over once more to see him.

"What are you doing?" Panic heightened Cole's voice. "No, stop. Wait!"

The pair of shears were the kind used for cutting branches off the tops of tall trees, and by leaning over the railing, he was able to wedge the blade between the first knot in the rope.

Cole's thrashing resumed. "You mad bastard! Let me go!"

"Grief will do that to a person, you know. It'll literally drive them mad. Make them do things they'd normally not even dream of."

With the shears, he snipped a knot.

One.

"No, please!"

"Say you're sorry."

"I'm sorry. I'm sorry. I'm sorry!"

"Not good enough." He cut another knot.

Two.

"What are you sorry for?"

"I'm sorry I killed your little girl."

"What about how you killed her. What was the reason you didn't stop?"

His voice was a high-pitched shriek. "I wasn't insured. I knew I'd get in trouble!"

"Bullshit. You'd been drinking all day."

He wedged the blade between the third knot. Snip.

Three.

"Argh! Stop! Stop it!" He was sobbing now. "Please, don't do this. Show some mercy."

The remaining knot strained against the weight it held.

Ryan's heart froze over.

"Like you showed my daughter mercy."

He didn't need to cut the final knot. As he watched, it unravelled, and the rope gave way.

Cole Fielding fell—down, down, down—and hit the rushing water beneath, vanishing into the dark.

Ryan sucked in a breath then slowly blew it out again. He trembled all over, his heart beating wildly, but it was done. It was over.

Almost.

He left the rope where it was, tied to the railing, the end loose. The pieces he'd cut away had fallen into the river and would be long gone by now. He hoped, should someone find the body, they'd assume the ligature marks were caused by a failed hanging, and, when the hanging had failed, he'd let himself fall.

Finally, he taped the note Cole had written to the railings.

First thing in the morning, Detective Ryan Chase would drive the car to a local crusher who he knew would be happy to take cash and keep his mouth shut.

He got in the car and drove until he spotted one of the few red telephone boxes that remained in this time of mobile phones. He'd kept some change in the cupholder for this purpose. He fished it out, then went into the phone box and called his ex-wife.

Donna answered on the second ring. He'd known she wouldn't have been able to sleep.

"Hi, it's me."

"Ryan? Is everything all right? Do you know what time it is?"

"Yes, I'm fine. I'm sorry about calling so late, I just needed to let you know something."

He sensed her sitting up in bed.

"Let me know what?"

"That system that failed us... I finally made it right."

ABOUT THE AUTHOR

M K Farrar had penned more than ten novels of psychological noir and crime fiction. A British author, she lives in the countryside with her three children and a menagerie of rescue pets. When she's not writing —which isn't often—she balances out all the murder with baking and binge-watching shows on Netflix. You can find out more about M K and grab a free book via her website, https://mkfarrar.com

INNOCENCE LOST

D.K. GREENE

When her son goes missing, a terrified mom uncovers a horrific kidnapping scheme disguised as a summer camp.

1

Mackenzie cursed the fog. Though she'd driven the route earlier, the twisting road was unfamiliar in the murky night. Static crashed through the music, adding to the misery as she snaked through a switchback. She smacked the radio. A pothole jolted the car, forcing her hand back to the steering wheel.

"Damn you, Barnacles," she muttered, and chanced a glance at the slouching form beside her. If she had weaned her son off his lovey before signing him up for camp, she wouldn't be braving the unlit mountain pass to deliver the forgotten bundle of fluff.

She squinted over the steering wheel. The twin pine columns that marked the campground entrance loomed on the shoulder like ghosts, and her blinker pulsed yellow on their bark as she turned between them. Mackenzie gritted her teeth. The fog was thicker here, collecting on her windshield like morning dew, diminishing her view beyond the car's nose.

The silhouette of the camp office materialized. She parked, rushed to the porch, and groaned as she reached the padlocked door. Mackenzie trudged back to the car, preparing to face Ryan's inevitable plea to abandon camp and return home.

Driving deeper into the compound, it seemed odd there were no lights glowing from the cabins or illuminating the communal toilets.

The dash clock read almost eleven. Most campers would be asleep by now, but the pudgy bear in her passenger seat promised one boy lay awake, consumed by fear of the dark.

Mackenzie counted the buildings. She parked at lodge nineteen, killed the engine, and waited for someone to investigate her arrival. The night was eerily still, a stark contrast to the noise and bustle when she'd dropped Ryan off that afternoon.

She cradled Barnacles against her chest and opened her door.

The damp chill pricked her skin. She pulled her jacket closed and listened for the telltale sounds of a slumbering camp. Her straining ears were met with silence. Pushing away an irrational panic, she retrieved her flashlight and clicked it on. Gravel crunched beneath her feet, amplified by the hollow night as she approached the blackened porch.

Her tentative knuckle tapped the door. She moved to the window, pressed her flashlight to the glass, and gasped.

"Hello?" She scanned the rows of unoccupied bunks, then knocked on the window. "Is anyone there?"

She hurried to the next cabin, refusing to accept her growing dread. Tears stung her eyes when she found it was uninhabited, too.

Heart slamming against her rib cage, Mackenzie searched the next building. Empty, as if the children and staff she'd seen hours before had never existed. She swallowed hard, willing her dry throat to function, and sprinted to another cabin. "Ryan? It's Mommy! Can you hear me?"

Only that terrible silence replied.

Each locked door protected nothing but empty beds. Mackenzie tripped and lost the flashlight. It hit the ground, then sputtered and went out. A cry of terror tore through her, shattering the night.

Her son was gone.

She must have missed something. She retraced her steps, telling herself all those people couldn't have vanished. But every empty path, abandoned building, and darkened trail told a different story.

Cold and confused, she tried to filter the thoughts bouncing around her head. Was this a Chernobyl inspired evacuation? Had the rapture happened while she was driving? Either way, shouldn't someone have called her?

The thought of her phone forced her back to the car. When it came into view, the driver door hung open and the dome-light cast a pale-yellow hue over the seats.

She tossed the bear onto the passenger seat, scrambled behind the wheel, and berated herself for leaving the key in the ignition. The impotent starter clicked and the dome light flickered. She grabbed her cell phone from the center console and dialed 9-1-1.

The line beeped three times and disconnected. She tried again. The three tones repeated, rattling her soul. Help wasn't coming.

Engulfed in anger, she threw the phone at the passenger door. It hit the armrest with a loud crack. Mackenzie ignored the impulse to dive after it and switched off every knob and button on the dashboard. She grasped the key again.

Please start.

The engine croaked twice and sprang to life. Mackenzie hugged the steering wheel like an old friend. She turned on the headlights and squinted at the wall of white fog.

The tires kicked up gravel when she turned toward the main road. The fog thinned at the edge of the treeline, opening the world to her again. Mackenzie flew onto the pavement and the car fishtailed, drifting across the pavement. She jerked the wheel and quickly realized her mistake. The rear tires skidded the opposite direction. Heart in her throat, she slammed on the brakes and held on for dear life until the car stopped sideways across the center line.

Usually steady and unflappable, Mackenzie was the family anchor. She handled broken arms and lost pets, schoolyard shakedowns and family drama. For nine years she'd escaped sleepless nights, soccer games, and PTA meetings in the pages of mystery novels.

The hero was always calm, following clues wherever they led. Mackenzie might not have a rakish detective hat, but she could tell the panic screaming inside her to shut up while she figured out what had happened.

At the bottom of the mountain, lights held the promise of a nearby town. Mackenzie pressed her foot against the gas pedal.

It was nearly one in the morning when she passed the first streetlamp. She found the police station and pressed the brakes too late, hopping the curb before the car stopped. Mackenzie peeled her fingers from the steering wheel and wiped her sweaty palms on her jeans.

The tiny station's lights were dim, like a small-town store that had closed up shop. Mackenzie grabbed her purse and retrieved her phone. Barnacle's eyes reflected the dome light, making them shine like they were about to burst into tears. She could hear her son beg her not to leave him behind and panic threatened to overtake her again. She took a deep breath, tucked the bear under her arm, and made her way to the station's narrow glass door.

"Hello? Is anyone here?" Her heart sank when she took in the unmanned information counter and empty desks.

A door opened in a nearby hallway, and a middle-aged man in uniform emerged. "I'm Sergeant Binn. Can I help you?"

"My name is Mac Jones," she sputtered. Her throat felt like it was full of gravel. "My son is missing."

Sergeant Binn glanced at his watch. "The bars don't close for another hour. Have you checked there?"

Mac's features tightened, and her voice rose a panicked octave. "He's nine."

"I'm so sorry. Where was he seen last?"

"On Trask Mountain." Mac set the bear down and searched her purse for the paperwork she'd signed that afternoon. She handed the packet over.

Sergeant Binn glanced at the address printed across the header. "Camp Kapsualla? When my daughter went there, it was Camp Broderick. It closed five years ago."

"It's open now. Here's their website." Mac jabbed the page while fighting the urge to scream.

The sergeant carried the paperwork to a computer. He typed, frowned, and turned the monitor toward her.

404 Page Not Found

"You did it wrong." Mac rounded the desk and typed the address herself. Dread filled the marrow of her bones when the error returned. She tried again. "It has to be there. I dropped him off this afternoon."

Sergeant Binn pulled the keyboard away. "Tell me what happened."

With her purse clutched in a white-knuckled grip, she told him about finding the camp deserted.

He entered the details in the computer. “You left your son at a closed campground, then when you went to pick him up it surprised you no one was there?”

“It wasn’t closed. There were counsellors and kids running around everywhere.” He looked unconvinced, and she used every ounce of willpower she had to not smack him. “It’s a summer camp.”

“If all these kids are missing, where are their parents? Why aren’t they filing reports?”

She took in the abandoned station. A shuddering breath rattled her lungs. “They don’t know.”

He raised an eyebrow. “How’s that?”

“It’s a week-long camp. Today was the first day,” she said.

“Why did you go back tonight?” Sergeant Binn asked.

“Barnacles.” At his confused expression, she added, “Ryan’s bear. I found him at home.”

Sergeant Binn’s eyes softened. “You drove up there in the middle of the night over a stuffed bear? Why not wait until morning?”

“Ryan can’t sleep without him. You said you have a daughter. Wouldn’t you do the same thing?”

He nodded, mouth a grim line. “Who else knew about this place?”

“My husband, Sam.” Mac’s heart froze. The responsibility of being the family messenger soured her stomach. She covered her mouth and whispered, “Oh, God. I haven’t told him Ryan’s gone.”

She searched her purse for her phone and burst into tears when she found it. A spiderweb of cracks rippled across the screen. She touched the display and it scattered in a rainbow of useless pixels.

“Use the phone in my office.” Sergeant Binn pointed to the room he had exited. “I’ll be right there. I need a few minutes to make copies of your camp forms and file a report with the county and state police."

Mac dragged herself to the office. His landline sat at the edge of the cluttered desk. She swallowed hard, picked up the handset, and dialed Sam’s number from memory.

While the phone rang, she practiced what she’d say. She should ask how Robby was doing. Sam had volunteered to stay home when their youngest son came down with a stomach bug. She’d been so glad to leave him behind to clean up puke. But now she needed him to tell her everything would be okay.

The call switched over to voicemail. Mac tried again. When the recording played a second time, she slammed the handset against the desk.

It was late. He wouldn't recognize the station number. The battery was dead, or he left the phone in his car, or the ringer was on vibrate. None of those possibilities made her feel better.

Mac restrained herself from throwing Sergeant Binn's phone and dialed the number one more time. Angry tears blurred her vision when the voicemail message played again.

"Sam?" She wound her fingers in the phone's cord. "It's Mac. I'm at the Carlton police station. Ryan is missing. All the campers are. I've filed a report and the police are checking the place out. I broke my phone, so you won't be able to reach me, but I'll call back when I know more." She didn't know what else to say about her living nightmare and added, "I hope Robby is feeling better."

Sergeant Binn appeared in the doorway with a coffee cup in each hand and a sheaf of paper tucked under his arm. "Were you able to get through?"

Mac shook her head. She accepted a mug of coffee and sat in a chair near his desk. "What do we do now?"

Sergeant Binn untucked the paperwork from the crook of his arm and dropped it on his desk. Ryan's camp forms peeked from behind a typed report. "We wait. Oregon State Police are sending a couple patrol cars to look around the camp. They've notified the missing persons unit. Search and rescue will head out at dawn."

Anger seeped through her veins like poison. "My son vanished, and we're just going to sit here and wait?"

He raised his hands in surrender. "Like I said, I got the report in front of the right people. I'd drive out there myself, but in case you didn't notice, I'm the only one on duty. I can't do much until I hear from OSP."

"You think something more important than a bunch of kids disappearing will happen in the next few hours? We've got to go up there. You can't abandon my son!"

Sergeant Binn's voice was firm. "Even if I had someone to cover the desk for me, I'd wait. It's not safe to hike the mountain at night."

Mac gestured to a photograph of a young girl on the wall. She had a broad smile and held a trophy up in the air. "What would you do if your daughter were missing?"

He frowned. "I'd get some rest."

Mac yanked the photo off the wall and slammed it onto the desk. "Maybe you're a heartless bastard who can shut off worrying about your kid, but I don't have that ability. I'm his mother."

A pair of Oregon State Police officers were sent to the campground. They came by the station afterward to ask Mac a few questions. They took the picture of Ryan from her wallet and said they hadn't found anything suspicious on the mountain.

They'd asked her to call Sam, probably hoping she'd hallucinated the whole campground story so they could send her home. The call went to voicemail again and she handed the phone to one of the officers to leave a message. Now, she rested in the empty holding cell. She pulled a wool blanket over herself and stared through the open door.

Though exhausted, Mac couldn't sleep. Time floated by in a cloud of misery until she heard unfamiliar voices. She hurried through the building. A slow stream of men and women flowed through the front door.

The group wore a mixture of the forest green button-downs of the Yamhill County Sheriff, blue and white jackets of the Oregon State Police, and hunter-orange coats of Search and Rescue.

Sergeant Binn noticed Mac and called her over. "Everyone is getting ready to head out." He gestured to a man in blue with deep frown lines. "This is Captain Shearer from Oregon State Police. He's taking the lead on your son's case."

Mac shook his hand. "Thank you so much for coming. I hope you find all the kids missing from Camp Kapsualla."

"Your son is our priority. He's the only one missing as far as the paperwork is concerned." Captain Shearer turned away.

Mac refused to let him ignore her. "Ryan isn't the only one in trouble. There were dozens of kids already at camp when I dropped him off. They need help too."

"Mrs. Jones, can you even describe these other kids?" Captain Shearer asked.

If he intended his words to make her feel small and scattered, she wouldn't take the bait. "They looked like kids."

"Do you have a way to contact their parents?"

"How could I?" The more the captain questioned her, the less he appeared to listen.

The captain wore an impatient grimace, "Your son is the only child reported missing. I can't tell my crew to look for other kids if we don't know how many there are, how old they are, or what they look like. I can, however, give them details about your son. When did he go missing?"

"Yesterday between noon and eleven p.m." Mac watched everyone check their gear and realized she needed to grab her stuff before it was too late. "Do you want me to ride with someone or drive my car?"

Captain Shearer sighed. "I know you want to assist us, but we'll take it from here."

With her hands on her hips, Mac gave the captain her scariest mom scowl. "I want to help."

"You can. Call your family and friends. See if Ryan is with them. Runaways usually go somewhere familiar."

"My son isn't a runaway," she said through clenched teeth. "Somebody took him."

"Until we have evidence, we keep every option open." Captain Shearer turned away. His voice boomed over the room's chatter. "Okay, everybody. OSP is heading this investigation. If you find anything, bring it to me. We leave in five minutes."

Mac raised her voice to catch his attention again. "I can show you where I dropped Ryan off, and the cabin they assigned him to."

He pulled a notepad and pen from his breast pocket. "Great. Write it down for us. That'll be a big help."

He walked away. Mac cussed under her breath. Her hands trembled while she sketched a map of the camp. Erratic smears threaded through the ink while she imagined stabbing the captain with his stupid pen.

When she finished, she gathered her things and delivered her map to the captain. "Here are my notes. But I can't sit here and make phone calls. I'm coming."

A thin-lipped frown accompanied Captain Shearer's hooded eyes. "Thank you for the information. To be honest, if you come, you'll be in the way. I'd hate to charge you with obstruction."

He waved the Sergeant over. "Binn, will you get Mrs. Jones a landline and a computer?"

"Of course," Binn said. He waved her into the heart of the building. "Come on. I've got a desk you can use."

"He's giving me busywork. Ryan isn't at a friend's house," she complained.

"Captain Shearer knows what he's doing." Binn led her to a small wooden desk with an ancient computer.

She dropped her purse and sat down. The computer's keyboard was yellow with age, and the tower's fans chugged sluggishly while it came online. Binn went to the station coffee maker and returned with a cup brimming with thick, black sludge.

"Thank you." Mac wrapped her hands around the hot mug. The coffee might be the worst she'd ever had, but it held the promise of caffeine. He returned to his office, and she spun in the chair.

Time to play detective.

She pulled her copy of Ryan's camp forms from her purse and flipped through the pages. The packet held schedules, his cabin assignment, and waivers for a variety of activities.

She read the event descriptions, reabsorbing the promise of a summer camp that didn't exist. When she got to the liability release, her eyes glazed over. With two kids, she'd signed enough waivers to wallpaper a house. She'd stopped reading them years ago, assuming they were all the same. Now, she forced herself to study each clause.

Halfway down the medical release form, her breath caught. She tapped the spacebar on the computer's keyboard and clicked the mouse. A security screen popped up. She grabbed the paperwork and rushed to Binn's office. "I need the computer login."

"Oh, right." He scrawled a password down on a Post-It and handed it over. "Do you know somewhere he could be?"

Mac dropped the packet on his desk. "No. You know the clause that gives event staff permission to take kids to the hospital in an emergency?"

"Yes."

She showed him the form. "I thought that's what this was. But it says I enrolled Ryan in a medical research program."

"What?"

"I need to know who's running this camp." Mac ran her hands through her tangled hair, restraining the urge to yank it out.

"When county records open, we can have them pull the name of the owner."

"I'm not waiting." She grabbed the papers and returned to the computer out front. The sergeant followed and hovered over her shoulder while she logged in.

Mac typed the campground street address into the search bar. It didn't take long to find the name of the family that ran the camp before it closed.

She typed the name in the search bar. "Look at this. There's a family with this name here in Carlton."

"Great work, Mac. That will help the girls in records track down some contact information." Sergeant Binn patted her shoulder.

"You seriously think I'm going to wait for regular office hours? There are what... thirty people in Carlton? I don't need help to track them down." Mac scrawled the address on the back of the camp forms and shoved them in her purse.

"We have two thousand people, actually." Binn crossed his arms, appearing offended. "Remember what the captain said about obstruction? You're supposed to stay out of the way."

Mackenzie gritted her teeth. "You don't want me to look for my kid in the woods. You don't want me to talk to someone who might know where he is. What am I supposed to do, Binn? Sit on my thumbs and hope for the best while some stranger does God knows what to my son? That's bullshit." She slung her purse over her shoulder. "Are you coming with me?"

"No. But... wait a minute." He left for his office and came back holding a small black cell phone. "I pulled this off a kid dealing pot at the high school. It's one of those prepaid things they buy at Walmart with cash. It's unlocked. No code to use it. Take it."

"Does it work?"

He punched a number in and the phone in his office rang. "Looks like it's still got some minutes. I don't know how many, but hopefully it'll get you through a couple calls."

Mac accepted it and started toward the door. She paused when an idea came to her that might help win over whoever she was about to wake up. "Is there a place in town that sells actual coffee? Something thin enough I don't have to drink it with a spoon?"

"Yeah. Go down Main a couple blocks. The coffee stand is on the right."

Mac exited the building, got into her car, and pulled off the curb. The undercarriage dropped into place with a jarring clunk when her wheel hit the pavement. She pressed her foot to the gas, determined to find some answers.

With coffee trembling in the cup carrier on the floorboard, Mac sped over a lazy road through fields of grapevine. She pulled around the circular driveway of an elegant farmhouse surrounded by a vineyard. The leaves glowed crisp and green in the early morning.

Someone looked down at her from the second story. When Mac got out of the car, they disappeared.

She peered into the house through the glass-panes of the double doors. A young man descended a wide staircase and opened the door. "Can I help you?"

"Hello. I'd like to talk with someone from the Broderick family."

"I'm Justin Broderick." He frowned. "What do you want?"

She introduced herself. "I'm hoping you can help track down some missing kids. Your family came up in my investigation and I'd like to ask you a few questions." Mac lifted her drink carrier like a sacrificial offering. "I brought coffee."

Justin stepped outside. He gestured to a pair of overstuffed deck chairs. "Let's sit out here, if you don't mind. I don't want to wake anyone up."

Mac set the drinks on a short table between them, using the moment to sort her thoughts. She wanted to scream at him, demanding answers. But he might clam up and throw her out. She had to stay calm. He took the black coffee, and she picked up the caramel macchiato.

"What were you saying about missing kids?" Justin asked.

"My son, and a lot of other boys and girls, have gone missing up on Trask Mountain." Mac took a drink, watching him over the rim of her cup for any hint of guilt.

"That's a long way from here," he stated without emotion.

"The kids were at Camp Kapsualla when they went missing. People called the property Camp Broderick a long time ago. Do you know anything about that?"

"Kap-su-al-la?" Justin repeated the name a couple times, drawing out each syllable. "That means... 'stolen', I think. Or maybe... 'to steal.'"

Mac set her drink down so quickly she nearly dumped it over. She scrambled to pull a pen and paper from her purse. "What language is that?"

"Chinook," Justin said. "At least a version of it used in trade. Before I got into grapes, I studied Pacific Northwest languages. Unfortunately, alcohol makes more money than linguistics."

"Who in your family owns the camp?"

"Nobody, really. It's held in a trust. My grandpa passed the camp to my dad and uncle. They wanted us kids to take it over, but I'm not interested in being a camp counsellor and my cousin moved overseas five years ago."

"That's when it closed?" Mac asked. "The sergeant at the police station said his daughter went there until it shut down."

Justin nodded. "Since then, I don't know what they've done with it. But I know who does. I'll be right back."

He went inside. Mac's anxiety leeched out of her in small fidgets. Her foot tapped the ground and her finger drummed against her half-empty coffee cup.

When Justin returned, he held a business card. "Here's the number for my dad's attorney. He'll know more about the property than anybody. I hope you find your son."

"Me, too."

The lawyer's office hid in an unassuming brown house. Only a hand painted sign hung near the sidewalk marked it as a business.

Mac got out of the car, a current of nervous electricity running beneath her skin. She made the short walk to the front door and rang the bell. A young woman in a fitted skirt suit answered.

"Hi, Rita? I called a few minutes ago. I'm here to see Davin Richards," Mac said.

"Come on in. Davin is waiting for you."

Rita led Mac to a set of doors at the rear of the sitting room and pushed them open to reveal an office. A short, balding man sat behind the oversized cherry wood desk.

"Mrs. Jones!" The attorney tottered around his desk to shake her hand. "Rita tells me you're interested in the Broderick property on Trask Mountain."

"Yes. I have some questions about it."

"Of course." Davin returned to his seat and offered Mac a chair. He pulled a thick folder from his desk and flipped it open. "When would you like to lease it?"

Leaning forward, she saw a monthly calendar. Her heart stopped at the large, red X's marked in a row through the current week. "You rent it out?"

"Isn't that why you're here?" Davin drew his finger across the page. "It's booked through the end of the month. If you don't mind waiting, we can fit you in for a retreat before the end of summer."

Notes scrawled in illegible handwriting filled the margins of the calendar. "Are all the rental bookings managed by your office?"

"Yes. The property was owned by a friend of mine. His son isn't interested in running the place, so it's being held in trust for the next generation. I rent it for my clients to cover property taxes and upkeep."

Mac flexed her hands, fighting the urge to leap over the desk and snatch his notes. "Can you tell me who is renting it now?"

Davin lifted an eyebrow. "If you'd like references, I have several repeat customers you can call. The camp has become quite the corporate destination."

"I need to know who's using it this week. Whoever is running the summer camp took my little boy." She scooted forward an inch, drawn to the calendar like a magnet.

"I think you may have the property mixed up with another camp. We only rent Camp Broderick to corporations and religious groups. Right now, it's being used for a team-building retreat."

She pulled the camp forms from her purse. "Last week, I signed my kid up for summer camp. I dropped him off yesterday. When I went back, the kids had vanished."

After glancing at the forms, Davin called out, "Rita, can you come in here?"

His assistant appeared in the doorway. "Yes?"

"See what you can find out about Camp Kapsualla. They appear to be using the Broderick address."

"There's nothing," Mac stammered. "They've taken down their website. I have no other records of them."

Davin rested his elbows on the desk and steepled his fingers against his chin. He narrowed his eyes at her as if trying to read her mind.

"I know it sounds crazy, but the police are searching the woods for my son. I tried to tell them about the other kids, but I don't think they believe me." Mac realized she'd been wringing her hands. She clasped them together and tucked them between her knees to make them stop.

He flipped through the folder's pages. "This week's rental is for a pharmaceutical company. They said their research teams needed some bonding time." He looked at Mac with wizened eyes. "But that's not what they're doing, is it?"

"No," she answered, breathless. She flipped the paperwork to the medical release page. "They advertised a summer camp, but this form says we signed the kids up for some kind of research program."

Davin read the fine print, then fixed his gaze on Mac. "How many campers went missing?"

"I don't know. Fifty? A hundred? I didn't count. But the place was full."

He dragged a hand over his face. "We need help."

"Oregon State Police, Search and Rescue, and Yamhill County Sherriff's office think they're helping, but they're looking in the wrong place."

Davin handed the papers to Rita. "Copy these for me and call the police station. Tell them I may have evidence of a mass-kidnapping."

"You believe me?" Mac's heart swelled. She could almost kiss him just for listening.

Davin wrote on a legal pad. "As the saying goes, the jury is out. But I'm more inclined to believe a frantic mother than a corporate giant. We leased the property to Persicer Pharmaceuticals."

"Aren't they the ones doing malaria research?" Mac asked. She sifted through her memory, pulling the details from the dark corners of her mind. "They wanted families to sign their kids up for test trials. My husband and I joked about signing our two boys up. With how much they were paying, we could have taken a nice vacation."

"Did you?" Rita asked her.

"No." A lump of emotion caught in Mac's throat as an image of Ryan strapped to a medical table flashed in her mind. "Do you think they're testing the vaccine on the kids?"

Davin handed her the paper he'd written on. "Practicing law taught me people will do anything to get what they want. This is the address for their lab, and the direct number for their C.E.O., Joseph McDonald. He's the one who signed the rental forms."

"Why are you helping me?" Mac asked. "What about lawyer-client confidentiality?"

"Persicer Pharmaceuticals isn't my client. The Brodericks are. I won't see their name dragged through the mud." Davin's eyes darkened. "Plus, I'm a grandfather. If anyone pulled a bait and switch on my family, I'd want answers, too."

"Thank you so much for believing me. I've been wandering around feeling like everyone thinks I'm an idiot," she said.

Davin walked her out. He rubbed his chin thoughtfully. "We'll make a few calls and see if we can't talk some sense into someone working your case. Get them off that damn mountain and over to Persicer. What are you going to do?"

"I'm going to get my son."

Mac sat in the lawyer's driveway and stared at Joseph McDonald's name and number. Deep down, she knew he'd taken the missing kids. If he hurt her son... she'd kill him. A fog of emotion smothered her thoughts while she strangled the steering wheel.

She was going to Persicer Pharmaceuticals but wasn't sure what she'd find there. Mac pulled Binn's spare phone out and dialed Sam's number, put it on speaker, then backed the car onto the road.

His voice was frantic when he answered. "Hello? Who is this?"

"It's me," Mac said. "Have you talked to the police?"

"Yeah. I'm trying to find someone to take Robby so I can go to the Carlton station. Where are you?"

"On my way to Salem. I think I know where the kids are." Mac pulled around a slow-moving tractor on the two-lane road. "I'm going to find Ryan."

"Mackenzie," Sam drew her name out long, "go back to the station. I'll meet you in a couple hours."

"I'm not going back. Everybody thinks I'm some crazed housewife stepping on their toes. I have to see this place and find out if Ryan is there. I love you."

She hung up. At a stop sign, Mac dialed the number the attorney gave her. A woman answered. "Joseph McDonald's office."

Mac made her voice calm and airy, "Is Joe in?"

"He's on his way to a meeting. Can I take a message?"

"Sure. Tell him I know about Camp Kapsualla." Mac turned onto the narrow highway and headed south.

"Please hold."

Soft music played before the line clicked. "This is Joe McDonald. Who is this?"

Mac tightened her grip on the steering wheel. "I want to know where the kids are."

"I don't know what you're talking about." McDonald's voice was low and tense.

Mac's cheeks burned. "Let's say you were making a children's vaccine, but you couldn't sell it until you proved it was safe. What would you do if you couldn't convince families to volunteer?"

The line got so quiet Mac checked to see if the call had dropped. He spoke again. "What are you, a reporter? Our research programs are the best in the country. I'd be happy to e-mail you a press kit."

A scream built in Mac's throat. She swallowed hard, forcing the knot of emotion down, and hung up on him. A few miles later, she pulled the phone's call history and re-dialed Binn's number.

He picked up on the second ring and babbled excitedly the moment she announced who she was. "Mrs. Jones! I'm glad you called. I just got off the phone with a lawyer who thinks a medical company set up a fake summer camp on Trask Mountain and took the kids for some kind of experiment."

"No shit? If only someone had mentioned a bunch of missing kids last night," Mac said.

"I know, I know. You were right. Captain Shearer is processing the report now. He just got off the mountain. They found child-sized shoe prints all over the property. Tire tracks for a couple big vehicles, too. Where are you? He wants to ask you some questions and compare your tires to the tracks at the scene."

"If he wants to check my tires, he'll meet me at Persicer Pharmaceuticals." Mac turned east on Pacific Highway.

"Mac, come back to the station."

"Why? If Captain Stuffshirt was going to listen to me, he should have done so last night. I'm going to Persicer to find out whatever I can. You're welcome to join me whenever you're done sitting on your ass, waiting for instructions."

"We don't have a warrant," Binn said with an exasperated tone.

"Well, maybe you should work on that." The desire to see where Joe McDonald worked propelled her forward. A flustered cop on the phone wouldn't stop her now.

"We have procedures to follow." His tone was firm. "Captain Shearer will form a plan once we have all the facts."

Mac's voice cracked with worry. "Ryan can't wait that long."

"We're all concerned about him. Let's figure this out together," Sergeant Binn urged.

"If you're worried, you'll meet me at Persicer in thirty minutes."

She hung up and drove through Salem's industrial district. She found the Persicer campus and pulled into the parking lot. The modern building was a towering block of mirrored glass.

Mac parked and watched the building. People in casual office attire passed through the doors. She wasn't sure what to do next. She couldn't simply walk in. Should she have waited for help?

No. She couldn't ignore her instincts. He was here. She could feel it. And there was no telling how much damage would be done to her son before the police turned up. He needed her.

An unpinned semi pulled around the corner of the building. Mac considered the unburdened truck while it crossed the parking lot. She left the car and walked casually through the narrow lane the truck had taken. On the back side of the gleaming office, she found several worn industrial doors attached to the loading area. An unattended trailer stood beside the dock.

A door into the building looked open. Mac crept closer. Someone had left a rusty coffee can at the edge of the dock, and a small box shoved between the door and its frame held it open.

Mac whispered, "God bless smokers."

She inched up the stairs to the platform and tiptoed toward the door. The muffled voices inside were barely audible over her pounding heart. Taking a deep breath, Mac gathered her courage and placed her trembling fingers on the handle.

The door's rusty hinges squealed. Mac flinched, but no one came to investigate. She hurried inside.

Beyond the door was a small warehouse. Pallets of cellophane wrapped boxes lined rows of heavy-duty shelves.

Mac turned away from the sound of chatter. A forklift drove past the opposite end of the aisle, and she jumped behind the shelves. When the machine turned, she dodged across the gap.

She moved cautiously across the room. Hugging the stacked pallets, Mac crept to the end of the aisle and peeked around the corner. A modular office with wide windows faced the rows of pallets. Beyond the office, a metal door led deeper into the building.

Hands balled into fists, Mac fought with herself over what to do. She could retreat, call Binn, and wait for help. But she needed to know what was on the other side of that door. After another glance around the corner, Mac ran to the office, then dropped to crawl below the window. She made it to the painted steel door and scurried through into a long hallway.

A series of doors and windows punctuated the stark corridor. She marched toward the first door and noticed the card reader mounted in place of a handle. She peered through the nearby window.

The room was dark, but Mac made out chairs set in neat rows, like a classroom. She kept going, passing empty rooms until she hit one with the lights on. Mac pressed herself against the wall and peeked around the window's edge.

A short, brown riot of hair bobbed across the bottom of the window. Mac leaned closer and held her breath.

The room was full of young girls. Some walked a narrow path along the edge of the room. Others sat in groups of five or six atop a sea of sleeping bags. Mac heard the lock click before the door opened an inch. She sprang back against the wall in hopes the door would shield her from whoever was exiting.

"Eat your lunch. This will all be harder if you starve yourselves," the familiar voice of Joseph McDonald commanded.

"Yes, Mr. McDonald," the girls replied in chorus.

Mac kept herself from lunging at him while the door pulled itself shut. McDonald walked away, talking to a woman beside him. "We should be ready to start vaccinations this afternoon."

She hurried through the closing door. The lock clicked when it settled into its housing. Dozens of wide eyes stared at her. In a voice just above a whisper Mac asked, "Are you from Camp Kapsualla?"

Slow nods around the room sent goosebumps racing across her skin.

A tall girl in a t-shirt and shorts came closer. "Who are you?"

"My name is Mac. Do you know my son, Ryan Jones?" She searched the girl's face for some hint of recognition.

"No. There are a lot of kids we didn't meet before we got on the bus. I'm Sophia. Do you know my mom?"

"No, honey. I don't." The girl's glassy eyes split Mac's heart in two. She felt Sophia's need for her mother deep in her bones and reached an arm toward her.

"Don't," Sophia warned. She looked over Mac's head. "The camera will see you."

Mac lifted her gaze. A security bubble hung above her. She pushed against the door, but it didn't budge.

"You need a card." Sophia pointed to the badge reader.

Ice ran through Mac's veins. She scanned the room. The girls had sleeping bags, pillows, and backpacks. A pile of lunch sacks lay untouched below the window. Trying not to panic, she pulled the cell phone from her pocket and redialed Binn. The call went to voicemail.

"Sergeant, it's Mac Jones. I'm inside Persicer Pharmaceuticals. I found some kids. They're locked in a room. I am too, actually. I hope you're on your way." A lump formed in her throat and she ended the call. She tried to smile at the surrounding girls. "Okay, kids. Let's get out of here."

"We can't," Sophia said. "I tried running away the first time we went to the bathroom. Now they won't let us out."

Mac hadn't noticed the makeshift toilet. A yellow bucket with a hazmat sticker and a roll of paper towels sat in the corner.

A tiny girl in a stained dress whispered in Sophia's ear. She nodded and walked away. "I have to move, or they'll think something's going on."

Mac watched the girls for a moment. A happy squeal pulled her attention to a couple of girls hiding under the sleeping bags. "I have an idea," she announced. "Who likes trampolines?"

One girl raised a tentative hand. "I have one at home."

"Great. We're going to build one."

Mac coaxed them into bringing her an unzipped sleeping bag, and soon she laid beneath it. She'd instructed the strongest girls to pull the edges and stretch the fabric flat. Sophia's small friend climbed aboard the taut bedding.

"Let it go loose, then pull it tight all at once." The sagging lump of the little girl dropped dangerously close to Mac's prone body. The kids counted to three and pulled the edges taut. Squeals of surprise filled the air when the body above Mac rose a few inches. The entire group fell into giggles. They tossed the little girl higher.

The lookout at the window screeched, "Someone's coming!"

"Don't stop," Mac said. The girls threw their companion in the air again. Between their legs, Mac saw the door fly open. A set of adult feet rushed into the room.

"What are you doing?" a man shouted.

Mac scrambled to her hands and knees. Just like they'd planned, she charged the gap between the kids and threw her arms around his knees. "Push him over!"

The closest girls sprang at him. He fell backwards, pulling Mac to the ground. Her jaw snapped shut when he kicked out and smacked her chin with his knee. Despite the jarring shock, she tightened her grip.

"Sleeping bag!" Mac yelled. Before she lost her hold, they flung the undone sleeping bag over him and a pile of brave children pinned him down.

At her instructions, a pair of girls brought belts from their luggage. Mac used them to wrap his limbs together. She unlocked the door with his key card, then pushed it open and pointed toward the warehouse. "Run!"

The girls rushed the door. Once the last kid headed towards the back room, Mac let it shut. The lock let out a satisfying click before a dull thud sounded from inside.

She ran deeper into the building. A group of boys pressed their noses against the next window. She skidded to a stop and swiped the key card through the reader.

"Get outside, boys!" She directed them toward the storage area. Her heart stilled while she searched their faces, but Ryan wasn't among them.

Mac emptied two more rooms of children before security guards crashed through a door at the end of the hall. She hesitated. There were three rooms left to open, and still no sign of Ryan. The guards were closing in fast.

"Shit!" Mac spun on her feet and ran back the way she came.

She tripped on the threshold of the warehouse door and fell in a world of chaos. Boys and girls scrambled through pallets while workers ran after them. Mac scrambled to her feet and raced to the other side of the warehouse, screeching, "This way!"

Kids streamed into the aisle from all directions. Mac led them to the loading dock exit. She burst through the door with a wave of children behind her. The tide of bodies pushed her down the steps, and her kneecap hit the pavement with a sickening crack. Her pain-filled scream got lost in the thundering feet of scattering kids.

She had to get them away from here. Once the kids were safe, maybe one of them could tell her where to find Ryan. Struggling against the fire of pain, Mac gritted her teeth and pulled herself across the asphalt until a circle of security guards yanked her to her feet. Stars flickered behind her eyes when another ravaging bolt of pain cut through her knee.

Feeling helpless, she sagged in the guards' arms while a man with a devilish grimace approached. His voice was familiar when he said, "You've disrupted my child research."

"They aren't your kids to experiment on," Mac spat. She yanked an arm free to punch Joseph McDonald in the face. Her injured knee buckled, sending her off-balance, and she swung wide.

McDonald stepped back and laughed when the security guards let her fall. The pavement scraped her cheek, filling her skin with grit and her eyes with tears. The will to fight dissolved in a sea of failure. They'd recapture the kids, and now they had her, too. Would they punish Ryan when they realized he was the reason she'd come?

A far-off shout drew everyone's attention, and a string of police cars careened around the building. McDonald spun on his heel as though making a run for it, but Mac clamped her arms around his ankle. He struggled, but she hung on, refusing to let the bastard get away.

A police cruiser skidded to a halt nearby. Its doors flew open and Sergeant Binn leaped out, weapon drawn.

McDonald threw his hands up in surrender, and Mac finally let go. Her heartbeat pulsed through every strained nerve in her body when she tried to stand. She had to find her son.

After another officer cuffed McDonald and led him away, Binn holstered his gun and helped her up.

"You made it," Mac croaked.

"We couldn't sit back and let you have all the fun." He looked her over. "You look terrible."

"I feel worse. Has anyone gotten inside yet? I think more kids are in there. Have you seen Ryan?" She scanned the crowd around them.

"Mom?" Her son's voice rang through the air.

Mac's heart stopped. Just beyond her reach were the puffy cheeks, tousled auburn hair, and brooding eyes she'd so desperately searched for. Ryan leaped, tangling his wiry limbs around her until she could hardly breathe. She held his trembling body close while every fear and worry escaped in a torrent of tears.

Binn went to his car and reached inside. "Hey, you forgot something."

A smile tugged at Mac's lips when he returned with a stuffed bear. Mac tapped Ryan on the shoulder. He pulled away, face lighting up when he saw his fuzzy friend.

"Barnacles!"

Ryan hugged it to his chest and buried his face in its soft fluff.

Mac smiled at Sergeant Binn. "Thank you."

"I should thank you. If you hadn't figured all this out, we might've been too late." He considered her a moment. "Have you ever thought about joining the force?"

"Why? Are you trying to recruit me?" Mac snickered at the absurd question.

"Maybe. That was some impressive detective work," he said.

Mac might not have had the grit and swagger of a detective, but the boy in her arms was evidence she had good instincts. She turned the idea over in her mind. "I'll think about it," she said. The overwhelming relief of having her son safe left her mind fuzzy and her body drained. Thoughts about anything beyond the feeling of his little body pressed against her could wait. "Right now, I just want to take Ryan home."

She squeezed him tighter, vowing to never let him go again.

ABOUT THE AUTHOR

D.K. Greene became obsessed with the psychology of crime after police arrested the Green River Killer near her home. She has since watched way too many true crime documentaries, consumed countless books about criminal behaviour, and grew up to become the author of the *Killers Club* crime fiction series.

Greene lives with her wife and son in Washington State. She enjoys taking them on macabre day trips disguised as family outings so she can research locations for fictional felonies. They frequently drift off to look at souvenirs, pretending they don't know her when she says things like, "This would be a wonderful place to dump a body."

You can find more about Greene and her work at https://kawaiitimes.com/d-k-greene/

THE NINTH MAN

JEFF SHELBY

A man with a reputation for being able to find anyone joins forces with a woman seeking to avenge her daughter's death.

1

"You're the one, right?" Kara Safford said. "Joe Tyler? The one who finds the missing kids?"

I nodded.

She leaned back in the chair and studied me. "I've read a lot about you."

"A lot to read."

"You used to be a cop?"

"I used to be a lot of things," I said.

"You're still looking for your daughter?"

I nodded again.

"I'm sorry," she said.

"Did you take her?"

She sat up straighter, startled. "No."

"Then nothing for you to be sorry for," I said. "Why did you call me, Ms. Safford?"

She blinked several times, then cleared her throat. "My daughter. Luna. She was taken a year ago."

"From where?"

"She was on her way to work," she explained. "She was fifteen. They took her right off the street. Her bike was still lying there hours later."

"They?"

She glanced toward the window of the coffee shop, the Rio Grande just visible. "The cartel. On the other side."

"In Mexico?"

She nodded. "Yes. She worked in a coffee shop like this, but over there. Luna's father is a Mexican citizen. We've been going back and forth for years." She paused. "We used to."

"How do you know who is responsible?"

She smiled, but there was no warmth behind it. "Because it's the cartel and because they sent me pictures of her. After they'd killed her."

I shifted in the chair. "I'm sorry."

"Why? Did you kill her?"

I didn't say anything.

"It's what they do," she said. "They want to make sure you know it was them. You get pictures. Sometimes videos."

"Why was she targeted?" I asked.

She picked up the porcelain mug in front of her, took a long drink, then set it down. "My husband was...involved with them."

I looked around the coffee shop. I'd been in El Paso for a day. I'd come from Dallas, chasing down what ended up being a dead-end related to my daughter. Chasing dead-ends had become my life. I'd been doing it for several years. But I'd gotten into the business of helping others find their own missing family members. Helped pay my bills and pass the time while I wondered what happened to my own daughter. The irony was not lost on me that I could find other kids but not my own.

I turned back to her. "You already know what happened to your daughter. I'm not sure why you asked me to come here."

"There were nine men involved in my daughter's death," she said. "I've found eight of them on my own. I've committed my life to avenging Luna's." She studied me again. "We're alike in that way. When I read about how you gave up everything to find your daughter, I knew you were the man to help me."

"But you already know what happened to her," I said again.

"I don't need you to help me find my daughter, Mr. Tyler," Kara Safford said. "I need you to help me find the ninth man."

I got up to order another cup of coffee from the barista at the counter and mull over what Kara was asking me to do. I wasn't entirely comfortable with the scenario, but I'd learned to live with being uncomfortable. I headed back to the table and took note of a teenage boy wrestling with a flattened bike tire at the curb on the other side of the window. Parked on the opposite side of the street was a gray Chevy Suburban with blacked out windows.

I sat back down, but angled my chair just enough so I could see out the window.

"The amount I'm willing to pay is significant," Kara said. "I understand that what I'm asking is...different."

"I need to make something clear," I said. "I'm not willing to kill anyone or be a part of killing anyone. I'm not a bounty hunter and I'm not an assassin."

"I'm not asking for that."

"Sounds like you are."

"The other eight men?" She stared at me. "I found them and turned them over to authorities. I had no interest in killing any of them. My goal has always been justice for my daughter."

"What happened to them?"

"I can't say for sure," she answered. "Seven of them I found in Mexico. I turned them in to the local police. I have no idea if they've been held or charges filed. Information isn't always easy to get from the authorities there. My objective was to let them know that I'd found them and that I knew what they'd done." She shifted in her chair. "But I'm fully aware that the cartel's tentacles are wrapped tightly around the local police in Mexico. It's fully possible that they are back on the street. I don't know."

I glanced out the window. The boy had the bike upside down and was pulling an inner tube out of his backpack. The Suburban was still parked, the windows still darkened.

I turned back to Kara. "What about the eighth?"

"The eighth I found here in El Paso," she said. "I got lucky and got a tip from someone that he was in a barbershop about three blocks from here. I called a police detective I've established a relationship with, walked into the barbershop, and announced who I was." She smiled. "He was sitting in the barber's chair, a cape tied around his neck, his face half-covered in shaving cream. The police arrived about ninety seconds later. He's being held at the county facility while they work out...the details." She frowned. "Because it occurred in Mexico, there are jurisdictional issues and, quite honestly, it's not like I'm going to sit around and wait. I looked him in the eye and told him I knew. That's what I wanted."

The boy at the curb now was using a hand pump to inflate the inner tube.

The Suburban hadn't moved.

"What am I supposed to do when I find him?" I asked. "Again, I'm not a bounty hunter. I'm not going to cuff someone and bring them to you."

"Call me," she said. "I have a contact over there and they'll send local authorities to arrest him."

"If you have law enforcement involved and you've been successful in tracking these men down, why do you need me?"

She tucked a loose strand of hair behind her ear. "I'm sure you can imagine how much work this has entailed. To find these men. Maybe not at first, but after I located the first couple, the word was out. I was wearing disguises and creating fake identities to get to these men. Now, I'm sort of notorious. They know I'm out here. I can't get close enough at this point anymore." She paused. "But an outsider? Someone they don't know?" She pursed her lips. "That person can get to him."

The kid was still fiddling with the inner tube, trying to fit it around the rim.

The brake lights on the Suburban flashed.

So there was someone inside.

"I have an idea of where he is," Kara said. "A friend of a friend has shared some information with me. It seems he's in a small neighborhood on the south side of Juarez. Once you're across the border, it's a twenty-minute drive. He's been seen at an auto shop, which makes sense because he's done some work as a mechanic. And he's been seen at a bar there, which makes sense because he drinks regularly. I can send you to those places. I just need you to be able to tell me if he's there. I, for obvious reasons, can't just walk in and look for him."

"You should just call the police," I said. "If you can pinpoint him like that, call them and send them in."

"But then I don't get to look him in the eye." A sad smile crept across her lips. "And that is the most important part for me." She leaned forward. "I don't know what happened to your daughter, Mr. Tyler, but I'd imagine that you'd very much like to look into the eyes of the person responsible for her disappearance. Don't tell me you haven't imagined it. People like us, we think about it day and night. Maybe it's the only thing we think about."

She wasn't wrong.

"And my fear is that he's going to run," she said. "He has to know I've found the other men, so he's on guard. My concern is that he's going to leave and he'll be in the wind and I'll have to start from scratch." The smile reappeared. "And I will. I just don't want to."

The kid outside the window was rummaging through his backpack, looking for something else to help with the tire now, the inflated tube lying next to him on the ground.

The brake lights on the Suburban were still illuminated.

There was something she wasn't telling me, but I wasn't sure what it was. I was fairly certain, though, that a piece of the story was missing.

"I can write you a check right now," she said. "You can call the bank and verify the funds while we sit here. I would've brought cash, but cash makes you a target."

"You don't know what my fee is."

She nodded. "True, but I'm prepared. There isn't a number you can give me that will surprise me."

I gave her the number.

She reached into her bag, pulled out her check book, and scribbled. She tore the check off and slid it across the table to me. "Bank's phone number is near the bottom."

I glanced at the check. "This is for more than what I asked for."

"Consider it a signing bonus. You can call the bank. I won't be offended."

I folded the check in half and put it in my pocket. "We're good. I don't think you'd be dumb enough to write a bad check to a guy who specializes in finding people."

"We have an agreement then?" she said.

I looked toward the window again.

The kid was still fishing in the backpack.

But the Suburban was edging away from the curb.

I relaxed a fraction.

That was a mistake, though.

Because as the SUV pulled away, the kid with the bike yanked an automatic weapon from the backpack and pointed it at the window.

I took Kara Safford to the floor as the glass shattered. Bullets poured in above us and the noise was deafening as everything went to shit in a single moment.

I pulled the table we'd been sitting at onto its side as a de facto shield and rolled onto my stomach. Kara was already army crawling toward the back of the café. I followed her, moving as quickly as I could. Shouts of panic mixed with the gunfire and glass crashing to the floor. We reached the coffee counter and scrambled around the side of it, got to our feet, and sprinted into a narrow hallway.

The gunfire stopped for a moment, then started again.

More yelling and broken glass.

"My car's back here," Kara said as we reached an exit door at the end of the hallway.

"Hold on." I grabbed her arm. "They might be on the other side of that door."

She shook her head. "No. That was a single kid they hired. If it was a hit, we'd already be dead." She shoved the door open before I could say anything else.

The sunlight seemed brighter than before and I squinted as we rushed out. I followed her toward a white Lexus sedan in the small lot behind the café. She slid in behind the wheel and I managed to close the passenger door just as she floored the accelerator.

The car lurched forward and she made a hard right into the street, then ran a stop sign, her foot still pressed to the floor.

I checked the passenger mirror.

"No one behind," I said.

She nodded, then swung the car hard left, and I had to brace myself against the door.

She drove like that for a solid two minutes before she finally eased off the accelerator. Her eyes drifted toward the rearview mirror. "I think we're okay now." She cut her eyes in my direction. "I told you they're aware of me now."

"That was pretty bold, coming after you in coffee shop on this side of the border."

She nodded. "Yeah. But they don't send a teenager with a bike if they want to finish a job. That was just a message."

I kept my eye on the mirror. "You've been doing this since your daughter died? Playing cat and mouse with the cartel?"

"It took me two weeks after I got the pictures of her to gather myself," she said. "I felt like I had nothing else. I needed something. So I just decided to...do this. I've been shot at, chased, threatened, everything you can think of." She paused. "But they took Luna from me and I can't forget that."

Hunting these men was the one thing that gave her oxygen each day. I knew the feeling. Ever since my own daughter had been taken from my own front lawn, I had thought of nothing else but her and what might have happened to her.

She pulled to the curb. We were just outside of the downtown area, next a square park with patchy grass and a brightly colored play area.

"If you don't want to do this, I understand," she said. "This isn't tracking down a missing kid. There's a different...element."

I looked toward the park. A small girl was in the swing and a woman was pushing her. The girl was kicking her feet and giggling.

Kara was right. There was a different element to this. But I sympathized with the death of her daughter and I'd already taken her money.

I turned back to Kara. "I'll find him."

Kara told me that if he was still around, I'd find Eduardo Sanz in a neighborhood called Calles de Dolor.

Streets of Pain.

She gave me some more particulars and then dropped me at the border crossing. I elected to walk over because it was faster than driving and it gave me time to clear my head and make a plan.

The Juarez side of the border didn't feel that much different than the El Paso side. Businesses lined the paved streets, and people were moving about like they did in any normal American city. U.S. residents made a big deal of crossing into Mexico, but the only way that you knew you were in a different place was because you had to wait in a very short line to cross and most of the billboards were in Spanish.

I found a rental car agency and rented an old Volkswagen Jetta for fifty bucks a day. The woman behind the counter spoke near-perfect English and encouraged me to purchase all of the extra rental protections. I did so without objection and then asked her for directions to Calles de Dolor.

She eyed me for a long moment. "Sir, that is not a place you want to visit."

"Why's that?"

"Is not safe," she said. "Is not safe for me. Definitely not for you."

"Because I'm American?"

"Because you're an outsider," she said. "You're not from there. That place is for La Mafia. The cartel." She shook her head. "No one goes there on purpose."

"How far is it from here?" I asked.

She hesitated. "Maybe thirty kilometers. Is just south of the city. But, please. Do not go there if you do not need to. There is nothing there but problems."

I took the keys to the rental car off the counter and held them up. "I'll have these back to you tomorrow. And thanks for the advice."

"I am not kidding, sir," she said. "Many things get exaggerated about Juarez. The news makes it sound like all of Juarez is bad and that's not true. There are many good places to visit." She paused. "Calles de Dolor is not one of them."

Kara Safford said that Eduardo Sanz spent his time in two places in Calles de Dolor: the auto shop where he worked and the bar where he drank. I typed the name of the auto shop into my phone and saw that the woman at the rental counter had been exactly right. It was thirty-one kilometers away.

My phone led me through the city, and even though I'd never visited Juarez, I felt like I'd been there plenty of times. Strip malls. Traffic. Restaurants. Business parks. It was nowhere near the foreign land that Americans often tried to make it out to be.

The neighborhoods began to change, though, once I made it through the middle of the city. The buildings appeared less cared for. There were more abandoned storefronts. Fewer people walked the sidewalks. And traffic lightened considerably.

My phone indicated that I was only five minutes from my destination when I noticed the first group on the corner.

I was at a red light and there were three guys on the opposite side of the street. They were sitting on a stone wall, doing nothing other than watching. The middle one, a kid in a Nike T-shirt and jeans, pulled out a phone when the light turned green, and I pulled away.

At the next light, there was another group on the corner. Four this time, and they were older than the previous group. They didn't bother to hide the fact that they were watching me. No smiles, no curiosity, just hard looks. And at least two of them had bulges on their hips that indicated they were armed.

I nodded at them and pulled away slowly when the light turned green.

Verde's Auto Shop was at the end of a one-way road. The sign on the street was lit neon pink even in the middle of the day. Most of the repair bays were empty as I pulled the Jetta to the end of the road. I parked and got out.

There was a small office attached to the long row of bays and a small bell chimed when I pushed open the front door. The small waiting area smelled like tire rubber and motor oil. A single register sat in the middle of the counter and a box fan hummed in the corner.

I stood at the counter and waited.

Thirty seconds later, a guy in a red polo shirt and jeans emerged from the door on the other side of the counter. I put him in his late twenties. His jet-black hair was shaved on the sides and swept back on top, and his skin was flawless other than the diagonal scar that ran through the middle of his left eyebrow. A thin, gold chain hung from his neck, just inside the shirt and an oversized, silver watch hugged his right wrist.

"Help you?" he asked.

"Uh, yeah," I said. "Looking for a mechanic."

He looked over my shoulder. "That Jetta yours?"

I nodded. "Yeah. It's making a rattle of some kind. When I turn."

He moved his eyes back to me. "Yeah?"

"Yeah. Was told Eduardo was the guy to see?"

"Eduardo," he said. "You know him?"

"No, but a friend gave me his name."

The guy smiled. "Eduardo. He has a good...reputation."

"Guess so."

"You live down here?"

"No. Visiting."

"Family?"

"Friends."

The smile stayed on his face. "Same friends that told you about Eduardo?"

"That's right."

He nodded and laid his hands on the countertop. "We don't see many guys like you down here. This is why I ask so many questions."

"Sure."

He squinted at me. "Well, Eduardo is not here right now. But maybe I could take a look at your car for you?"

"Are you a mechanic?"

More of the smile. "Sure."

"I'd really prefer if Eduardo could take a look at it," I said. "No offense."

He held his hands up. "No offense taken, hermano. Cars are like our kids, right? We're very...particular about who gets near them."

"I'm glad you understand," I said. "Any idea when he might be back?"

"Probably soon," he answered. "But maybe you could go convince him to come back sooner." He lifted his chin. "He's just taking a long lunch over at El Cuchillo."

"El Cuchillo?"

"Bar across the street," he said. "Just go out way you came and you'll see it. Walk in and ask for him." He smiled. "Someone will find him for you. And no worries, hermano. I'll keep an eye on your car while you're gone." He winked.

"Ah, perfect," I said. "I'll head over there and see if I can talk to him."

"You do that," the guy said. "I'll be right here."

I walked out of the shop and headed back out the way I'd come in. I had no idea what I was walking into, but I was sure that I wasn't going to just walk into a bar and find Eduardo Sanz. Whoever I'd just talked to was setting me up. I was fairly confident he didn't even work there.

Because I'd never seen a mechanic with such clean hands.

I pulled out my phone and called Kara Safford as I walked.

"He's supposedly at a bar," I told her. "El Cuchillo."

"Who told you that?"

"Guy at the auto shop."

"There's no way they'd just send you to him."

"I know that."

"So what are you doing to do?"

"Unless you're going to call your law enforcement contact and tell me my work is done, I'm going to El Cuchillo."

The line buzzed for a moment. "I need you to get eyes on him."

"That's what I assumed. So I'm going to the bar to see what I can see."

"You need to be careful, Mr. Tyler," she said.

"I assumed that, too," I said. "Will let you know what I find. If you don't hear from me in an hour, maybe call your contact." I hung up.

El Cuchillo was a cinder-block rectangle with an empty parking lot and no windows. A small, hand-carved sign hung precariously over the entrance, and a banner was tacked to the exterior of the building, advertising 2 for 1 Tecates.

I walked around the back and found a rear door and a trash dumpster. I wasn't looking for anything in particular, but I wanted to have at least a superficial lay of the land. I wasn't crazy about walking into the bar unarmed, but the Mexican government frowned on bringing unauthorized weapons over the border. I could handle myself just fine, but walking into the unknown was an uncomfortable feeling.

I walked back to the front of the bar, pulled open the door, and stepped inside.

It took a moment for my eyes to adjust to the dim interior. A bar ran the length of the room to my left, with mismatched stools underneath it. Half a dozen tables filled the rest of the space. A neon Dos Equis sign hung behind the bar and a guy the size of the Incredible Hulk stared at me from beneath the sign.

I took the first stool and nodded. "Get a beer?"

The guy didn't move.

I looked around the room. We were the only two people there.

I waited for a few seconds. "No beer?"

The Hulk licked his lips, then moved toward the tap handles. He reached under the bar and came back up with a sawed-off shotgun. It looked like a twig in his massive hands.

"No beer, I assume?" I said.

The corner of his mouth twitched.

"Are you Eduardo?"

"Don't move and shut the fuck up," he said.

Thirty seconds later, the door to the bar opened, sunshine streaming into the dark interior. I didn't turn and look for fear of having my head blown off.

A man sat down on the stool next to me. He wore a light blue button-down shirt loose over a red T-shirt. His khaki pants were wrinkled and dirty at the knees, but not as dirty as his work boots. His black hair fell nearly to his collar and he hadn't shaved in several days. A diamond stud glinted in his left earlobe.

"Carlos, this our man?" he asked, keeping his eyes on me.

"Motherfucker walked in three minutes ago," the Hulk said. "Asked for a beer."

Something that felt distinctly like the barrel of a handgun pressed against the back of my skull. I had no idea who was holding it there.

"What's your name, boss?" the man on the stool asked.

"Joe."

"Joe," he said, smiling. "Regular old Joe. What are you doing here, regular old Joe?"

"Came in for a beer."

"Yeah, but first you went over to Verde's with your shitty rental," he said. "Mario said you were looking for somebody to work on your car." He raised an eyebrow. "Kind of weird that you're looking to get a rental worked on." He smiled. "And that you have a personal mechanic."

"Rental started acting funny as I was driving," I said. "Didn't wanna keep driving."

He studied me for a long moment. "Stand up, Joe."

I moved slowly, the pressure of the gun still against my skull and Carlos still aiming the shotgun at my face.

The man stood up. "Spread your arms."

I did as he said and he patted me down, pulling my wallet from my back pocket and my phone from the front. He flipped the wallet open, examined my driver's license, then tossed the wallet on the bar. He put the phone next to it. "Least you're not lying about your name."

I started to ask him what he thought I was lying about, but he buried a hard left hook into my ribs. Stars exploded behind my eyes and I gasped for air, but I stayed on my feet. He drilled me again in exactly the same spot and this time I did drop to a knee.

The man squatted down so he was at my level. "Look at me, Joe."

I tried to find some air, but managed to look at him.

"She send you?" he asked. "Kara?"

I coughed and spat on the floor, the pain spreading along the entire left side of my body.

He put a finger under my chin. "Joe. Listen to me. I'm Eduardo. She sent you, right?" He smiled. "You wanna live a little longer, you better fucking answer me right now."

"I came to fix my car," I said.

Eduardo chuckled and shook his head. "Dumb fucking gringo." He stood and pulled my phone off the bar. He grabbed my hand and pressed my finger to the screen until it unlocked. He dropped my hand and started scrolling through my phone.

He chuckled. "Man oh man. You were on the phone with her ten minutes ago. You sure you wanna stick to that car story, Joe?"

I didn't say anything.

"Get up, motherfucker," he said.

I got to my feet. My ribs throbbed, but I was starting to inhale and exhale normally. A hand shoved me toward the bar and I stumbled toward it. I sat on one of the stools. For the first time, I saw the guy that had been behind me. It wasn't terribly surprising to see the guy I'd met at the auto shop in the red polo shirt pointing a gun at my chest.

"What's the play here, Joe?" Eduardo asked. "Why did she send you?"

I didn't say anything.

"She got the others, but she ain't getting me," he said, shaking his head. "So you're gonna help me." He grinned. "Or I'm gonna keep working those ribs." He held my phone out. "Call her."

"You want me to call her?"

He nodded. "That's right. Tell her you found me. Tell her you fooled me and you have me. She can come and get me. Tell her to come to the auto shop." He grinned again. "Tell her to get here and you'll hold onto me and then she can do whatever she wants with me." He squinted at me. "I'm guessing you're some sort of hired gun, right?" He laughed. "She's so predictable." He reached over and tapped the screen on the phone. "Here. I'll even dial for you." He pushed my hand toward my face. "Just tell her you've got me and to come. But you say anything else here and my boys are going to paint the walls with you. Got me?" He touched the speaker icon on the phone. "And this way we can all hear."

The phone rang twice before she picked it up. "Mr. Tyler?"

Eduardo grinned and nodded.

"I have him," I said. "I have Eduardo."

Eduardo gave me a thumbs up.

The line buzzed for a moment. "Really?"

"He was at the bar," I said. "I've got him at the car place now. Come if you're coming."

The line buzzed again. "Alright, I'm on my way. Give me about forty-five minutes."

The line went dead.

Eduardo took the phone out of my hand. "Well done, Joe. Now, we'll head on over to Verde's and wait on that bitch. I want you to watch her die before we kill you." He slapped my shoulder. "So relax a little bit. You've got some time left."

I had no doubt that Kara knew something was wrong. Having her come and having me hold Eduardo in custody wasn't part of the deal. So she had to know something had gone awry.

I was just hoping that I hadn't underestimated her and where she really was.

"Now, this is what's gonna happen," Eduardo said. "The four of us are gonna walk back to Verde's. Nice and easy. Get some sunshine and fresh air. We're gonna wait for Kara. You try anything outside and one of my boys is gonna put holes in you." He grinned. "Can I trust you, Joe?"

I stood up from the stool. "Let's go."

Eduardo studied me for a moment. "You hear me right, Joe? No bullshit. They'll aerate your body and then some if you try to run."

"I'm not running," I said. "What's the point?"

Eduardo nodded. "Bueno. Let's go."

Carlos came around the bar and stood by the doors. Eduardo motioned for me to turn and walk and I did so. He took me by the elbow. Mario brought up the rear.

"You a dumb motherfucker, Joe," he said. "Walking in here like this."

We were about to find out if that was true.

A fine mist hit my face and my first thought was that I didn't recall rain in the forecast.

And then I realized that Carlos was missing his head and the mist on my arms was red.

His body crumpled to the ground.

I pivoted and drove my elbow into the side of Eduardo's head. He stumbled to his left and I tackled him to the ground just as something zipped behind my head. Mario let out a yelp and then I heard a thud. I scrambled off Eduardo, grabbed Carlos's shotgun, and spun to where I thought the shooter was.

Kara Safford emerged around the backside of a Honda Odyssey, a sniper's rifle in her hands, still trained in our general direction.

"It's me," she yelled, crossing the road. "It's me."

I moved the shotgun to cover Eduardo lying on the ground.

"Are you alright?" she asked.

I nodded. "Yeah."

"We need to get inside and off the street," she said. "Can you get him up?"

I jerked Eduardo up by the back of his shirt.

"Auto shop," Kara said.

The three of us walked quickly and silently until we were inside Verde's. I turned the deadbolt on the front door and Kara motioned for Eduardo to sit.

"Think I'll stand," he said.

Her rifle flinched, a whooshing noise filled the space, and Eduardo stumbled to the side. A bright red streak bloomed on his left ear.

"Okay," she said. "You don't want to sit. Let's go back to the bays."

His hand covered his bleeding ear, but his face went pale. "I'll sit."

"No, don't," she said. "Why prolong this? Move or the next one will hit more than your earlobe."

Eduardo's jaw tightened, but he turned and walked slowly behind the counter. I followed them both through the door that led to the bays.

But the bays didn't resemble an auto shop in any way. There were no industrial strength lifts or old tires or tools or anything else you'd normally find in an auto shop. It was a large warehouse with immaculate concrete floors and a couple of chairs in the middle. I would've wagered that not a single car had ever been driven into the space.

Eduardo walked to one of the chairs in the middle of the room and sat. He pulled his hand away from his ear, which was now caked with dried blood. The color hadn't returned to his face.

"Did you know?" Kara asked, holding the gun on Eduardo, but glancing at me.

"That you were here?" I said. "I had a feeling."

"The whole time?"

"Never saw you, but the story about calling the police and then you'd come never made sense." I paused. "And if it had been me, I would've followed you."

I knew that something hadn't felt right to me when we talked in the café, but I hadn't been able to put my finger on it at the time. The more I'd thought about it, though, I was certain that she was tailing me because she would've been worried about the lag time of me notifying her and then her getting there.

Fortunately, she had.

"But I told you in the café," I said. "I'm not going to be a party to killing someone."

Eduardo shifted in his chair.

Kara held the sniper rifle out to me. "Here. Hold it on him. Because I guarantee if you don't, he'll do something."

I hesitated, then took it from her, and trained it on him. "So what now then?"

She walked over to a shelving unit in the corner and returned with several bungee cords. "First, I'm tying him to the chair." She went over to him and secured his wrists and feet to the chair. "You know what they use this place for, Mr. Tyler?"

"No."

"Killing," she said, turning back to me. "Obviously, you can see it's not what it's designed to look like. It's a killing space. They bring people in here, murder them, then clean up." She rubbed her toe on the concrete. "Spotless. But it works great because it's in a neighborhood people are afraid to come to and it's out of the way and it's secluded and no one asks questions." She looked at Eduardo. "Right?"

Eduardo said nothing.

"Their own little torture chamber," she said.

"Kara, I meant what I said," I told her. "I'm not here to kill, and I didn't agree to help you. I won't."

"I remember," she said. She walked backed over to the shelving unit and pulled off a rolling cart with what looked like two black scuba tanks on it. She wheeled it to within ten feet of Eduardo, who looked as if she was approaching him with a cobra. His feet were kicking and his body wiggled, but he couldn't free himself from the chair.

"Kara," he said. "Come on."

"Shut up," she said. She reached behind the tanks and removed what looked like a really long Nerf gun that was connected to the tanks by a hose. She shook out the hose until it was fully extended. "You know what this is, Mr. Tyler?"

"No."

"It's a flamethrower," she said. "They keep it here and use it regularly. To make people talk. To kill them with." She smiled at him. "Right, Eduardo? I remember you telling me that."

I shifted the rifle in my arms. "You've met him before?"

"I did more than meet him," she said. "I married him."

"Eduardo is my ex-husband," Kara said. "He was also Luna's father. He's the ninth man." She glanced in my direction, noticed the look on my face. "I told you that her father was involved with the cartel, did I not?"

I nodded.

"He was involved because he was taking their money," she said. "For a long time. Eduardo was a cop, but not a good one. He was on the payroll. And unfortunately for him, he screwed up one time. And one time is all it takes with the cartel. They have a zero-tolerance policy."

She pulled the trigger on the flamethrower and fire roared from the nozzle, nearly reaching Eduardo's feet. He jerked back and the chair squeaked against the concrete.

Kara smiled. "There's a joke about a hot foot here somewhere. Anyway. Eduardo screwed up. A deal he was supposed to keep his fellow officers away from went bad and his cartel buddies got arrested. You can imagine how well that went over with his bosses. They told him he had to pay." She paused. "And the payment was our daughter."

Eduardo looked down at his knees.

"He told them where she worked and when she'd be there," she said. "Because he's a coward. It's not that I couldn't find him exactly, Mr. Tyler. But I was always saving him for last." She shook her head. "I've spent two years to get to this moment. I've learned how to shoot weapons. How to tail cars. How to disguise my voice. How to create phony identifications. How to sneak into neighborhoods like Calles de Dolor. I found those other eight men that were a part of Luna's murder and I didn't lie to you, Mr. Tyler. I turned them in and I didn't hurt them." She paused and stared at Eduardo. "But this one's going to be different." She pressed the trigger again and the flames tickled his shoes.

"Jesus, Kara!" he yelled. "Come on! Don't do this!" He looked at me. "Yo, dude. I've got more money than you know what to do with."

Kara looked at me. "You wanna hear the best part?"

"Not really," I said.

"I don't blame you," she said. She turned back to Eduardo. "Tell him who took the pictures. Of Luna."

"Jesus, Kara, I—"

The fire spewed from the gun again and he yelped as it touched his knee.

"Tell him," Kara said.

Tears streamed from Eduardo's eyes, but he wouldn't look at me. "I took them."

Kara looked at me. "So. He gave up our daughter. He arranged for her murder. And then he took the photos that were sent to me. I want to make sure you have all of that straight. You understand?"

I did. It was horrific. I'd long imagined what I would do if I ever found out who'd taken my daughter and in my darkest moments, my imagination had gone to scenarios just like the one I was actually standing in the middle of now.

"So I know what I told you and I know what you said," Kara said. "I'm sorry that I lied to you. But now you know why. And now you know why I'm going to kill him. I understand you don't want to be a part of this. But you have two choices. Kill me or walk away." She paused. "Because I'm going to make him pay for what he did to our daughter."

I had never been a party to hurting or killing anyone for as long as I'd been searching for my daughter. I had no plans to make it part of my repertoire. And I wasn't going to help her kill Eduardo.

But I understood where she was coming from.

I bent down, laid the rifle on the ground, and headed for the door.

"What are you doing, man?" Eduardo screamed. "Come on! She's gonna fucking kill me! Don't do this!"

I reached the door and turned back around. I nodded at Kara. She nodded back.

Then I stepped outside, Eduardo's screams echoing in my ears, as I walked out of Verde's and Calles de Dolor.

ABOUT THE AUTHOR

Jeff Shelby is the bestselling author of over 50 mysteries. He divides his time between Texas and Minnesota. You can learn more about his books by signing up for his weekly newsletter at www.jeffshelby.com

THE LAST ASSIGNMENT

DOUGLAS DOROW

The last assignment for a Military Working Dog Handler and his four-legged partner is more than just another day in the field.

1

Everything appeared quiet through the magnified view from the binoculars. Weeds and rocks were larger than life in this focused view of the world. It was quiet; no wind, no buzzing of insects, no roar of aircraft flying overhead. Just the soft panting of his partner.

A prickly sensation tickled the back of Stevens' neck. It wasn't sweat dribbling down from the heat of the midday sun. He might be in someone's sight as he lay prone, studying the surrounding area. He wriggled to his left and pressed further into the shadow in the recess under the rocky overhang, almost a cave, making himself harder to see. Rupert moved along with him, maintaining contact against his legs, guarding the area behind them.

He checked his watch. The operation should be moving ahead soon. He was used to waiting, setting up in positions and watching, observing. That's what he did. He and Rupert moved into this spot in the dark and hadn't seen anything move since they settled in. From his position about fifty yards up the slope of the mountain, Stevens had a view of the dirt road that wound through the Afghan valley and the surrounding area. He spoke into his headset, "Dugout, how long until the stagecoach comes through?"

"Still clear?"

"Alpha clear, but I have a feeling we're not alone."

"Maintain position. Stagecoach is two klicks out maintaining route alpha unless you call a change."

Stevens was here, because if he was going to attack, he'd do it from here; a narrow passage with little chance of escape. The movement of the prisoner wasn't public knowledge, but info always got out. It's just who knew.

He moved his binoculars through positions like a second hand ticking on a watch. First position, clear. Second position, clear. Rupert moved from resting to alert as he sensed the change in his handler's body. Third position, clear. Fourth position, clear. Stevens whispered, "Rupert, Bewaken. Zwijg." The Dutch commands produced an immediate response. Rupert, a Belgian Malinois, Stevens' partner for the past twelve months, rose into a crouch, ready to charge. He watched the opposite direction to the south, alert and quiet. Stevens could focus north, knowing that Rupert had his rear.

This was Stevens' last assignment, his last day with Rupert. A day he'd been dreading since he got notice he was going home. He couldn't imagine what tomorrow would be like without his partner.

Rotating through the remaining positions, Stevens radioed, "Alpha clear." Over his shoulder to the south, a dusty plume rose from the road as Stagecoach, a caravan of two Humvees, barreled along. "Stagecoach in sight."

The Humvees passed the intersection in the road, a gravel path veering off to the right from the road they were on, and proceeded ahead, passing beta, committed to route alpha. Two vehicles. It wasn't clear which held the Taliban leader they'd captured. That was the plan. Two vehicles reducing the chance that the enemy would know which to attack. A fifty-fifty chance. Stevens knew he was in the lead vehicle.

He continued to click through positions up and down the slopes bordering the valley, checking for attackers. He glanced at the caravan. It continued on the path, kicking up dust in its wake.

Rupert growled. Stevens looked back to see what alerted him. Something moved. Rocks clattering down the slope told him someone was there. Stevens twisted and swung his assault rifle around. Through the scope he spied about a half dozen fighters moving among the rocks. "Contact!" he said into the radio. "Enemy on the slope south of my position. Two hundred yards." The fighters moved down the slope, scrambling over the rocks. What's their plan? Where had they come from? They wouldn't stop a couple of Humvees by themselves. An IED in the road? How would they control which Humvee triggered it? A remote to set off the explosion? He turned back and studied the road to the north to see if an enemy vehicle was heading this way. The road appeared clear.

A second group of fighters scrambled among the rocks to the north of his position. "Fighters to the north of me. One hundred yards." Without looking, he knew the Humvee drivers were accelerating to move past the area, the engines changing pitch. He focused on the group in front of him. A fighter crouched and raised a rocket-propelled grenade launcher to his shoulder. "RPG!" Stevens radioed. He exhaled, calmed himself, focused, centered the fighter in his sights and pulled the trigger, all in a couple of seconds. He hoped to shoot the fighter before he launched the grenade.

Smoke shot from the launcher as the fighter sent the grenade toward its target. The fighter went down. From his shot? Stevens didn't know. The sound from the launcher echoed off the mountain slopes. Stevens turned from his rifle's scope to see where the grenade would hit, hoping the aim was off. The grenade flew past the nose of the second Humvee and hit the base of the rocky slope on the other side of the road. Rocks flew, and the explosion echoed along the walls.

The targeted Humvee swung to a stop facing where the RPG had come from, the smoke in the air revealing the position. The gunner in the Humvee turret engaged the Taliban fighters with the fifty-caliber machine gun. Stevens radioed, "Gunner. I'm on the slope about one hundred yards south of your target." He heard machine gun fire behind him. "I'll take the bad guys behind me to the south. You have the north group."

"Roger," the gunner replied.

Stevens twisted to face the other direction. The Taliban fighters were firing at the Humvee, about two hundred yards away from behind boulders on the slope. He was still a ghost in his hiding place. They hadn't heard his shot. They didn't know he was there. From his vantage point, he had a pretty clear shot at them. Soldiers from the Humvee were firing on this group from the road, protected by the vehicle's body. The lead Humvee returned to join the other, stopping twenty yards from it. The turret gunner from the lead Humvee fired on the south group of fighters.

One Taliban fighter stood, defiantly firing at the targets below with his automatic rifle. Stevens lined him up in his scope. From this range an easy head shot. He pulled the trigger. One fighter down. Two remaining fighters in this group scrambled back up the slope to escape the fifty-caliber gunfire. One ran across the slope toward Stevens, probably seeking the protection of the rocky overhang.

Rupert stood and growled. It was a low, menacing growl from deep in his throat, sounding the alarm that a bad guy was coming at them. Stevens fired a quick shot at the enemy. Rupert charged the bad guy, protecting his partner. Stevens aimed for a second shot, but Rupert was in the way. He yelled the command to get down, "Rupert, Af!" The Taliban fighter stopped and shot automatic fire toward Rupert and Stevens' position.

Stevens felt a sting in the back of his leg. He winced, then ignored it, his goal to protect Rupert.

Rupert ignored Stevens' command and launched himself at the fighter like a battering ram. He knocked the attacker to the ground and clamped his teeth into the arm holding the gun. He wouldn't let go until Stevens issued the command to release as long as the enemy struggled.

The attacker pulled a knife from his belt with his free hand and stabbed at Rupert. The pointed blade bounced off the dog's protective vest. The second stab drew blood from Rupert's shoulder. Stevens zeroed in on the attacker through his scope and knew he had to take the shot to save his partner. He pulled the trigger before the fighter stabbed Rupert again.

Rupert maintained his grip on the attacker's arm. Stevens called out, "Rupert, Laas los. Af!" The dog obeyed and released the attacker's arm and lay down. Stevens knew his partner needed medical attention, but he couldn't help him until it was safe.

The fighting to the south seemed to have stopped. "Hold your fire on the south group!" Stevens yelled into the radio. "The fighter is down. My dog is out there. Don't shoot him."

Automatic fire from the north group started again. Stevens fought the urge to help Rupert. The north group had to be stopped first. He turned and scanned the rocks through his scope. The fifty-caliber gun downed a few fighters. Behind a boulder, Stevens spied the fighter with the launcher. He must've missed him with his first shot. He wouldn't miss with the next.

A grenade stuck out from the end of the launcher, and the fighter was moving into a position to fire at the Humvee again. Stevens exhaled, calmed himself, gently placed his index finger on the trigger and fired. The Taliban fighter with the RPG launcher was down before he could send the grenade at the Humvees. "Target down," Stevens radioed.

The gunfire ended. He heard the rumble of the Humvee engines. Stevens scanned the area to the north. Nobody moved. He turned and looked to the south. Nothing moved. "I'm coming out to get my dog," Stevens said into the radio. "Don't shoot me. Watch the slope above me for any stragglers."

"Come on out. We got you covered."

Stevens worked his way across the rocky slope toward Rupert, staying low to make himself less of a target. He scanned the slope above him and ahead of him. He made it to Rupert and curled up next to him.

Rupert panted and whined. He twisted to try to lick the wound on his shoulder. Stevens rubbed Rupert's neck. "You okay, buddy? Let me take a look." He held Rupert's neck with his left hand in case Rupert didn't like what he was doing and tried to nip him. With his right, gloved hand, he spread the fur at the wound. Rupert whined, but didn't protest too much. Blood oozed out slowly. A good sign, maybe. Stevens spoke quietly to Rupert. "You're going to be okay. We're going to patch you up temporarily until we can get down the hill and take a better look." He pulled a leather muzzle from his pack and fit it over Rupert's nose. Then he pulled some white packing material out and held it over the wound. He wrapped tape around the shoulder to hold it in place.

"That should do it. Let's get down to our friends." Stevens crouched next to Rupert and scratched him behind his ear. "You're going to be okay. You ready?" He lifted Rupert up and pressed him over his head. The dog was seventy-five pounds of muscle and heart. Rupert whined. Stevens lowered him onto his shoulders, Rupert's body across the back of his neck. His front legs stuck out to the left, his back legs to the right.

He worked his way down the rocky slope with Rupert on his shoulders, his feet sliding with each step on the loose stones. They were about halfway down the slope when he heard an RPG launch to his left and up the slope. "No," he said to no one. He dropped to a knee and swung Rupert onto the ground. Then he swung the rifle hanging from his shoulder into a shooting position in one move. He turned to where the RPG launch sound had come from. The sound of the exploding RPG filled the air, but Stevens focused on the telltale smoke in the air, found the shooter in his scope, and pulled the trigger.

After he saw the shooter go down, he scanned the area for other fighters. Seeing none, he turned his attention to the road. The trailing Humvee took the hit. Soldiers around the vehicle sought cover behind it. The soldier in the turret appeared to be injured.

Stevens worked his way down the slope and joined the men standing behind the Humvees. The gunner manned the turret in the undamaged Humvee, keeping an eye on the mountain where the Taliban had been. Stevens had to almost yell to be heard over the loud idling vehicle. "Hey, who's the medic? My partner's injured."

"He's over there. I'll get him," one of the soldiers said. He yelled over to a group by the lead Humvee. "Hazen, we need you over here."

Stevens knelt and gently lifted Rupert off his shoulders and laid him on the ground.

A big man came over. He could've been an offensive lineman for Army's football team. "What's up?"

Stevens stood and shook the giant's hand. "I need you to look at my partner. He's been stabbed. I bandaged him up quick, but I think he'll need more."

"I'm not a vet. Just a medic."

"And he's not a dog, he's a soldier. A medic is just what he needs."

Hazen glanced at Stevens' leg. "It looks like you need some help too." Stevens' pants were torn and wet with blood.

"Worry about him first," Stevens said. "I think I got hit by some rock fragments or something." He crouched and held Rupert's head again so the medic could check him out.

Hazen knelt by Rupert's head and cut the tape holding the packing. "Hold him down. I'm going to flush out the wound. It'll probably sting a little." He spread the fur covering the wound with his fingers and poured some water over it to clean it out. "Can he walk?"

"I'm not sure. I carried him down here," Stevens said.

"We'll bandage him up again until we can get to someplace to look at it better."

"You're a good boy, Rupert. You're going to be just fine." Stevens spoke softly to the dog and gently held him down while Hazen finished bandaging the wound.

A shadow fell across Rupert's body. "Thanks for the intel and the over watch. You helped make this a short skirmish."

Stevens looked up to see a man in camo with a patch on his chest with black letters – FBI.

"One shot got through. Is everybody here okay?"

The FBI man said, "We're all alive. A couple of injuries. One Hummer not running."

A couple of soldiers were inspecting the damaged vehicle. The other operational Humvee waited, doors open, the turret manned with a gunner.

"Sorry about your partner," the FBI man said. "I'm Special Agent Kiley."

"His name's Rupert. Looks like he'll make it," Stevens responded.

"I'm done here," Hazen said.

"Thanks," Stevens said.

"Now for your leg wound."

"I'm okay."

Hazen stood over him. "Drop your pants."

"Rupert, Blijf," Stevens said, commanding his partner to stay. Then he stood and unbuckled his belt and dropped his pants. He returned his attention to Agent Kiley while Hazen worked on his leg. "So, you're FBI. Intelligence for this mission?"

Kiley nodded. "Yep. Intel and anti-terrorism are my areas."

"Well, your intelligence sucked." Stevens took a step toward Kiley.

"Quit moving," Hazen said. He grabbed Stevens' thigh and slapped a sticky bandage on the wound. "That'll hold you until later."

"Thanks," Stevens said. He pulled up his pants and secured his belt.

Hazen grabbed his medic bag and headed back to the Humvee.

Stevens refocused on Kiley. "Rupert and I are wounded. A Humvee's hit by an RPG. Soldiers are wounded. Your intelligence sucked."

Kiley stood his ground. "It wasn't too bad."

Stevens squeezed his hands into fists. He raised his chin and stared directly into Kiley's eyes. "Is there even a prisoner in the first Humvee?"

"What makes you think there isn't?"

"We're sitting here. Not in too much of a hurry to move and nobody seems to be keeping an eye on the lead Hummer." Stevens watched Kiley to see how he'd respond.

Kiley stepped closer to Stevens and checked over each shoulder. "Between us, we were a decoy and a test on mission security. I'm sorry about your partner and your wound. But, we've proved there's a leak. The Taliban attacked the second vehicle, thinking the prisoner was in the lead."

"Why you telling me?" Stevens asked.

"I checked out your file before we started. I know you're not the leak and I'm going to need good people I can trust to complete the mission."

"There's still a mission? There's a prisoner to transport?"

Kiley cracked a smile and nodded. "You in?"

Stevens didn't even think about it. "They stabbed my partner. Let's complete this mission, my last assignment before rotating home. Stevens looked over at Rupert resting on the ground. "His last one too now, I guess."

Rupert lay across Stevens lap in the rear seat of the Humvee. They bounced along down the rocky road, dust floated in the cabin. The constant roar of the engine worked its way into Stevens' head. He pulled a tennis ball with a foot-long rope threaded through it, out of a pocket. Rupert's tail started wagging. Stevens held the ball in the palm of his hand. He unbuckled the leather muzzle and offered the ball to his partner. Rupert grabbed it with his teeth and started chewing on it. Stevens turned to Kiley sitting in the seat to their right. "It's his favorite toy. His reward."

"Everybody needs a reward," Kiley said. He reached for Rupert. "Can I pet him?"

Stevens grabbed Kiley's wrist and held tight. A low growl came from Rupert's throat. Stevens shook his head and pet Rupert's side with his other hand. "Normally, I'd say yes, after introductions. But, I don't know how he'll react since he's injured." He let go of Kiley's wrist.

"Okay, then." Kiley folded his hands. "Maybe later."

The Humvee rumbled along. They backtracked to the beta route and stopped where the main road intersected with a side road. "Another truck is going to meet up with us. The prisoner is in that one. We were going to have two vehicles accompany it to the base, but we'll do with one. When we get to the base we'll interrogate the prisoner and prepare him for transport."

"You think they're done?" Stevens asked. "They aren't done." He knew the fighters wouldn't let them take this prisoner. Not if he was the leader they said he was. With the information he had, he was too valuable of an asset to let the CIA, FBI or other US intelligence officers have time to interrogate him. They didn't get lucky and just happen to be covering the road the first caravan was on. They probably had multiple routes covered. There weren't that many.

They stopped at the intersection and waited for the following truck. "How'd you catch this guy?" Stevens asked. "Guns, girls or money?"

Kiley smiled. "Money makes the world go round. We made him an offer he couldn't refuse. And when he came to get it, we captured him."

"Since the first attack failed. They'll try again. The next one might not be a rescue mission. It might be a kill mission so you can't interrogate him."

"That's why we need to be successful and get him back to the base where we can talk to him."

"The truck's coming," the driver said.

A Toyota truck pulled up next to them and stopped. "We're going to shuffle the deck here," Kiley said. He opened his door and got out. He stuck his head back in and said, "You coming?"

Stevens opened the door. Rupert was still on his lap. Stevens took the ball from Rupert's mouth, swung his legs out and slid Rupert to the ground. Then reached back in the Humvee to get his rifle. When he turned back, he found Rupert on his feet, his right leg bent to keep the weight off it. "Can you walk, buddy?" The dog took a couple of steps, limping on his front right leg while he followed. He was a fighter.

A couple of soldiers from the truck were taking their places in the Humvee. At the truck, Kiley got in the front passenger seat and Stevens lifted Rupert to get in the seat behind Kiley. To his left behind the driver was the prisoner. He had a black hood over his head. He wore the Afghan dress of pants and a robe-like top. His hands were in his lap, bound with flex cuffs.

Rupert sniffed at his pants. The prisoner flinched from the sound or the touch of the wet dog nose. Rupert turned his snout to the front and settled in for the ride on Stevens' lap.

"Where're we going?"

Kiley twisted around. "Time to get him to the base."

"But, which route?" Stevens asked.

"It has to be random. I still don't know if we have someone who gave up the initial route or not." He narrowed his eyes. "Pick a number between one and five."

Stevens stroked Rupert's neck. He wasn't sure if Kiley was playing with him or what. "Four."

"Four it is," Kiley said. He turned to the driver. "Sigma route. Just tell the other driver to follow us. Don't tell him which route." He turned back to Stevens. "Now, we're the only ones who know where we're going." The driver radioed the Humvee to follow and then pulled a U-turn and headed south.

The prisoner sitting in the seat next to Stevens remained quiet, still. Stevens used the time to shut down and re-energize. It had been a long day so far, and it wasn't over yet. He worried about Rupert, but he seemed to be doing okay. They were lucky not to lose anyone in the last skirmish. Getting through the day was now the goal, and getting the prisoner to the base. Stevens didn't know who he was other than some high-ranking fighter. To have Kiley here from FBI counterterrorism and the troubles they were going through to get this guy to the base, he had to be a valuable asset.

They weren't on routes alpha or beta. Sigma was just a designation, but for which route? There weren't a lot of options to get to the base from this side of the mountains. There was the long way or the longer way. And the longer they took, the later it got and the darker it would be. Stevens would rather fight in the light of day.

Kiley twisted around again. He nodded at Rupert in Stevens' lap. "How's he doing?"

"He seems okay."

"Is it true you can communicate through thoughts?"

"What?" Stevens asked.

"I hear with some teams, dogs can almost read their handler's mind."

Stevens continued to rub Rupert's neck. "It seems like it sometimes. We practice a lot of different scenarios and the dog starts to read my actions, my body, the tenor of my voice in addition to the voice commands. He knows what he's supposed to do." Stevens thought back to some of the times Rupert had surprised him in performing. Seeming like he read his mind. "In the end, it all comes down to reward, attention, his favorite toy, and play time or a treat. He doesn't know why we're doing what we do, but he knows the game."

"I'm just glad he's on our side," Kiley said.

The driver slowed the truck. "Contact ahead."

About a quarter mile ahead of them there was a beat up pickup truck stopped in the middle of the road. There was very little room on either side of the road to squeeze past because of the boulders that lined the road at the bottom of the valley that formed the path between the mountains. "Stop here," Kiley said. He raised a pair of binoculars to his eyes. "I don't see anybody."

"That's not good," Stevens said. "We can't just sit here. A moving target is harder to hit." He scanned the hills on either side of the road for signs on enemy fighters.

Kiley said to the driver, "Have the Humvee pull ahead of us. Tell the gunner he might have to shoot the truck off the road for us."

The driver slowly pulled ahead and to the right side of the road to give the Humvee room to pass. As the Humvee passed, Stevens cracked open the truck door.

Kiley looked back. "What are you doing?"

"I can't be a target," Stevens answered. "This isn't just a stalled truck and they aren't going to let us pass easily. We'll recon and cover until we're sure we're past this." He pushed the door the rest of the way open and stepped out with his right arm wrapped around Rupert. He grabbed his rifle with his left and pushed the door closed. He lowered Rupert to the ground until he had his legs under him. He glanced back along the road in the direction they'd come from. It was clear. He watched the Humvee pull ahead along the road and hoped if the enemy was out, they were watching it. He issued a command, "Rupert, Rechts," and crouched and jogged to some rocks up the side of the hill. Rupert followed on his right side, limping and keeping up with a three-legged trot.

They scrambled up the slope and around a pile of boulders to find a spot they could use to hide while Stevens scanned the area for the enemy. He settled in and swept the area, trying to identify where he'd hide and ambush the convoy from if that was his mission. "Kiley," he radioed. "I don't see anything."

Kiley answered, "We're rolling ahead. Going to blast the pickup and either go around it or push it out of the way."

"Why aren't they attacking?" Stevens asked. "We've stopped and we're easy targets. Give me a minute to move up a little higher and closer to the pickup."

"You've got a minute. But, don't go too far. We need you back in here when we're ready to roll."

"Roger," Stevens answered. "We'll be there. We don't feel like walking." They moved among the boulders, past Kiley's truck, almost in line with the stalled truck. "We're in position and still don't see anything."

The gunner in the turret fired on the stalled truck. Tires flattened, glass shattered and the sides shredded. No explosion. The Humvee pulled forward to push the stalled truck out of the way.

Stevens scanned the mountain slopes looking for any sign of the enemy. Why was the stalled truck there? It wouldn't stop them. Slow them down? The Humvee's bumper touched the back of the truck. Kiley's vehicle pulled forward. And then it happened. The stalled truck shot into the air from an explosion beneath it. The Humvee's front end rose, and the force pushed it back. The hood of the armored vehicle was gone. The gunner in the turret was thrown onto the road.

A remote trigger or triggered by pressure when the Humvee pushed on the truck, Stevens didn't know, but he was on alert, looking for the enemy. He saw Kiley down below, jump from the truck and run toward the smoking Humvee. The gunner lay still on the road. A soldier stumbled from the Humvee and fell to his knees.

An old Jeep with three Taliban fighters drove toward them from up the road, beyond the exploded truck. Stevens got comfortable on his stomach and took aim. He fired on the approaching Jeep. It didn't slow.

Stevens checked on Kiley. He reached the downed gunner and fired at the Jeep. The driver from Kiley's truck got out and crouched behind the engine and fired on the Jeep as well.

Not sure if this was a rescue mission or a suicide squad coming to take out the prisoner, Stevens continued to fire on the Jeep. One fighter slumped over. There was still the driver and another fighter. The Jeep continued forward through the hail of fire, the glass headlights exploding, the front, right tire flattening. The Jeep continued toward Kiley and the truck, swerving back and forth as the driver struggled to drive with a flat tire on the rocky road.

Stevens tracked the driver through his sight, leading him slightly, and pulled the trigger. The driver fell over and the Jeep swerved hard to the right and ran into a boulder on the side of the road. Kiley continued firing on the Jeep and the remaining fighter until he was killed.

The truck driver rushed forward to make sure the fighters in the Jeep were no longer a threat and to help Kiley with the injured. Stevens started down the slope and noticed the prisoner in white, running the opposite direction, away from the battle. Rupert stood whining, alert and ready. "You want him? A little payback for you getting stabbed?" He jabbed his hand in the direction of the fleeing prisoner and commanded, "Rupert, Revier," rolling the R at the end, drawing it out. He followed with, "Rupert, Transport."

Rupert took off in the direction of the prisoner. His injured leg hardly slowed him down. Stevens was confident that Rupert would run down the fleeing prisoner and return him to the truck. Especially after seeing how the man reacted to Rupert in the truck earlier.

Sliding down the slope to the road, Stevens joined Kiley and the driver as they tended to the soldiers from the Humvee. "Everyone okay?" he asked.

"Everyone's alive. Some injuries," Kiley replied. "Where's your partner?"

Stevens jerked his head down the road. "He had an errand to run. He'll be here in a minute. Your prisoner got out and tried to make a run for it."

"What?" Kiley said. He anxiously glanced down the road past their truck.

"Rupert will bring him back. Don't worry. Get these guys ready so we can get out of here." Stevens watched the mountain slopes around them while Kiley and their driver worked on bandaging the injured soldiers from the Humvee.

Rupert's barking got their attention and they all turned and watched as he barked and nipped at the prisoner's legs and butt, herding him past the truck toward them. The prisoner stumbled forward, trying his best to avoid Rupert's prodding.

Stevens grabbed the prisoner's arm and pulled him down until he sat on the ground. "Rupert, Braff." He scratched his partner behind the ears to reward him. "Rupert, Erop." The dog turned his attention to the prisoner to guard him.

"I'll go get the truck," Stevens said. "We'll need to squeeze us all in to get to the base since the Humvee's out of commission. The sooner we get out of here, the better."

The sun dropped behind the mountains to the west, making it seem later than it was as they pulled into the base. The driver stopped the truck behind a wall for protection and concealment. Stevens said to Kiley, "I don't think you need any more help with our friend here, do you?"

"No, I got him."

"Can you point me to the medical area? I want to get Rupert checked out."

"It's the third building up on the right," Kiley said. "We'll get these other guys over there."

Stevens held Rupert in his arms, both under his stomach, and carried him from the truck to the medical building. "You take it easy, buddy," Stevens said.

At the medical building, he found a doctor who set him up in an examination room.

Rupert's tongue hung out of the corner of his mouth. He was relaxed from the painkillers and tranquilizers they gave him so they could work on him while keeping him quiet. His shoulder was bandaged and wrapped. Stevens sat in a chair next to the bed Rupert slept on. They'd been lucky. Rupert had been injured before on a mission, but those were minor scrapes and strains compared to this. A cut with some potential nerve damage. Not good. Stevens placed the ball with the rope through it in the bed next to Rupert so he'd have his favorite toy when he woke up.

Agent Kiley walked into the room and stood at the end of the bed. Stevens stood and stretched. "Everybody else okay?"

"They'll be fine."

You done with the prisoner already?"

Kiley shook his head. "My job was to find him, capture him and transport him. Someone else is doing the interrogation."

"It was quite the adventure getting him here."

"It was," Kiley said. "Thanks to the two of you for the help."

They both watched Rupert on the bed, twitching, panting and whining. "Looks like he's dreaming of his own adventures," Kiley said. He turned to Stevens. "So, this is your last assignment?"

"Yep, this was it. I'm going home." Stevens nodded at Rupert. "The doc says it's his last assignment too. I'm going to see if I can bring him home with me. He was scheduled to be assigned to another handler. But, I'd love to get him rehabbed and retired with some time in the woods or on the beach."

"I'll see what I can do to help and maybe get him assigned to you,"

Kiley said. "I don't know what you're planning to do after you get home. But, after Rupert recovers and rehabs and you get tired of relaxing and drinking, if you decide you want to keep chasing terrorists and bad guys, give me a call." He pulled a card out of his vest pocket and handed it to Stevens. "The FBI's Hostage Rescue Team could use a pair like you on one of their teams."

Stevens studied the card and put it in his pocket. "Give us a few months. We'll see."

ABOUT THE AUTHOR

Douglas Dorow is an FBI crime thriller writer from Minnesota. Learn more about his FBI thriller series and his Critical Incident series at www.douglasdorow.com. While you're there, get Short Thrills, a free box set of four short stories. Read for the *THRILL* of it!

MINE

MICHELE PW (PARIZA WACEK)

No good deed goes unpunished.

1

The girl was nervous.

Her head kept whipping around as she strode down the darkened street, trying to take in everything at once. The death grip she had on her purse reminded me of a how a drowning person might clutch a life preserver, as if she were praying it would somehow save her from whatever lurked in the shadows of the alley.

But she didn't need that purse.

She had me.

I would protect her.

Clearly, though, I needed to have a firm conversation with her about how dangerous it is for a woman to walk by herself at night even with the light of a full, bright moon in a clear night sky. Even in a town as safe as Redemption.

We would have that talk as soon as I was able to safely introduce myself.

She tripped on a crack in the sidewalk, her arms flailing for a moment while she righted herself. I paused, letting her catch her breath, trying to ignore how much she reminded me of Jenny. Jenny was such a klutz, too. If I hadn't spent so much time saving her over and over again, who knows ...

No, I had to stop. I promised myself I wouldn't think of Jenny anymore.

Tonight was about the girl.

She started walking again, her heels clicking briskly on the sidewalk. She appeared to be paying more attention to where she was walking now, increasing my approval. If I wasn't around, she would need to be more concerned about her environment, but with me right behind her, it was acceptable for her to focus on watching her step.

She was approaching another cave-like alley, dark with shadows. The hairs began to rise on the back of my neck as a shiver went down my spine.

Something was wrong.

I peered into the shadows, squinting to get a closer look. Was there something there? A predator hiding in the dark, motionless and silent, patiently waiting for its prey?

The girl continued on her way, blissfully ignorant of the danger lurking just up ahead.

I had to do something.

But what? I couldn't blow my cover. It was too soon. I couldn't make that same mistake again.

But I couldn't allow her to walk blindly into danger, either.

I quickened my steps, careful to keep them light. Her heels were so loud on the pavement, they sounded like miniature firecrackers.

Maybe she wouldn't notice. Maybe it would be fine.

I held my breath as I moved closer, trying to stay as quiet as possible. It seemed to be working; she gave no indication she had any idea I was behind her.

At that exact moment, my foot came down on a branch lying on the sidewalk. I cursed myself—if I hadn't been so focused on her general lack of awareness, I would have noticed it.

Instead, it snapped under my foot, as loud as thunder. She spun around, her eyes wide, her expression suspicious.

I held both hands up, palms out, trying to look harmless. "Sorry," I said with a friendly smile. "I didn't mean to scare you."

She didn't answer, just continued to watch me.

I cleared my throat. "You know, it's never a good idea for a woman to walk by herself at night. If you'd like, I'd be happy to accompany you to wherever you're going."

"Why would you do that?" Her voice was low, throaty. It reminded me of one of those black-and-white movie actresses, like Lauren Bacall. "You don't know me."

"Just being a good Samaritan."

If anything, she looked even more distrustful. "Are you following me?"

"What? No, of course not! I just wanted to help ..."

She started to back away. "Stop following me. I mean it."

This was not going well at all. I took a few steps forward. "No, wait. I'm just trying to help ..."

"Stay away from me," the girl shrieked before turning and starting to run.

"Wait," I called out, but I could already tell she wasn't going to listen. She was an awkward runner—slightly bent over clutching her purse and steps heavy on the pavement. Jenny ran like that, too. Why didn't they teach girls how to properly run in gym class? Yet another thing wrong with our educational system.

Enough. This was not the time. I had bigger problems.

What to do now?

I briefly wondered if I should just let her go. Give her a few days before approaching her again and see if I could maybe explain myself better.

But no. I had to protect her. What if something happened to her while I was letting her cool off? I would never forgive myself.

I started after her, trotting so I could keep her in sight. She must have sensed something, because she threw a terrified glance back at me, then veered to the right.

My heart leaped into my throat.

She was turning down the alley—full of shadows and blood.

Shit. This wasn't good.

I sped up to a jog, and then a run. I had to keep up with her.

She darted around the corner, disappearing into the dark, as if she were swallowed by a giant maw.

I kicked up my speed another notch, practically flying across the pavement as I rounded the corner toward the alley. I was about to plunge into the darkness after the girl when the hairs at the back of my neck stood up again, and all my senses went on high alert.

Danger.

I skidded to a stop at the mouth of the alley. The light was poor, but I could just make out the shapes of multiple dumpsters. The stench of rotting food and garbage that wafted toward me confirmed it.

I stood for a moment, listening and watching. It appeared to be otherwise empty.

But looks can be deceiving.

I knew I needed to check it out. The girl may need my help. But I also wasn't going in without protection.

I patted my front pocket where I kept my switchblade. Would it be enough? It might have to be if I couldn't find anything else.

Silently, I crept forward, breathing through my mouth as I approached the dumpsters looking for some sort of weapon. Nothing near the first, but I got lucky at the second. Leaning against the side was a thick two-by-four with a bent nail on one end.

That should work.

I had just picked it up when I froze. Had I heard something? It sounded like a small, muffled cry. I cocked my head, trying to listen more closely, but the blood was pounding so loudly in my ears. I strained to gaze deeper into the alley, but as far as I could tell, nothing moved. All was silent.

That didn't stop my skin from prickling. I wasn't alone. I was sure of it.

I started forward again. If that soft sound came from the girl, she was in trouble.

I was about halfway through the alley when the voice came.

"Stop right where you are."

It was a male voice, quiet but full of menace. The voice of a predator. Whoever it was clearly meant business.

I paused. "Are you talking to me?"

"Who else would I be talking to?"

"I have no quarrel with you," I said as I carefully took a step toward the voice. "I'm looking for a girl who ran in here. Have you seen her?"

"Why do you think she wants anything to do with you?"

I continued to ease my way forward, straining my eyes to see where the voice was coming from. "Why do you think she doesn't?"

"I told you to stop!"

Finally I was able to see which direction the voice was coming from. If I squinted, I could just make out what looked like two bodies pressed against the alley and a scrap of white that I assumed was from the girl's shirt. "Maybe let her tell me," I said.

There was sudden movement to my right, and two men materialized out the gloom. I took a step back, shifting my stance to face them.

"Maybe you need to rethink that," said the voice as its owner stepped forward, dragging the girl with him. Her shirt was torn in front, hanging open and exposing a lacy bra. Her eyes were wide with terror.

"I don't think she's all that into you," I said, eyeing what I could now clearly see as three men. They were all thin and relatively scrawny, the biggest one of them holding the girl. I subtly hefted the two-by-four in my hand.

I could take them.

The man holding the girl took another step forward, and the two underlings followed suit. "This doesn't concern you," he hissed. "Walk away. While you still can."

I took another look into the girl's wide, frightened eyes. "I think not."

Then, I dove into action.

I moved fast, lunging forward and swinging the two-by-four at the nearest man. He awkwardly ducked, clearly caught by surprise by my swift attack, but he wasn't quick enough, and the board slammed into this shoulder, knocking him over. At the same time, I leapt to the side, avoiding the second man's bullrush. He stumbled, flailing for a moment, and I slammed the board against his head, dropping him like a stone.

I pivoted back to the first man, kicking him in the chest and head to keep him down while I dealt with the leader.

He had shoved the girl against the wall and was coming after me. I caught a glimpse of something silver in his hand. A knife, its blade wickedly sharp.

I swung the board at him, but he easily sidestepped the blow, knocking me off balance. Before I could recover, he was on me, swinging the knife at my chest. I grabbed his wrist right before the tip hit its mark. He was close enough for me to see the flat expression in his eyes, and his lips were pulled back in a snarl. We struggled for a moment as I watched a drop of sweat streak down his hairline.

I released his wrist as I rolled to the side. His body crashed to the earth, and before he could recover, I slammed my fist into the back of his head. His forehead hit the ground, and he went limp.

Quickly, I scrambled to my feet, searching the alley to see if either of the other two men had regained their legs, but all were still. I glanced back toward the wall and saw her.

She was huddled near the bricks, too frightened to move.

"Hey," I said, holding my hand out. "We have to go."

She started, shooting me a distrustful look as she tried to step backward.

"None of that," I said, trying to keep the impatience out of my voice. "We have to go. Now."

She pressed her lips together. For a moment, I thought she was going to refuse, but then she took a few tentative steps toward me.

I nodded in encouragement, reaching out to grasp her arm. Her bones were so tiny and fragile, I feared I might snap them in half if I squeezed too hard. I could feel her shy away, but I didn't have a choice. Every cell in my body was screaming at me to leave *NOW*, and I had to get her out of there.

"I'm sorry," I said in her ear as I hurried her out of the alley. "But we have to move faster. I don't know how long we have until they wake up."

She didn't answer, but her pace quickened as she staggered after me.

I didn't let up until we were out of the alley and back on the street under a bright streetlight. We still weren't completely safe—we wouldn't be until we got out of there completely—but at least we were more likely to attract witnesses in a more public area.

"Hold on," the girl said, flailing against my grip.

I released her reluctantly. "We still need to go. We're not safe."

"I'm not going anywhere with you until I get some answers," she said, shaking her wrist as she simultaneously grasped at her shirt to hold it in place.

"All right, what do you want to know?" I asked, trying to keep my frustration from creeping into my voice.

"Why are you even here?""

I blinked. "What do you mean?"

"Here! Why did you follow me? Why did you attack those men?"

"I attacked them to save you."

"Yeah, but why?"

I stared at her, flummoxed. How could I answer that? Tell her I was drawn to her from the first moment I saw her sipping a glass of wine by herself in the Tipsy Cow? That she reminded me of someone close to me? Or would she find that strange and disconcerting? "Because it was the right thing to do," I said, hoping that would satisfy her.

It didn't. Her frown deepened. "But you were following me before I was attacked. How did you even know?"

Why the twenty questions? I wanted to shout. Aren't you glad I followed you? Look what would have happened if I didn't. With effort, I shoved the words down. The last thing either of us needed was a fight. "I just ... had a feeling," I said. "Something didn't seem right with that alley. I felt like you were in danger."

She gave me a suspicious look. "You *felt*?"

"Yeah, I just ... didn't have a good feeling about any of this. Look, I didn't mean to scare you. I just wanted to make sure you were safe. That's it. Can we go now?"

She studied me for a moment longer. "Okay," she said finally. "You can walk me to my friend's. That's where I was going. It's a couple blocks away. She's expecting me."

"Okay," I said, relieved. I shot another quick glance at the mouth of the alley. Nothing appeared to be moving in the shadows, which was good, but I still couldn't shake the uneasy feeling coursing through my body.

She fell into step next to me, fishing through her purse for her phone. She held it at an angle as we walked, so I couldn't see what she texted.

I wanted to tell her to pay attention—that her obliviousness to her surroundings was part of the issue. Instead, I gritted my teeth.

"Okay," she announced, dropping her phone back into her purse. "My friend knows we're on the way and will be there in a few minutes."

"Good," I said, trying not to let her see me watching her. She appeared to be remarkably cool after what had almost happened to her. Other than the slight tremble of her hand clutching her torn shirt, no one would have guessed she had just almost been raped.

I found myself grudgingly admiring her for that.

"How are you doing?" I asked.

"How do you think?" she shot back, her slim hand tightening on her shirt.

"If you want to talk or anything ..."

"I'm okay," she said. She gave me a quick, sideways glance from underneath her long eyelashes. "But thanks for asking," she said, softening her tone. "Actually, thanks for everything," she added awkwardly. "I probably sound like a bitch, but I think I'm still in a little shock."

"Totally understandable," I said. "And, really, I meant it. I'm here if you want to talk."

"I appreciate that, but I think I just need to get to my friend's house. If you don't mind."

"Of course," I said gravely, but inside I was smiling. The door was open now. Maybe just a crack, but that was all I needed. "I'm Tom, by the way."

Her face puckered, and my heart stuttered. Was she going to refuse to tell me her name? But then her expression cleared so fast, I wondered if I had imagined it. "I'm Adele."

Adele. I rolled the name around in my mouth. It suited her. "Nice to meet you, Adele," I said. "Although I would have preferred it not be under these circumstances."

A ghost of a smile touched her lips. "That's for sure. This is me." She gestured toward a fourplex down a side street. "Thanks for walking me home."

"You're not home yet," I said, but she shook her head firmly.

"I'm fine," she said. "You've done enough. Thank you."

I was clearly being dismissed, and I could feel the anger starting to build inside me. *How dare she? After all I had done for her?* But I pushed it down. Now wasn't the time. She had a bad fright and probably just needed some rest before she could start seeing things clearly.

"Do you want my number?" I called out, but she was already hurrying toward the fourplex.

I stood on the corner and watched her as she disappeared inside the house. Two lights were on in the upstairs windows. I wondered which one of those rooms her friend lived in, but at that moment, I saw the curtain twitch on the right-hand side.

That was probably the one.

I wanted to stay longer, to keep an eye out, especially if she decided to leave again, but I forced myself to turn and walk away. The last thing I wanted was for her to see me.

There would be time enough for that later.

It was nearly a week before I found Adele again.

She was sitting by herself in the Tipsy Cow, a locals' favorite, a glass of white wine in front of her. Her head was down as she messed with her phone, so she didn't immediately see me.

I watched her for a few minutes. She looked even more beautiful than I remembered, this woman who had replaced Jenny in my dreams, causing me to wake with her name on my lips. Her wheat-colored hair was slicked back into a high ponytail, bringing out the sharp, elegant angles of her face. Her long, graceful neck was further emphasized by a black mock turtleneck.

Now, staring at her in the dimly lit bar, I realized even my dreams had not done her beauty justice.

Taking a deep breath to steady myself, I carefully approached her. *There's no need to be nervous*, I told myself. *It would be silly not to say something after the experience we shared.*

The experience we shared. I liked how that sounded.

I was nearly at the table when she glanced up, the crease of a frown gently pulling at her forehead. The moment she recognized me, it seemed to deepen, and something shifted in her eyes ... an emotion I couldn't immediately identify. Then it hit me—anger.

But just as fast as it appeared, it dissipated, making me wonder if I had seen it at all. Perhaps she was just remembering the details surrounding our last meeting. That would cause anyone to feel upset.

"Tom! You startled me," she said. "I didn't realize you were here."

"I just walked in," I said. "I thought I'd have a drink. Can I buy you one?"

She hesitated and glanced at her phone. A surge of jealously shot through me. Was she on a *date*? After all I'd done for her, would she really go on a *date* with another man?

"I'm supposed to be meeting my friend," she said. "But she's running late."

She. I could feel the tightness in my chest relax. "I can keep you company until she gets here."

"You could," she said slowly.

I wondered why she was being so reluctant. She must have seen something in my expression because she rushed to continue. "It's not that I don't want to have a drink with you. It's just that I don't think she'll approve."

"Approve?" I raised an eyebrow. "Aren't you old enough to make your own decisions?"

She flushed, the pink staining her cheeks, making her even look more adorable. "Of course. That's not it. She was the friend whose house I went to that night. She's been really concerned and protective of me since then. She keeps telling me to keep a low profile for a while ... to not do anything to bring attention to myself. I just think it might be easier to, you know, avoid having to answer a bunch of her questions right now."

"I can understand that," I said, even though I was really thinking how controlling her friend sounded. We would have to eventually have that discussion, too. "Does anyone else know what happened?"

What I really wanted to know was if she had told the cops. We hadn't discussed the option that night, and I was still kicking myself about it. I had used one of my aliases, so they really shouldn't be able to trace me anyhow, but you can never be too sure.

She shook her head. "No. No one. I was too embarrassed. Which is another thing she's upset with me about."

"That you didn't tell anyone, or that you're embarrassed?"

"Well, both, in a way." She laughed a little self-consciously. "She really wanted me to go to the cops, but I didn't want to. I just wanted to forget about it. You know?"

"Makes sense to me," I said, trying to keep the relief from showing on my face. "So, you don't want to do anything to start another argument."

"Exactly." Now it was Adele's turn to look relieved. "She's been really helpful. I don't know what I'd do without her, but she's also driving me crazy. And I know if she sees you here, she's going to pepper us both with all sorts of questions, and neither of us need to deal with that. Right?"

"Understood." I was disappointed, but aware that these things take time. It was months before I could have a conversation with Jenny. So really, this relationship was moving faster than I had dared hoped.

"But," she continued, a thoughtful expression on her face. "Let's do this. She should be here in a few minutes. Why don't you go out back and wait for me there?"

"Wait for you?"

"Yeah. Give me five or ten minutes. I'll tell her I'm not feeling well or something, and then meet you out there in the back of the bar. We can go somewhere else for a drink. Would that work?"

"Sure," I said, flabbergasted. Could it really be that easy?

She smiled then, nearly taking my breath away. It lit up her face, practically caused her to glow. "Okay, then. It's a date." She glanced down at her phone and frowned. "Oh, you better hurry. She's almost here."

"I'll see you in a bit," I said, turning to quickly stride out the door. I couldn't believe my luck. Everything was working out so perfectly. I had known, the minute I had laid eyes on her, that she was meant to be mine. I just had to convince her.

Apparently, doing so was easier than I had expected.

I circled around the bar to the back. It was dark back there, darker than I had expected. It smelled of garbage, flat beer, and cigarette smoke.

I felt a prickle of unease tickle the back of my neck and instinctively shoved my hand into my pocket to find my knife. I didn't like this at all. Maybe it was just because it reminded me of our first encounter, but it didn't feel ... right.

I started to back up slowly, sensing it would be better to wait for her out front. I could stand under a streetlight, so she would quickly see me. Even if she was taken aback by my not following her instructions, once I explained why meeting there was a bad idea, she would surely understand. In fact, she would probably thank me. There was no way she would possibly have wanted to meet back there if she had known what she was asking ...

"Well, look who's here." An ugly voice declared from behind me. "I think we found ourselves the hero."

I whirled around, all my senses on high alert. I would have recognized that voice anywhere. It was the leader of the gang who had attacked Adele.

I immediately pulled my knife out of my pocket as two shadows detached themselves from the mouth of the alley. "We don't have to do this," I said. "I can walk away."

"Oh, did you hear that? He can walk away," the other voice chuckled in response as the shadows continued to advance. I wondered if the third man was with them again, or if there were only the two. I flicked my wrist to open my switchblade as I continued to slowly back up toward the dumpsters. "Maybe *we* don't want to walk away. Ever think about that?"

I was starting to worry that Adele might show up in the middle of this altercation. I had to lead them out of there, and fast, but as far as I could tell, they were blocking my only escape route. Was there a way to distract them, so I could run past them? It wasn't that far to the front of the bar, and at least there would be light there, and other people. Adele might even be able to see what was happening and stay inside where she was safe. I just needed to get them away from her, as far away ...

Two strong arms grabbed me from behind, pinning my arm to my side. The third man must have snuck up behind me, under the cover of the shadows. There was no more time to think.

I slammed my head backward, hearing a satisfying "crack" as the back of my skull connected with the man's face.

The arms holding me loosened, and I twisted to the side, but at that moment, a fist plunged into my belly, doubling me over.

"We're not done yet," the voice came with a knee to my face. The arms behind me grabbed me again, this time holding me firmly as the leader began landing blow after blow to my stomach. "We've been looking for you. We've got some business to finish now."

My stomach was a wall of pain. I couldn't breathe. Everything hurt.

The leader paused. "Oh, and once we're done with you, we're going to find your pretty little girlfriend and finish what we started."

"You bastard," I gasped, trying to free my arms, but the punches resumed. My last thought before I blacked out was praying to a God I didn't believe in to keep herself safe until I could protect her again.

I winced as I approached Adele's friend's house.

I still wasn't completely healed from my ordeal.

After I had blacked out that night, I woke up in the hospital with broken ribs, a ruptured spleen, and a concussion.

I was immediately frantic. Was Adele alright? Was she the one who had brought me to the hospital? The doctors weren't able to tell me anything. Later, I learned from a nurse that someone had apparently called an ambulance, and the EMTs had delivered me to the hospital.

It had been tricky to navigate my medical and legal issues simultaneously. The cops of course came by for a statement, and I told them as little as possible.

I was jumped for no apparent reason.

Why was I behind the bar in the first place?

I couldn't remember. It was all fuzzy.

The cop, an unattractive young female with frizzy brown hair and gold-rimmed glasses didn't look particularly convinced, but since I also said I couldn't describe who had jumped me, there was nothing for her to do. She finished her interview, gave me her card, and told me to get in touch if I remembered anything before walking out the door.

Hopefully, that would be the end of it.

It took a couple of weeks before I could re-initiate my search for Adele, and when I was able, I couldn't find a trace of her. Every night, I walked the streets of Redemption, looking. I spent hours at the Tipsy Cow, nursing a beer for as long as I could make it last, waiting for her to appear.

Nothing.

And every night that I came up empty, my terror grew. Had they gotten to her? Was she hurt? Or even worse?

I couldn't eat. I couldn't sleep. I called the hospitals. I poured over every issue of the *Redemption Times* looking for a clue.

Finally, I couldn't stand it anymore. I had to make sure she was okay. And the only lead I had was this house.

I knew it wasn't the best plan. I had no idea how her friend would react, especially considering how 'protective' Adele said she was. For all I knew, she would slam the door in my face and call the cops.

But I had no choice. I had to know if Adele was alright, and this was the only way.

I opened the front door of the building and stood in a foyer facing a staircase. It appeared to be divided into four apartments—two on the bottom and two on the second floor. The night I had walked Adele here, it seemed she had likely entered the one on the right, so that was where I was planning to start.

I rubbed my chest and started to slowly climb the staircase. It still hurt to take deep breaths, but what else could I do?

As I climbed, I marveled at how quiet the building was. There were no sounds of footsteps, music, television, talking. Nothing at all. Either the walls must be super thick, or some of the apartments were vacant.

The second option seemed more plausible. I had spent some time watching this building, pretending to walk around the block several times each night, hoping just to catch a glimpse of Adele coming in or out, but I had never seen anyone entering or exiting.

By the time I reached the top, I was starting to wonder if Adele's friend was the only person actually living in the building. Even the air smelled stale and dusty.

I walked over to the door to the right, listening to the floor creak beneath my steps, and knocked. In the quiet, the sound was amplified, almost like gunshots.

I stood there, straining to hear. But there was nothing.

I knocked again. Still nothing.

I took a step back and stared at the door in frustration. Was it possible Adele's friend had moved? Maybe I could contact the owner.

I turned back to the staircase to make my slow way back down when I spied the door across the way.

The second light that night. Maybe the neighbor would know if Adele's friend was still living here, and if not, where she had moved.

Despite my lack of hope, it was certainly worth a shot.

I walked over to the other apartment and knocked on the door.

The doorknob turned, and there was Adele.

I blinked, so surprised I couldn't say a word.

Adele was equally surprised. She was wearing black leggings and a black tee shirt, her hair pulled back in a tight ponytail. She wore no makeup, and her naked face stared up at me with absolute vulnerability.

"Tom," she said. "What are you doing here? And what happened to your face?"

I blinked again, reaching up to touch my cheek that was still bruised. "Don't worry about that. How are you? Are you okay? And what are *you* doing here?"

"I'm fine," she said. She was still clutching the side of the door with one hand. The other was hidden behind her leg. There was a faint frown on her face, "Why wouldn't I be?"

"Because I got jumped," I said. "That night I saw you at the Tipsy Cow. Those same guys who attacked you had apparently followed me. They jumped me in the alley."

Her eyes widened. "Oh, I'm so sorry. I had no idea what happened to you. Would you like to come in?" She stepped back, holding the door open wider.

"Thanks," I said, relief flooding over me. I had found her, and she appeared to be healthy and whole. I stepped across the doorway and into the small landing space. Behind me, Adele shut the door, locking it with a "click."

And just like that, I could feel the hairs stand up at the back of my neck. Something was wrong. The apartment was too dark. Other than the light on in the landing, I could see nothing.

Why would she be sitting in her apartment, alone, in the dark?

Maybe she wasn't alone.

I turned to ask her what was going on just in time to see her lunge at me. With the hand she had kept hidden, she plunged a needle into the flesh on the side of my neck, and I staggered back in pain.

I grasped at the needle as the edges of my vision started turning black. "What did you do?" I choked out, trying to pull it out of my flesh. "What did you do?"

She watched me, her eyes flat and hard as I dropped to my knees, my limbs unable to support me any longer. Everything around me swam before my eyes, the shapes and colors indistinct.

How could she do this? How could she betray me like this? I had done everything for her, everything! Why would she do this to me?

She leaned over as I sank to the ground. I saw her lips part. "Justice," she said, her voice echoing as if she was speaking from far away.

And then, everything dissolved into nothingness.

The first thing I became aware of was pain.

My chest hurt, my arms hurt, my head hurt. It felt like my body was on fire. My mouth was dry and parched. I wanted—needed—something to drink.

I tried to move, to open my eyes, but my body felt heavy and thick. A clanging type of noise I couldn't identify reverberated around me. What was going on? I knew I needed to think, but my brain was too foggy to focus on anything other than the pain.

"Ah, there you are," said a voice. "Took a bit longer than I anticipated. I was getting a little worried I may have overdone it with the dose, which of course would have ruined all the fun."

I forced my eyes open. Adele was sitting cross-legged on the floor staring at me with an amused expression on her face. The room we were in was bare of furniture, and there was something odd about the walls behind her I couldn't quite figure out.

But the room was the least of my worries. My thirst was all I could think about. I licked my dry lips. "Water," I rasped.

Her eyebrows went up. "Oh, are you thirsty? Yeah I read that was one of the side effects." She picked up a bottle of water and held it out. "Is this what you want?"

I nodded as pain shot through my head and neck.

"Then take it."

I tried to move one of my arms, and a bolt of pain shot through my chest, making me gasp. It was then that I realized my arms were tied tightly behind my back, so tight they were stretching my broken ribs in painful ways. I licked my dry lips again. "Why are doing this to me?"

She cocked her head for a moment, still holding out the water bottle.

"Jenny."

I stared at her. She couldn't have said "Jenny." I must have misheard her. Or my brain was misfiring. She couldn't know about Jenny.

"What are you talking about?"

She unscrewed the cap on the bottle of water and took a long drink. A dribble of water ran down her chin. I gazed at it longingly, my desperation for a drink nearly making me mad.

"You know who I'm talking about," she said when she finished swallowing. She wiped her mouth with her arm. "The woman you murdered."

My eyes went wide. "I didn't murder anyone."

"You murdered Jenny."

"That's a lie. I loved her, and she loved me."

Her face darkened, and she leaned forward, putting her hands on her thighs. "She was *terrified* of you. You stalked her, and you killed her."

"No! I tried to save her! It wasn't my fault she ran in front of that car."

"She was trying to get away from you."

"No!" I howled, my throat on fire. "You lie! You don't know anything about it. How do you even know Jenny?"

A slow, ugly smile stretched across her face. "Jenny was my sister."

Aha! Proof she was lying. "Impossible," I said, triumphantly. "She didn't have a sister named Adele."

"You're right. My name is Julie Adele."

I froze. The pain in my body was suddenly overshadowed by the creeping realization that something had gone very wrong.

Her smile widened. "Oh? You didn't think to research her sister's middle name? Or did it just slip your mind?"

I tried to swallow, but there was no saliva in my mouth. The more I looked at her face, the more I could see the resemblance. The high cheekbones, the lips shaped like a little bow. My mind flipped back to all the details that had reminded me of Jenny ... all the things I had tried to push away.

How could I have been so sloppy?

"You have to believe me," I said. "I loved your sister. I would never hurt a hair on her head."

Her expression darkened. "You *stalked* my sister. You *terrorized* her. And the cops did nothing. Nothing! Even after her death, they told us there's nothing they can do. But you get to walk free ... to stalk and terrorize some other poor, innocent woman. No ... not anymore."

My blood felt like ice in my veins. "What do you mean?"

She smiled again—the triumphant grin of a predator cornering its prey.

There was a knock at the door.

"Oh, good. Just in time," she said, scrambling to her feet as I began frantically struggling with my bonds, ignoring the pain roaring through my body.

"Help," I screamed as loud as I could. "I'm in here, and I need help!"

She glanced disdainfully over her shoulder as she walked to the door. "Scream all you want," she said. "No one else lives here."

I stared at her as a creeping sense of horror began to fill my body.

She nodded at the walls. "We soundproofed the walls, too, so no one is going to hear you outside, either."

That was why the walls looked so odd. They were covered with a thick, white padding.

She disappeared from view, and I began to struggle again in earnest. I could hear her open the door and greet whoever was there.

She came back into the room.

"Tom, or, actually, is that even your name? I meant to ask. You're a tough one to track down. A lot of aliases. Makes me suspect Jenny wasn't your first. But never mind that now. You remember our guests, don't you?"

I glanced back at the entrance, and my eyes widened in terror. The three men who attacked me, who had attacked Adele—no, Julie—stood there.

Julie smiled. "I don't think you've been properly introduced. This is Jack, our older brother. Oh, didn't you know Jenny had an older brother? I'm not surprised. Technically, he's our half-brother. He lives with his father. My mom had him before she met and married our father. But we're still close. Luckily, my mom and his dad both believed strongly in family and made sure we spent time together growing up."

"You set me up," I said. "How could you do this to me?"

"It was easier than you think," she said as she moved to the next man. "The hardest part was finding you, but once we did that, it didn't take much at all to catch your eye and lead you down that dark alley. I figured once you 'saved' me, that would seal the deal, and boy was I right. Now, let's continue with the introductions. This is our cousin, Levi. You probably didn't know about him, either. Remember what I said about my mother believing in family? Well, we spent a lot of time with our cousins, as well.

"And last but not least," she said, moving to the leader, the biggest one in the group. "This is Grant."

I blanched.

She nodded as Grant folded his arms across his chest. "Ah yes. I thought you might remember that name. Jenny's fiancé."

"She loved me," I said, but my voice was hollow, even to my own ears. "She didn't love you. She wanted to be with me."

"Keep telling yourself that," Grant said. "You and I both know the truth."

"Well, now that we've all gotten acquainted, I'll leave you boys alone." Julie started walking to the door. "Try not to have too much fun."

"Wait," I gasped. Julie paused and glanced at me. "You can't leave me. They're going to kill me."

"They're not going to kill you," she corrected. "At least, not right away. Which is actually unfortunate for you. You'll wish they would, before this is all said and done. I'll see you all later. Well, maybe not you." She gave me a pointed look as she headed to the door.

"Wait," I called out. "Don't leave me. I'm sorry. I'm sorry about Jenny."

Her voice floated back to me. "I'm sure you are. But not as sorry as you will be."

There was a "click" as the door firmly closed.

For a moment, there was silence.

I eyed each of my captors, my mind desperately searching for a way out.

There *had* to be a way out.

I wasn't meant to die here.

There had to be a way.

Then Grant cracked his knuckles and gave me a nasty smile. "Well. Shall we get started?"

ABOUT THE AUTHOR

Michele PW (Pariza Wacek) taught herself to read at three years old because she wanted to write stories so badly and ended up writing everything from marketing copy to magazine articles to business books and more. Her latest work of fiction is the award-winning Secrets of Redemption series, where nothing is ever what it seems. You can start your visit to Redemption for free with *The Secret Diary of Helen Blackstone* novella at https://mpwnovels.com/sign-up.

NO REASON

STEVE DAVISON

When a hostage exchange goes wrong, special field operative Louis Cane is forced to take matters into his own hands.

1

Sânandrei, Romania

The man pointing a Glock 19 at my face is called Reisman. He's fat, and wears a gray boiler suit that's open to the waist. His skin is sweaty and red; I can smell his sour odor. His round face shines beneath the fluorescent lights. I check his expression for any signs of anxiety. There are none.

My eyes slide to the right, to the corner of the room, where a young woman, half-naked and shaking, is tied to a metal chair. Her name is Justine Grenhall. She is twenty-five years old and works as an agent for British Intelligence. She's bloody and ragged, and her mouth is stuffed full of cloth.

I don't know her personally, but I've spoken to her father. He is beyond scared, and for good reason—Reisman is a psychopath. I can only guess at what he's done to her. I think of my own daughter. Had she lived, she'd be sixteen years old now.

"Worried about her?" Reisman smirks, tapping a stubby finger over his lips, as if contemplating a deep puzzle. His voice is high and stringy, with a strong accent and guttural inflection.

I don't answer. There are lots of things on my mind. The angle of the Glock, for one.

"Why did they send you?" he asks.

I remain silent. This is deliberate. I don't want him to get comfortable. He must surely know I'm not an ordinary operative, but he will assume that I will follow protocol and plead for the girl's safety or appeal to his human decency. Not an unreasonable deduction.

"What are you hiding?" he asks.

An interesting question. It's as if his well-honed survival instinct is kicking in. I shrug. "Nothing."

"Take off your clothes," he says suddenly.

I pull off my jacket and drop it to the floor. I do the same with my shirt. Then I step out of my pants and socks and add them to the heap. I stand before him in my boxer shorts. He looks me up and down for a long moment. I wait for him to notice the prosthetic, but his eyes flick away, and he says, "What's your name?"

"Louis Cane," I reply.

"Okay, Louis Cane, where do I find Mace?"

"In a farmhouse."

"Where?"

I gesture to the pile of clothes on the floor. "Jacket, inside pocket. There's a key to the front door and instructions on how to get there."

He thinks about this for a long moment, then he drags the pile toward him with his foot. His eyes never leave my face, and neither does the Glock. He squats down and reaches for the jacket.

"Was it worth it?" he asks.

"What?"

"Volunteering to get killed. You must have a reason."

I shake my head. "No reason. And who says I'm getting killed?"

A broad smile breaks over his face, and I see his yellow teeth. "You'd be amazed at the number of people who've said that same thing to me." His fingers feel for the pocket opening. "They were all wrong."

"What about the girl?" I ask.

"What about her?"

"She's released to me now. That's the agreement."

He shakes his head. "I want Mace. If I don't get him, I'll kill her."

Our eyes lock as his hand disappears inside the jacket pocket.

I wait for the snap. It comes quickly. A clean sound like the crack of a whip as the hammer is triggered and smashes into his fingers. His eyes bulge a second before he lets out a guttural roar.

In the split second of confusion, I rush at him. He leaps up, and I watch the trajectory of his arm as it lowers.

Good.

He pulls the trigger twice. Both shots rip into my chest, and blood gushes in an urgent spurt. I tip away and roll over, coming to rest on my front with my head turned toward him. I lie motionless, bleeding out.

He has splatters of my blood on his face, chest and hands. He glances at me briefly, while his brain calculates my state of health. He must have concluded that I'm finished, because he grabs my jacket, rips the pocket open at the seam, and reveals the trap with the key nestled beside it. He carefully removes the key and tag with a location written on it.

Hurrying over to the girl, he unties her from the chair and pulls her up by her hair. They lumber to the door, then they are gone. Outside, I can hear a van's engine roar to life, then tires crunching over the dirt as he drives away.

I wait a short time, then sit up, turn my wrist over, and tap a receiver on my watch. Within moments, I hear Randolph's voice. It's breathy and urgent.

"Cane?" she asks.

"Yes."

There's a small beat, and I hear her breath exhale. "Jesus," she says. "You survived it."

I *did* survive it. I always do.

"Did he take the key?" she asks.

"He went for all of it."

"The Kevlar?"

I smile. "I thought he'd realized."

"He shot you, though?"

"Of course."

Silence.

I grope at the space between my chest and my armpit, feeling for the edge of the prosthesis, teasing it away. The fake skin and putty peel back as I pull the chest plate free. I turn it over in my hands. A plastic bag, neatly fixed behind the Kevlar composite, is now empty, its contents dispersed. A neat job. Hours in the make-up chair to achieve it. My life prolonged because of it—and, hopefully, Justine Grenhall's too.

"Can you send someone to get me?" I ask.

"We're on our way."

I ring off and look about the room. It has corrugated-iron walls, a concrete floor, and metal beams stretching across the ceiling. I glance down at my feet. I'm standing in a shallow lake of pig's blood from the bag, my toes stained red. I toss the chest plate aside, and move toward a sink in the corner of the room to clean up.

Outside, the sun is high and hot. I'm standing in acres of grassland, vast swathes of parched straw stretching for miles in every direction. I wait under a tree, out of the heat, and think through what Reisman will do next.

He'll go straight to Mace, of course, but, after that, his movements will be unpredictable. If it were me, I'd head to the nearest city, probably Arad, or even circle back to Timisoara. Both locations will make it difficult for us to track him. The biggest worry is Justine Grenhall. Will he do what he says he'll do?

Somewhere in the distance, I hear the low whoop-whoop of the helicopter before I see it moving in my direction from out of the sun. It settles on the grass, and the doors swing open. Randolph and Wakefield run toward me.

Randolph is a redhead. That's the first thing you notice about her. She's lean and taut like an athlete, strong and determined too. Her superpower is organization; she overlooks nothing but also has a soft side. She throws her arms around me in a rare display of emotion.

"Worried about me?" I ask, trying to lighten the tension.

She holds me close for a moment, then pulls away and uses the back of her hand to dab her eyes.

Wakefield extends his hand. "Nice job, Cane," he says, "and before you ask, I *was* worried about you." He flashes me a smile. His ivory-white teeth contrast sharply with his dark skin. He pushes his round spectacles up high onto the bridge of his nose. Wakefield is techy. He can do almost anything with a computer.

"Ready to debrief?" asks Randolph, back to her usual normal, focused self.

We make our way to the chopper and climb inside. There are two rows of seats facing each other. I take one side; Randolph and Wakefield take the other. We buckle up, and soon the aircraft lifts high into the air. Randolph pulls out a thin digital note-pad, fires it up, and a map rushes in to fill the blank screen.

"Okay," she says, pointing to a blue dot on the map. "Here is the position of the corrugated hut. And here," she adds, pointing to a flashing red light about 4km north of that position, "is our man."

"The GPS in the blood splatter is working," I say.

"For now."

I turn to Wakefield. "How long will it transmit?"

"Two hours normally, but in this heat it may be less."

"Assuming he doesn't shower," says Randolph.

I picture Reisman's rancid flesh, peppered with the blood. "I think we're safe on that front."

The chopper soon drops onto a grass apron. We are in an uninhabited space, fifteen miles south of the farmhouse where we've left Mace. This is our temporary operations area, and it's basic: a single canvas tent, 6ft high and 20ft wide, tethered to the ground, it's inside kitted out with technical gear— all of it powered by a generator hooked up to a transit van.

The heat hits my face as soon as I enter, the monitors and cables all chucking out warm air. Members of the backup crew, dressed in khaki, are huddled together in tight cliques around WIN-T screens.

"Okay," I say, "so far, so good. Now we have two major unknowables. What happens after Reisman collects Mace? And will he take Justine Grenhall with him?"

"Or will he spare her?" puts in Randolph.

"Or kill her," I say.

Wakefield adjusts his spectacles. "If the transmitters in the pig's blood continue to work, the first part is no problem."

"It's the second part that worries me," I reply.

"What does the decision maker say?" asks Randolph.

The Decision Maker is an algorithm Wakefield designed. Developed originally for psychological profiling, it interfaces with military grade geospatial software to assess what decision a target in the field will make next. It's extremely accurate.

"He'll take her," says Wakefield.

There is a brief moment of silence, which I break. "What's happening at the farmhouse?"

"Maddox and Johnson are there. No movement yet."

"Still think he'll head for Arad?" asks Wakefield.

"That's where I'd go."

In the center of the tent is a white board. Stuck to it are three 6"x4" glossy photographs. One is of Reisman, one of Mace, and the other of Justine Grenhall. My eyes flick between them. Reisman looks fat and unhealthy, while Mace is lean and cold-eyed, with hair buzzed close to his scalp. He stares into the camera like a fish from a bowl. I've seen his type before—detached, socially dominant, psychopathically violent. The network of crimes for which he's been responsible stretch from Romania, across Western Europe, to the US. Human trafficking, drugs, money laundering, and murder.

Last is Justine Grenhall. She's pretty in an unconventional way, with a small, elf-like face, keen eyes, and a cute smile. Her appearance belies her bravery. I've learned a lot about her over the last couple of days. An agent working for MI6, originally as a field operator, then as an undercover agent, she infiltrated a ring that was transporting girls from Romania across Western Europe. Mace had her as a "runner" between borders, making sure transportation from one country to the next ran smoothly. She's the reason MI6 caught Mace in the first place, and why we've set him free. Once his crew discovered who she really was, she was in deep trouble.

Adams, our commander, ducks into the tent, his smooth forehead creases into three deep lines. The reason becomes clear when I see the man following behind him. Justine Grenhall's father is tall and gray, his shoulders are hunched forward, as if the troubles of the world are bearing down on them.

His presence here is highly irregular, but not entirely unexpected. The man is a politician, not a prominent one, but he is old-school, and will have used whatever leverage he has to get here. I don't blame him for that, I would have done exactly the same had our roles been reversed.

Adams turns back to me. “Do you have a minute, Cane?”

I don’t, but I nod. “Of course.”

I move to join them, and Justine’s father takes my hands in his. “Louis, did you see her?”

“Yes sir, I did.”

“How was she?”

I think of the frightened creature, half-naked and shaking in the chair, and reply, “She’s coping very well, sir.”

“Did she say anything?”

I shake my head. “There was no chance, but we made eye contact.”

He searches my face for something—anything—from which he might derive comfort.

I adopt a well-practised expression—somewhere between confidence and empathy. “She was in control. Focused on the job. A true professional.”

He watches me for a long moment, then nods slowly, as if what I’ve said has hit the spot. “You will get her out, won’t you?”

“Absolutely.”

Adams clears his throat, places a hand on Grenhall’s shoulder. “Let's leave these people to get on with it.”

Grenhall pulls his eyes away from mine. I watch them go. A father in despair. I can relate to that. Nothing prepares you for losing a child.

“You okay?” asks Randolph.

I nod. “Yeah.”

Reisman hauled Justine Grenhall out of the corrugated hut, bound her with decking rope, and tossed her into the back of his van. He called Mace’s crew and gave them the farmhouse’s position.

His priority was Mace. It always had been, even when they were kids.

The plan was simple. He'd go to the location by way of a town called Hodoni, then drive 30 miles north to Arad, where the police sub-commissioner would help him vanish. The man was so deeply ensnared in Mace's network, he had no choice. The fate of the Grenhall girl would be up to Mace. She'd been the one responsible for putting him behind bars in the first place.

Before that, though, there was the matter of Justin Grenhall's dinner companions. When he'd raided her apartment, he assumed she'd be alone. However, she'd been having dinner with a couple of women.

He didn't know who they were, not that it mattered much—the only question had been whether to leave them or take them all. The first option risked identification at a later date, the second meant an organizational headache.

He'd chosen the latter.

He had tied the two women to a steel post in a warehouse he owned two miles south of Hodoni. That was nearly a week ago. He had no worries about them being discovered—the warehouse was remote, and people in Hodoni knew better than to interfere in his business.

He turned off the 692 at Carani and took a narrow road that cut deep into the countryside. After three miles, he came to a deserted area, about an acre in all, bound by a three-bar fence. The warehouse was the only building on the site. Once an agricultural depot, Reisman had acquired it for a different purpose. Many of the women he'd trafficked, especially from the remote villages, were stored here whilst waiting for transportation to their final destinations in Western Europe.

Pulling the van to a stop, he took a leather valet case from the passenger seat, and got out. He peered down at the dry soil. The sun was still high; he could feel droplets of sweat peppering his neck. He opened the back of the van and looked at Justine Grenhall. She was tied up like a mummy, the cloth still firmly stuck in her mouth, her eyes wide and fearful. The temperature in the back of the van was in the high 80s, yet her pale, naked skin was puckered like gooseflesh. Fear did peculiar things to people.

He leaned in and pushed his face next to hers. Cheek to cheek. He felt her recoil—a conditioned reflex; one that made him feel powerful.

He closed the back of the van again, leaving her inside, and turned to face the warehouse. It was a timber-framed construction, solid, befitting its original purpose. The iron chain on the double doors at the front was still firmly in position. He released the lock and entered. The space inside was high, wide and hot. At first glance, the dimly lit space looked completely empty. It smelt damp, and a rancid smell of sewage.

Reisman used a torch he'd left inside the door to pick out the two women, who were still chained to the metal post at the far end. As he angled the light, he could see both of them—on the floor, semi-conscious. The source of the smell then became obvious—they'd defecated right where they were lying.

In the system they were worth around $30,000 each. Not an inconsiderable sum. One of them was naturally thin, the other fatter and more rounded. On paper, the thin one would fetch more, although food deprivation and drug addiction would soon bring the other one into line.

Being Westerners, their final destinations would have to be much farther afield. Perhaps Asia or the Middle East. They'd have to be fully broken-in, of course, but that was not an insurmountable problem, either.

He opened the valet case and rummaged around for the syringe and vials of Midazolam. 2mg each should be enough to start them off. He injected the liquid into the median cubital vein of each girl, then called the organizer in Mace's crew.

Vulpe answered quickly.

"I have two more for this afternoon's transportation," Reisman told him.

"Where?"

"Hodoni."

"I'll pick them up."

Randolph and I are watching the GPS signal emanating from the blood spatter on Reisman's skin. He has made an unexpected diversion toward a town called Hodoni. I've read a lot about Reisman—his file is extensive—and there's one thing about which I'm clear. The man is devoted to Mace.

"What's he doing?" she says. "Why isn't he going straight to the farmhouse?"

"He must have a good reason to stop."

"A pre-designated plan?"

"Maybe."

I go through some scenarios in my mind. A pick-up is the most obvious one. If that's the case, then who or what is he picking up? And what does it have to do with Mace's freedom?

"Anything important in Hodini?" I ask.

Wakefield shakes his head. "We have nothing on Hodini. Just a village. Not important."

"It is, for Reisman," I say, watching the GPS signal on the pad.

Wakefield removes his spectacles and cleans them on his shirt. We watch the pulsing light on the pad and wait. Five minutes pass, then ten, before he's on the move again. Retracing his route back to the 692, he proceeds northwards, toward a town called Vinga—and the farmhouse.

Adams comes back in; his smooth head is shining under the fluorescent lights in the tent. "Okay. Almost showtime." He flicks his eyes at Randolph. "How far from the farmhouse is he?"

She watches the pad. "A mile."

He looks at me. "We can take you two miles south of Arad. That's as far as the chopper's allowed."

"Two's better than five. When did they change their mind?"

"Just now," he replies. "We offered to donate the Land Rover to whatever good cause the *poliția* thought worthy."

"That it?"

He shrugs, and turns to Wakefield. "Back-up in place?"

Wakefield nods.

Adams looks back to me. "Then it's down to you, Cane. In the meantime, check on Maddox and Johnson."

"I already have," says Randolph. "They're still reporting no activity at the farmhouse."

Adams seems to weigh this up in his mind. "Thoughts?" he asks, turning to us.

"I'm surprised," I say. "I thought they would form a choke point at the farmhouse."

Randolph curls a strand of her hair behind her ear. "They're not stupid. They must have a plan."

Adams looks at me. "What are you thinking, Cane?"

I shrug. "Who knows what the psychos might do. They may not go to the farmhouse at all. That way, the crew is safe, and they'll just allow the current actors to play it out. Or they might just be clearing the site."

"Of what?"

"Of anyone who shouldn't be there."

Adams falls silent. I can almost hear the cogs inside his mind working.

"This operation's a mess," he says finally. "It's been conceived too quickly."

There's no denying that. When Grenhall was compromised, things escalated fast.

"I hate pandering to Mace's crew like this," he continues. "The location, the farmhouse, you meeting Reisman in the hut—all of it suboptimal."

Another man ducks into the tent. I know him from the London office. Colt is his name. Small and neat, with quick movements, he's an administration officer, high-ranking, with an eye for detail. He gestures to us with a formal nod of his head, and says to Adams, "Can I have a word, sir?"

Adams moves away, and they begin talking in hushed whispers.

My mind turns to Maddox and Johnson. They are good operators, but in this terrain, with not much time to prepare, they are vulnerable. And something else, too—something that strikes me as odd.

"How are they communicating with you?" I ask.

"Usual way," Randolph says. "BOWMAN voice transmission."

"When was the last time you heard from them?"

"Fifteen minutes ago."

"Using the usual subscriber nodes?"

"Yes."

"Ask them to input again."

She moves to the WIN-T interface and evokes a communication stream. I watch her and wait.

Nothing.

She tries again, with the same result, then glances at me. She looks worried.

Adams returns. The color has drained from his face, replaced with a waxy, yellowish tone. "We have a problem," he croaks.

"What?"

"Mace has been pulled from the farmhouse."

"Pulled?"

"The Americans want him for an information exchange. They've taken him out."

"So they've got him now?"

Adams nods. "He's on his way back to jail."

"What about Grenhall?"

He opens his mouth to say something, then closes it again.

I can't believe what I'm hearing.

Adams regains his composure. "She won't be harmed," he says, quickly. "If Reisman touches her, he'll never see Mace again."

"He's *already* harmed her," I say through gritted teeth. "I saw her thirty minutes ago."

He rubs his forehead with the back of his hand. "I'm in an impossible position. They've taken it out of my hands."

"*You're* in an impossible position? What about Justine Grenhall?"

"What do you expect me to do, Cane?" he says, raising his voice.

"Who agreed to it?"

"Command in London."

"When?"

He turns to look at Colt, who is standing at the tent's entrance, who says, "Earlier. I've just received the message."

"Verifiable?"

He nods solemnly.

My brain feels like it's smacking against the inside of my skull.

"What do you think Reisman will do when he realizes Mace is not at the farmhouse? Just shrug his shoulders and carry on, as if nothing happened?"

Silence, which I fill. "He'll kill her."

Adams' jaw sets.

"You've told her father?" I ask.

"No."

I walk about the tent, trying to collect my thoughts. "No interference from anyone. That was the deal."

Adams watches the floor.

"Who else knows we're here?"

"A handful of people," Colt says softly.

"Only in London?"

"In Virginia, too."

I glance at Randolph. "How far is Reisman from the farmhouse?"

Her eyes flick down to the pad. "He's there."

"Ok," I say, getting back in the zone. "Reisman is a psychopath. Getting Mace was possibly enough to keep him from killing Grenhall. But not now."

"Agreed," says Wakefield.

"What's happening with Maddox and Johnson?" I ask Randolph.

She shakes her head. "Nothing's coming back."

"We can assume they're dead. Which means Mace's crew are in and around the farmhouse. Which begs the question—how did the Americans get Mace out?"

I look at Adams. Behind him, Colt clears his throat. "It's my understanding," he says softly, "that Mace was removed soon after we left him."

"Before Maddox and Adams arrived?'

He nods.

I picture a scene in my mind: Reisman's Glock is pointing at my face, the Kevlar composite stuck in position, waiting for him to make his move.

My voice is a low growl. "So I risked everything to give up a man who had already been removed?"

Colt averts his eyes; Adams rubs his temples with his palms.

Randolph cuts into the silence. "Cane, focus. What do you want to do?"

I think about Justine Grenhall cowering in the back of Reisman's van. Her father is somewhere outside this tent, worrying about his baby, and I know what that feels like.

"The next move is clear. I'm going in to get her."

Reisman was a mile from Mace's location when he got a call from Luca, one of Mace's inner circle—a man almost as close to him as Reisman himself. He'd found two agents within half a mile of the location and assumed they were hostile.

"What did you do?" asked Reisman.

"Injured them, then hung them upside down from a couple of telephone poles."

This made Reisman smile. "Are they dead?"

"Not yet."

"OK. Don't do anything else until I get there."

Reisman turned westward onto a small track. He could hardly quell his excitement at the prospect of seeing his brother again. A scene flickered through his mind like an old movie. Two young kids sitting in a bath. The water is colored red by blood. Their mother slumped dead over the side, stabbed through the chest for a heroin debt.

Reisman had always been protective of Mace. Back then, he'd hugged him tightly, told him everything would be alright.

As it turned out, he had been correct. Everything *had* worked out. That was, until they came for Mace. A rat in the organization is difficult to legislate for. At least, that's what he told himself, though, deep down inside, he knew it was his fault. He should have been onto Grenhall much earlier. He'd let his feelings for her get in the way.

He glanced over his shoulder into the back of the van. Justine Grenhall looked like a plucked turkey—puckered and dumb, and all trussed up. He felt nothing but contempt for her now.

He came to a steep gradient, and the van bounced around in the dirt. Up ahead, he could see a building on top of a hill. It wasn't a farmhouse at all. More like a bunker. Cube-shaped and windowless.

The crew were huddled together over to one side. Reisman pulled the van to a stop, and got out. Luca came jogging over. His shaved head shone in the sunlight and beads of sweat were peppering the dragon tattoo on his face and neck. Jerking his thumb over his shoulder, he said, "These two are ready for market."

Reisman's eyes drifted in the direction of where the crew were standing. Two poles were positioned about 30 feet apart. Hanging upside-down from each of them, with rope around their ankles, were two men in khaki gear. The gang members were swinging them from side to side like cow carcasses on a butcher's hook. The one on the right was in particularly bad shape—even from where Reisman stood, he could see the blood caked on the side of the man's face.

"Not yet." he said, turning his attention back to the farmhouse and rummaging in his pocket for the key. "Come with me."

The door was heavy duty, probably steel. It had three metal arms: one at the top, middle, and bottom, each secured by an industrial-strength padlock. Reisman placed his key in the first lock and turned it. It popped open, and he hooked it off easily. He did the same with the second and third locks.

Then he pushed the large door inward. Inside was a clean, illuminated area, with a wooden floor, white walls, and spotlights on the ceiling. In the center of the space was one desk, an upright chair, and a sofa. Ductwork snaked across the ceiling and dived into an air conditioning unit.

But, most importantly, no Mace.

He spotted a door in the far corner. Running across to it, he swung it open. Inside was a small bedroom with a single bed in the center, which had been made up as if waiting for a hotel guest. To the left, a tiny en-suite with a toilet and shower.

All of it empty.

He spun around and ran back into the living area. There was nowhere to go or hide. Mace was not here. Reisman's world slowed down as he tried to make sense of it.

"Did you see anyone here earlier?" he asked.

Luca shook his head.

No Mace meant what exactly? A trick? Why, though? He still had the girl, and he was sure they didn't want to lose her. A trap, then?

He hurried out of the farmhouse and looked around the grounds, half expecting it to be surrounded. He could see no one. Some of the men were still huddled around the telephone poles. Others were leaning up against the SUVs, smoking and talking. He strode toward them.

The shock of Mace's absence quickly turned to anger, which was tinged with another emotion, one he hadn't felt since he was a child: *humiliation.*

It bubbled inside him like gas from a stinking sewer. Mace had always taken the lead; Reisman had been fine with that. Mace was bright and strategic. Now he was in charge, and they'd outwitted him. Messed with his mind.

He glanced over at Luca and clicked his fingers. "Knife."

Luca pulled a hunting knife from his belt and handed it over. The blade was long and jagged, and the crew parted as Reisman stormed forward. The man hanging from the left-hand telephone pole was wriggling to get free. His face was red and puffy, engorged with blood. As Reisman approached, the man's eyes flicked up to meet his. Perhaps he hoped that this was his rescuer.

He was wrong.

Reisman plunged the blade deep into the man's belly and dragged it down toward his neck. He did it with such force, the man's chest gaped open like a curtain. Blood pumped out onto the dirt. Reisman quickly moved to the next man. This one was already in trouble; he helped him on his way by stabbing the knife into his neck so that it went all the way through.

Then he turned back to the crew. There was immediate silence. They stared at him with an awed diffidence that violence commands.

"No one messes with me," he said bluntly. "Understood?"

The men said nothing.

Reisman tossed the van's keys to a short, stocky man called Suta, who had a scar that ran the length of his right cheek. "Go and get the girl. And bring the case from the front seat."

Then to Luca: "Vulpe is escorting a transportation of product passing through Felnec tonight. I want her on the truck with the rest of them. Can you arrange it?"

Luca grinned. "I'll take her myself. Might even have some fun with her on the way."

Suta hauled Grenhall out of the van and carried her to where Reisman and the rest of the men were standing. She was crying. He dropped her to the ground, and Reisman hunched down next to her and pushed her flat onto her back. "Hold her legs and arms," he said, wiping the knife on his sleeve.

The blade glistened in the sunlight. He moved it up to her stomach, and flicked his wrist. She let out a high-pitched scream as blood began to ooze. He carved the letter "S" into her skin. Then he continued to move the knife from her stomach to her chest, carving an "O", followed by a "B", then an "OLAN". One word: SOBOLAN. It took him eight minutes to finish it.

Rat in English.

When it was done, he stood up and watched her. She lay supine, shaking so violently her teeth were rattling in her skull. The blood from the wound in her chest trickled down onto her ribs, then dripped onto the dirt like a faulty tap.

"Give me the bag," he said, clicking his fingers.

Suta handed it over, and Reisman rummaged inside it. He pulled out a bottle of surgical spirit, unscrewed the lid, and poured the liquid over Grenhall's chest.

She gasped as the deep burn of the alcohol seared into her wounds. Next, he pulled out a vial of Midazolam and sucked 2mg into a syringe. He squatted down next to her and grabbed her arm, injecting the liquid into her vein.

He turned to Luca and said, "Get her in the SUV. Make sure she makes the transportation."

Luca hauled her up from the dirt and carried her to his vehicle. He climbed into the driver's seat, with a weird expression on his face—something close to anticipation. Reisman watched the tires kick up dirt as the vehicle spun around and sped away. He checked his watch. Fifteen minutes to Arad, if he put his foot down.

I change into black jeans, black t-shirt, and a denim jacket, then I duck outside the tent. The heat of the afternoon throws up a haze over the ground in the middle distance. Much of the discussion we've just had centered around the choice of vehicle I will use.

Land Rover or Kawasaki?

I've chosen the Kawasaki. Modified for military use, of course. A competent vehicle for what I have in mind. Randolph is at my side. So is Adams and Wakefield.

Randolph hands me a Glock 17, which I place in a holster under the jacket. "Got a Kevlar vest on?"

I nod.

She slaps two throwing knives in my palm, like a surgical assistant. These are not regulation supplies, but I always carry them. I ease them both into my back pocket. "Make sure you get people out to the location in Hodoni," I say, "I want to know what Reisman was doing there.'

Adams says, "Regular contact as per the protocol."

I clip in my earpiece, and fire up the bike.

Colt appears from inside the tent and hurries over. He has the pad in his hand. "I thought you should know," he says, 'the GPS signal has split."

I glance at Randolph.

"Grenhall?" she asks.

One of the reasons for using the pig's blood was what Wakefield termed "cross-contamination". If Reisman's skin got close to Grenhall's—and I knew it would—small droplets of the pig's blood would transfer, along with the nano-transmitters.

"So, they've split up," I say.

Randolph nods. "Which means we can track her independently."

"One signal's heading east," says Colt. "Toward Gelu. The other is on the E671, heading north."

"Arad?"

He nods.

"That's Reisman." I'm certain of it.

"He's handed Grenhall off to someone else," adds Wakefield.

I look at Adams. "Or he's killed her, and they're dumping the body."

The group goes silent.

I glance at Randolph, and she mouths, "Good luck."

I let out the clutch, and the Kawasaki leaps forward. Soon I'm out on the main road, the wind rushing at me, the countryside passing by in a blur. It reminds me of another hot day five years ago. I was on a motorcycle then too, heading to a private military hospital.

There's a small crackle of static in my earpiece, and Randolph's voice comes on the line: "Cane?"

"Yeah."

"The second signal is now moving north toward Mailat. I'll guide you when you get nearer Vinga."

"Okay."

She detaches.

On the motorcycle, the memories come flooding back, unbidden. Dr. Krist's office—which was expensive, with oak paneling on the walls, and a view over acres of grassland. Portly and studious, he was a kind man, who'd wanted to know about my feelings. He had dozens of questions about anxiety, guilt, and grief. Was I on the edge, or at the center of life? Feeling strong or weak, detached or engaged?

I told him I'd felt nothing.

But that was not true. As soon as I saw the bodies of my wife and child, strung out and bloody, murdered by a man I should have killed years before, I knew what my life would now be: destroying people like him before they got to the innocent, or the vulnerable or the weak.

The feeling had kicked in immediately; it was like taking a drug, a clarity injection that kept me focused. No anxieties, no worries, and nothing to lose.

"You must have a reason to carry on," he'd said.

"Why?" I'd asked.

"Because otherwise you'll go mad."

I'd shaken my head. "I won't, and I don't need a reason."

"Cane?"

Randolph is back in my ear.

"Yeah."

"Take the next left-hand fork. It'll take you around the edge of town."

"Where's Grenhall now?"

"The signal puts her three miles north of Mailat. She's heading to the 682."

"Where does that go?"

"From east to west."

"Follow it west. Where does it end up?" I ask her.

There is silence for a long moment as she scrolls along its route. "Serbia, then Austria and Germany."

"Okay, stay with me."

I turn east onto an unmade dirt road. The bike bounces around as I move quickly up a gradual incline. Finally, I see the farmhouse on the right-hand side. Its cubic, prison-like appearance belies its name. It's deserted. Something catches my eye over on the left-hand side. I push the motorcycle on, and into a flat dirt apron. There are two poles, about thirty feet apart, with telegraph wires going from one to the other. Hanging upside down from each pole is a man in khaki gear.

I stand the Kawasaki up, get off, and move the first man. His body has been ripped open by a blade, in a vicious slashing action. Below his hanging corpse, the earth is sodden with blood. The other man has taken a fatal wound to the neck. Probably by the same knife.

"Randolph?"

She's back on immediately.

"You'd better get a team to the farmhouse. It's not pretty."

"Maddox and Johnson?"

"Stabbed to death."

The line goes silent.

The next 15 minutes passes in a blur as I follow Randolph's directions. The terrain is unmade, much of it dirt tracks that cut through agricultural land. Eventually, I hit the 682—a two-lane tarmac road with flat featureless fields on either side.

"Okay," says Randolph. "The signal is two miles west of your current position."

I open up the throttle on the Kawasaki and start to burn up the distance. Randolph counts me down. Half a mile, one quarter, 200 yards, 100 yards. Ahead of me is an articulated truck. It's painted dark-green, and looks brand new. Painted on the back is a yellow logo—two stripes, between which is printed *JCL Transportation*.

As I move up behind it, Randolph says, "You're right there. The signal is on top of you."

"It's a truck." I pull the Kawasaki out of my lane, and accelerate so that I'm level with the cab. The man nearest the window glances down at me, and I recognize him immediately. This is not good. I decide to take immediate action.

I pull in front of the truck and slow the bike down. Then I turn on my hazard lights and wave my arms, pointing to the wheels as if something is wrong with them. Reluctant to stop, the driver leans on the horn. I give them another chance, waggling my arms frantically, as if I'm a concerned fellow citizen who's spotted a defect in their vehicle.

Up ahead is a turnout, and I gesticulate in its direction. The truck slows, and pulls in behind me. I stand the bike up and get off, while they all get out together. Two from one side of the cab, two from the other. They move toward me in a line, and I get to see them properly for the first time. I recognize them all. We've had their photographs for months—members of Mace's crew. The one on the left is called Rosu, he's the smallest of the four. As wide as he is tall, his face looks like it's been squashed into a jar. Next to him is a man called Grasi. He wears his hair long and looks like a biker in a black vest and jeans. Then comes Luca, whose shaved head is perspiring in the sun. He has a full beard, and a dragon tattoo that runs around his neck and finishes up above his eye. The last one is Vulpe. Average-looking, normal haircut, regular clothes, and clean-shaven. He's almost respectable. Undoubtedly the most dangerous of the four.

My fingers brush the knives in my back pocket to ensure they are in position, then Luca says something to me in Romanian. His tone is aggressive. I don't understand any of it.

"I speak English," I say.

They look along the line to Vulpe, who studies me closely. I can sense the cogs in his brain turning. "What do you want?" he says finally, in a thick accent. I take a few steps forward, still playing the concerned citizen.

"Your back tire," I comment.

"What's wrong with it?"

"Flat as a pancake." I push my palms together to make the point. "It could blow out at any time."

They make no move to investigate. Which means they do not believe me.

I take a few more steps forward. "I'll show you."

Still, they don't move. I calculate the distance between us to be around twenty feet. My throwing accuracy is decent at this distance, although the power I generate will be low. My target will be Rosu. He's so wide that even from here it will be like hitting a barn door.

"Who are you?" Vulpe says suddenly.

"Gareth," I respond, still playing along, still moving forward. "Gareth Jones from South Wales." The distance is now around eighteen feet. "I'd hate to see your tire blow."

I will have to initiate the action very soon, before they do. So I execute two things at once.

I gesture to my bike with my right hand, saying, "I'm on a motorcycle holiday across Europe." At the same time, I grasp a throwing knife from my back pocket with my left. I bring the knife over my shoulder and throw it forward in one smooth movement, like a pitcher at a baseball game.

As soon as I release it, I'm running. The blade flips through the sunlit space like a glistening star. It hits Rosu's chest with a muffled thud, and his eyes go wide. I pull out the Glock 17 and fire immediately at Vulpe. He's smart, though, and is already moving downwards and into a roll. The bullet passes by him. My arm swings left, and I get two off into the face of Grasi, sending pieces of bone and blood into the space above him.

Luca's eyes are glazed. He has a gun in his hand. A Glock. He pulls the trigger, and I take my chances. The bullet smashes into the Kevlar. I feel the impact but keep moving. A fact that seems to surprise him. He fumbles, and I hurl the second knife as I did the first. It hits him in the side of the neck, which he claws at with his fingers. I turn back to Vulpe. He's ten feet from me with a Glock 17 pointed at my head.

"Drop the gun," he says calmly.

The frantic energy of the last few seconds dissipates instantly.

"Drop the gun," he repeats. "I won't make the mistake of firing at your chest."

I do as he says.

"Who are you?" he asks.

"Does it matter?"

He watches me for a few moments, thinking that one through. I, in the meantime, examine my options. He'll pull the trigger—there's no doubt about that. The real question is what I should do about it. Against a skilled marksman, it would all be over for me no matter what decision I were to make. The question is, is he skilled? He's evil—I know that from his record—but that's not the same thing.

My preferred move would be to fall backwards, roll away, pick up my gun from the floor, and fire at his legs. Sudden movement may give me half a chance. How well will he perform under pressure?

I'm about to instigate it when two things happen simultaneously. First, the sound of a vehicle's engine. It's close by, and roaring. Second, the appearance of a black Land Rover veering across the road and ploughing into the side of Vulpe. His body is thrown twenty feet into the air, and lands like a rag doll in the dirt by the edge of the road.

The Land Rover screeches to a stop, and the door swings open. Wakefield steps out. His dark face is concentrating hard, glistening with sweat. He pushes his spectacles higher on the bridge of his nose. I pick up my Glock from the floor and move toward the cab of the lorry, jump up into it, and grab the keys from the ignition.

"What now?" asks Wakefield, coming up on my shoulder. He is breathing hard.

"The back of the truck has barn-door locking," I say, holding up the keys. "Grenhall is in there. Our problem will be whomever she is with."

We move around the back. I assume the crew will have a code between them, so I hammer on the tailgate with my fist. Two taps.

We wait.

Two taps come back in response.

I move close to Wakefield and hand him the keys, whispering, "The doors open outward. Unlock it, and pull your side open. Then stay out of the way."

He inserts the key into a fat lock, and the mechanism opens. He grabs the handle and glances at me. I nod, and he pulls it open. I wait a second, then swing into view.

I process the scene instantly. Three men, all armed. One at the back, and one at either side. Between them are six dirty mattresses arranged in a semi-circle. On each one is a naked girl, unwashed and drugged.

I fire immediately at the man to my right. He goes down like a stone. The one at the back doesn't have the stomach for a fight and drops his weapon immediately, holding up his hands. His colleague follows suit. Everything in me wants to shoot them. They stare at me, pleading for their lives.

I'm immediately transported to another time and place. A scene not dissimilar to this one. Colors, feelings, and smell wash over me like a wave.

"Cane," says Wakefield.

"What?"

"They're unarmed."

I scan the girls on the mattresses and recognize Grenhall; she's sprawled unconscious on the mattress furthest away from me. Strung out, and halfway broken in by the men who now want me to spare their lives. I lower the angle of the Glock, so that it's pointing at the legs of the man on the back wall and I pull the trigger—the slug rips into his knee. He screams in agony and clutches at the wound. I move my arm in a wide sweep and point it at the last man standing. He is shaking his head and muttering in Romanian, pleading for forgiveness or mercy or some kind of redemption. I shoot at his leg, and the flesh on his thigh pops through his jeans like a flower. He sprawls against the side of the truck, his mouth gaping open.

Wakefield gets up into the box and drags the men out by their legs. Their heads smash against the dirt as he hauls them off to the side of the road.

I step into the box and smell sweat and urine. I squat down gently next to Grenhall. She looks pale and undernourished. Her eyes flicker open.

"It's okay," I say. "You're safe."

Then I check the other girls for ominous signs. All are alive but one of them looks to be in trouble. I check her pulse. It is thin and reedy.

Randolph's voice is in my ear. "Cane," she says.

"I'm here."

"Status?"

"I've got Grenhall. Tell her father she's okay."

I hear her let out a breath. "Is Wakefield there?"

"Yes," I say, glancing at him outside, standing over the two injured men. "We need police and medical personnel out here. There are five girls besides Grenhall. One is in very bad shape."

"I'm on it."

I call out to Wakefield. He has an IV kit in the Land Rover. He hurries to fetch it and I hook it up the best I can. I make several failed attempts to get the cannula in. The veins in the girl's arm are too flat; a sign her blood pressure is low. I find one eventually that will accept the needle and set the saline drip going.

I leave Wakefield at the scene and get back on the Kawasaki. I'm now heading east toward Arad, and Reisman. I need to get there quickly before he learns what has happened.

It's late afternoon when I arrive in the south of the town. The main thoroughfare is a four-lane highway, with cheap high-rise apartments and industrial units either side of the road. The afternoon sun throws up a misty haze from the tarmac.

"His signal is two miles northwest of your current position," says Randolph in my ear.

"Is he on the move?"

"No," she replies. "Been static for the last twenty minutes."

I wonder how Reisman is processing events. Not finding Mace will have messed with his mind. If it were me, I would go directly to The Ranch, a remote farm fifty miles northeast of this position, which has served as a base for Mace's crew for many years. Once there, he is untouchable. It's remote, patrolled by gang members who are always fully armed, and it has the protection of the local police, who are either bribed or blackmailed into acting as his security firm.

So why has he not gone there yet? I wonder.

"Next left," says Randolph.

I follow her instructions and I'm quickly into a warren of criss-crossing roads set back from the main drag.

"Take the next right, and you're on top of him."

I slow the bike down and turn sedately into a narrow road. I see him at once and realize why he has not gone north.

He's not worried. He's surrounded by his own people in his own backyard. He's untouchable.

He sits outside a bar in a space reserved for al fresco drinking. There are leafy green plants and sun umbrellas with tables and chairs. He sits against a wall drinking from a beer bottle, still wearing the boiler suit that he had on at the hut. There are six men seated around him, laughing and talking loudly. I recognize most of them as crew members, but there are other people there too. At another table, an elderly couple; next to them, a family with two young kids; on a table nearest the road, three teenage girls who look like students.

These people have nothing to do with Reisman, so I don't want them caught up in whatever comes next. I must target only Reisman himself.

This also means not causing a scene.

I'll simply wait.

He's got another beer in his hand, so it won't be long. I take a linen handkerchief out of my pocket, scrunch it up into a ball, and watch. He gets out of his seat after ten minutes and goes into the bar. I climb off the bike and jog across the road, past the tables where the crew are drinking and into the dimly lit building.

I check for anyone following.

All clear.

I see the sign for the bathrooms and follow it. Inside, Reisman is standing at a stainless-steel urinal. I move up next to him, a bit too close for comfort, in fact, and he glances at me. I smile, and the recognition on his face is instant.

Now he has a problem: he is in mid-stream and I am not, so I bring my elbow up and smash it into the side of his face. The blow sends him sprawling sideways. Urine splatters his trousers and shoes. He bounces against the wall, and his right hand moves toward the chest area of the boiler suit. I suspect he's going for the Glock but he's not quick enough. I'm already into my next play. He's fat, so his knees will be vulnerable. I kick downward into his left patella and hear a crack as the bone dislocates.

The pain from this maneuver is always horrendous for the victim. He screams, and I push the scrunched-up handkerchief into his wide-open mouth to dull the sound. Then he slides down the tiled wall and slumps onto the floor.

"Was it worth it?" I ask.

He mumbles something through the cloth. His good leg vibrates like he has a neurological disease. I came to kill him, but as I look down at his bloated, broken frame I change my mind. He watches me. His eyes are wide and full of fear. I check the inside of the boiler suit and reveal the Glock. It's the same one he used on me. I store it in my jacket and then grasp his left arm and pull it toward me. His pinky finger is red and puffy. I yank it laterally with a whipping force until it pops. Then I hold it fast for three seconds to increase the level of discomfort. I hear the squeal of muffled pain through the cloth.

I change arms and this time he struggles. He knows what's coming. I step on his dislocated knee and rotate my shoe as if I'm stubbing out a cigarette. He moans through the cloth again and offers me his other hand. I wrench the pinky finger off to the side until it too snaps. Again I hold it fast and once again he lets out a muffled scream.

I open the bathroom door and check the bar. To my right is where I came in, to my left is a fire exit. I duck back in and grab him by the collar, spin him around, and drag him across the tiled floor.

That's the easy bit. Getting him out of the bar is more difficult because of his weight. I haul him up and order him to hop. He complies and I bundle him through the fire exit and into a parking area beyond; on the far side of the space are three industrial-sized refuse bins. I push Reisman forward, and he hops toward them. I get him down and out of sight behind them, and join him.

"Randolph?"

"Here," she says.

"Can you still see the signal?"

"Yes."

"Good. I've got Reisman. Come and get him."

"I'm on it," she says.

We wait in silence, and I wonder how long it will take his crew to realize he is missing. At one point I hear the fire exit door bang open, and so does Reisman. We stare at each other for a long moment. He doesn't make a move. Had he done so, it would have been his last.

In the end, their searching is irrelevant, because two military vehicles full of armed soldiers swing into view. The soldiers have Reisman on board within a few seconds.

I travel back to the camp with Randolph and Wakefield.

Smiling, Randolph hands me a flask of coffee. "Thought you might need it."

I take a sip and turn to Wakefield. "Thanks for the intervention back there."

He shrugs. "You'd have gotten out of it, wouldn't you?"

"You think?"

His grin gives away exactly what he thinks. "No chance."

The camp is buzzing with people when we arrive back. Not only ours but also local officials.

Adams appears. He is brisk and nervous and stands awkwardly in front of us. "Well done all of you. A professional job under very difficult circumstances."

"Under *unacceptable* circumstances," I correct him.

He nods in agreement. "It won't happen again."

He goes to leave then stops and says: "remember the two other women who disappeared at the same time as Grenhall?"

"Her dinner companions?" asks Randolph

He nods. "They were also in the truck."

"They okay?" Randolph asks.

"One is," he replies. "The other didn't make it."

There is silence.

I watch the camp and drink my coffee. A short distance away, Grenhall is being carried out of a tent on a stretcher toward the chopper. She has a saline drip going into her arm on one side and her father, clutching her hand tightly, on the other. He glances over and our eyes meet. He makes a gesture with his face. It conveys a thousand feelings all jumbled together. He's exhausted, relieved, grateful...on the verge of tears. I feel relief that it ended this way for them. That is always my plan. I smile back and think of my own beautiful family. Saving his doesn't take away my own grief, but it helps to ease it a little and reminds me of why I carry on doing what I do.

They board the chopper and it rises then banks to the west and drifts away into the setting sun.

ABOUT THE AUTHOR

Steve Davison graduated in Immunology from King's College, London. He then completed his MPhil in Molecular Genetics at Cambridge, UK. He lives near London with his wife and children.

He is the author of the Amazon bestselling "Varcy and Kendrick" series, which follows the adventures of two hard-nosed London detectives as they work the most intense cases around London.

www.stevedavison.net

DEATH AND DOLLARS

JONATHAN SHIPPERLEY

Coast Guard Special Agents Frank Dalton and Jessica Carter pick up the trail of "El Doctor" a notorious cartel capo wanted for an attack on a U.S. Embassy, but Dalton wants him for his own reasons.

1

I was cutting it close to nautical twilight as I came round the last bend in the marina and saw the hazy outline of a woman standing on my dock. I cut *Serenity* back to idle and moved my pistol from its cubby by the helm to the small of my back. No one knew where I was.

When I got closer to the slip, I cut speed and drifted in under control, nudging the helm and throttle as necessary. Almost another lifetime away I could still hear the coxswain at my first unit say in his broad Chicago accent, "Don't forget, Frank, speed kills. Don't be one of those assholes that races to the slip and then slams her astern." I still heeded his advice.

"Grab the bow line, Carter." I yelled, as I saw who was waiting. I couldn't resist adding, "That's the one on the dock toward the front of the boat."

She gave me the finger as she took the bow line, wrapped it around *Serenity's* forward cleat and back to the dock cleat in a neat figure-eight pattern before I'd even secured the stern line.

"Nice," I said, when I looked up. I'd taught my partner, Coast Guard Special Agent Jessica Carter, how to sail, and I was starting to think she was better than me. I secured the engine, leaned over the port side and gave her my hand to help steady her as she stepped on board.

"Thanks, Frank," she said.

"How d'you know I was here?"

"I know where you live, you idiot. What happened to your nav lights?"

"I'm Coast Guard, navigation lights are optional."

"They're broken, aren't they?"

"Yeah. Fritzed out on the way in. I was trying to beat twilight. Anyway, to what do I owe the pleasure? We're not back on again 'till next week."

"Something came up, and I didn't think you'd want to wait. Grab me a beer and I'll show you."

Curious, I did as she asked, going below and returning with two open Heinekens. I handed one to her, taking a swig of mine as we sat. Carter pulled a manilla folder from her bag and placed it in front of me on the table.

"Am I going to be sorry if I look at this?" I asked.

Carter shrugged.

I opened the file. Glaring back at me from a mugshot was Cardona Perez, also known as, "El Doctor." My hand jerked from the file as if it was hot, my vision tunneled. Scenes from memories played in my head. The pungent odor of scorched human flesh, my eyes thick with tears, black smoke everywhere, and screams from every corner that still echoed through my soul. I was on my knees. There was nothing left of Penny. Blood trickled down my face, marking a path through the soot. I was too late.

"Frank, Frank!"

I jerked back to reality and Carter was sitting next to me, gently shaking me. "Hey, hey, snap out of it, big guy."

"Why'd you show me this, Jess? You know what this guy did to me, the embassy bombing."

"I know, Frank. I wouldn't bring it up unless I had a reason. I think this time we have him."

I balled my fists, "Where?"

I parked in the back of the new Coast Guard Sector Corpus Christi building and was already sweating by the time I levered myself out of my car, dripping by the time I punched the code into the security door, and chilled as soon as I stepped through, the air conditioning running full blast and causing my damp shirt to stick to my chest.

I preferred the old building, in the heart of downtown, with the best damn egg and bacon breakfast tacos in the basement cafeteria you'd ever hope to eat. Now, although we had a shiny new galley, they staffed it with people that didn't like their jobs, didn't want to be in Texas, and couldn't care less about the product they dished up. The one saving grace was the coffee was good and always ready, so I swung through, poured a mug, ignored the sign that said to not leave the galley with galley property, and headed for my office on the second deck.

I plopped down in my chair, slid my CAC card into the computer reader, bashed the keyboard a few times to wake it up and logged on, accessing the secure server. After accepting and ignoring all the dire warnings about accessing a DOD server and if I did anything squirrely, they'd lock me up forever, my name, Special Agent Frank Dalton, popped up on the screen along with the Coast Guard Investigative Service (CGIS) banner. I resisted the urge to check my email, knowing that would be a rabbit hole I wouldn't escape from for hours. Instead, I clicked a few buttons to find the file on Cardona Perez.

After reading for a few minutes, I was pretty sure Carter had been presumptive in saying we knew where he was. The best I figured is we may have a somewhat tenuous lead. Carter walked into my office and I glared at her as she sat down.

"We don't exactly have him, do we?" I said.

"No, and I know that face. Before you go all special agent on me," she said, "Hear me out. This is the closest we've ever been. I didn't think you'd want to wait another week until we were on call again to find out we let the only potential lead we have walk on by."

I took a swig of coffee. "So, the boys in Brownsville arrested some guy that might have a link to Perez?" I said. "Is that about the size of it?"

Carter shook her head. "Give me some credit, Frank. I wouldn't get your hopes up for nothing. The scuttlebutt from the field agent down there is they got Ortega in a sting, he's the link to Perez. He was trying to sell undercover agents equipment to print TWIC cards, social security cards, driver's licenses and so on."

"So, a, what do you call it a—" I said, snapping my fingers.

"Document mill."

"That's it."

"They also found a nice stash of high-powered weapons—Tec 9s, AR-15s and AKs."

My eyebrows popped up. "Nice haul. So, what's the intel on what they were doing?"

"A false Transportation Workers Identification Card could get someone into a secure area inside a port. Combine that TWIC with the right cover, say ship agent or techie, and someone could easily get on board a tanker or gas carrier. Blow one of those babies up and you've scuttled the port for weeks, probably months. Do that around the country and you've crippled the U.S."

"Yeah. I've thought about that before. So, what's our angle? How does this link to Perez?"

"Perez and Ortega both work for the Sinaloa Cartel, and both go back a long way. After the embassy bombing it went sideways for Perez, he thought it would be his crowning achievement, but the cartel bosses were furious, thought it would bring too much attention on them. They were right. Perez should have been executed, but they exiled him instead and he's been gone for years, but his ties to Ortega stay strong. There're rumors Perez wants to reclaim his title, be El Doctor again. The old guard isn't getting any younger, it's ripe for a takeover."

"And Perez will remember his faithful and take them along for the ride."

"You got it."

"Ok. It's certainly worth a shot." I opened my desk drawer and took out the G-ride keys. "Let's do it. We'll go talk to Ortega and see what drops. Grab your go bag in case we have to stay overnight." I stood up and walked to the door. "Also, call the lead agent and tell them we'll be there in two hours."

"Are you driving?"

"I have the keys." I jangled them at her.

"Then I get to pick the tunes. I'm not sitting in the car with you for two hours while you subject me to your shitty music."

"I'd be wary, Special Agent Carter, that you don't insult my choice collection of 80s and 90s superior girl band singers." I said, smiling. "But fine, you can DJ. Oh, and Jess?" I stopped and looked at her. "Thanks for staying on top of this. It means a lot." I brushed past before she could reply and headed to the galley to return the mug.

It was an uneventful trip from Corpus Christi to Brownsville; south on Highway 77/I-69E. Once passed King Ranch it was one flat road looking at flat scenery in an arid flat landscape, dotted with the occasional worn giant billboard, tumbleweed and 7-11 until you get to the town of Harlingen, just outside of Brownsville.

Light traffic and a lead foot got us there with daylight to spare, and we headed to the Customs and Border Patrol office off of the expressway. Thanks to Carter, they knew we were coming, and we were ushered into the inner sanctum, straight to the director's office.

"Thanks for seeing us on such short notice, director, we certainly appreciate it," I said shaking hands with him as he came around his desk. "Special Agent Frank Dalton and Special Agent Jessica Carter, we're CGIS agents out of Corpus. Heard you'd caught one of Perez's main men, Ortega."

"Sam Kerger," the director said, shaking hands with Carter. "Please, sit down, make yourselves comfortable. Can I offer you coffee? Water?"

I looked at Carter. She shook her head. "No, we're fine thanks."

"So, what is it I can help you with?" Kerger said. "We rarely get agents from Corpus coming down this far."

"We'd like to interview Ortega. I understand he hasn't said anything yet, and I've had some success with, ah, let's say, interviewing less than helpful subjects."

Kerger steepled his fingers together and swiveled his chair to look out the window. He had a massive desk, more fitting a CEO of some Fortune 500 company than a CBP regional director. The walls were an off yellow color with several generic government paintings, two standard office chairs which we were sitting in, bookshelves with various industrial looking tomes and tucked away in the corner a small mini fridge with a coffee maker on top. The desk looked like it was the only touch of personality in the office, no personal plaques, awards, mementos, love me wall–nothing.

Kerger swung back around and faced us. "Sorry, I do my best thinking when I'm looking outside. It sets me free. I'm sure you understand."

I didn't. I looked at Carter, she shrugged.

"Unfortunately, I can't let you talk to Ortega. He's in our custody and if something should happen to him, it well, it just wouldn't look good for our office."

"I'm not sure I'm following you, director. We only want to interview him, it's not like we're going to get out the thumbscrews."

Kerger flashed a tight smile, almost a grimace. "Quite. But under the circumstances, the answer remains the same. Ortega is too valuable an asset to let another agency mess around with him."

"What do you think is going to happen? We're all federal agents here, all on the same side," Carter said.

"I believe, Agent Dalton," Kerger said, ignoring Carter, "That your reputation precedes you. An alarming number of people you interview seem to end up in the morgue—"

"With all due respect, director, this was a joint op that took Ortega into custody. CGIS agents were on scene with your guys, it could easily have been our office that held him."

"But it isn't, is it?"

"Listen—" I stood and leaned over his desk.

"No, you listen, agent, and get out of my face before I have you removed from this office. You're being disrespectful and insubordinate. Now, I've entertained your request and after due deliberation your request is denied. I'm sorry for the inconvenience, but that's just the way it is." Kerger pressed a button on his desk phone.

"Jarvis? The two Coast Guard agents are leaving. Could you escort them out, please?"

"Yes, sir," came the tinny reply, "Be right there."

Carter stood, and we walked to the door. I was fuming.

Jarvis knocked and opened the door. "Agents, this way please."

I glanced back as I went through the door and Kerger was already on the phone, laughing at something. Fucker.

I leaned in and whispered to Carter, "You get the feeling that something stinks around here?"

"Yeah. You know, we are like ten feet from Mexico, the director's been here a while, maybe he got too cozy."

"Yeah, maybe."

Jarvis stopped. I was looking at the floor and nearly ran into him. He looked over my shoulder, then hustled us into a small room off the corridor we were in. It must have been an old storage room as there weren't any windows, just a couple of dusty file cabinets. He closed the door behind him.

"You wanted to talk to Ortega, right?" he said.

I nodded.

"And the director shot you down."

I nodded again.

"I think it's bullshit, but they made the deal within an hour of us picking him up. I just wanted to tell you not all of us agree with that," Jarvis said.

"What deal?"

He narrowed his eyes and rubbed his hands through his hair, stopping mid rub when he realized what I'd said. "Shit. What did the director tell you?"

"Nothing much. We just got in a pissing match. What gives?"

He shook his head but stopped and said, "Fuck it. Sure. You know about the op where we took him, right?"

I nodded. "In a warehouse sting, right?"

"Yeah. We read Ortega his rights, he didn't say a word. Didn't even lawyer up. Someone must have leaked we had him in custody though, as within the hour in waltzes John Melendez, all smiles and brown leather briefcase as if he owns the place. He's a high-end counsel for the Sinaloa Cartel. What's weird though is he didn't spring Ortega, he worked with us, more specifically the director, to get him into witness protection, says Ortega's gonna spill, but only after a DA signs the order."

"Wait, that's not right." I said, "If he's a lawyer for the cartel, he'd want the opposite. He'd want to spring Ortega, so he didn't talk, not get him into WP. Jess, what do you think?"

"I think you're—" Carter said, but was cut off by the fire alarm.

I looked at Jarvis. "That can't be good."

He opened the door and thick smoke flowed in. "Shut the door," I screamed as my eyes and lungs instantly burned. Jarvis slammed the door closed, and we all moved as far away as we could, coughing.

"CS gas," Carter said, wiping her nose with her sleeve.

The distinctive percussion of automatic weapons fire came from down the hallway. "Jarvis, how many people do you have in the building?"

Jarvis wiped his eyes, then blew snot out of each nostril onto the ground. "Seven total, including me and the director."

"Carter, call for backup," I said.

"I tried Frank, no signal."

"They must have a blocker. Probably cut the landlines too."

"I think we can assume they're after Ortega. Makes sense now why they tried to get him on the witness protection program. They had no intention of him squealing, just wanted to give their boys time to mount an attack. That must mean he's way more important than we realized. Okay. What do we know? Carter?"

"These kill squads usually come in groups of four. It enables them to move fast. They don't want prisoners. They'll find us and take us out if we don't react soon."

I nodded. "Jarvis?"

"Agreed. We need to move," he said.

"I'm guessing the door we came in is the only way out?"

Jarvis nodded.

"Alright," I said, looking around. "Grab what you can to cover your face, stay low to the ground and try not to take deep breaths. Jarvis, you'll lead us to where Ortega's being held. Weapons free, normal rules of engagement. Ready?" Both nodded. "Let's go."

I pulled my pistol from my gun belt and held it at weapons ready, watching Carter and Jarvis do the same. Jarvis opened the door a crack. The CS gas had dissipated, and we had a clear line of sight down the corridor as we followed him, crouching down and moving fast. We moved past the reception area and saw a CBP officer on the ground.

"Jess, check the doors."

Jarvis crawled up to the officer, but I could see the through and through had taken out his throat. At least it was quick.

"No good, Frank. The doors are chained closed."

I tapped Jarvis on the shoulder, "Gotta go, man."

He nodded, and we proceeded to a closed fire door about halfway down the corridor. There was a small glass window in the door's top and Jarvis risked a peek. He signaled it was clear, eased the door open, and we continued. The lights flickered once, twice, and then cut out. It was pitch black for a second, and then the emergency lights kicked on. It was already creepy. Now it was eerie too.

"How much further?" I whispered.

"Two more turns. If they're expecting us, it'll be around the next corner."

A shiver ran down my back. I don't get spooked easily, but you could hear a pin drop. The fire alarm had cut out and gone were the sounds of a normal office at work; no phones ringing, no doors slamming, no laughter or loud conversations, no whispers at the water cooler, no footsteps. Just a dead silence. The gunfire had stopped, I wasn't sure if that was a good thing or not. I hoped it meant the customs officers had holed up somewhere, but I feared the surprise attack had caught them out.

We stopped at the corner. Jarvis signaled with his fingers, gesturing for me to take a quick peek low, while he went high. I stuck my head out and back. The eyes might register nothing for the brief millisecond you were looking, but if you gave your brain a second to decode the images, you could usually figure out if there was danger. We stepped back a few feet so we could talk. Heads huddled.

"I saw an open door, the brig? Didn't see anything else," I said.

"It's the cell where he was being held," Jarvis said. "I didn't see anyone either."

"Alright, same plan. You go high, I'll go low, Jess cover our six. Ready?"

We stepped out at the same moment, moving fast, and made it to the door of the cell. I went in low and to the left, Jarvis went high and right, Carter made fast at the entrance. The room was empty except for a small table smeared with blood.

"Where's the exit, Jarvis? They've got what they came for, they'll be making tracks," I said.

"More importantly," Carter said from the doorway, "Where're the rest of your officers, and where's that scuzzy director of yours?"

"Must be in the garage. It's underground. If anyone is still here, they're probably holed up there," he said.

The way down to the garage was elevator or stair access; we chose the stairs. I opened the heavy steel door, soundproofed like everything else, and we descended, covering each other. Stairs were a great way to get ambushed. As we got closer to the garage door, we could hear the muffled reports of gunshots. We moved faster. There was one more steel door between us and whatever was happening in the garage.

"Someone's alive," Jarvis said, and flew down the stairs.

"Jarvis," I hissed. "Stop. We don't know where the friendlies are."

I raced after him but was too slow. In his hope that his colleagues were still alive, he'd forgotten all his training. The adrenaline must have been spiking at massive levels as he yanked open that steel door like it was a kitchen cabinet. Like in slow-motion I saw the glare of the emergency light shine down on him like a stage spotlight as the door opened wide, I yelled, "No," which came out in an elongated, "Noooooooo," he made three giant slow-motion steps before gunfire concentrated on his torso, sprays of blood rising in an arc blown from his back, his body jerking like a marionette with each successive shot, Carter pulling me down to the ground and back away from the door, the door slowly closing on its spring muting the gunshots.

"Fuck," I yelled, punching the wall and instantly regretting it. "Goddamnit. Why didn't he wait?" I took a deep breath. "We need to get out there."

"I don't suppose it crossed your mind that we could just sit this one out? Stay right here. Barricade the door?"

Carter stared at me. I stared back.

"Shit," she said. "How do we do it?"

"We know there must be some good guys out there. They must be near this door, as the enemy fire came from a distance." I thought for a moment. "Here's the plan. We prop open the door, see where the bullets are going. All the hits on Jarvis were center mass. I don't think that's 'cos they're ace shots, they're probably barricaded up, and that's the best line of fire they have. If so, we can crawl out and join whoever's left."

"I think that's a shit plan."

"Ready?"

She nodded. I crawled to the door, reaching up and holding it open, but staying behind it. Bullets slammed into the stairs behind us, but as I thought, all the shots remained above waist high. Good enough.

I shouted out the door, "Any CBP officers out there?"

"Who's asking?"

"Agents Dalton and Carter, CGIS."

"We're to the left of the door."

"Is it safe for us to come to you?"

I could hear a low but furious conversation and then, "No. It's not safe. But if you want to come, we're about fifteen feet from the door. Behind the crash barriers. Stay low."

"What do you think, Jess?"

"Can't stay here."

"Right. Don't get shot."

"Likewise."

I crawled on my elbows and knees, keeping my ass low, and shuffled over to where the officers said they were, Carter right on my heels. I stopped and Carter banged into my feet making a muffled curse and then she came around my side and saw why I'd stopped. Two officers had their guns trained on us.

"Hi guys. Can we join your party?" I said.

"ID."

"Back pocket. Reaching for it now," I said, still prone on the floor. I pulled out my ID and tossed it over. The first agent took the ID, opened it, studied the picture and then stared at me.

"You've looked better, Agent Dalton."

"I'm sure. We good?"

"Yeah. Sorry, couldn't be too sure. I've had my fill of surprises for the day." A shot rang out, pinging off the barricade, and we all instinctively ducked. "Keep your heads down." He looked strained, unsurprising with the day he was having. The officer continued. "We were doing okay, pinned the bastards down here, holding our own, but then the director comes out gun drawn. Thought that with his help we might have enough people to do something. Should have known he was a bitch ass traitor 'cos the shooting stopped while he got over to us, then started again. He was here for all of ten seconds before he shot two of our own in the back before we realized what was happening and took him down."

"Motherfucker."

"Yeah. That's what we thought. Why are *you* here?"

"We were here to interview Ortega, but the director shot us down."

The agent winced.

It took me a moment. "Shit. Sorry. Bad expression. Sorry about your agents and Jarvis. He seemed a good guy. I tried to stop him from running out."

"Thanks, man." He turned and gestured across the parking lot, all business again. "We have three of them, plus Ortega pinned down. They can't get out without passing us, we can't get over to them."

"Backup? What about the exit?"

He shrugged. "Everything's down. They have a cell phone blocker, radios are out, landline is static. This entire building is soundproofed. The exit is right over there. We can't get to it, but neither can they. We're on our own until the next shift comes in," he looked at his watch, "In about four hours. If we hold out that long. We're running short on ammo. How about you guys?"

"We both have three full magazines, fifteen rounds each. Haven't had anybody to shoot at 'till now."

He nodded. "Jared, by the way. This is Luis."

We nodded back. "Frank and Jessica. What's the plan?"

"This is it. Hold them if we can. Don't get killed."

"Solid. But I think we can do more," I said.

"Be my guest," Jared said.

"Jess, what do you think the chances are for a full-frontal assault?"

Jared and Luis both snorted. Luis mumbled, "I thought he said he could do more?"

Carter knew me better. "What are you thinking?"

"We hot-wire one of those cars over there and ram it into the fuckers."

"Don't you think we thought of that?" Luis said. "They'll just shoot you or disable the vehicle before it gets there."

"Maybe, maybe not. I've done something similar before."

"How did that work out for you?" Luis asked.

"I'm here aren't I? Anyway, I'm not going to be inside it, I'm going to be behind it." I looked over at the vehicles. "That Ford Bronco looks pretty sturdy, I'll use that."

"That's mine," Jared said. "Use something else. It's brand new."

"Seriously? You have insurance, right? Gimme your keys. It'll be quicker than trying to hot-wire the damn thing."

Reluctantly Jared handed over the keys, and I crawled over to the Bronco. I could see why he didn't want to part with it, it was a sweet ride and it looked like he'd had some aftermarket parts added, seriously beefing it up.

I stood, protected for the moment from a direct shot by a concrete wall that stuck out near where the bastards were cornered.

Carter crawled over and joined me. I sat inside and started the Bronco up. "Look for a length of line and something heavy, or a big stick." I said.

Carter came back with a wooden broom and some twine. "Perfect."

"There was a janitor's closet. I almost took the steel mop buckets as head protection."

"You'd have looked cute, I'm sure." I snapped the broom handle, cracking it just where I wanted. "I'm going to point this truck in the right direction, then I'm going to wedge this stick on the accelerator and against the wheel and tie it all together, so the wheel and stick don't move. We don't need to go fast, just faster than walking speed. Once it gets going, we'll stay right behind it."

"What's preventing them from shooting out the wheels or us, when we get closer?"

"We won't be behind the Bronco."

"We won't?"

"Nope. This is going to give us cover, they'll think we're behind it, but we won't be. See that wall by them?"

She nodded.

"They can't see us. We're coming at an angle, and I'm going to cut the Bronco in as close to that wall as I can. When we get close, we'll move from the truck to the wall, they'll be focused on the truck, they won't see us."

"I can see how that might work in your head, but are you sure it's going to work for real? Sounds a bit, I don't know, fucking crazy? And that glint in your eye tells me I'm close to the truth. Wouldn't it be easier to wait until backup arrives?"

"Of course it would, but you heard Jared. It'll be four hours. I'm betting those cartel fucks know that too. They can't risk us getting reinforcements, so they're going to have to make a break for it, and they probably don't care if they die trying. I don't see we have any other options. Trust me?"

Carter reached out and touched my hand. "Not in a million years. Let's do this."

It was one of those rare moments that go beautifully to plan. I nudged the Bronco back and forth until it was pointing where I wanted, got my jury-rigged stick and twine in place, put it in drive and jumped out, leaving the door open. The truck crept along at about six miles an hour with us behind it. Shots rang out when they saw the truck, but nothing could get through to us. When we were over halfway there, I looked over and gave Jared and Luis a maniacal thumbs up. They looked at us with disbelief, shaking their heads, but both gave us a thumbs up in return.

A shot rang out puncturing the radiator, and I was stepping on antifreeze as the truck rolled onward. The Bronco wouldn't have much left before it overheated and the engine seized. I hoped we could squeeze another thirty feet.

The truck lurched to the right as the right front tire was shot out, I panicked for a moment as the gap between the wall and the truck widened, increasing our chances of being seen, but then they shot out the left-hand tire and the truck straightened again. It was about the only time I was thankful they were on target. I could hear a hissing sound coming from the engine in between the gunfire, and there was a burnt sweet odor noticeable above the acrid bite of gunpowder. We didn't have many more seconds before a piston seized.

As we came level with the wall, the open driver's side door hit the edge of it and gave us the opportunity we needed. Jared and Luis gave us covering fire, and we moved to the side, unseen, as the truck continued to roll. The hitmen continued to shoot at the truck, opening up a deafening volley that reverberated through the garage as the truck rolled to a stop at their makeshift barricade.

Now. I slipped low around the corner, Carter right behind me, gun at the ready. I wouldn't give them a chance to surrender. If we didn't take them by surprise, we were all dead. There was no other way. I shot two of them in the back, Carter tagged a third in the head and another in his shoulder.

It was over. The air was thick, clouds of gunpowder smoke hung low in the garage. I couldn't hear a damn thing. I'd be mostly deaf for a few minutes until my hearing adjusted.

I gave the all clear to Jared and Luis and they ran over, keeping low, pistols out. I kicked the gun clear from the man Carter had nailed in the shoulder, he seemed to have been hit in the leg as well, probably from a ricochet, while Carter, Jared and Luis checked the others. I was glad it was over, but it was a fucking mess, and now our lead to Perez was gone.

"Shit," Jared said. "That one's Ortega."

I looked where he was pointing and it was the guy Carter had shot in the shoulder. Our luck just went up.

"Jared, Luis. I know this isn't protocol but as soon as your backup arrives, we'll be mired down in paperwork and interviews for hours if not days. We need to move fast on this while we still have a chance. I want to take Ortega with me. Can you guys stall?"

Jared and Luis looked at each other, silent communication, and an almost imperceptible nod. "Normally, no. But seeing as you guys just saved our asses, yeah, take the fuck. I can hold them off for twenty-four hours. It'll probably take the crime techs days to sift through all this shit."

“Thanks. Last request. Do you have a med kit? I don’t want him bleeding out in the G-ride until we deal with him.”

As if on cue, Ortega writhing on the floor wailed, “I need a doctor!” He didn’t look so tough now his boys were dead. I kicked him.

“And perhaps something to gag him with?”

Jared smiled, “Sure, I’ve got just the thing. A nice stinky gym sock should do the trick.”

“Perfect.”

The Coast Guard weren’t in much need of safe houses to stash people, but I called in a few favors from my feebee friends hoping Ortega was worth it, with the promise that I’d drop them a bone if there was anything useful. We’d patched up Ortega for the ride and stashed him in the back of the G-ride, on the way to Robstown, a small town just on the outskirts of Corpus and a perfect place to hide away for a few hours or days.

I pulled into the garage, closing the door behind us and got Ortega out, slapping him to wake him up and half carried half dragged him to the basement. I gave him a shove down the stairs and chained him up to a steel chair bolted to the concrete floor and left him there, walking back up to the kitchen. They’d left it fully stocked, so I put a pot of coffee on.

“What’s the plan, Frank?” Carter said.

“It won’t be pretty, Jess. We don’t have the luxury of taking our time. I might have to break a few rules to get him to talk. If you want to leave, I’m okay with that. I won’t blame you. Then you can say that you didn’t—”

Carter closed the gap between us. “Stop,” she whispered, putting her hand on my chest. “First, thank you for getting us out of there. It scared me. Second, I’m here, with you. Whatever it takes.”

I reached up and held her hand in mine for a moment. “Thanks. For the record I was never scared.”

Carter pushed me away and punched me lightly on the arm. “Jerk,” she said, but she was smiling.

I didn't give Ortega a chance to talk. Didn't ask him questions. Didn't play good cop bad cop. Didn't play at all. Didn't say a word. I walked right up to him. Looked him in the eye and broke his little finger on his right hand. I let him scream. Then I broke his little finger on his left hand.

"Fuck you, cop," Ortega spat out.

"I'm not a cop," I said, and broke his ring finger on both hands.

Ortega passed out.

I threw a bucket of water over him. Broke the other two fingers. He passed out again. More water.

I dragged a chair over and sat down in front of him. He was a blubbering, snot filled mess. His fingers were at crazy angles. Must have hurt like a son of a bitch.

"I'll ask you once. I think you know I don't play games. Where is El Doctor, where's Perez?"

Ortega spat on the floor and sniffed. "If I tell you, he'll kill me."

"I think you know the next line in this play, Ortega. I say, you don't tell me, I'll kill you. But we both know that's stupid as I'm not going to kill you."

Ortega looked up in momentary hope.

"Nope," I leaned in close and grabbed two of his broken fingers, grinding them backward. He screamed.

He broke in the next twenty minutes. I don't want to have to tell you what I did. It disgusted me. It's a slippery slope down to hell and I could feel myself falling, and honestly, not giving much of a shit. Penny was in my head more and more. Had been since Carter told me we had a lead on Perez. The flashbacks were getting worse, blurring and blending with reality.

They'd used a Narco Tank. A friggin' SUV that was reinforced with steel plate on the outside, a battering ram at the front, holes cut out for automatic weapons. Monstruo the Mexicans called them. Monster. The Sinaloa Cartel had a reported five hundred of them. They'd used one to plow through the barricades. I was fifty feet away when I saw her in the courtyard. Saw it happening.

Too junior, too fresh, too untrained, I froze. And then I yelled. Instead of running, she turned to me—turned to *me*. She didn't see it happen. I remember the confused look on her face. The monstruo had cleared a space for another car to follow. It came in close. It was a *coche-bombas*, a car bomb, a new tactic in the narco war. The monstruo took off, diesel engine gunning. It was quiet for a moment. Then it wasn't.

They estimated the car had seventy-five pounds of explosive. The blast blew me backward, cuts and bruises, mild concussion, nothing more, but it destroyed Penny. Then came months of sifting through data, crime scene reports, intel chatter. Until then they'd kept to killing each other. This change in tactics was Perez's attempt to prove himself worthy. What he couldn't have foreseen was the backlash the cartel got from killing American citizens. They couldn't shit-can Perez completely, so they relegated him to the cartel equivalent of Siberia.

I'd been chasing down every lead on him ever since. Now he'd surfaced. Trying to reclaim what he'd lost. I was going to make sure it stayed lost.

I'd waited until Carter had left the basement. Then I'd squeezed Ortega for all he was worth. I bit down the bile, steeled myself against his screams, and I'd got an address.

I went back upstairs, asked Carter to get Ortega some water while I said I was going to use the head and clean up. While she was in the basement, I bailed on her. Took the G-ride. Felt guilty. I owed my partner so much, but I couldn't drag her into this. She was already in enough trouble following me. She had her entire career ahead of her. I had to do this myself, I didn't want her to have unsanctioned blood on her hands.

Perez was holed up in a small compound at the end of a dirt road just outside of Alice, a little less than an hour west of Corpus. I parked down the street out of sight. Normally an op like this would take days or weeks of intricate planning, I didn't have that luxury. Perez was probably already planning to move out. This was my one chance. I should have called for backup, but I wanted Perez for myself. They'd only lock him up. He'd have the best lawyers. Witnesses would disappear, eventually he'd escape or get off on a technicality, I'd seen it far too often, and with the CBP Brownsville director on the take there was no knowing how far up the chain Perez's influence went.

I loaded up from the trunk, put on a vest, added spare magazines for my pistol, and grabbed the riot shotgun which I loaded with five shells. I stuffed a handful more in my pocket. Keeping the wall of the compound on my left, the shotgun hid on my right, I hoped I could get close enough to the front gate. I'll admit, it wasn't the best plan.

"¡Hola, amigo!" I said as I approached, waving with my left hand, keeping my right side hidden. The guard was suspicious but didn't aim his weapon at me. That was his mistake. "Lo siento, mi auto se averió. ¿Puedo usar su teléfono?"

"¡No mames! Vete a la chingada," he said, dismissing me and turning away. It was all I needed.

I broke into a sprint, raising the shotgun. He heard me and turned back raising his weapon. I pulled the trigger first, now within ten feet. My aim was off as I was running. I was aiming for center mass but took his head off instead. He sank to his knees blood spurting from his neck. He must have had his finger on the trigger as a burst of automatic fire came from his Tec-9. I dove to the ground, but his bullets went into the air.

I could hear shouts from inside the compound. I ran through the guard shack, saw two guys running to me, two snap shots and they fell. Chunks of dirt flew up next to me as I was running. I'd forgotten to look up. A man on the roof was taking aim. I dropped the shotgun and took out my pistol. He was about thirty yards away. I stood in a Weaver stance, aimed. His shots inched closer. I breathed out half way, held it, fired three times in rapid succession. He fell. I resisted the urge to blow down my barrel and ran on to the front door.

I stood to the left of the door for a moment to catch my breath. So far, I'd taken out four guys. It would have been good to know how many were left.

The front door opened, and a pistol followed by an arm stuck out. I grabbed the arm and pulled him out the doorway simultaneously stepping in and raising my left elbow smacking him in the face, crunching his nose. Blood spurted. I turned into him, kneed him in the balls so he doubled over then kneed him in the face, smashing his nose again. He went down. I grabbed his weapon in my left hand and moved inside.

In front of me was a dramatic sweeping staircase with a landing on either side. Two guys were up there, one on each side, aiming at me. I shot both simultaneously, a gun in each hand, both went down. Bucket list item crossed off.

I didn't know where Perez was, but as two thugs were upstairs, it was a good bet he was too. I ran up the stairs, guns out at both sides covering the landing. I didn't see anyone else. I turned right and ran to the end of the landing where I saw a door.

In my haste I missed a recessed door. It hadn't looked like a door, I guess that was the point. Normally we'd have a team and take our time, clearing as we go. Thermal cameras, the works. Me? Not so much. I heard and felt it at the same time and went down hard. Someone had nailed me in the calf. Whoever it was was a lousy shot, as they could have seriously fucked me.

I rolled when I hit the floor and let out two shots. One went wide, but one nailed him in the gut. His gun went flying. It was Perez. Gotcha.

I dragged Perez down the stairs by his leg, his head thudding on each stair. I'd ripped part of my shirt to tie round my leg. It wasn't bad, the bullet had only grazed me. I limped across the floor pulling Perez as I went, out the front door and into the front yard. He wasn't going anywhere.

I sat for a minute a few feet from him to catch my breath. There was no one left in the house. I hadn't looked but figured they would have shot at me by now if there was. Not the most effective method of clearing a house, but well, fuck it.

"Tengo dinero," Perez rasped.

"I don't want your money, fuckbreath."

I crawled over to him, rolled him over onto his front, cuffed his hands behind him and rolled him back, then slid something I'd been saving out of my pocket and jammed it into the hole in his gut where

I'd shot him. He screamed. I smiled. He jerked around but with his hands cuffed couldn't do anything and he soon stopped, a look of panic on his face. I lit the fuse, watched for a second to ensure it would not go out, then stood up and limped away.

"Boom, motherfucker," I said under my breath.

In retrospect I probably should have thought that last part through some more. I heard the blast of the dynamite as the force of the concussion washed over and through me - I was that close - and only just got my hands in front of me before I landed in a heap of jumbled limbs. It felt like a wrecking ball had slammed into my back. Deep down, I knew I needed a medic. I tried to move my arms and legs, but no bueno. Head felt like fifty pounds of spaghetti.

I came to, coughing my guts out, face down in the dirt. My ears were ringing, couldn't hear a damn thing. That was becoming an unpleasant habit. I rolled over onto my back and looked back at Perez. There wasn't much to see. Just his smoking boots. I'd wanted Perez to go down the same way Penny had. Mission accomplished.

I rolled back to my stomach and slowly got to my knees then stood up, taking a second when I had my feet under me to stop swaying.

Flashing lights in the distance were getting closer. The cavalry arrives. The lead SUV screamed through the gates, smashing them open, drove right up to me and in one simultaneous move the vehicle skidded to a stop as the driver side door opened and Carter flew out and into my arms, causing me to stagger back a few steps. That had to be hell on the transmission. Never buy a government vehicle.

"Are you okay?" she said, taking a step back so she could see me, but still holding onto my arms.

"Yeah, yeah, I'm fine. How d'you find me?"

Carter slapped me on the cheek, hard. "You stupid motherfucker. They could have killed you. Never scare me like that again."

"I-"

She slapped me again. The same cheek.

"Don't, Frank. Just shut the fuck up," she said, supporting me, "Come on. Let's get you looked at by medical." I could hear a few whoops and jeers from the agents she'd brought with her that were now getting out of their cars. Carter stopped and let go of me, hands on hips. "You fuckers better not be laughing? 'Cos if you are, you'll be next." They turned and pretended to be busy.

I smiled and relaxed as she helped ease me into the vehicle and strapped me in. Carter was right, it could have gone sideways at any point, but it didn't and here I was. I thought of Penny as Carter started the car. It wasn't happy dancing and sappy end credits, riding into the sunset, but maybe now she could rest, maybe I could dream without nightmares. I wasn't proud of what I'd done, didn't want to think of the shit storm that was waiting for me back at the base, but for a few minutes I had a respite. I rested my head on the back of the seat and closed my eyes.

ABOUT THE AUTHOR

The author is an Active Duty Coast Guard Chief Warrant Officer who may have finally found his forever home in Rhode Island but can't live there yet as he's stationed somewhere else. He just returned Stateside from two arduous years in the U.S. Virgin Islands where he did more drinking than writing, but he's now getting back down to it. He writes novels and short stories loosely based around his full-time job in the Coast Guard which consists of drinking coffee, taking naps, sometimes inspecting boats and investigating things that seemed to be a good idea at the time. He likes to think his stories are better than the popular TV show NCIS and if you think so too you can find his novels for sale on Amazon or on his website at www.ShippWrites.com and join his email list at jonathan@shippwrites.com

SASQUATCH HUNTING

KES MCDANIEL

Stopping for snacks puts Jake Daely's life in the hands of the mythical Sasquatch.

1

Hands down, this was the fanciest convenience store I've ever seen. The clerk wore suspenders and lederhosen to match the festive feel of the town. Little Bavaria is a picturesque slice of German countryside airlifted to central Washington.

Rooting through the energy bars and packages of nuts, I heard a loud growl and wondered if there was a dog in the store.

I shuffled toward the cash register holding my snacks, a towering display of corn chips blocking my view. The noise repeated. I heard the clerk say, "What the fuck are you supposed to be?"

Bent over, holding a bulky pile of snacks against my chest, I turned the corner and smiled. A seven-foot-tall Sasquatch lurked at the counter. That explained the gorilla noise. I relaxed—a prankster—no need for me to be on high alert.

Then Sasquatch turned slightly, and I saw the pistol which held the clerk's wide-open gaze. The poor kid looked terrified. The robber twitched, waving the gun in broad sweeps as he danced in place, uttering random noises.

Well, crap, a fucking robbery.

The clerk's eyes darted wildly, then focused on me. Looking for help? I took a step backward, hoping the robber hadn't noticed me.

No such luck.

"You. Freeze," Sasquatch said, wildly waving the gun in my direction.

I gotta calm this guy down. He's too shaky—too unpredictable.

I keep my service weapon clipped in the small of my back, not nearly close enough.

"I said freeze!" the robber demanded. He turned to the clerk, gesturing with the gun. "Gimme the cash—stick it inna bag. Don't try nothing."

He's never done this before.

The clerk opened the register.

"All of it. Hurry." The pistol circled the room. A shot might land anywhere.

I eased back a half step while the clerk distracted his attention.

"You!" Sasquatch swung back to face me. "Your wallet. Fast."

I let the groceries crash to the floor and held out my open hands.

"Yes, sir. No problem. My wallet is in my back pocket."

He let out another growl.

This guy is bat shit crazy. I have to calm him down.

"Here, just take the money. No need for anyone to get hurt." I kept my left hand up and reached behind me with my right, shifting my body slightly to the left.

"He's got a gun!" the clerk shouted.

Oh shit...

I saw the muzzle flash and felt the punch to my chest. Then my body slammed into the door of the freezer case, and all went black as I fell.

I opened my eyes to an EMT who checked my pulse and breathing.

I tried to speak, but what came out was barely audible. "What...?"

"Quiet. Don't move," the EMT said.

He turned to yell over his shoulder, "He's awake."

"I've got a single shell casing over here," said another voice. "Twenty-five caliber."

"Sir, you must stay here until they can interview you," someone said.

Who was he talking to?

"I need to check him first," the EMT said and cradled my head while he poked and prodded.

Someone had shot me?

A muffled memory... a gunshot—a blinding blast of pain. Screams. Yelling. "You actually shot him! You killed him, you idiot!" *Who'd said that?*

The clerk moved into view, peering down at me, his long blond hair falling forward.

"He'd fallen onto his side. The robber grabbed something from this guy's back before running out of the store. I couldn't tell what it was—his wallet, I think. As soon as the robber left, I knelt about where you are and checked for his pulse. Then since I knew he was still alive, I rolled him onto his back to look for the bullet hole, but... but I couldn't find one! I was still looking when Officer Shelby showed up, and you were right behind him."

The same voice I'd heard yelling? I couldn't be sure.

"How was he lying when he fell?" the EMT asked.

"On his side."

"Which side?" I heard a strain in the voice.

"Oh! His right side. He'd been reaching for his wallet and kind of turned his body, and the guy just shot him. But—I couldn't find any blood. Maybe it was a blank."

Yes, it was the same voice. He's lying—that wasn't what happened. What was going on?

I felt the EMT's gloved hands on my chest. My shirt was open. A bead of sweat dripped off his head and landed on my stomach.

"Massive bruising," the EMT said. "Wasn't a blank; something hit him."

"Roger that," a deeper voice responded. "Could it be in his clothing?"

"Nothing obvious. You can examine his clothes after we're sure the patient is stable." He raised his voice. "Clear the path! We're moving him."

I floated up and over, then abruptly rose with the EMTs and felt the current of air across my bare skin. Someone put a mask over my face, the air tasting strange with a metallic tinge, then covered me with a blanket. A clamp squeezed my arm.

The room spun. *Where was I?*

"He's going into shock," were the last words I heard before waking up in a hospital bed.

"You're fortunate," said a person hovering over me. My blurred vision made out a figure dressed head to toe in pale blue. Male? Female? I couldn't tell.

"You're hurt, and your body is in shock," the speaker continued. "You're going to be very sore, but you aren't seriously injured. You might have hit your head when you fell. Let me know if you feel you're going to throw up."

The sensations washed over me. Antiseptic smells. Pounding pain. Dizziness when I lifted my head.

I opened my mouth to speak, but nothing happened. I cleared my throat and tried again.

"Thanks."

"Can you tell me your name?" the person in blue asked.

I focused, concentrating on their face. Male, I thought. Why was he blurry?

"Daely," I said. "Jake Daely." I stopped to lick my lips. "Federal agent. ID is in my wallet."

"You didn't arrive with an ID," he said. "Are you feeling dizzy? Nauseated? Any confusion?"

All the above, I thought but kept my focus on his face. "What happened?" I asked. It hurt to talk. "What's wrong with my voice?"

"A robber shot you in the chest, but the bullet deflected. You have massive bruising, but it appears no damage to your ribs. You may also have a mild concussion. We're monitoring."

He lifted each lid and looked closely into my eyes while shining a flashlight into them.

"Dilation is normal," he said, removing the light. "I want to check you in for overnight observation." He turned away. "Tell the officer he can come back now."

My vision cleared the more I blinked. It helped not to have that light in my face.

A burly uniformed police officer appeared at the cubicle opening, carrying a notebook and speaking into his radio.

"About to interview the victim. Ten-six for about twenty."

"Officer Benbright from Little Bavaria," he said, pulling up the lone guest chair. "The doctor said you were alert and communicative. What can you tell me about what happened?"

"The bastard shot me," I said. "I was reaching for my wallet, and he shot me."

That was going to be my official story.

"We found no wallet in your possession. Can you tell me your name?"

"My name's Jake Daely," I said. "I work for the PDT out of Seattle. Son of a bitch took my wallet after I went down. Took my service piece, too. I'm federal. ID is in the wallet. Call PDT in Seattle; someone will confirm."

I felt my sore chest and noticed my neck was bare. "Asshole stole my medallion, too. But you want a description." I tried to draw enough breath to talk. "Seven foot tall and hairy," I said. "He was wearing a Sasquatch mask. Don't know how he could see through it, but he saw well enough to shoot me."

I shook my head to clear it and immediately regretted that choice. I closed my eyes to visualize. "Extrapolating from his shoulders, suspect's height is between five-foot-ten and six feet tall; Caucasian, slender build, wearing faded jeans with a hole in the left knee, dark brown or black work boots, and a long-sleeved gray hoody, no logo observed. I caught a flash of color on his right wrist, tattoo, or birthmark. Agitated, very nervous. Voice was high-pitched, sounded young—and scared. Possibly his first armed robbery. Didn't get the stoned vibe, but erratic."

That's what I tried to say. My mouth was dry, and talking was difficult. My chest hurt. I was breathing shallowly and speaking slowly and quietly to avoid more pain.

Officer Benbright was scribbling in his book. "The clerk at the scene said you seemed dazed and incoherent. Someone will come back to interview you later today or in the morning before you're discharged. The doctor has your name as Jake Daely. Is that correct?"

I stared at him and gave the tiniest of nods.

He stood. "Take it easy and recover. You're lucky to be alive."

I stared at his departing back. Had he heard a single word I said? I'd heard myself speak—but had it all been in my head?

Time passed. I had to get out of this hospital. Where were my clothes? I pushed myself upright on the hospital bed, then gripped the mattress to avoid tipping over.

A nurse flew in. "Stop! Here, let me help you lay back down. Transport is on its way to take you over to the general wing for observation."

"No," I said. I didn't have a concussion; the hospital didn't need to monitor me. A lineman had knocked me out once, playing football. This didn't feel the same, plus my head was clearing.

She stepped forward, raising one gloved hand to place behind my back.

"I said no," I repeated, clearing my throat.

"You're refusing further treatment?" she asked, bafflement coloring her tone.

"I do not wish to check in overnight," I said, my voice getting more assertive. "But I would like a prescription for pain relief."

"You have a brain injury," she said. "You need adequate rest, or you won't heal properly."

"I understand the process," I said. "I don't need to be here to rest. I'll get a motel."

"That's not a good idea. If you fall, you could injure your head worse, and no one would be around to help you."

"I need to make private calls," I said. "I need my laptop and my cell phone. I can't do what I need to do from a hospital bed."

Damn, I hurt—but mostly my chest, not my head. The pain was from the shock and bruising.

"You can't leave without filling out the patient paperwork," the nurse said. "If you promise not to get up, I'll tell the doctor you're alert and also notify the front desk."

I lifted my hand in the Boy Scout salute. "I'll behave."

Now that I could talk clearly, the ER doctor agreed with my assessment of no concussion and canceled his admittance order. The paperwork took a lot longer.

"Oh, there's an officer in the waiting room, wants to talk to you. I'm to let him know as soon as you're released," the nurse said.

The same guy, Officer Benbright, that I'd tried to talk to before was waiting. The hospital clerk led us both to a small private conference room.

"We use this for family consultations," she said. "Stay as long as you need."

I took a seat at the small table.

"Are you sure you're feeling up to this?" Benbright asked. "You seemed very disoriented before. Can I get you anything?"

"Something with sugar," I said. "And then maybe a ride back to my car when we're done?"

"I'm surprised they're not keeping you overnight." He went to the door briefly, talked to someone, and then returned with a cold can of cola, which he handed me.

"They tried. I declined. What can you tell me about the asshole that shot me?"

"Sir, I'm here to get your statement. What do you remember?"

Right, he wouldn't tell me anything before he got my version; they would look for contradictions.

"When I walked into that store, I was carrying my federal ID and my service pistol, a Sig 357," I said. "Both are now missing. That's a big problem, and I need to notify my chain of command. Also, the shooter was a guy wearing a Sasquatch mask that made him look seven feet tall."

I took several long gulps from the soda, then repeated the description I'd tried to give him earlier. Sitting upright was clearing my headache, and the sugar also helped.

"Do you remember anything after he shot you?" Benbright asked.

"Bits and pieces," I said. "Someone was leaning over me. I heard yelling. Once everything stops hurting so much, I can probably do better."

"The clerk said the robber took your wallet after you fell. He didn't mention a handgun."

I frowned; the clerk certainly knew I'd been carrying. Why wouldn't he have mentioned that? I put my hand to my chest. "He also stole a medallion I wore under my clothes. Did the clerk mention that?"

Benbright looked through his notebook, frowning. "No. The clerk thought you were dead and was afraid he'd be next. He said he ran to the back so the robber wouldn't shoot him too."

He flipped a page. "Then once the robber had fled, he said he checked for your pulse then rolled you over to find the bullet wound." He looked up. "We found a twenty-five-caliber casing. That medallion you said is missing—probably saved your life—or at least some broken ribs. Hard to tell with a Saturday-night special. Sometimes they're deadly, sometimes they bounce off."

"My lucky day. Yours too, if Saturday-night specials have made their way out here. Cheap, easy to hide, and as much a danger to their users as their victims. Did the surveillance camera show anything?"

"The camera was disabled; it looked like a rat chewed through the cord." Benbright turned to a new page in his notebook. "Tell me about this medallion."

"It's a 1924 Liberty silver dollar mounted in a collar that I wore on a stainless steel chain. My neck hurts like hell where the guy broke the chain taking it." I paused. "It was my grandfather's, made from a coin from the year he was born. The coin is not valuable to a collector; its only worth is sentimental and maybe for the silver. Not sure even a pawn shop would offer more than face value. I can't think of any good reason for anyone to take it. Especially now if it's got a dent in it. Pretty easy to track."

"A trophy," Benbright said. "He won't pawn it. He'll keep it handy to remind himself how brave he was to shoot and rob you—and it will be the nail in his coffin when we take him to trial."

"I'd like it back," I said. "Even dented. I don't have a lot of family heirlooms. This one means a lot to me."

Benbright nodded. "We'll catch him." He closed his notebook. "You're looking better. Want me to give you a lift to your car? Then you can officially show me your backup ID and make my paperwork easier."

"I'd appreciate it." *Then I get to start my paperwork.* "Will you email copies of what you have?"

He nodded. "Insurance companies commonly request copies as proof of loss. There won't be any problem getting them to you."

I dozed while he drove, ignoring his radio chatter. I had some unpleasant paperwork of my own to look forward to, and I needed a plan to divert the upcoming shit storm.

Benbright waited until I had retrieved my cell phone and laptop, and he was sure he could contact me.

"Don't drive home." He handed me a voucher. "Go to this motel; it's on the far end of town. This will cover you for a night's stay. Little Bavaria takes care of its crime victims. Get some rest. We'll talk tomorrow. Do nothing foolish."

I thanked him and watched him drive off.

He appeared to be under the mistaken idea that I'd leave this investigation to others. Not when it's my ID and my gun in the wind. There will be hell to pay if I don't recover those before they hit the black market.

Along with my personal backup piece, I keep my credit cards and emergency cash in a lockbox permanently bolted to the inside of my trunk; the lock keyed to my thumbprint. Also stashed are full-color copies of my wallet contents and my passport. I was not unprepared.

I'd take the motel room—it would serve as a base while I clean up and report the theft. A police report from a small town was not adequate at the federal level. I had two more days until I was due back on duty, enough time to track down a small-town would-be killer.

The motel was adequate—with your run-of-the-mill bed, desk, and shower. I booted my laptop and hopped on the VPN. Filling out the form reporting my lost ID, I marked the police report as "pending," then checked my email on a hunch before submitting.

Benbright had come through—he'd sent me the preliminary report. I copied the file numbers into my official document. That would help minimize the fallout. After finishing, I sent a secure email to my boss.

I let the hot water wash over me and forced myself to relax. The painkillers from my saved stash kicked in, and the steam also helped.

I replayed the scene, slowing it down as I mentally reviewed details of the shooter.

I'd recognized the pistol with one glance. Few handguns are as small as a twenty-five, and the robber's large hand had dwarfed it. The guy was physically large, not a smaller man wearing an oversized mask to seem more imposing. Benbright would be interested in that detail.

Then I remembered the clerk had shouted, "He's got a gun." The words had felt off; I could see the gun plainly. And then it fired...

The scene unfolded. The clerk had glimpsed the holster in the small of my back. He thought I'd been reaching for it and was warning the robber.

The clerk and robber were partners.

Now the oddities in the police report made sense. I hadn't imagined the clerk's actions. The clerk had flat out lied to cover his participation. Which one of the two actually robbed me? How long had I been out?

I felt my scalp carefully. No bruises, no tender spots. I hadn't hit my head. I'd blacked out from the pain of the bullet hitting me, but not until after hitting the floor. I must have instinctively tucked my chin.

To find Sasquatch, all I needed to do was follow the clerk.

Do I tell Benbright this? An odd niggling feeling told me not to. I was still missing something. But the part about the hands? That, he needed to know.

I reread the police report before calling. Two witnesses had seen the shooter, still wearing the mask, drive off on a motorcycle after putting something in his saddlebags. One would think that a Sasquatch on a Harley would be easy to find, but this was a tourist town. Observers might think it was a publicity stunt.

From the business card he'd given me, I entered the phone number into my cell and hit the phone icon.

"Benbright," his deep voice answered.

"Daely here," I said. "I've remembered something about the shooter."

"Tell me."

I described the oversized hands holding the tiny pistol. "They look small in most guys' hands, but this was excessive. His finger was almost too big to fit inside the trigger guard."

"I'll add it to the report," Benbright said. "My nephew mentioned nothing about that. Maybe this will jog his memory."

His nephew?

"Your nephew is the clerk?" I asked. "Roger Calloway?"

"Yup, that's why he knew enough first aid to help you. I make all the kids in the family get certified every two years. Roger had some rough spells growing up, but he's turned into a fine young man. I was proud of the way he jumped right in to help you."

"I'd like to swing by and thank him," I said. And get a better read on the kid in person. Troubles in the past? Perhaps they weren't all put behind him.

"Store's still closed. The crime scene guys finished, but my sister wanted to get her cleaning crew there before reopening it.

"Your sister owns the store?"

Benbright gave a small snort. "Hey, it's a small town, once all the tourists go home. I worked there myself, back in the day."

"So, where might young Roger be hanging out?"

"Oh, he'll be at the store. Sara will have him cleaning up the mess and mopping the floors while she does all her insurance paperwork. He's part of the cleaning crew—along with his sisters."

"Was anything taken from the store beside the cash?"

I heard Benbright shuffling. "Some alcohol maybe, hard to tell, lots of breakages—not typical behavior for a robbery. We think our man might be high on meth or PCP."

Or in a rage, I thought. Much was becoming apparent.

"Oh, almost forgot to tell you! We found the Sasquatch head. A tourist called it in. It was sticking out of the brush under the North River Bridge. We had the area searched—found a fair amount of trash, but not your wallet. Sometimes we get lucky, and the thief dumps everything but the cash. I got someone tracing the mask. If we can figure out where this head came from, we might get a line on our suspect."

I nodded. Tracing the head would lead to Roger's friend, the one he'd conspired with.

After the call, I replaced the laptop in my trunk and headed back into town. An upscale deli had parking available, and I collected several sandwiches and bottles of water to go. I devoured one sandwich while I drove the rest of the way to the scene of the crime.

The closed sign was prominent, but the small parking lot was full.

I pulled into an empty spot on the street and surveyed the parking lot while I ate another sandwich, drank more water, and studied maps of the area on my GPS. Two young women came out the back of the store, climbed into a minivan, and drove away toward the direction of my motel, leaving two vehicles in the lot—a new SUV and an older, badly beat-up Jeep.

Bingo. Roger left the store and headed to the Jeep. I clearly saw his expression; he was not a cheerful man. Didn't like mom making him clean up his mess? His sisters had looked more tired than angry. Roger was angry.

As I had hoped, Roger pulled out of the parking lot and headed out of town in the same direction I was facing. I allowed another vehicle to pass before pulling out. We still had a good hour of daylight left at this time of year; I did not expect following him to be complicated.

It wasn't.

He led me several miles out of town, turning onto side roads that twisted through the mountains. I was only in danger of losing him once when he took a turn while out of sight, but I spotted the dust hovering in the air over the rutted trail. I reduced speed to avoid damaging my car's undercarriage; Roger's Jeep was definitely a more suitable vehicle for this terrain.

The road wound through the trees as we slowly rose in elevation. Roger was getting further ahead, but I accepted the risk. I didn't want him to hear or see me tracking him. About three miles in, I caught a glint of reflection as I rounded a corner, then braked to a full stop, still in the shade of the fir trees.

I watched for a full minute, seeing no movement of any kind. I rolled my car slowly up to the unoccupied Jeep and parked behind it, verifying no armed man was hiding in the vehicle.

A clearly maintained two-foot-wide trail led off into the woods.

Looking closely at the footpath, I spotted telltale tire tracks in the softer dirt where the pine needles gathered—a motorcycle. Was it still there?

Time to suit up. I donned my Level II body armor with an exterior gear harness, stuffed additional magazines in the ammo pouch, strapped on a heavy-duty flashlight and handcuffs, double-checked my phone was on vibrate, and surveyed the area. I didn't want to charge down the trail with one or possibly two armed killers lying in wait, but dusk was descending and the shadows lengthening. This needed to be a stealth approach, as with deer hunting, although I doubted my prey would catch my scent.

Confronting Roger and his confederate without backup was beyond foolhardy. Procedure dictated that I call in my location and my suspicions and let the local force investigate—or not—as they saw fit. I would have made the call if I had a connection.

I could drive down the mountain until I found a signal. I paused at the trailhead, considering.

Going in without backup was never a good idea.

Which is when I heard the gunshot.

I took off at a run.

Ten seconds later, I burst into a clearing and saw Roger aiming a handgun at what appeared to be a figure hiding behind the log shelter's back wall.

"Come out here, you asshole. Come out here and face me like a man!"

He shot another round into the logs, narrowly missing the motorcycle parked nearby.

"You lied to me," came the answering shout. "You told me you loaded the gun with blanks. You made me kill that guy!" The voice rose in pitch, ending with a childlike sob.

"He didn't die. You didn't even get that right," Roger said, moving toward the end of the wall.

"You told me he was dead."

"I lied." Roger moved closer to the corner, ready to shoot.

"We agreed on a prank. Why'd you put real bullets in the gun? I could have shot you instead of him."

"So it would look real, you idiot!"

"It was an effing prank! It wasn't supposed to look real."

I crept toward the shelter, making my moves while the two argued. I wanted to see who the other man was, to see if he was armed.

Getting in the middle of a shootout was not on my bucket list. I worked my way to a covered vantage point where I could peer around the corner. I reached my spot at the same time Roger rounded the wall. A large man stood in the shadows at the corner of the shelter's two solid walls. As Roger aimed and fired, the other man dashed around the corner, out of sight.

I must have made a noise. Roger whirled and fired at me as I left the shelter of the thick fir tree. He was less than ten feet away. Half a second more, and I'd have gotten the jump on him.

So close there was no way he could miss.

I took two shots to the center of my chest.

Shit, that hurt...

He expected me to fall, not to take a step backward, recover, and keep coming.

I leapt to tackle him, jumped on his side and back, and slammed his gun hand against the ground, sending the pistol flying. I twisted his arm behind his back and jabbed my knee hard on his forearm, holstered my pistol, grabbed my zip-cuffs with one hand, and wrenched his other arm backward with the other.

Once he was secure, I put my foot on Roger's pistol while scanning for the other man, my gun again in hand.

"Come out with your hands up," I called. "Roger is done shooting for today."

A massive pale hand waved around the corner of the wall. "I'm not armed. I'm coming out. Don't shoot me."

A bulky young man, several inches over six feet tall and with broad, heavy shoulders and short muddy blond hair, followed the hand.

I sized him up against what I remembered from earlier.

"Sasquatch, I presume?"

His face scrunched in the dimming light. "You're the cop," he said, leaning back against the wall. "I thought you were dead. Roger said you were dead. Roger said I'd killed you."

Already looking unsteady, the man slid down the wall and sat staring at me. "Roger told me he loaded the gun with blanks. And then you fell—and he yelled that I'd killed you. But just now, he said you're weren't dead. I thought he was lying." He stared at me, wide-eyed. "Praise Jesus, you're not dead. I didn't kill you. I'm not a killer. I'm not."

Then he leaned forward, put his head in his hands, and started sobbing and crying out incoherently.

At no point did it seem to occur to him that had he stayed behind the wall and started running through the woods, I hurt too much to give chase. He could have escaped clean. At heart, he was not a criminal. He was a scared man-boy, in over his head, looking for salvation.

He'd come close to killing a man—me.

Only I could grant him absolution.

I holstered my weapon; this person was no threat. I pulled out my cell phone and began taking video. First, I filmed the boy against the wall, then Roger lying cuffed face down in the dirt, and the pistol he'd used a few feet away.

I pulled an evidence bag and a pair of latex gloves from my harness pocket and picked up the handgun Roger had used. As I suspected, it was my service piece, the serial number etched in my brain. I cleared the Sig, bagged it along with the ejected ammunition, and then placed the sealed bag back in my harness. With it secured, I could deal with my two suspects.

My chest hurt like hell. *How was I going to get both of them back to town?*

"What's your name, son?"

He looked up, blinking. "Huh?"

"What's your name?" I repeated. "My name is Jake Daely. What's yours?"

"Oh," he looked blank for a moment. "I'm Dillon. Dillon Griswold."

"Lean back against the wall and stick out your feet," I said.

When he did, I set my phone down, still recording but leaving my hands free. "Tell me what happened, Dillon. How did you get into this mess?"

"Roger asked me to help him prank his mom after he found this mask. It had to be me because I'm so big. He said it would be good publicity, and people would love it, and I'd get a full-time job as the town mascot. I'd be on TV."

Dillon stared at me. "I needed the job, man. I thought the robbery was pretending, just a prank."

"Where'd the gun come from?" I asked, sensing that Dillon needed prompting to keep talking.

Roger, who had kept silent except for loud gasps of air, found his voice.

"Shut up! You lying sack of shit."

I took a step backward and started reciting.

"Roger Calloway, you are under arrest. You have the right to remain silent."

He swore at me throughout the process. Didn't matter to me; an audio recording would hold in court.

I kept myself from reacting when he claimed I had no authority as he was a "sovereign citizen."

Roger continued to rant, but lying on his front, he couldn't get the lung power to achieve his desired volume. I had him incapacitated, and with concrete evidence of his assault on Dillon, I could afford to ignore his raving long enough to deal with Dillon.

I double-checked that my phone was still recording and stepped closer to Dillon, kneeling near his feet. This was the moment for delicacy—I needed him to talk, and I needed him not to be afraid. He'd returned his face to his hands. Hiding from the world or just me?

"Tell me what happened." I put my hand on his foot gently to get his attention. "Go back to the beginning. When did you first talk about pulling a prank on Roger's mom?"

He lowered his hands and looked across at me, his face dappled in shadows. "I dunno. A couple months ago, Roger was at my house."

"Are you and Roger good friends?"

"Not really, but he drops by a lot. I think he's trying to impress my sister. Keeps joking around with her, pretending to ask her out and laughing when she turns him down."

"Okay," I said. "Did the idea start as a joke?"

"Yeah, my sister made a crack that she'd go out with Roger when Sasquatch walked through downtown Little Bavaria. So Roger hunted around on the internet and found this mask, but once he got it, it was too big for him, so he convinced me to wear it."

"That's a long way from armed robbery," I said. "What changed?"

Dillon rubbed his forehead. "I dunno. Roger's plan kept getting more complicated. He's a steamroller when he wants something. He keeps pushing and pushing until you do what he wants so he'll shut up."

"What happened?"

"Roger swore it would all be on camera, and I was to only growl and wave my arms. Then he'd put the video on the internet, and we'd be famous, and more tourists would come to town, and the city would hire me to walk around in costume—a summer job. I need a regular job."

"That all sounds good. Where'd the gun come in?"

"I don't know where he got it. He told me he loaded it with blanks and that I should wave it around and act like I was crazy—that the video would get more views if I looked dangerous."

Dillon wiped his eyes with the heels of his hands. "He lied, and then he yelled at me."

Dillon looked me straight in the eyes. "Man, until you fell, I thought the whole thing was a big joke. And then, he said you were dead, and I panicked. Roger knocked over some bottles, put a couple in a sack, grabbed some other stuff, and told me to get the hell out of town. I had to hide. He said he'd tell me when it was safe to come back but to get rid of the mask and come out here and hide until he could clear things up."

"What did you do with the gun? And the other stuff he gave you?" I asked.

"I drank the liquor," he said. "He didn't give me enough to make the buzz last, and that cheap crap always gives me a headache."

He rubbed his face. "Can I have something to drink? There's a bottle on the table, next to the money bag. Your wallet is in there, too." Raising his jaw, Dillon looked at me. "Sorry about that, dude. Shooting you was bad enough; robbing a dead body is just cold."

"Roger knew I wasn't dead," I reminded him. "What about the gun? The one you used in the robbery?"

"I threw that in the river when I got rid of the mask. I wasn't keeping that thing a minute longer than I had to!"

More paperwork. Probably need a diver from the State Police for the recovery.

"And my medallion?"

"What medallion?"

I looked at Roger laying on the ground, still struggling against the zip-cuffs, cursing life and me in particular. He was secure for the moment.

"Stand up," I said to Dillon.

"Why?"

"I need to search you for weapons."

Dillon struggled to his feet. "You won't find anything. My pocket knife is by my bike. After you search me, can I have that water?" His voice wasn't quite a whine. "Can you give me a hand up?"

"You know better than that," I said, wondering about the mental age of this man-child. "Stand up, face the wall, spread your legs, and put your hands up wide and lean forward."

I found nothing unexpected. I stepped backward, resuming my position between Dillon and Roger. "We'll move inside, and you can get your drink, then sit down again. You're going to convince me you won't try to run away when you help me take your buddy back to my vehicle."

"What's the point of running? You know who I am. Mom's going to kill me if you don't first. My sister is going to hang me with this for the rest of my life. She never liked Roger—wouldn't go out with him like he wanted."

I made a snap decision.

"Help me get this meatloaf out to my car. I will not cuff you, not if you don't force me to." I shook my head, looking at this foolish young man. "Help me get him to town, then turn yourself in. I'll make sure they know you cooperated and Roger duped you."

"You'd do that for me?"

Seeing the bare hope in his face gave me a jolt.

"You made some poor decisions. Learn from this, then put it behind you."

I won't kick puppies.

I leaned down to search Roger. As I suspected, my medallion was in his pants pocket. I bagged it as evidence, noting the asymmetrical bulge in Liberty's face.

I motioned to Dillon. "Help me get him to his feet. We have a long night ahead of us."

I need pain killers. I think I broke a rib.

"I still can't believe I almost killed you, and you don't hate me."

"My guardian angels helped me see into your heart." I stashed the bagged coin and looked heavenward at the few stars now visible with the dusk. *Thanks, Dad. Thanks, Grandpa.* "Come on, kid. Waiting won't make this easier on any of us."

Another Sasquatch sighting debunked.

ABOUT THE AUTHOR

Kes McDaniel writes action-packed crime thrillers and jumps at any excuse to find adventure: by land (traveling to 46 states and 17 countries), sea (scuba diving in 2 oceans and 1 sea), or air (zip-lining in 3 different countries).

She's an Army veteran, where she learned to operate heavy equipment, which was useful when she and her husband built a four-story geodesic dome as owner/builders; started in 1995 with an expected finished date of 2030.

https://kesmcdaniel.com/

AN INSIDE JOB

IAN W. SAINSBURY

An attack on a family woke the monster inside his head. It won't sleep again until it takes revenge.

1

Her name is Margarita, but when she buzzes the intercom she announces herself as Justine.

Justine, she repeats to herself while she waits. It's the details that can catch you out. *Justine.*

"Where's Consuela?" The voice of the nanny. Mrs. Lloyd always left for the office before dawn.

"Sick. Upset stomach. She hopes to be back tomorrow."

"I see." The intercom crackles. "Ah... Justine, please don't be offended, but..."

Margarita smiles into the camera. Shrugs. "Please. Call Consuela. I could be anybody, right?"

"Thank you for understanding."

Margarita looks away from the camera and examines the wrought-iron gates. The initials of the mistress and master of the house are worked into the design; when the gates close, they come together in a symbol of everlasting love. That bullshit statement probably cost more than Margarita's two-bed apartment.

"Sorry to keep you."

The gates don't open, but there's a click and a person-sized door swings back within the design. A gate in a gate. Margarita steps through.

Much of the house's exterior is obscured by a huge mimosa tree, budding with pink flowers.

The door, blinding white, besieged by verdant creepers, is open. A wheelbarrow stands nearby and a huge man, broad, heavily muscled, pulls weeds from the borders. He shoots a glance at her but says nothing, returning to his work.

"Hello." A pale, tall, scrawny specimen in her forties holds out a hand for Margarita to shake. Brown hair pulled into a ponytail. Sensible shoes.

"I'm Anna, Mr. and Mrs. Stone's housekeeper. Nanny to Charlotte."

The nanny—no one likes to use the word *servant* in Austin—doesn't need to introduce herself to Margarita, who has already memorized the information. Other than Anna, and the near-mute gardener, Tom, there's only Carlson Lloyd and his daughter Charlotte at home. It's almost too easy.

Margarita keeps her eyes down. Would a curtsey be too much? "Pleased to meet you."

"Follow me." Anna trots across a marble-floored lobby dominated by a staircase straight out of *Gone With The Wind*. The kitchen smells of coffee and fresh bread, then they step into a room full of washing machines, dryers, vacuum cleaners, floor polishers, and mops. Shelves loaded with chemical cleaners and cloths.

"Consuela never mentioned a niece."

"She and my mother argued, many years ago. I hope they reconcile. My mother is very sick."

"Oh. I see. I'm sorry." Good. The nanny is embarrassed. Perhaps she'll leave. But no.

"Will your aunt be well enough to work tomorrow? She sounded terrible."

Margarita didn't doubt it for a second. Hector had pushed the barrel of a gun into Consuela's mouth while describing what he would do to her and her kids if she deviated from his instructions.

"By tomorrow," says Margarita, "everything will be fine. Trust me."

Once the housekeeper leaves, after telling the new cleaner which rooms need attention this morning, Margarita fills a bucket with hot water, squirts in detergent, and carries it through to the main lobby.

The marble floor turns out to be much easier to clean than twenty-year-old linoleum.

It's seven-fifty. Consuela's shift ends at nine-thirty. If Margarita cleaned for a living, she has no doubt she'd be able to mop all the downstairs floors, and dust the living room as requested, but she has a different agenda. She skims the mop across the lobby floor to give the appearance of cleanliness, doing the same for the kitchen and utility room. She finds a basket full of dusters and polish and takes it through to the enormous living room. The couches are white, as are the rugs. White. Unmarked. It looks like a photo shoot. Maybe the kid isn't allowed in here.

Aimee Lloyd is a big shot tech company CEO, and her husband trades stocks from home. Hector's information, which he says is good, suggests the girl—Charlie—spends more time with the nanny than her parents. Margarita almost feels sorry for her. Even rich kids have shitty childhoods. The difference is, they have the money for therapy to get over it later.

"Taking Charlie to school, Justine."

Margarita is a little slow looking up, forgetting her fake name. A shy, gap-toothed smile from the kid, who's holding the nanny's hand. She's got that solemn, fearful look some kids have. Like she expects something bad might happen. She doesn't know it yet, but she's on the money today.

"Mr. Lloyd is working in his basement office. Please don't disturb him. If you need anything, Tom is outside. He doesn't speak much, but he understands just fine. Please give my best wishes to Consuela. I hope she feels better soon. Thank you for filling in."

"No problem." Margarita winks at the kid.

Thirty seconds later, a car starts up outside, and the gates swing open to let the Mercedes leave. The gardener waves, and a small hand returns the gesture from the back of the car.

By the time the gates close, Margarita is moving.

There's a flatscreen television on the kitchen wall, the key tucked behind the soundbar. At the far end of a walk-in store cupboard crammed with cans of Italian olive oil, bags of flour, and shelves full of wine bottles, she turns the key in a small door.

Inside is a desk, a computer, and six screens showing the exterior of the property from cameras mounted just below the gutters. Any television in the house can show the views from these cameras, linked to a high-tech alarm system.

All of which can be overridden, but only by someone who has the password. Time to find out if the information they bought is good.

Margarita taps in letters and numbers. The screen goes dark. She holds her breath, then smiles when the welcome message appears. Inserting a thumb drive, she uploads the malware, watching the screens. The gardener is turning over soil in the flower bed. As for Carlson Lloyd, Hector says the man of the house will only quit his basement if the place is on fire. There's a bathroom down there, a fridge, a microwave, and a bar. Lloyd gets up in the early hours to catch the Asian markets and often sleeps through the afternoons.

Margarita pulls out the thumb drive, shoves it back into her pocket. The clock is ticking now.

She locks up, replaces the key, goes through to the living room and sprays the air with polish. It'll smell clean, at least.

The gardener glances up as she walks back past the mimosa, gives her a nod. The blue bandana across his bald head is wet with sweat, as is the white T-shirt that clings to his frame. He's not ripped, exactly, more like he lucked out in the genetic lottery and ended up with the frame of a heavyweight boxer.

Very much Margarita's type. But she's here on business, not pleasure. By this time tomorrow, she'll be on her way to Mexico with enough money for her own marble-floored palace, not that she has the poor taste to build one.

She fires one last glance at the gardener as the door in the gate closes behind her. He's looking at her, but there's nothing flirtatious in those dark green eyes. There's not much of anything there at all. But she hopes they won't run into him tonight. It would be a tragedy if such a fine specimen got caught up in the mess.

The hour after supper is Tom Lewis's favorite time of day. Supper means hot chocolate and a story on the back porch. For the first few weeks after he started working here, drawn to Anna's voice, he always found a job within earshot. One evening, Charlie, the Lloyds' daughter, hearing movement, hopped off the wooden boards mid-story. She found Tom by the rose bushes, entranced, holding secateurs he had no intention of using. Recognizing a kindred spirit, another cup was procured, and he became a regular guest at story time.

Tonight, it's too humid for hot chocolate, but a ritual is a ritual, and Charlie—like most six-year-olds—expects consistency. She takes the swing seat, Anna the wicker chair, and Tom, still in overalls, fingernails dark with soil, sits on the step, his back against whitewashed wooden panels.

Anna reads from *The Secret Garden*. Much to his—and Charlie's—delight, the book features not just a garden, but a gardener, with the bonus that the main character is female. Charlie's personality is far from the feisty Mary Lennox, but Tom likes the fierce smile that creeps onto the child's face while she listens.

The thirty minutes pass too fast. Once Tom has washed his hands, he and Charlie play hide and seek.

At six-foot-three and built like a linebacker, there are a limited amount of hiding places for Tom. Charlie finds him in sixty seconds flat, giggling at his attempt to conceal himself behind a row of mops and brooms with a bucket on his head.

"My turn!" and she's gone, sprinting away.

Tom begins his count, hearing Charlie skid past Anna in the kitchen. The housekeeper calls after her. "Downstairs only."

"I know," comes a distant shout, originating from upstairs. Tom reaches ten. It's supposed to be thirty, but he sometimes gets lost after twelve, so Charlie agreed to ten so long as he counts slowly.

"Just one game tonight, Tom. Mrs. Lloyd will be back early." The big man makes a show of looking in kitchen cupboards, opening and closing them loudly enough for Charlie to hear.

"Okay, mm, got it."

He stumbles over words more rarely these days. It's over a year since Bedlam Boy last came, and, in his absence, Tom is changing. Not only is his speech less hampered by a stutter and the constant struggle to find the right words, but his confidence is growing. There's a fresh clarity in the way he thinks. Some nights, Tom runs his fingers along the pages of Charlie's old books, sounding out words. And he's making progress.

"You can't find me, you can't find me."

Tom heads upstairs, following the broad anti-clockwise curve of the banister, homing in on the smothered giggles.

The master bedroom, three guest bedrooms, and a home gym are on his left. To the right is Charlie's room, a fourth guest bedroom, Aimee Lloyd's home office, and—overlooking the garden—Anna's bedroom.

"Hmm," says Tom, with exaggerated confusion. He opens the store-room door, prepared for a few seconds of fruitless and noisy searching. A car blips its throttle outside. Mrs. Lloyd's Porsche.

He skips the preliminaries and goes to Anna's bedroom. Books piled on a bedside table, a photograph of her parents, a crucifix on the wall. A neatly made bed.

Tom doesn't step inside. It wouldn't be right.

"I g-give up," he says, feigning amazement when the six-year-old slides out from under the bed.

"I win. This is the absolute best hiding place ever, ever, ever."

She skips ahead to the top of the stairs to inform Anna of her triumph. Neither Anna nor Tom point out Charlie hides in the same spot every night.

"Go clean your teeth, Charlie. Your mother is home."

Tom makes for the back door. He's happy in Anna and Charlie's company, but awkward with anyone else. The Lloyds are fast-talking and busy. Kind, too: they gave him a job, and somewhere to live. But he can't keep up with their conversation, preferring the tranquility of the garden or boathouse when they're home.

The basement door opens and Carlson Lloyd emerges. Tall, thin, bearded. Pale from lack of sunlight.

"Hey, Tom, how's the ol' bucolic lifestyle treating ya?"

Mr. Lloyd can't seem to stop himself peppering every sentence with long words.

Lloyd smiles. "Don't mind me, Tom, I'm just jealous. I see you as our very own Thoreau, philosophizing in our backyard, sitting out there nights, gazing out across the Colorado. Don't deny it."

Unsure of what he would be denying, Tom is saved from answering by the front door opening.

"Mom!"

Charlie, with a drum roll of bare feet on marble, hugs her mother. Aimee Lloyd, glamorous in a sharp trouser suit, sunglasses, and a headscarf, plants a kiss on her daughter's tousled head.

"Sweetpea. Sorry I'm late. What have you been up to? Tell me everything. No. Change of plan. Go brush your hair, get into bed, and I'll lie down with you while you tell me. Deal?"

"Deal." The little girl flashes a smile at Tom and Anna on the way upstairs.

Tom uses the distraction to back towards the door. Unlike her husband, Aimee doesn't feign interest in Tom's life. She pushes her sunglasses onto her forehead. The bruised-looking hollows around her eyes are testaments to the hours she's been keeping.

"The beds out front look great, Tom. Thank you. Goodnight."

"Goodnight." Tom moves his head to include all three adults, reserving a smile for Anna, before opening the door and heading for the boathouse.

It's the last time he'll see two of them alive.

Tom keeps his shower short, the water cool, and he leans a glass against the door in case anyone tries to come in. It's a Bedlam Boy habit that Tom hasn't broken even now, fourteen months after last seeing him.

The mirror, when Tom wipes the mist from its surface, shows a broad face which has an asymmetric charm. His nose might have seemed aristocratic had it not been broken three times. A strong chin, movie star square, but his lips are thin and his distinctive green eyes are hooded, haunted.

After shaving, he rubs oil into the scars that give his head its unique geography. They rise in moon ridges along the plane of his scalp, creating shadows where the bullet made its crater, shards of bone knifing away from the epicenter.

He climbs the wooden stairs to the open-plan bedroom. It has a bed, a sink, a rocking chair, and a microwave. There are two windows. One looks back towards the house, venetian blinds painting honeyed slabs of light onto the floorboards. The window facing the river is enormous. Tom wakes with the dawn, bathed in light, the ceiling dancing with reflections of the ever-changing water.

He exercised before showering. A run along the riverbank; stomach crunches, push-ups, and sets of pull-ups on the boathouse beams. Then a series of moves similar to Tai Chi. These routines, Tom knows, are Bedlam Boy's, not his own, but his body craves the ritual.

Outside, the roses are fading, anticipating the Texas heat that will come later this month. He'll prune tomorrow - it'll help them avoid fungal disease. And it's a good time to collect and dry the seeds of the dead and dying wildflowers, ready to plant in November. Tom wonders if he'll still be here in fall. He thinks of hot chocolate, Anna's stories, hide and seek with Charlie, and he dares to hope so.

Before sleep, he reviews the day, grateful for its riches. His has been a life marked with tragedy, violence, and retribution. Tom's family is dead, and any friendships have been shallow or temporary. His only constants are his first name—his surname changes with each new identity—and Bedlam Boy's presence. Distant now, yes, but never absent.

As late evening sinks into night, Tom sleeps. The Boy may not be here, but his memories color Tom's dreams, steeped in blood and pain. There's no avoiding the dreams. The best Tom can hope for is that he will wake up without remembering them.

When Tom opens his eyes, his body is already moving, legs curling out of bed, feet on still-warm floorboards. To his left, the river, the house to his right.

He's sitting facing the Lloyd residence, looking through the slats of the blind. All is quiet. No lights. What woke him? He pushes a button on his watch and the green digits flash on, then fade.

03:17

He mouths the numbers in order. It's too early for Carlson Lloyd to be at his trading screens.

Tom holds his breath, shuts his eyes. Listens.

When he first moved into the boathouse, every sound woke him. The splashes of fish breaking the surface of the Colorado, the snuffles of racoons. For the first few weeks, any change in the frenzied maraca shakes of the katydids snapped him awake.

Now, the nocturnal soundscape is so familiar it has become a lullaby. And its absence woke him. A break in the night-time song.

He stands, places each foot, approaches the window. Puts his face to the blind, a wooden slat resting on one eyebrow. Sees nothing. Hears nothing. Blinks, yawning. Is about to retreat when he sees it; the tiniest point of light. An orange pinprick by the backdoor, glowing brighter, fading, then moving down, almost disappearing. Ten seconds pass, and the cycle repeats. Tom knows what he's looking at. A cigarette.

No one in the house smokes.

Tom dresses fast, descends the wooden stairs barefoot. The katydids' concert continues unabated as he pulls on his work boots.

He lifts a wooden oar from a bracket on the wall. What he thinks he's going to do with it, he's not sure, but Tom doesn't want to arrive empty-handed.

He keeps to the edge of the grass, staying in the shadows to conceal his approach. His eyes adjust fast. It's a rare cloudy night, one of the last before Austin heads into summer.

Tom uses the glow of the cigarette as a marker. When it drops and is snuffed out, he stays where he is for one long breath before continuing.

He's twenty yards from the house when it happens.

A flash of light and a sound like someone clapping their hands twice. He looks up. Anna's room.

Suppressor on a handgun. A year ago, a thought plucked from Bedlam Boy's memory would have barely registered. Now, it jars and disorientates him.

The sound comes again, twice, each dull crack accompanied by a flash. A scream fills the gap between the first two shots and the rest. It's short-lived, cut off almost immediately.

A child's scream.

Charlie.

The presence of the smoker forgotten, Tom drops the oar and sprints for the house.

The smoker turns his head at the sound of the shots.

The fraction of a second when he looks away saves Tom's life. That, and the fact the watcher on the porch is a smoker. The man's gun is in its holster, and—as he pulls it out—two hundred and thirty pounds of brawn barrels into him.

Tom isn't trying to attack. He wants to get through the door, up the stairs, find Charlie and Anna. The scream echoes through his mind, and he can't, he won't, think about what it means.

The smoker takes evasive action, which works up to a point. He drops into a squat, turning shoulder-on against the impact. When Tom hits him, the weapon flies out of his hand, skids across the porch.

More shots from the house, louder now.

Tom's knee hits the smoker's shoulder, and his upper body pivots, hitting the porch deck hard. He doesn't stop, scrambling towards the screen door, crawling on all fours. Tries to get to his feet, but a heavy boot sends him sprawling, a searing pain spreading across his ribs. Rolls onto his back and sees the smoker clearly for the first time. A heavy man in his forties, bearded, bushy black eyebrows flecked with white. He kicks Tom again, and this one connects below the ribs, driving the breath from his body.

Tom rolls, gulping like the catfish he's seen anglers pull out of the Colorado. If he can just get his breath, he can protect Charlie and Anna. He doesn't want to think about that scream.

All he knows is that he has to get up. He must.

Where is Bedlam Boy? Something terrible is happening, and darkness surrounds Tom, so the Boy must be close. It's been so long, and he didn't think he'd ever need him again, but he needs him now, Charlie needs him, and he has to come now, now, please, come now.

Gasping with pain, Tom stares into the darkness, searching for the figure in the deep shadows; the creature who lives there, waits there, the only one who can help.

No one stares back.

Tom scrambles forwards. He doesn't register the bearded man picking up a terracotta planter. Doesn't notice him raise it over his head and take three short steps, shuffling because of the weight.

The planter hits Tom between the shoulder blades, driving his face into the deck. One of his molars is punched out of his gums as his lower lip splits.

A man's voice says something from the kitchen. The screen door opens and shuts. Tom is alone. He tries to speak, but the whisper he produces isn't even strong enough to cause a ripple in the blood pooling under his cheek.

Hector Barcia is checking his watch when the job turns into a nightmare. All four of the crew work to a clock. They've been in the house fifty-eight seconds. He stands in the lobby. Margarita and Tony are upstairs, Raoul out back, watching the rear of the property. Jimmy waits in the van, lights off. One advantage of hitting a Westlake house. No near neighbors to worry about.

Now, in his mid-forties, and his name known to the Austin police department, Hector is ready to retire. The mythical one last job that proved the undoing of so many careful criminals is well known to him, so he researched this gift horse thoroughly.

Margarita had sought Hector out. They had worked together before, trusted each other, and her pitch was straightforward.

The house belongs to Aimee Lloyd. Her tech start-up just took on new investors. One weekend next month, she'll have eight million dollars in the company bank account. We break in, threaten to kill her kid. She transfers the money to an account we set up, which transfers it to wherever we want. The first account then deletes itself.

Sounds expensive.

Ten thousand dollars to a pimply kid in Houston with a laptop.

And how much of the eight mill are you taking, Margarita?

Four million is already accounted for. We split what's left. I'm not greedy.

Accounted for?

I have an insider. That's how we get in, that's how I know the layout of the house and the security passwords. There's no score without her, and she wants four million.

No. I'll need a crew, and they'll need to lie low for a good while afterwards. Austin PD will be all over something like this. I want three. You'll be able to live pretty well on a million dollars.

Jesus, Hector, you know there are other criminals in town? You're not so special.

Yes I am. That's why you're here.

Listen, this is a score we can retire on. I've made my calculations. I need two million.

This insider, you're sure the information is good?

Yeah, I'm sure. And I'll be the one uploading a program into their security system.

Another job for your pimply kid?

You got it. Look, on the night, if we turn up and the gates don't swing open, we just drive away.

Ok. But I won't do it for less than three million.

Not gonna happen.

If that's your decision, that's your decision. Unless we talk about the elephant in the room.

What elephant, Hector?

Eight million divided by two is a much more satisfying figure, don't you think?

Margarita wasn't difficult to convince. Hector avoids unnecessary violence, but to stay as lucky as he has, sometimes there's no choice. Even without the extra money, it makes sense to get rid of the insider. She's an amateur, an unknown. She might ID Margarita if this all goes south. Better for everyone if she's dead.

When he hears the child scream, Hector takes the stairs two at a time. At the top of the stairs, he freezes. More shots, this time from the master bedroom.

Margarita, in a blonde wig and glasses, is in there pointing a gun at the Lloyds. No one's supposed to get shot.

Tony backs out of the nanny's room, shaking his head when he sees Hector.

"Sweet Mary, Mother of God." Tony's left hand brings the crucifix hanging from his neck up to his lips. His right hand still grips the handgun.

"What have you done?" Tony doesn't answer. Hector pushes past him, barely noticing the bloody sheets, or the dead housekeeper staring at the ceiling. Only one thing in this room is moving. A child's bare foot, sticking out under the bed, twitching. Hector squats, putting one hand on the carpet to stop himself falling, and sees the small pink toes, the dinosaur pajamas, the head flopping to one side, the spreading pool of blood.

"No."

He has to stand up, but he can't move, can't look away. Can't think.

Tony recovers first, walks across the landing towards the Lloyds' bedroom, hisses, "Salma. Salma!"

They choose different nicknames for every job, but Margarita doesn't respond to hers. Hector grips his gun, walks towards the master bedroom, ready to kick the door open.

Jimmy's shout from downstairs stops him.

"Someone called it in. Cops on their way."

Hector tries the door. It's locked from the inside. A woman's voice, shouting. Not Margarita.

"I have a gun. Get out of my house. I've called the police."

Hector raises his gun. "Salma. Answer me."

The door explodes an inch above the handle, a bullet knocking a chunk of masonry out of the wall behind him.

"Move," comes the call from downstairs. "The van leaves in thirty seconds." Jimmy has the coolest head of any man Hector knows, so he responds to his urgency, grabbing Tony by the collar, half-dragging him down the stairs.

Raoul is already in the back of the van. Hector pushes Tony inside and slams the door. Jumps in alongside Jimmy up front. They pull away fast.

Three minutes later and the van slows. They're driving a private ambulance which, as every cop knows, means someone died. Lots of old rich folk in the Westlake area, so their vehicle won't attract the wrong attention in the early hours.

Hector exhales. He thinks about his brother, constantly warning him to abandon crime before he winds up in jail, or dead. After two decades of earning ten times Carlos's car mechanic salary, Hector always greets his sibling the same way, "Still free, still alive, *hermanito*." With the sirens fading behind them, he wonders if Carlos might have a point.

"What happened, brother?" Jimmy's bass voice rattles the windows. Hector usually finds it reassuring. Not tonight.

"I don't know."

"Margarita?"

"Dead, probably."

"Shit, man. What now? What we gonna do?"

"There is no 'we', Jimmy. Too much heat. We're done."

Jimmy, who has just seen his hopes of a huge payday vanish, sums up his feelings with admirable brevity.

"Shit."

Tom spits out his tooth and groans. Brings his fingers up to touch his mouth; wishes he hadn't.

"Argh!"

His thoughts are sluggish, more confused than normal. His entire upper body hurts, his stomach aches as if he's been throwing up.

Why isn't he in the boathouse? The memories bob to the surface and he remembers the shots inside the house, the man on the porch. The scream.

"Charlie," he says, using the wall to steady himself as he stands. His whole head throbs now. After two stuttering steps, he drops to his knees, vision blurring then clearing, blurring then clearing.

Shots inside the house mean more intruders.

He senses the figure arrive behind him, although it makes no sound as it glides out of the dark garden onto the porch. It moves with the grace of a nocturnal predator; deadly, unforgiving. Beautiful.

He heard Tom's call.

Bedlam Boy is here.

Even as Tom turns to face him, his mind loosens and dissolves. He sees the wooden boards of the porch, wet and sticky, smells the copper of his own blood and a faint scent of coral honeysuckle, hears the chorus of katydids—distant now, as if afraid—but none of it has any meaning.

The last vestige of Tom is an image of Charlie, listening to Anna read from *The Secret Garden*. The man who rises to his feet, opens the screen door, and enters the house, is Bedlam Boy.

An engine starts, spinning wheels dislodging loose stones as a vehicle accelerates away. The Boy breaks into a run, flings open the door in time to see a private ambulance race through the open gates.

In the sudden quiet, he hears sirens coming closer. Two minutes out, maybe less.

Behind him, Aimee Lloyd's voice cuts through the sirens, a ragged, unbelieving shriek of raw pain as she screams her daughter's name.

Bedlam Boy makes his decision, runs back through the house and out onto the back porch, pausing to pick up his bloody tooth.

Back in the boathouse, he shoves clothes and his phone into a backpack, tosses it into the rowboat Carlson Lloyd never uses, unhitches the rope.

As he rows away, he looks back at the house, the sky now lit by strobing blues and reds.

He doesn't know what happened tonight.

He doesn't know who fired the shots in Anna's bedroom, who made Charlie scream, who drove that private ambulance. But he will find out.

And they'll pay.

Three months after the break-in

No one knows why the bar is called The Kinky Squid. The previous owner wound up in an unmarked grave after falling behind on protection payments. When the new owner changed the name, the same protection guys claimed they were fond of it. The old sign was repainted and still hangs outside the building on the eastern fringe of Austin's Montopolis district.

Raoul has ordered a bottle of tequila—the decent stuff—and three cold beers. When Jimmy and Tony arrive, they clink shot glasses together, drain them, and nod, saying, "Margarita."

It's the first time they've met since the night she died. Hector left town that week. None of them expect to hear from him again. His luck ran out, and he took it hard.

"Good news," rumbles Jimmy. He tosses his phone onto the table, its screen showing a local website.

Lloyd murder investigation makes no arrests. Austin police chief cites lack of physical evidence and disappearance of key witness.

A link proclaims: *Cops claim attempted robbery was inside job: cell-phone hidden in housekeeper's room sent passwords, security details, house layout to perpetrators.*

Tony manages a nervous smile as he scrolls down the article.

“She's OK. The kid, I mean. She moved away with her mom."

"Yeah." No one mentions that Charlie Lloyd, while surviving the bullets that cut through the nanny and into her midriff, isn't expected to walk again.

"Wasn't anyone's fault," says Raoul, keeping his voice low. They are sitting at the back, in the last booth, the music loud and the bar teeming with regulars. "But Margarita? I don't buy it."

Jimmy shrugs uneasily. Tony, too. What happened in the Lloyds' bedroom makes little sense. The official report claims Carlson Lloyd kept a gun. When he went for it, Margarita shot him dead, only for Aimee Lloyd to grab her dead husband's gun, roll off the bed, and shoot three times. According to the post mortem, the first shot was fatal, taking out half of Margarita's throat.

Margarita was an experienced gun user, calm under pressure, and smart enough to arrange the Lloyd score.

Raoul gives voice to what all three of them are thinking. "How the hell did Aimee Lloyd get the jump on her?"

The job had been rehearsed, every second decided in advance. Tony and Margarita reached the top of the Lloyds' stairs at the same moment. Twenty seconds later, he entered the nanny's bedroom and fired into the sleeping Anna Washington, unaware of the child under the bed. Margarita burst into the master bedroom at the exact moment of the first shot, flicking on the light, pointing a loaded gun at the stunned couple. Carlson and Aimee Lloyd, one a trader, the other a CEO, were confronted with an armed robber, experienced and good with a gun. How did that end with Margarita dead?

No one has an answer.

"I need the bathroom." Raoul stands up, slides out of the booth, and walks away.

Ten seconds later he's back, eyes wide, fists clenched.

"He's here."

"Who?" Jimmy and Tony speak at the same time.

"The guy who disappeared. The gardener I beat up."

A stunned silence greets his words. Then Jimmy speaks.

"He recognize you?"

"He didn't see me. But what the hell? Margarita said the guy is retarded. Now he shows up the same day the cops drop the investigation?"

"What do we do?" Tony looks up at Jimmy, the closest thing they have to a leader now. Jimmy doesn't take his eyes off Raoul.

"He's a big guy, you said. But not much of a fighter?"

Raoul slides back into the booth. "I don't think he'd ever been in a fight before. Any of us could take him, easy. How we gonna play this?"

Jimmy pours himself another shot, but only sips it this time. He points at Tony.

"You and me, we're gonna head out through the back door. Raoul, give us five minutes, then leave. Go out front. Make sure he sees you. Act scared. Cross the street and into the alley by the basketball court. We'll take him there."

Raoul half-stands. Jimmy places a big hand on his arm, and he sits down again. "Raoul. Tony. Maybe Hector was right to skip town. I don't know how this guy found us, but if he can do it..."

He doesn't need to finish his sentence. He looks from one to the other. "Whatever goes down, you should get out of Texas. That's what I'm gonna do. Tonight."

They nod, all the celebration drained out of them.

"Good. Let's kill this asshole."

A skinny kid selling crack, clothes hanging off him like hand-me-downs from a guy twice his size, eyes Jimmy and Tony as they emerge from The Kinky Squid and cross the street. His initial appraisal of them as potential customers takes a knock when he sees the expression on their faces, and when Jimmy grunts, "Get lost," the kid takes his advice.

Three feet into the alleyway, the shadows swallow them. On one side, the wire fence of the basketball court, on the other the graffiti-covered bricks of an apartment building. A dumpster hugs one wall, melted on one side, puddling in drug-related paraphernalia and broken glass like a surrealist art installation.

Tony is jittery, hand constantly going to his jacket pocket. Jimmy grabs his wrist.

"No guns. You crazy? We do this quick and quiet, we put the body in the dumpster and we leave town."

Tony's head bobs in agreement. Jimmy has never seen him this wired. He hasn't been himself since the girl got shot. Jimmy wonders if Tony is using chemical help to silence his conscience.

"You got a blade, Tony?"

In answer, Tony pulls out a folding knife, opens it. Jimmy pulls a telescopic baton from his pocket.

"Eyes front."

Raoul steps out of the bar, head down, crosses towards the apartment building. He's slipping between two parked cars when the door of The Kinky Squid opens again, and their quarry appears. He scans the area, hands held by his sides. Jimmy's brows come down as he appraises the man Raoul left unconscious on the Lloyd's back porch. Whatever he expected to see, this isn't it. Years back, Jimmy was a bare-knuckle boxer. His most dangerous opponents had an inner stillness about them, able to control the adrenaline rush that accompanies physical confrontations. This guy, even at this distance, radiates danger. Jimmy experiences a novel emotion for no good reason. He's afraid. He looks at Tony, but he's oblivious, bouncing on his toes like a middleweight with a shot at the title.

Raoul plays his part perfectly, firing a nervous glance over his shoulder, crossing the street, ducking into the alleyway.

"Good job," whispers Jimmy.

Raoul puts his hands in his pockets, brings them out with brass knuckles on his fingers.

Jimmy points, and the three men move into position. The alleyway is wide enough to accommodate two adults shoulder to shoulder, so that's what Jimmy and Tony do, hanging back. Raoul stands ready near the mouth of the alleyway, fists up. A well-placed punch to the face, augmented by the metal protecting his fingers, can break bone. The three of them against one disoriented opponent who, Raoul says, had all the finesse of a distressed elephant when they last met.

Five seconds go by. Six, seven, eight. Jimmy raises his baton, ready to strike. Ten seconds, twelve, fifteen. Something is wrong. Jimmy frowns. No footsteps. They saw the guy step off the curb before they backed further into the darkness. Since then, not a sound.

Raoul turns. Jimmy pats his shoulder, points at his eyes. Raoul nods his understanding, takes a step forward, then one to the left, so he can see The Kinky Squid and most of the street. He pauses, then leans out.

It happens so quickly that neither Jimmy nor Tony react. Raoul's head snaps to one side, there's the sound of bone meeting brick, then he's back in the alley, coming straight at them. Only he's not, not really, he's being propelled by the figure behind him, he's stumbling backwards, and his head lolls to one side.

Jimmy moves first. The situation has changed, but there's no time to think. He has a height advantage, and his baton is already raised. One blow will do it, now, before his opponent's eyes adjust to the darkness.

He steps in, aims at the gardener's bandana. Holds nothing back. The baton sends shock waves along his forearm as it cracks bone, rearranges an eye socket, sends the soft organ within rocketing sideways, crushed against cartilage.

The body that drops at Jimmy's feet, brain already shutting down, is Raoul's. Shit. He raises the baton a second time, but a punch to his sternum sucks the air from his lungs. His lower back hits first, his spine rolls up the wall, and the back of his head thumps so hard into the bricks that the night fills with stars.

He drops the baton and sinks to his knees, wheezing. Tony makes his move, right hand slashing as he dodges and weaves to keep out of the gardener's longer reach. Jimmy blinks, willing his vision to clear. All he hears is the dull rush of his own blood, and what he sees can't really be happening.

The gardener twists and turns, avoiding the dancing blade, but every move looks calm, unhurried, as if he knows where the knife will end up before Tony moves. The flurry of unsuccessful strikes only goes on for five or six seconds, but time stretches the inevitable conclusion out, and—when it comes—Jimmy's blurred vision is clear enough to witness Tony falter, off-balance, as his opponent grabs his wrist. Another big hand cups the back of Tony's skull, pulling his head forward as the knife, twisted back towards him, buries itself in his throat.

The gardener lowers Tony's twitching body alongside a broken syringe and a beer bottle, his eyes on Jimmy, who flattens himself against the wall as the stranger draws himself up to his full height. Jimmy, at six-foot four, is taller, but right now, he doesn't feel it.

"Where is Hector Barcia?"

The fear Jimmy tried to dismiss returns in a sickening wave. Jimmy spent eight years in the pen; put three men in the ground. He's always accepted his future might not involve a retirement plan and dozens of grandchildren. But he never thought he would face the moment of his death as a coward.

"I... I don't know."

The gardener looms. Jimmy looks into the other man's eyes and regrets it. He's faced down killers before. The trick is to show no fear, to hide your doubts in a place so deep the other guy will think twice about taking you on. No chance of pulling it off with this man. It's not just that there's no fear in those dark pupils. There's a chasm there, a void, an emptiness so profound that Jimmy's mind can't accept it, instead trying to fill in the gaps. So he sees fury there, driven by a will more powerful than he can imagine, a will forged in the darkest furnaces of hell.

Jimmy says the rosary. Whispers the words.

"Hector Barcia," repeats the gardener. "I won't ask again."

"No one knows where he is," says Jimmy, his voice strange to his own ears, a shaky wheeze, more air than sound. "I swear. He left town. That's all I know."

Those terrible eyes stay locked on his.

"Dios te salve, María," gasps Jimmy, "llena eres de gracia."

Eyes closed, he senses the gardener move away. Dares to hope he might be spared. Hears a gritty, wet, tearing sound, and doesn't have to open his eyes to know it's Tony's knife coming out of his dead friend's throat. When it slides between two of his ribs, pinning his heart to the muscles in his back, he embraces death with relief if it means he'll go someplace this monster can't follow.

If there is a hell, Jimmy is certain it's his destination. This thought destroys his relief, and he coughs out his last breath with a rictus of fear contorting his features.

What if the gardener follows me there?

Even before he answers the phone, Hector knows. He stares at the device vibrating on the plastic table next to his half-finished coffee, and he knows.

His brother's name comes up on the screen. But it's Sunday morning. Carlos goes to church Sundays, as his wife Yolanda is a deeply religious woman. So religious that Carlos didn't even see her breasts before he married her, a fact he confessed to his brother a year later.

"Not until our wedding night," Carlos had said, voice hushed with wonder, whether at the memory of how long he had waited, or the quasi-religious awe in which he held his wife's chest, Hector wasn't sure.

So Sunday mornings are for church. This call means an emergency. There's only one kind of emergency that would make Carlos call Hector, after he discovered his brother led the attempted robbery that ended up with two people dead and a child crippled.

Hector looks out of the cafe door to the sun-baked street. Mexico, the land of his ancestors, borders Texas—a five-minute bus ride would see him back in the States—but it might as well be another planet. He moves through town breathing his own atmosphere, a ghost in a spacesuit.

Like he's waiting for something; but what?

He picks up the phone. Maybe this?

"*Hermanito.*"

"He's taken her, Hector, he's taken her. You must come. Now."

Hector remembers the tear-streaked face of the ten-year-old Carlos, when he'd had his lunch money beaten out of him for a week straight.

"Who? Slow down, little brother, you're not making sense."

"He has Yolanda."

"Who does?"

"I don't know who he is. He sent a picture to my phone. Oh, god. He says he won't hurt her if you come."

Hector had found the bullies, beaten the crap out of them. They'd donated their own lunch money to Carlos for a year. Today's problem, he suspects, won't be as simple to resolve.

Raoul, Tony, and Jimmy are dead. Two nights ago, their bodies dumped in an alleyway. Now this.

"He says you have until three." It's ten-forty-five. If Hector leaves now, he'll make it, but only just. No time to organize any kind of plan, no time to do anything other than jump on his bike and go. It's almost as if whoever did this knows where Hector has holed up, or has made a very good guess. Either way, the thought isn't a happy one.

He leaves the rest of his coffee, walks outside to start the dusty BMW; opens the throttle, and points it towards Texas.

Carlos is standing in front of his house when Hector parks the bike alongside his brother's ten-year-old SUV.

His brother acknowledges Hector's arrival with little more than a slow blink. He's standing as if being court-martialed, dark curls plastered to his sweating forehead, clutching a cellphone. As Hector turns off the engine, the phone rings, and Carlos answers with shaking hands.

"Yes? Yes, he just arrived. Please, please, don't hurt her. Please... yes, of course. I understand."

He hands the phone to Hector.

"Who is this?"

"My name is Bedlam Boy. I'm the man who killed your crew, Hector. Raoul, Tony, Jimmy."

There's nothing strange about the voice, nothing Hector can pinpoint to explain the conviction that takes hold of him as he listens. The man speaking, with his stupid name and his generic accent, is deadly. His admission of murder isn't supposed to frighten Hector. He recites their names like a shopping list. Hector, who hasn't stepped inside a church outside a wedding or funeral since he was fifteen, fights an urge to cross himself. If the devil had a voice, it wouldn't be the rasping, bass-enhanced growl of a movie monster. It would sound like this.

"What do you want?"

"I find myself in a position to ensure your actions have consequences, Hector. Now hand the phone to your brother. His wife needs him. If you do anything other than follow my instructions, you die. If you run, someone dies in your place. Yolanda, perhaps, or Carlos. Nice bike, by the way."

Hector doesn't respond, but when he hands the phone back to Carlos, he scans the dense belt of trees that begins across the street, rising to a low crest half a mile further back, before descending to the dried-up stream that lends Williamson Creek its name. This Bedlam Boy could be anywhere. His forehead itches, as if he can feel the crosshairs resting there.

Carlos listens, then hangs up. He gives the phone to his brother.

"Hector. I am going to get Yolanda. You have to stay here." He hesitates with his hand on the door, and the brothers lock eyes. There's too much to say, so they say nothing. Carlos runs into the house, returning a minute later with his three children. The twins see Hector's bike and ask questions, but Carlos snaps at them, and they scramble into the back of the car. Juanita, five years old, scowling beneath her curled mop of brown hair, spots Hector, and squirms out of her father's grasp.

"Uncle Hector, Uncle Hector!" She flings herself into his arms, wraps brown arms around his neck, and squeezes. "We didn't go to church today. Mom is visiting a friend. Where have you been? I drew a picture of you at school, do you want to see?"

Hector inhales his niece's warm skin, a mixture of soap and freshly laundered clothes. Kisses her cheek, sets her down.

"Maybe another time, honey. Say hi to your mom for me."

"I love you, Uncle Hector." She kisses his nose, and he watches her skip to the car. When it reverses into the street, he waves until it's out of sight.

The phone rings. He speaks before the other man can say anything. "Have you hurt Yolanda?"

"You think your sister-in-law's life is more important than the lives you have taken?"

Every word is a cold finger walking Hector's spine. There's no good answer to the question.

"If you're going to kill me, you'd better do it."

"Turn around."

"What?"

"You heard me."

"And if I don't?"

No answer. Hector thinks of his brother. Of the twins. Of Yolanda. Lastly, of Juanita. The breeze is a soft hand on his cheek. A lawn is being mowed nearby. Traffic hums along the interstate.

He turns around. The voice speaks one last time.

"You should thank your niece. She changed my mind."

Hector's knees buckle as something punches him in the small of his back. The sound of the shot reaches him just before the cellphone hits the concrete.

He drops sideways, coming to rest facing the cracked screen. There's no pain, but when he puts his hand to his spine, it comes back wet.

He's floating. The driveway is a mountain range. He's floating above the concrete mountains, the highest mountains in Texas.

The lawnmower has fallen silent, and its owner is leaning over him. He's wearing a red shirt, and his beard is white.

So this is where Santa Claus lives in summer.

"I've called nine-one-one. Hang in there, son. Take my hand."

Tears collect in the corner of Hector's eyes, blurring the mountains. He grips Santa's rough, dry hand.

Nine-one-one. Ambulance. Cops, too. Thanks, Santa, but no thanks.

Hector takes a breath, holds it, pushes down on the driveway, gets his elbow onto the concrete. There's a doctor he knows takes cash and doesn't ask questions.

"Don't try to move," says Santa, but Hector isn't listening. If he can just crawl to the bike.

"You're shot, son. Lie still."

Ignoring him, Hector rolls. Falls. Tries to move his left leg. It won't cooperate. He tries the right, but it's the same story.

The old man huffs and puffs. Now that Hector is on his front, Santa has a clear view of the entry wound.

"How bad is it?" hisses Hector, trying to flex his toes. His skull buzzes and his vision fades to black for a second. His legs don't belong to him anymore. That's how he can float over the concrete mountains. He left his legs behind.

Santa shakes his head. He's practically hyper-ventilating, looking everywhere other than at Hector.

"I'm sorry, son, I'm sorry."

Hector drifts. It's night, and he can't see the mountains. Time stutters, and he hears voices, the sound of an engine, the shriek of a siren.

"He's stable."

"Bullet wound."

"Spinal trauma."

"Significant damage."

"He'll live, but let's hope he doesn't love running."

"Or cycling," says a second voice.

"Or walking."

They scratch his arm. A soothing warmth spreads and sleep pulls Hector away, down into darkness.

Five months after the break-in

To live close to the sea in California's famous Big Sur region takes money. To possess one of the symphonies of glass, metal, and brick that cling to the cliffs costs upwards of a seven-figure sum.

Aimee Lloyd wasn't making a statement when she bought Eagle's View. She wasn't trying to impress anyone. She wanted solitude with superfast broadband, and it had to be wheelchair accessible.

Eagle's View ticks all the boxes, and they moved in two months ago. Aimee didn't bring a single stick of furniture from their Austin house. Time for a fresh start. For Charlie, too.

An elevator connects the lower levels. Charlie, who is getting used to the electric wheelchair, can get around most of the house without help.

The only place Charlie can't reach is Aimee's small suite at the top, and this is where Aimee spends her evenings, once Charlie is asleep. Earlier, sometimes. Charlie's full-time carer, Lauren, is so good with her daughter that Aimee often leaves them together, drawn to her semi-circular bedroom and its balcony, which looks out across the Pacific Ocean.

She scoops ice from a bowl, dumps it into a glass, pours herself a vodka. Aimee rarely bothers with tonic.

Before heading out to the balcony, Aimee turns down the volume on the intercom to Charlie's room. Her daughter's nightmares might punctuate the hours until dawn, but she doesn't have to hear them.

At first, Aimee spent nights on a mattress in Charlie's bedroom, which—despite the bright wallpaper and Disney posters—looks like a hospital room. The drugs in daily pill boxes, the oversized bed with its remote control. The diapers for a child long grown out of them. The sweet smell of disinfectant.

When Charlie woke during those first few weeks, it was Aimee who stroked her forehead, told her everything was all right. It was Aimee who held the sobbing child as she screamed Anna's name over and over until exhaustion claimed her.

Charlie doesn't want her mother. She wants the dead nanny.

One morning, Aimee told Lauren to take the mattress away. She's slept upstairs ever since.

She slides open the doors and steps onto the wide balcony. This is her favorite spot at night. During the day, the view is picture postcard perfect. At night, she can hear waves crashing below, taste salt spray on the wind that carries the distant screams of gulls. Behind her is the new house, her daughter, and—sixteen hundred miles beyond the driveway with its adapted minivan and Aimee's Ferrari—the bullet-ridden house in Austin. She keeps her eyes fixed west, staring over the endless ocean.

Aimee has rules. She won't allow herself the first vodka of the day until after lunch, and she still takes tonic with that one. Sobriety has become an unappealing proposition.

She takes a gulp of the vodka, toasts her dead husband, a man who —on paper—should have been perfect. A rich orphan with a substantial inheritance. But he had proved a disappointment, and his inept forays into stock trading made serious inroads into their joint bank balance.

By the time Charlie came along, the Austin house, with its personalized gates, spectacular mimosa tree, mature gardens, and boathouse, was all they owned. After three months with the baby, Aimee took matters into her own hands. She wasn't ever going to be poor again.

Aimee proved to have a sound instinct for business. At first, at least. With the house refinanced, she bought into a struggling tech company with an innovative idea for a phone app. She paid off their debts and gave them six months to get the product market-ready while she set up meetings with potential clients.

Early success was followed by a winning streak that continued for five years, before a string of poor decisions and failed projects brought everything crashing down. She hid the damage while trying to repair it, but doors that had once been flung open were now shut in her face.

She faced ruin. The answer, when it occurred to her, was shockingly simple. She fleshed out the idea, checking for weaknesses, making adjustments. Aimee Lloyd had a reputation for being thorough, and she scrutinized every detail of her plan. It couldn't fail.

And it didn't fail. Not exactly.

Finding the right people without revealing her identity took three months and fifty thousand dollars. Then it was just a case of moving the pieces around the board.

Aimee had two tasks on the night itself. The first—hiding the burner phone in the nanny's room—was straightforward. While Anna was in the bathroom, Aimee concealed the incriminating device at the bottom of the nanny's closet.

The second task might have been difficult for someone other than a Wisconsin girl who'd shot rats, rabbits, and deer since she was old enough to pull a trigger.

She slipped Carlson a sleeping pill that night, so he was groggy when Margarita burst through the bedroom door. Aimee, kneeling at the foot of the bed, handgun in a secure two-handed grip, shot the woman three times. Then she put on a pair of gloves. When her husband sat up, dazed and disorientated, she shot him dead using the intruder's gun. Removing her gloves—now containing the necessary gun shot residue to make the story convincing—she pulled them onto the intruder's hands. Aimee dropped the weapon next to Margarita's body, and bolted the bedroom door. Her last shot through the door at Hector was that of a terrified woman protecting her family.

How could she know Charlie would hide under the nanny's bed? How could anyone have foreseen it?

Aimee gulps the vodka. One more glass should do it. Most mornings she wakes up in her clothes, but it's nothing a few cups of coffee and a swim in the pool can't fix.

She takes one last look out at the view she can't see, then turns around to face the house bought with Carlson's life insurance.

The man standing between Aimee and her bedroom is silhouetted by the light behind him. The sight of him, huge, silent, unmoving, is so unexpected that Aimee doesn't even drop her glass. She stares, her mouth hanging open, then shuffles left until the bedroom light illuminates one side of the stranger's face.

He's not a stranger.

"Tom?"

The gardener disappeared the night of the robbery, giving the police a dead end to pursue. Aimee was glad he'd escaped. Tom, a brain-damaged stray who was wonderful with plants, had been no trouble.

Until now.

"How did you get in here?" Eagle View's security system is even better than the Austin house. "What do you want?"

She puts her hand on the back of one of the cast-iron chairs, glancing down to make sure her shaking fingers don't miss. She's drunk, she knows, but not so drunk she can be imagining this.

When she looks up, Tom—who had been about four feet away—is inches from her face. She looks into his eyes and realizes she's made a mistake. There's none of the gardener's placid, dull-witted good nature there. Rather, she sees a fierce intelligence. The vodka has dried up her throat, and she swallows, tries to look away. She can't do it. The eyes, darker than the deep invisible ocean, drill through her facade, lay bare her secrets, scoop her open. She sees the judge and the jury in those eyes.

She sees the executioner.

"Tom, please."

His voice is not the hesitant, gentle sound she expects. It cuts into her.

"My name isn't Tom."

That's when she knows. The deaths of the men who were there that night, the last left paralyzed. It was Tom.

His fingers close around her wrist. He pulls her away from the chair to the iron railing separating them from a one hundred and thirty-foot drop.

He places his other hand in the middle of her back. Aimee can't move. She thinks of the vodka bottle on her dressing table.

"Charlie needs me. She needs her mother. I'm all she has. Please."

Even if she survives this moment, it's brought an awful clarity. Aimee doesn't love Charlie. She doubts Charlie loves her. For Aimee to love her daughter would mean facing what she's done to her, and she's not sure she'll ever be ready for that.

God, she needs a drink.

The hand remains on her back, but he doesn't push. Not yet. Seconds go by, then minutes. Tom leans closer.

"How old are you?"

Aimee answers without thinking. "Twenty-nine."

"Anna Washington was forty-five."

The pressure of the hand on her back increases, and the fear, held back by the alcohol, flares into life. Aimee tries to speak, but her throat won't cooperate.

After another oppressive, terrifying few minutes of silence, Tom speaks into her ear.

"I'm going to kill you, Aimee Lloyd." Tears slide down her cheeks. She would never have guessed that someone could literally shake with terror, but she has the evidence now.

The hand leaves her back. Aimee closes her eyes, expecting it to return with a shove, sending her over the railing, spinning and tumbling through the California night until her body breaks on the rocks below.

It doesn't happen.

Tom's voice comes from the doorway.

"Bring up your daughter well. I'll be checking in on you. And when you're forty-five, I'll come back, and I'll kill you."

The door slides shut, but it's another hour before Aimee moves. She walks past the vodka bottle in the bedroom, goes downstairs, slumps in the corner of Charlie's room, pulls her knees close to her body, still trembling.

She watches her daughter sleep.

ABOUT THE AUTHOR

Born at an early age, Ian W. Sainsbury soon learned to talk about himself in the third person, meaning a career in the arts was inevitable.

As a professional musician, Ian played piano on cruise ships before spending a decade singing in European piano bars. He also ran (and still does) a pub choir.

In the 2000s, Ian spent five years as a stand-up comic. He still writes music and material for ventriloquist Paul Zerdin, co-writing his Vegas show in 2016.

Since *The World Walker* appeared on Amazon in 2016, Ian has—to his amazement—found he can do what he loves for a living without having to sell a kidney.

In 2019, he won the Kindle Storyteller Award for his psychological thriller, *The Picture On The Fridge.*

He lives in East Anglia, UK with Mrs S, two children, and a flatulent dog.

Discover the Bedlam Boy series and more at ianwsainsbury.com

For a free Bedlam Boy story, visit http://tiny.cc/freebedlam

A DANCE WITH DEATH

DREW AVERA

How do you stop a killer when he's one of your own?

1

Desperation kills.

For Ryan Stepp, it was quickly becoming a part of life. With each turn he felt any sense of normalcy slipping further out of his control. A single gunshot had put him on a trajectory toward destruction.

In order for it to end someone else would have to die.

Ryan rounded the corner of the parking garage at MacArthur Center and stormed toward the stairs. He went down them two at a time, careful to breathe in through his nose and out his mouth like he had been taught at the academy.

The stairwell deposited him on a downtown Norfolk sidewalk. A line of restaurants and a popular music venue stood on the opposite site of the street. It was bustling with activity. He planned to use it to his advantage.

"Stop!"

Ryan turned and saw the older man pursuing him was out of shape and out of breath. But he also had more determination than Ryan gave him credit for. The old cop was a retired Marine, and Ryan was certain the detective's past life had taught him how to push himself and accomplish the mission at any cost. That attitude had been explained to Ryan during numerous coffee break chats at the precinct. If it was any other man following him, Ryan should have felt more at ease with each step farther that his pursuer lagged behind.

But not tonight.

Marty was something of a legend with the other cops, and Ryan now had a front row view of why.

Ryan forced himself to run faster. It was no easy feat after being dead legged by the former Marine. Sure, Ryan got a lucky punch in after the fact, but the old man knew what he was doing. They wanted their fugitive alive; a possibility that wasn't in the cards as far as Ryan was concerned.

He knew what would happen if he was caught. You don't take the lives of your brothers in blue and live out a prison sentence in peace. No, you received hate from both sides and looked over your shoulder until the bitter, inevitable end.

Justice always prevailed that way.

I'm not ready for that yet, he thought as he darted down a dark alley beside the Norva. Loud rock music emanated from inside the music venue, but it was a muffled drone behind the thick brick walls and through the roar of blood in his ears. He stopped in front of a tour bus and leaned against the bumper, trying to catch his breath.

He looked around, wondering if Marty had spotted him. He was running out of time and Ryan knew backup had to be on its way.

He didn't think he'd be able to make a clean getaway.

Hurried footsteps drove the fear of desperation like a stake into his heart..

Then Ryan did what he had tried to avoid up until that very moment. He pulled the gun from his waist and he stepped out from in front of the bus. His eyes caught Marty's and, in that final second, they communicated for the last time. Marty didn't look shocked. It wasn't horror. It was acceptance.

Ryan hated himself for what he was about to do. He knew this man. He knew what Marty stood for. He knew that once upon a time they had fought for the same cause.

But one of them had to die for the other to live.

Ryan Stepp pulled the trigger, and just like that his body count rose to five, solidifying what the media had reported about him.

Ryan Stepp, rogue police officer, was a heartless murderer who had to be stopped.

How do you stop a killer?

With hope and a prayer? Or maybe some unlucky sap using himself as bait?

Or a little bit of both, I thought as I exited the vehicle.

I had already called it in and backup was on the way. But I didn't want to wait. Besides, the sirens would alert the killer that we were coming. That would give *him* the advantage.

The element of surprise was my only edge.

It was a desperate plan, and maybe that was why I was so scared. I completed two combat tours in Iraq with the Army. I've been shot at numerous times; one time the enemy even connected, but that was just a flesh wound.

So, what was different?

"You have a wife and kid at home," I mumbled under my breath.

If this went sideways, I would probably be a dead man.

It was with that thought looming over my head that I decided to lean a little harder on the hope and a prayer part.

I entered the warehouse through the side entrance, careful not to let the door squeak as I pushed my way through. I was only a few steps inside when my eyes caught a flittering of movement. It was small, but it was enough to make the hairs on the back of my neck stand on end.

More importantly, it was enough to make that small voice in the back of my head scream one word.

Duck!

BANG!

The bullet exploded against the cinderblock wall where my head had been a moment prior. Shrapnel scattered, raining debris down on me as I braced myself for another shot, but it didn't come.

I glanced up and shuddered. There was no way he should have missed from that distance. I would have been another corpse without divine intervention, or whatever you call it when you know something terrible is about to happen.

Thank God I listened.

Regardless of what could have been, I was on borrowed time and wasn't about to let it go to waste.

I pulled my Glock 19 from the holster and pressed against the tightly fit row of fifty-five-gallon drums separating me from my would-be assassin. The shot came from above on the north side of the warehouse, but where was he now?

I listened intently, despite the ringing in my ears from the near miss. A few moments later the scratch of booted feet against the concrete floor caught my attention.

He was waiting for me.

Ryan Stepp was a former cop. I knew him from the academy. He graduated second in our class and everyone who knew him thought he had a bright future.

He was one of the good guys.

So why was he on a killing spree and taking out other cops?

That question got my partner, Marty, laid up in ICU less than twenty-four-hours ago, and it almost got my head blown off just now.

That question was going to take one of us to our grave.

I darted from behind the drums and kept my weapon trained on what I could see of the catwalk above me as I navigated the labyrinth of giant machines inside the warehouse. The smell of ocean water and grease wafted by as I drew close to Ryan's previous position. The stairs rose upward at a steep incline and I backed toward them, alert for movement. Ryan would have changed positions, but I moved with the notion that we were two hunters stalking our prey.

My instinct was to hold my breath, to force my heartrate down, but the adrenaline spike made that impossible. I was a rat in a cage, and there was a trap waiting to be sprung. The only question was when?

I should have waited for backup.

BANG! At first, I thought he had shot again, but I realized it was a steel door slamming against a wall.

And it sounded like it had come from the other side of the warehouse.

I spun on my heels and high-tailed it up the stairs, careful not to trip as I kept one eye over my shoulder. The second floor was open, save for clusters of work benches and giant rolls of bubble wrap strung from the overheads in what I assumed was the shipping department of the facility. On the far side of the space was a set of double doors.

An exit.

I sprinted toward the door but hesitated when I reached it. The push bar latch had not closed all the way and there was a tiny gap between the door and frame. Was he waiting on the other side?

I would be if it was me, I thought.

I aimed my weapon and kicked the door open, hard enough to make my teeth rattle when it crashed against the opposite wall. Nothing. But now the dark hallway leading away from my position posed a new threat. There was just enough light peeking through the barred windows to cast ominous shadows.

If he was waiting in the dark, then he would see me long before I did him.

What was worse, we had both gone through the same training.

Ryan knew what he was doing.

He knew what I was doing, too.

But our stalemate couldn't last forever.

Someone had to make a move.

But who?

I sucked in a deep breath and tightened my grip on the Glock. I pulled an LED flashlight from my pocket and rested my thumb against the switch.

Ready.

Set.

Exhale.

Go.

I entered the dark hallway and shone the light toward the opposite end. The light reflected off windows from numerous office doors, but I still caught the muzzle flash of Ryan's sidearm.

I ducked as it missed, but I would have been too late. The light must have affected his aim.

I returned fire, aiming in the direction of the flash.

My Glock boomed, sending two reports down the narrow hallway.

Ryan had to be in one of the offices, hiding behind a door, waiting for his eyes to adjust to my position. If I was lucky, I hit him and he was bleeding out.

Maybe it was all over.

Bang!

The bullet made contact and tugged at my left arm. I dropped the flashlight as I fell back. So much for it being over.

I was in the open. The light from the warehouse shone through the open door behind me. I grimaced and shifted my way toward it. I slammed it shut, blocking off what light there was until the only source was my flashlight, its beam angled more toward Ryan than me.

Was it enough to obscure his view?

"I hope you're enjoying this," Ryan barked. It was the first time I had heard his voice in months, and he sounded like he was in pain.

Had I hit him?

"There's nothing about this to enjoy. You know how this job is. More times than not, it's a kick in the junk on the best of days." I pulled off my jacket and inspected my arm. He had grazed me. There was a lot of blood and the wound felt like a hundred bee stings, but I would live barring this night getting any worse.

I glanced toward an outside window as the sound of distant sirens drew near.

"You called it in, huh? Smart man." Now there was a tremble to his voice. He sounded on edge, desperate.

"Give it up, Ryan. This can all be over without anyone else dying," I called back. It was a longshot, and I knew it. No one killed five cops and made it to prison. And Ryan didn't strike me as the self-inflicted suicide kind of guy.

This was going to happen the hard way. I had no doubt about that.

"How's Marty?" Ryan asked.

That hurt, though I didn't think he intended it as a jab. I could hear a tinge of regret in his voice. Or maybe that's what I wanted to hear.

"They're hoping he'll pull through," I said. It was the truth, but maybe it offered a glimmer of hope to a man at the end of his rope.

"Did he ever tell you I had a run in with him on my first year?"

What's this, small talk? I wondered. *Is he trying to buy time?*

"He never mentioned it," I said as I tossed my flashlight. I cringed as it rattled against the floor, but it was the only thing I could think of to keep from giving away my position. I felt like he was trying to disarm me, lure me into another trap. I couldn't shake that feeling.

"I was on patrol and directing traffic. Some guy in a lifted truck decided to hop the curb and cut off an oncoming vehicle. Marty was the driver who got cut off and he was on fire with rage. He had just bought that car and the guy in the truck had nicked his bumper." He stopped for a moment.

"What happened next?" I asked.

I heard movement and a groan, then he said, "Marty pulled the driver out of the truck and realized it was a teenager on a joyride. He started screaming at him like they used to yell at us at the academy. I'm pretty sure the kid peed himself." Ryan chortled, but cut it off quickly.

"What about his run in with you?"

"I think he was trying to put some of his anger at the kid off on me. He started in on me and I threatened to arrest him for causing a scene."

I couldn't fight the smirk from spreading across my lips. I could just see my partner's response. "Let me guess, he flipped out his badge and said he was going to report you?"

Ryan chuckled. "Verbatim."

"What happened?"

"Nothing. He was full of hot air. The next time I saw him was in traffic court. He shook my hand and told me I did a good job that day."

"Sounds like Marty," I said. "He's full of piss and vinegar one minute and then he's sweet like honey the next."

I heard Ryan sniff and then he said, "Until you shoot him."

Our conversation died and I let myself grieve what would be the sixth officer to lose his life this week. Ryan *was* one of us.

Cop cars skidded to a stop outside the warehouse.

"Time's running out," Ryan said.

"It doesn't have to be that way. You can put the gun down and go in quietly."

"And do what, rot in prison for the rest of my life?"

I understood. Not only would he get a life sentence, but prison would be almost impossible once the other prisoners learned he'd been a cop. Still, I didn't want more violence. It wouldn't be a good outcome.

"I know you're scared, but it's no reason to destroy more lives. There's been enough damage."

Ryan slammed something against the door near him and it took a moment for me to realize it was his sidearm. "Is that what you think of me? That I'm *scared*?"

I didn't want to answer with the truth so I said, "I would be."

"And that makes you weak." His tone had shifted from remorse to anger like a switch had been flipped.

"Then why do this?" I asked.

"Why not?" he replied.

I snorted derisively, and he must have heard me because he fired off two quick shots in my general direction. He missed, but he made his point.

"This is the way it has to be, Fox. There's no taking me alive, so be a man and do what you have to do."

Officer assisted suicide? That told me he *was* scared but too stubborn to admit it. *Why not just turn the gun on himself,* I wondered?

"Toss your weapon and give up, Ryan. We both know it's over. I'm not going to do what you're asking me to do."

"Why not? You've killed someone before. It's part of the job isn't it?"

I clenched my jaw tight to keep from spewing vitriol at him. He was trying to get to me, to force my hand.

Wasn't I doing the same, though?

"Is that what this is about? You feel guilty and you want to justify your actions by bringing up my mistakes? For what it's worth, he had a weapon aimed at me when I fired. I had no idea it wasn't loaded."

"And you think my situation was different?" Ryan spat back. "It was a setup. They were trying to take me down for it, but I saw through it. That's why I did what I did."

His explanation was madness. I knew he was being investigated by Internal Affairs, but no one was trying to take him out. Shootings happen, investigations follow. If it was by the book, then he would be cleared.

Maybe it wasn't by the book?

"Did you pull the trigger knowing the kid didn't have a gun?" It was a bold question, one that would light a fire in him if he felt guilty...if he was guilty.

Ryan spewed a flurry of expletives and fired wildly. Bullets splattered into the wall above where I sat sending chunks of concrete raining down on me. I tried counting the bullets. Was it three or four? I couldn't make it out due to the ringing in my ears and the pounding of my heart.

I couldn't risk giving him a chance to reload if he was empty, so I made my move. I scrambled to my feet and sprinted toward where I believed he was holed up. I fired every few steps as a deterrent until I found myself standing over him inside one of the offices at the end of the hallway.

His tear-streaked face was illuminated by the pale moonlight coming through the barred window. There was a pool of blood beneath him. I had no way to know if it was from my first shot or the last, but I hit him at least once.

"Don't move," I ordered as the dull thud of footsteps sounded behind me. I knew it was my backup. It was over.

"Finish it," Ryan said.

I shook my head.

"Then I will." Ryan Stepp lifted his weapon and leveled his gun at me.

I pulled the trigger.

Click.

My gun was empty.

A bloody smile curled his lips. "You should have counted your shots."

Time almost stood still as I stared at him. He thought we were the same, but I would go to my grave confident we were not.

His finger tensed. I closed my eyes.

The shot sounded like an explosion inside my brain.

I winced, expecting the darkness to burn. Instead, I felt hollow, cold, and heard voices.

"Are you all right, Detective?"

I opened my eyes and saw Ryan Stepp slumped over, this time blood poured from a chest wound. I blinked several times trying to make sense of what I was seeing.

"Hey, man, are you all right?" The man's voice came with a hand on my shoulder. I glanced over and saw a patrolman standing before me. "Can you hear me?" he asked.

"Yes," I muttered, trying to wrap my mind around the miracle that had occurred to me. Not so much for Ryan, though I expected it was what he wanted all along.

The patrolman grasped his radio. "Officer down at 4973 Boone Street. We have another officer wounded. Requesting EMTs. The scene is secure."

"Roger that," dispatch replied. *"Ambulance is en route."*

"Take a seat, man," the officer said pulling a chair over to me.

I sat automatically. A few moments later my attention was drawn to the involuntary shaking of my legs.

Was I in shock?

Probably, but the fog I found myself in seemed to come out of nowhere.

"Helluva night, huh?"

I glanced up at the patrolman and took note of his name "Yeah, it is, Humphrey. I'm glad you showed up when you did. I thought I was done."

He nodded and gave me a tight smile. "I've got your back, Detective. I'm going to document the scene. Let me know if you need anything."

I nodded and watched as he got to work. At some point the lights had been turned on and the room felt less like a crypt.

Several other uniforms arrived and the next thing I knew I felt a tap on my good shoulder. I looked up and saw an EMT looking down at me. “Detective Fox, my name is Robert Diedrich. I’m going to check on your wound. Is that all right?”

“Yeah,” I said, though it came out as a grunt. He cut off my shirt, careful not to drag the fabric across the wound. “Not your first rodeo, huh?” I joked, but it sounded forced.

“Not by a long shot. You’re in good hands. Do you have any other wounds?”

I shook my head and Robert started cleaning the wound. The burn was a staunch reminder that I was still alive, regardless of how hollow I felt minutes before.

“So, barring current circumstances, how was your day?”

The question struck me as odd, then I realized he was making small talk to get my mind off the pain.

“I spent most of the day at the hospital. He shot my partner last night. Thank God your people are good at their job; the doctors said the EMTs saved his life.”

“That’s good news considering the circumstances,” Robert replied.

It was, despite the situation that had brought me to this moment. This little dance with death wasn’t one I ever wanted to repeat.

I winced and withdrew my arm.

“Sorry,” Robert said, easing up the pressure. “The good news is that the bullet just grazed you. Maybe that’s your second blessing of the night?”

“Yeah, maybe so,” I said.

“You should be fine, but I recommend you get it looked at as soon as possible.”

“I’ve had my fill with hospitals today.” It was supposed to be a joke, but it landed like a water balloon.

“Go get checked out. If you want, you can ride in the back of the bus.”

“I’ll take him,” Humphrey chimed in. I looked up to see the patrolman approaching and my lieutenant walking with him.

"LT."

"Fox. I hate to see you banged up, but I'm relieved to see this is over." Lieutenant Stadl had a way of saying the right thing yet making it sound wrong. Was it over? It certainly didn't feel like it.

"Thanks, I guess." I kept glancing at Ryan and his dead eyes staring back at me. I couldn't help but wonder what he saw on the other side.

I couldn't help but wonder how close I came to seeing it for myself.

I stood outside the ambulance as they loaded Stepp's body. I wasn't surprised by the media presence, but I was thankful I was inside the perimeter of police tape and out of their view. The last thing I wanted was prying eyes formulating their own opinion about me while I stood there with a bloodied shirt and my arm in a sling.

The Public Affairs Officer could set the record straight after she was briefed. Until then it was best to stay out of sight.

"Get checked out and call your wife. There's no need to stick around," Lt. Staidl said, coming around a unit parked behind the ambulance.

"I feel obligated," I said.

He sat on the hood of the car and crossed his arms. The blue and red emergency lights reflecting off his bald head gave him an ominous appearance despite his upbeat nature. "I get that, but I feel obligated to take care of my people. I got enough of a statement from you to appease the captain in the morning. If I need anything more, I'll call you."

"I appreciate it."

I took a step back as the EMTs closed the back hatch of the ambulance, cutting me off from the monster who had destroyed six families' in just a few days.

"You ready to go?" Humphrey asked after pulling my car around. I had taken him up on his offer to drive me to the hospital, and arranged for his partner to pick him up later.

"I suppose so," I replied. "See you tomorrow, Lieutenant?"

He shook his head with an amused smirk. "Take a few days off. You have weeks of desk duty that isn't going anywhere. You did a good job."

I nodded, thankful he felt that way, because I certainly didn't.

Humphrey held the passenger door open for me as I slipped into the seat. He got in and pulled around to the far exit of the parking lot to avoid the zoo of spectators.

He drove in silence until he said, "I put in my application to transfer to homicide a couple of weeks ago."

I glanced at him and smiled. "Are you sure you're ready to give up the beat for the gold shield? The grass isn't always greener." I eyed my wound. He noticed.

"That could have happened to any of us," he said.

I resisted the urge to say it happened to me; that much was obvious.

"I'll talk to my lieutenant and put in a good word for you," I said after a pause. The small talk wasn't going well, and I wasn't sure if it was the seriousness of the situation, or if it was the blood loss that put me in a fog.

"I appreciate it."

We pulled up to the emergency room and I pushed open the car door.

"I'll park it over there and give the keys to reception," Humphrey said.

I glanced back at him and smiled. "Thank you. I don't know what would have happened tonight if it wasn't for you." But I did know.

I climbed out of the car, closed the door, and waited for him to drive off before I went inside.

I wasn't looking forward to getting poked and prodded again. And I certainly wasn't looking forward to calling my wife.

It was the second worse call a cop ever had to make.

I was just thankful she wasn't going to get the other one.

The soft beeps from the heart monitor welcomed me as a slipped into Marty's room. My partner was asleep, so I kept quiet as I made my way to the chair in the corner. I was relieved they had transferred him from ICU but seeing him laid up like this still filled me with fear.

The events of the day reminded me we aren't guaranteed anything in life. We can lose it all in the blink of an eye.

Or a gunshot.

Rows of balloons danced happily above the air conditioning vent and I stared at them until I heard a voice.

"You got him, didn't you?"

Marty.

"We did," I said, fighting the knot forming in my throat. I didn't want to tell him what it almost cost. I didn't want to admit I had rushed; that I didn't wait for backup, that I wanted to see Marty's shooter brought in.

"Good. Not good," Marty grunted, barely able to keep his eyes open.

"I don't understand."

Marty drifted back to sleep while I tried to figure out what he meant, but I'd be able to ask him later. He was on the road to recovery. Like they told them I was. What pushed Ryan over the edge? I wondered if I would ever find out, stop the next guy from it happening to him.

Or me.

ABOUT THE AUTHOR

Drew Avera is a Navy veteran and the bestselling author of The Dead Planet Series. Born and raised in Mississippi, Drew enlisted in the US Navy at seventeen. During his twenty-years of service he deployed four times in support of operations overseas. He began his writing journey in 2012 and published his first novel, Exodus, in 2013. You can learn more by visiting his website.

www.drewavera.com

CROSS YOUR HEART

G.K. PARKS

Who will survive when a private investigator's good deed places him on a collision course with a Russian gangster?

1

"Shit!" Blood and tissue dripped from Lucien Cross's once white shirt. He took a step back, hands raised. The woman he invited into the private room lay in a heap. They just met, and now she was dead. His eyes burned. A suffocating cloud of gunpowder had replaced the pungent haze of cigar smoke and fine spirits. Cross inched toward the table where he left his nine millimeter. If only he could reach it.

"I wouldn't recommend it." Vasili toed the woman's body out of his way, clearing a path to the oversized leather armchair which squeaked in protest under his massive frame.

"What would you recommend?" Cross asked. "Might I suggest Jenny Craig?"

"Do you think that's funny?"

"A little."

Vasili reached into the box for a cigar. He put his gun down and trimmed the tip of the Cuban. "Have you ever seen what one of these can do to loosen a man's lips?" Vasili held up the single blade guillotine, a wicked grin on his face.

"Can't say that I have." Cross glanced behind him. He needed to escape, but the Russian gangster had brought two of his enforcers along for the ride. They blocked the only exit. With no way out, Cross needed a weapon, but getting his hands on one would be tough. And taking out all three Russians without getting his brains splattered against the wall would be damn near impossible.

Cross couldn't count on help to arrive. The back room of the club was private. Soundproofed. But even if it wasn't, the pounding beats beyond the door would easily drown out weapons' fire. No one would interfere. Vasili could take his time. He didn't have to worry about the noise, which was exactly what he wanted.

Vasili examined the end of the cigar, put the cutter down, and struck a match. He rotated the Cuban, puffing slowly until the end glowed red. "Have a seat, so we can discuss your options, Mr. Cross."

What options? Cross thought. This wasn't a discussion. It was an execution, possibly a double-execution. He thought back, trying to clear his mind. What had he done to piss off the Russian? Only one thing came to mind. *Shit.*

"You should have called my office and made an appointment." Cross's gaze drifted to the dead woman. He didn't even know her name. Guilt and sadness flooded over him, but he held his emotions at bay. There would be time to mourn later, if there was a later. "You could have saved on the dramatics. We're both businessmen. We should behave as such."

"I wanted you to understand how serious this is and the peril you face." Vasili jerked his chin at the couch. "Sit."

Lucien stared into the woman's lifeless eyes and silently vowed Vasili would pay for this. "What do you want from me?"

"Cross Security intercepted one of my shipments and turned it over to the police. You have twenty-four hours to get it back."

"That's not possible."

"You will make it possible or unfortunate things will befall you and everyone you know." Vasili flicked the ashes off his cigar, letting them fall onto the dead woman's thigh. He lifted Cross's gun off the table, aimed, and fired a few rounds into her body. Then he unloaded the weapon and tossed it to Cross. "In case you were thinking of calling the police, don't, unless you want to explain why you shot and killed Svetlana."

Cross noted the gloves on Vasili's hands. The Russian had come prepared. He set this up. He even knew her name. "She was one of yours," Cross said, the realization coming too late. "Why kill her?"

"She stole from me. People shouldn't take what doesn't belong to them. Right, comrade?"

"I'm not your comrade."

"Have it your way, Mr. Cross. All that matters is you return my shipment. If not, I will destroy you. Piece by piece." Vasili puffed on the cigar.

Cross stared into the Russian's cruel eyes. "You should kill me now."

"Who said anything about killing you? I need you alive. Dead men can't follow instructions." His gaze dropped to Svetlana. "There are plenty of other ways to hurt you. Perhaps an anonymous call to the police for starters."

"You can't seriously believe you'll get away with this." Cross scanned the room, memorizing the details in case he had to prove his innocence. But he already knew the facts were against him.

"Me? That's your gun. Those are your bullets in her body. You're the murderer. No one will believe otherwise. Now retrieve what belongs to me. Meet me at pier nineteen at this time tomorrow. Don't be late." The big Russian nodded to his men, and they hauled Cross to his feet, dragged him to the door, and tossed him into the crowded club.

Cross stumbled backward, pinwheeling his arms to regain his balance. He knocked into several people on the dance floor. A couple turned to give him the evil eye, the annoyance on their faces quickly morphing into revulsion and fear.

I have to get out of here, Cross thought. He ducked away from them, removing his bloodied shirt and wrapping it around his unloaded weapon. He tucked the bundle against his stomach and hurried to the exit. Vasili wouldn't call the police. Not yet. But the gangster had gone to a lot of trouble to make sure Cross wouldn't either. However, the same couldn't be said for the nervous clubgoers.

As Cross pushed his way out the front door, he cautioned one final look behind him. Thankfully, his presence had already been forgotten. Vasili put him on a clock. But Svetlana's body posed an even greater danger. Once she was discovered, the police would come knocking. Cross needed a solution. And he needed it now.

Setting a timer on his phone, he slid into a waiting cab. He gave the driver his office address and dialed his assistant. "Justin, I need you back at work. We have a problem." Cross didn't wait for a reply before hanging up. He looked down, finding specks of blood and fluid clinging to his undershirt. A wave of nausea rolled through him, and he let his forehead rest against the cold window.

"Long night?" the cabbie asked.

"You could say that." Cross rubbed his eyes and shook out the tremors in his hands.

The cabbie alternated his gaze from the road to the rearview mirror. "You feeling okay, buddy? If you gotta hurl, let me know, and I'll pull over."

"I'm fine."

Cross forced his thoughts away from the sticky dampness he held in his lap. For the rest of the ride, he contemplated calling the police, but he'd had enough run-ins with them in the past. Given his history, he doubted they'd believe his story. Vasili was right. All the evidence pointed to him.

He tried to think where the security cameras were hidden in the club. He needed to see the footage to prove Vasili entered the room. He wouldn't be able to clear his name otherwise, and even that might not be enough. He sighed.

"Hmm?" the driver asked, eyeing Cross through the rearview mirror.

"Nothing."

The taxi came to a stop. "Here we are."

Cross tossed the money into the front seat and stepped out of the cab. So many thoughts went through his mind. He needed to focus. One thing at a time. The problem was he didn't know where to begin. After all, he'd never been framed for murder.

Unlocking the door, he went straight to the bathroom and stripped down, desperate to wash Svetlana's blood off his body. Flashes came to him as he showered, and this time, he couldn't contain the bile that burned his throat. He rinsed his mouth and remained under the spray for a few minutes longer, compartmentalizing the facts. Now it was time to get to work.

He dried off and dressed from the waist down. He shoved his bloody clothes into a zippered plastic bag and wiped his prints off the gun. That wouldn't solve much. The weapon was registered to him, but it might slow down the police, should they come knocking.

"Lucien?" Justin tapped on the door.

"I'm glad you're here. Find out what kind of security system Club Nova has. We have to gain access to their footage. And monitor the police frequencies. Listen for any calls pertaining to a homicide, female victim, blonde, mid-twenties."

"Right away."

Cross checked the countdown timer and turned to grab a fresh shirt, catching a glimpse of his angel of death tattoo in the mirror. He didn't get into this business to deal with death, quite the opposite actually. But death always found him.

He went into the outer office. "Justin, when you get a chance, get Almeada on the phone. It's about time my attorney earns his keep."

"Yes, sir." Justin glanced at the bag in Cross's hand. "Do you want to tell me what's going on?"

"No." Cross opened the top drawer in the cabinet. "Where's the Knox file?"

"Look under pending."

Cross shut the drawer and opened another one. "Got it." He took the folder and settled in behind his desk, scanning the contract he signed with Trey Knox. Nothing in the research indicated Knox's case involved anything other than recovering stolen property. It should have been simple. So what went wrong?

After turning on his computer, he poured a shot of bourbon. His fingers flew over the keys. How could he have missed Knox's connection to a Russian gangster? Why hadn't he done his due diligence? Why had he taken the man at his word? That was one mistake he'd never make again.

The intercom beeped. "Lucien, Mr. Almeada's on line one."

Cross grabbed the handset. "Hello?"

"Do you have any idea what time it is?" Almeada asked.

"This is an emergency."

"It better be. Tell me you aren't under arrest."

"Not yet. May we speak in hypotheticals?"

"I'm your lawyer, Lucien. This conversation is privileged. You know that."

"Hypothetically," Cross said, ignoring the declaration, "a man goes out to a club, meets a beautiful woman, and takes her into the private back room to get to know her better."

"I've heard this story before. Guy gets too rough, and the girl ends up dead. What does that have to do with you?"

"Different story, same ending. You left out the twist. The girl worked for a Russian gangster, who killed her to emphasize his point. And then he shot her four more times with the other man's gun."

"Your gun," Almeada surmised. So much for hypotheticals. "You realize I'm a lawyer, not a fixer, right?"

"Then bill me twice, or find someone who can deal with this."

"Do the police know?"

Cross peered into the outer office, but his assistant hadn't notified him of any radio chatter. "Not yet."

"Where's her body?"

"I don't know. Probably still in the back room."

"And your gun?"

"Here, along with my clothing."

"Any physical evidence placing you at the scene?"

"Plenty."

"DNA on her body?"

"Things didn't progress that far."

"All right. I can work with that. Fingerprints, fibers, we can explain those away. Bullets, not so much. Hopefully, the ME can determine which shot proved fatal. Ballistics will identify two guns, indicative of two shooters. It won't exactly clear you, but it should take murder charges off the table. The DA would have a hell of a time getting a conviction under those conditions, but they might still try. Your history works against you."

"I know." Cross sipped the bourbon. His focus divided between the conversation and the information on the screen. "So how do I proceed?"

Almeada weighed his words carefully. "As an officer of the court, I feel an obligation to tell you to trust in the law. You should report this to the police, turn everything over, and explain the situation. Things are likely to resolve in your favor."

"That's bullshit."

"You could go to your father. Tell him what happened and let him handle it."

"No."

"Christ, Lucien. He's the police commissioner. Let him help you."

"Help me? He'd be first in line to arrest me. What's option three?"

"Life isn't always multiple choice, my friend."

"Find me a third option. That's why I'm paying you."

Almeada mulled over the facts. Finally, he said, "The Russians wouldn't want the attention either. We're talking the ones who operate out of Brighton Beach, right? Little Odessa? They have their own clean-up crew, or so I hear. Are you sure the cops will even find her body?"

Cross stopped typing. "Maybe not. It depends on how willing I am to cooperate. Vasili has a gun to my head. I have to find a way to remove the bullets."

"We are talking in metaphors, right?"

"Yes."

"All right. Good." Almeada exhaled. "Are you sure you have your gun? Maybe it was stolen."

"Maybe." Cross knew what he had to do.

"That changes things. Make sure you report it missing first thing in the morning. The less evidence hanging around, the better off you'll be. An alibi might also come in handy in case her body surfaces, but it has to be airtight. Lies, if discovered, will only make you look guiltier. Are you sure the Russians will move her out of the club?"

Cross wasn't sure of anything. An image of Svetlana flashed behind his eyes. He should have realized she was a prostitute, but she didn't dress the part. And she certainly didn't approach him in typical fashion. Vasili had coached her. Planted her. And then he killed her. "The police won't find her unless Vasili tells them where to look. I should be in the clear as long as I give him what he wants."

"That sounds like wishful thinking. What does he want?"

"It's best if you don't know."

Almeada nearly choked. "Isn't it a little late for that?"

"Regardless, I won't be able to get Vasili what he wants if I'm under arrest, so the police won't find her body. Not right away. He'll have to move her. But in case I'm wrong, I need you to hold on to a package for me for a few days. Let's call it an insurance policy."

"I don't like the sound of that."

"Neither do I," Cross admitted.

"I know I can't talk you out of this, so I'll save my breath. Send the package to the office, just make sure it's sealed and contains explicit instructions. Label it for my eyes only. The last thing either of us needs is a legal assistant opening it. Then we're both screwed. I don't want my license revoked because of the dumb shit you've gotten involved in with the Russians."

"Thanks."

"And Lucien, try not to get yourself killed. I can't afford to lose your retainer and all the billable hours."

Cross snickered. "I'm glad my life means so much to you." After disconnecting, he stuffed his clothing and gun into a large bubble mailer, wrote out detailed instructions and a personal account of what happened, and brought it out to Justin's desk. "Have the courier deliver this to Mr. Almeada. Make sure you use our regular guy. I don't trust anyone else." He leaned over, reading the details on his assistant's screen. "Where are you on figuring out the club's security system?"

"Surveillance footage is stored on the cloud. We should be able to access it remotely, but I haven't had any luck getting past the firewall."

"Let me do it." Cross wasn't a hacker, but he had been a computer science major and a decent programmer before shifting his knowledge of the tech industry into making money on Wall Street. That was before everything went to hell and he decided to take a chance with private security. Oddly enough, that's when he made friends with a few elite hackers and picked up a couple of useful tricks. "Remind me we need to get a computer expert on the payroll sooner rather than later."

"Have you thought about taking your checkbook into the FBI training facility and offering an entire class of recruits a job in the private sector?" Justin asked.

"I have. But by then, it's already too late. They're brainwashed.

Indoctrinated with all those oaths, rules, and regulations. I can't work with people like that. I don't want idealists. I want realists. Life isn't black and white. It's messy." Just like Cross's current predicament.

Cross held his breath, waiting for the cursor to stop spinning. Bingo. He was in. He scanned the database for the footage from an hour ago. Clicking a video file, he watched the events play out on the screen. The club's back room didn't have cameras. But the main areas did. Plenty of footage had been captured of Cross with Svetlana, including him leading her into the private room and reemerging later covered in blood.

At certain times, the footage blanked out. Obviously, Vasili had gotten to the cameras first. According to this, no one else joined Cross and Svetlana in the private room. Vasili had covered his tracks and painted Cross as the killer.

Cross checked the current feed but saw nothing but a black screen. Vasili must have deactivated the cameras. He had to in order to move her body. "Are the video files also saved on the premises?"

"I don't believe so," Justin said. "Everything goes straight to the cloud."

It was a gamble. Vasili might have made a copy to use as blackmail, but Cross couldn't worry about that now. He pressed delete, replacing one fear with another. "You didn't see that."

"No, sir."

Cross returned to his office. One problem solved. One to go.

The steam rose from the top of Cross's coffee cup, and he blew on it before taking a sip. The air was crisp. In a few hours, the sun would burn away the early morning haze, leaving a clear sky and nothing but the brutal cold.

Cross shifted from one leg to another, wiggling his toes to regain feeling in them. *Come on*, he thought, *I haven't got all day*. He resisted the urge to check the time. No more than five minutes had passed since the last time he looked. Where was Knox? At this rate, the man would be late for work. Well, later, since Cross had every intention of detaining Knox until he answered a few important questions.

The front door opened. *Finally.* Cross bounced on the balls of his feet, preparing to intercept his client the moment the man stepped foot on the sidewalk. But Trey Knox didn't exit the apartment building. Instead, a gray-haired woman and her bearded schnauzer did.

The schnauzer strained against the leash, eager to go on his morning walk. But once he made it to the curb, he stopped. His ears perked up, and he stood as still as a statue. A deep growl emanated from within his taut body, and he bared his teeth.

"Buddy, you stop that right now." She whacked the pooch on the backside with the newspaper. "Where are your manners?" She offered an apologetic smile to Cross. "He never does that. I don't know what's gotten into him."

"It's quite all right. Dogs usually like me." Cross crouched down for the dog to sniff him.

But Buddy didn't budge. His ears flattening against his skull, and his sharp eyes zeroed in on something in the distance. He let out a warning bark.

"Quiet, Buddy." The lady tugged on the leash, but the dog didn't move. She scooped him into her arms and carried him past Cross. The dog's eyes remained on a fixed point as he continued to growl.

Cross turned to see what had caused the animal's unease. At first, he didn't see anything. The morning mist mixed with plumes of exhaust, limiting visibility. But as the icy vapor dissipated, Cross spotted two men in dark overcoats at the bus stop. One of them carried a shiny metal briefcase, and the other had what appeared to be a golf club inside a sealed duffel bag.

Taking another careful sip of the nearly scalding liquid, Cross returned to the food cart and pretended to study the menu while keeping one eye on the two men. He recognized them from the club last night. They were Vasili's enforcers. *Did they follow me?* Cross wondered. He hadn't noticed anyone outside the police station when he filed his report. His gut said they were already here. Waiting.

"You gonna stand around all day and stare, or are you actually gonna order something else?" the guy at the food cart asked. "I got other customers in case you haven't noticed."

"Right, um...give me a number six." Cross pocketed a few napkins, watching as the bus rumbled down the street. He grabbed the bagel and handed the man a twenty. "Keep the change."

The airbrakes exhaled, and the bus lurched to a stop in front of the Plexiglas structure. The doors opened, and a cluster of waiting passengers formed a line. But the Russians remained seated, their noses and cheeks rosy pink. Cross was right. They'd been here a while. And they had no intention of leaving.

Several people exited from the rear door, blocking Cross's view, so he headed for a nearby trashcan. Cross knew he shouldn't lose sight of the Russians. Doing so would be detrimental to someone's health, probably his own.

The crowd moved past. The line for those boarding continued to grow, but neither of the enforcers made any attempt to join the early morning commuters. Cross decided it'd be best to wait them out, at least for now.

Peeling back the wrapper, he bit into the sesame bagel, the toasty exterior offset by the cool chunk of cream cheese sandwiched in the middle. He swallowed and wiped his mouth, barely remembering to chew. His attention split between the Russians across the street and the apartment building behind him.

He thought about the classic cartoons he'd watched as a kid. This must have been how the moose and squirrel felt watching the two spies, except these Russians weren't watching Cross. As far as he could tell, they hadn't even noticed him.

Cross tossed the rest of his breakfast into the trash and searched for a better vantage point to stake out Trey Knox's apartment, away from the prying eyes of Vasili's men. A few minutes later, Knox exited the building, carrying a leather attaché case in one hand and a cell phone in the other. Cross peered around the thick trunk of the tree, feeling even more like he was trapped in an old cartoon. *Surely, this can't be happening*, he thought. Unfortunately, it was.

The moment the Russians spotted Knox, they split up. Cross lost sight of the one carrying the suspicious duffel. But the other headed directly for Knox.

The enforcer brought the briefcase up to chest height, held it flat, and popped it open with his thumbs. In a flash, he removed the hidden gun, knocked the lid closed with his forearm, and slipped his hand inside his jacket to conceal the weapon.

"Mr. Knox, we need to talk." Cross grabbed his client's elbow, spun him around, and led him in the opposite direction.

"Lucien, I don't have time for this. I'm already late." Knox tried to tug his arm free, but Cross held tight. "Let go of me."

"You don't want me to do that." Cross squeezed harder, using Knox's arm to steer him away from danger. He cautioned a glance over his shoulder. The man with the briefcase continued to follow them. "Last night, Vasili Petrov paid me a visit. Care to explain why?"

"Why would I know anything about that?" Knox stiffened, stopping short. "I'll call you back," he said to the person on the other end of the line and stuffed his cell phone into his pocket.

Cross pushed against Knox's back. "If you're going to lie, at least make it believable. Now keep moving, and keep your eyes facing forward."

"What's going on?" Knox asked. "Where are you taking me?"

The light at the crosswalk turned red. Cross spotted the Russian with the duffel bag waiting on the other side. Vasili's men knew what they were doing. They intentionally herded Cross and Knox in this direction. "Come on. We can't stay here." Cross jerked Knox away from the crosswalk. Since they couldn't move forward, they'd have to move laterally.

"Whoa!" Knox yanked his arm free, swinging his attaché case wildly. "Are you crazy? Are you trying to get me splattered across someone's windshield?"

"No, but Vasili's men are about to box us in. We're out of options." Traffic wasn't moving that fast. They could make it, if they hurried. "It's just like *Frogger*."

"What does that mean?"

"It'll be fun."

"Fun?" Knox's eyes grew to the size of saucers.

"Well, more fun than a cigar cutter to the genitals."

"Holy shit."

Cross glanced behind them. The Russian removed the gun from inside his jacket and held it down by his thigh. Vasili must have instructed his men to handle this quietly. Two silenced shots wouldn't be noticed, not on a busy street like this. If done correctly, Knox's body could be left on a bench or propped against a doorway, ensuring the Russians were long gone before the authorities arrived.

"Good news," Cross grabbed the attaché case from Knox's hand, "it doesn't appear Vasili has any intention of torturing you. He just wants to kill you."

Knox opened his mouth to speak, but they were out of time. Cross shoved Knox into the street, propelling him forward with a hand between his shoulder blades. The two darted through traffic, amidst a sea of honking horns, squealing brakes, and shouted profanities.

Knox tripped over the curb, skinning his palms on the pavement. Cross grabbed his client underneath the arm and hauled him to his feet. They had to keep moving. Cross had parked a few blocks away. If they could get to the car, they'd be safe.

"Lucien," Knox winced, rubbing his hands together, "you gotta get me outta here. I don't wanna die."

"I'm working on it." Cross turned to see where the shooter was, but he didn't spot him across the street. The other Russian remained at the crosswalk, waiting for the walk sign to illuminate. Hopefully, his comrade was doing the same. "Just stay close."

They only made it a few steps before the shooter hopped directly into their path from behind a parked car. The sun glinted off the silver suppressor. Cross reacted, swinging Knox's confiscated attaché case against the Russian's extended arm. The gun went off. The shot impacted against a tree, causing the birds in the branches to scatter.

Cross pivoted on his left foot and followed through with a hook. It connected squarely with the Russian's jaw. The enforcer stumbled backward, dazed by the unexpected hit. Cross grabbed for the gun, and the two banged into the parked car. The Russian lifted the weapon, and again, Cross batted it away with the attaché case.

The force of the strike caused the handles to slip out of Cross's hand. The momentum of the clunky leather bag tugged the suppressed weapon from the Russian's grip, and the gun skittered into the street and clanged against a sewer grate. The Russian cursed and headbutted Cross. Something snapped, and Cross's eyes watered.

Cross swung blindly. His jab connected with his attacker's ribcage. The Russian grunted, and Cross hit him again. And again.

"Shoot him," Knox urged as he dashed around the bench to grab the papers flying in the air. One of the compartments of the attaché case had fallen open, spewing Knox's work materials across the sidewalk and into the street. Passersby had taken notice. Most gawked from a safe distance, but a few had come to assist, only to find Cross and the Russian in the midst of a brawl.

A woman called 9-1-1 while several men shouted at Cross to back away. Cross delivered one final blow and shoved the Russian hard against the side of the car. He leaned in close and whispered in the enforcer's ear, "Tell Vasili I'll get him what he wants, but Knox is off limits. Got it?"

The Russian expelled a hot puff of acrid air into Cross's face and smiled, his teeth tinged red with blood.

"Got it?" Cross growled, but someone pulled him away before he got his answer.

Several men surrounded the now unarmed Russian, checking his injuries and asking if he was okay. Cross yanked himself free from the strong hands that held him and spun around, expecting to come face to face with the other Russian, but the man who pulled him away was nobody special.

The bystander held up his palms and stepped back. "Cool it, man. You're already in enough trouble. The cops are on the way."

Cross wipes his eyes, catching the briefest glimpse of the oddly shaped duffel moving down the sidewalk in the opposite direction. It was suddenly too hot for the Russians to carry out the execution. That meant it was also too hot for Cross to stick around.

He grabbed Knox, who was reaching for a folder that had fallen beneath the bench. "Leave it. We have to go."

"I'm really sorry about this," Knox said.

Cross smoothed the tape over the bridge of his nose and glared at his client. "You should be." He opened a pill bottle, shook a few into his palm, and knocked his head back, swallowing them dry. At least his eyes had stopped watering. Though, that was the least of his problems. "Vasili wants me to get his shipment out of police custody. Do you have any idea the kind of hell that will rain down if I do or the pain Vasili's prepared to inflict if I don't?"

"Shit."

"My thoughts exactly."

"Lucien, you gotta believe me. I didn't know this would happen. I needed the money. I didn't know he'd come to collect. I didn't realize he was behind the break-in. If I did, I never would have asked you to track down my stolen sports memorabilia. That championship ring alone is worth well into five figures."

"I know what it's worth. So does Vasili. That's why he stole it. You should have told me you owed the Russians money."

"Would you have taken my case if I did?"

Probably not, Cross thought. "At least I would have known what was at stake. You didn't keep up with your payments. You didn't even try to make good on your debt. That's why he took the ring."

Knox jittered his leg up and down, causing the floor to vibrate. "I didn't tell you to call the cops. You did that. That's all you. It's not my fault they confiscated everything in the freight container. It's not my fault Vasili's pissed at you."

Perhaps Knox had a point. But Cross didn't see it that way. "You lied to me." Cross held up a hand before Knox could protest. "A lie of omission is still a lie. Is there anything else I should know? Anything at all? Now's the time." Cross had sixteen hours until the deadline. And he still didn't know what he should do. But saving Knox's life and fighting off Vasili's enforcers hadn't earned him any favors with the Russian gangster.

"No," Knox shook his head for emphasis, "that's it. I swear. Cross my heart." He drew an x on his chest with his pointer finger.

"Do you owe anyone else any money?"

"No." Knox reached for the bottle of Irish whiskey and poured it into his coffee cup with shaking hands. "I thought I'd be safe. Isn't it bad business to kill a debtor?"

"Vasili's no longer worried about your outstanding debt. He wants revenge. You hired me to steal back your ring. You screwed him. You lied to me. And now here we are."

Knox took a swig directly from the bottle, capped it, and put it down beside the coffee cup. "Please, don't hand me over to him."

"I should," Cross picked up the liquor bottle and moved it out of Knox's reach, "but I won't."

"What are you going to do?"

"I wish I knew."

"Why did you call the police? According to everything I know about you, you despise them. You retrieved my property and returned it to me. Why didn't you leave the rest of it alone?"

That question had been on Cross's mind since the moment Svetlana's blood splashed against his face. At first, he blamed himself, but it wasn't his fault. Vasili would have killed her anyway. She had to pay for her betrayal, and her murder gave the gangster leverage over Cross. It would only take one anonymous tip for the police to find her body, just like it took one call for them to confiscate Vasili's shipment. Obviously, the Russian believed strongly in an eye for an eye.

Even if Cross was cleared of the crime, the suspicion might be enough to put off future clients and drive a larger wedge between his security firm and local law enforcement. If Cross's license was revoked, he'd be out of business. Vasili didn't have to kill him. He had plenty of other ways to make Cross's life miserable.

"Lucien?" Knox waved a hand in front of Cross's face. "You still with me? Why'd you involve the police?"

"Besides finding your ring inside the freight container, I also discovered several other interesting items."

"You thought the thieves had stolen from other people too?"

"I thought it was possible." But that was a lie. The bricks of cocaine and crates of assault weapons pushed Cross over the edge. He had to call in the tip. He couldn't turn a blind eye to that kind of contraband.

Cross's gut said the drugs were what Vasili wanted back. The Russian must have been in the midst of a deal, and with the merchandise gone, he could no longer deliver. Vasili's buyers would not be pleased. Maybe they threatened him. That would explain why the Russian was anxious to get his shipment back and why he'd gone to such extremes.

"I guess it doesn't pay to do the right thing."

"So I've learned." Cross returned the icepack to the freezer and checked his reflection in the mirror. He looked like a boxer who'd lost a fight. Maybe that would earn him some sympathy. "I'll take care of this. In the meantime, you need to stay here. Don't call anyone. Don't go out. Vasili wants you dead. He'll send more of his men to finish the job unless I can convince him otherwise."

Knox gulped. "Yeah, okay. No problem."

Cross held out his palm. "Give me your phone. Vasili could be tracking it. Tracking you. It's for your safety. When this is over, you'll get it back."

"Sure." Knox fished it out of his pocket. "I owe you."

"Don't worry, I'll send you a bill. I suggest you pay it this time."

Cross stepped out of the tiny back room and pulled the door closed behind him. He scrolled through the call logs, text messages, and contacts on Knox's phone, but nothing stood out. He went into his office and plugged the device in. While he ran reverse lookups on the numbers, Justin returned from running errands.

"You have a consultation with the plastic surgeon on Wednesday," Justin said in lieu of a greeting.

"Let's see if I'm still breathing by then." Cross rocked back in the chair. "If not, I'll need you to cancel."

His assistant laughed. "Will do."

Cross unhooked the phone from his computer and tossed it to Justin. "Hold on to this. I don't want Knox making any calls or contacting anyone. He's not the sharpest tool in the shed. He could compromise his safety and yours by doing something asinine."

"Okay. I'll keep an eye on him."

"Thanks." Cross climbed out of the chair, his shoulders and back stiff and sore. He winced, crinkling his nose, which made his eyes water again. He cursed, grabbing a tissue from the box.

"Lucien," Justin followed him out of the office, "are you sure you can handle this?"

"There's only one way to find out. In case I don't make it back, you know what to do."

"Rename the business and order new stationery?"

"Exactly."

Cross watched the reflected city lights dance across the water's surface. This was a bad idea. Possibly the worst one he ever had.

He had spent the day collecting everything he needed to pull this off, but he was starting to have doubts. He couldn't get Vasili's shipment out of police custody. With enough time and planning, he could have devised a scheme to steal what he needed from the evidence room, but he didn't have days or weeks to figure it out. So he went with plan B.

Except plan B required precise timing. Whenever Vasili showed up, Cross would have to get things moving. So hours before deadline, Cross arrived at the wharf and found a spot where he could keep an eye on pier nineteen.

Two large suitcases sat inside the trunk of his rented SUV. One contained an assortment of assault rifles. The other contained fifty bricks of white powder. Vasili should be pleased. These would replace what the cops confiscated, more or less. But Cross doubted the Russian would see this as a completed business transaction. He'd want more. Men like him always did.

Cross looked down at the unregistered gun on the seat beside him. Killing Vasili held a certain appeal, but he wouldn't do it unless he had no other choice. He flexed his gloved fingers, comforted by the familiar creaking of the leather. Then he checked to make sure the gun was loaded; something he'd already done a hundred times.

"You're losing it," he muttered, tucking the gun into his holster. His hands weren't nearly as steady as they should be on account of the caffeine and adrenaline, but on the bright side, he was awake and alert. When this was over, he'd probably sleep for days. Or all eternity. Either way, he'd get his rest.

Headlights bounced off the pavement, but the car kept going. Cross glanced at the neon display on the dash. It was too early.

Again, he considered phoning the authorities. But he didn't trust them. Power and money spoke volumes. Vasili would walk. He knew it in his gut, and once Vasili was a free man, he'd get his revenge on Cross and everyone who ever mattered to him.

Briefly, Cross's mind went to Jade. Her gorgeous eyes and fiery red hair brought a smile to his lips. For the first time since she left the city and left him, he felt relief. Vasili didn't know about her. He'd never find her. She was safe. No matter what happened tonight, she would be okay. That consoling thought bolstered Cross's confidence. At least he'd done one thing right in his life.

Settling into the seat, he checked the time again and reached for the burner phone. He typed out a message and hit send. Any minute now.

As if on cue, a black Escalade parked in front of the pier. Two men got out. Even in the dim lighting, Cross could see the machine pistols hanging at their sides. The one on the right opened the rear door, and Vasili stepped out.

Cross typed another text message, put the rental in gear, and drove the few yards to the pier. He parked at an angle with the rear corner facing the waiting Russians. Taking a deep breath, he opened the car door. It was game time.

"Mr. Cross," Vasili smiled, his accent more pronounced, "what happened to your face?"

"You should know." Cross glanced at Vasili's men but didn't recognize either of them. "What happened to Boris and Natasha?"

"Who?"

"Never mind."

"Do you have my shipment?"

"Did you get my message?" Cross waited, but Vasili held the poker face. "Trey Knox is off limits. You don't touch him. His debt is forgiven. Understand?"

"That matter doesn't concern you."

"Consider me concerned. How much does he owe you?"

"Twenty-five."

Cross tossed the MVP championship ring to Vasili. Sports collectors would pay through the nose for it, especially since it once belonged to one of the most famous players in the league. "Will that cover it?"

Vasili held the ring up, examining it beneath the dim lights. "Da." The Russian tucked it into his breast pocket. "I'll consider his debt paid in full if you delivered my shipment. If not," Vasili shrugged, "neither of you will enjoy what happens next."

"Everything's right here." Cross clicked the hatch release. The lights flashed, and the rear gate popped open. He took a step back and to the side, catching a glimpse of two approaching vehicles.

Vasili said something in his native tongue, and the man on the left lifted the hatch and pulled one of the suitcases closer. He unzipped it and took out an assault rifle. He examined it, put it to the side, inventoried the rest of the contents, and said something to Vasili.

"How'd you get them out of evidence?" Vasili asked.

"You know who I am. You know who my father is. How do you think I got them?"

"And you said it couldn't be done. This just proves anything can be done with the proper incentive." The Russian said something else to his men, and the one exploring the cargo hold checked the rifle and offered a response. Vasili frowned. "The guns are empty. Where are the bullets?"

"In the bottom," Cross said.

The enforcer peered inside again, finding what he was looking for and loading the rifle he had placed to the side. Then he lifted it out of the SUV and aimed.

Cross held up his palms, taking another step back. "Don't you want to see what's behind door number two first?"

"Ivan, not yet." Vasili shook his head, and the man lowered the gun. "Open the other bag."

Ivan unzipped the suitcase and held it open for Vasili to see. The white powder bricks practically glowed in the dark. The Russian licked his lips and eyed the police evidence labels, complete with case number and initials. This was their stash.

"All right, comrade. You've impressed me. The debt is forgiven."

Ivan zipped the second suitcase, hefted it into his arms, and carried it to Vasili's vehicle. He secured it in the back seat and shut the door. Then he returned to Cross's SUV and picked up the rifle.

"What are you doing?" Cross asked. His gaze darted to the two vehicles. By now, they had parked where he told them to. He thumbed the phone in his pocket, hoping to hit the right button to send the pre-typed text. That was one of the few benefits to flip phones, besides the price and disposable nature. "I thought we were square."

"You interfered in my business. You stole from me. No one steals from me, Mr. Cross. Not even you."

Ivan squeezed the trigger, confused when it failed to fire.

"Did I mention I removed the firing pins?" Cross pulled his gun and shot Ivan before he could switch to the machine pistol hanging at his side. The Russian stumbled backward. He didn't even hit the ground before Vasili and the second enforcer opened fire.

Cross darted around the side of the SUV, running in a crouch. Bullets impacted all around him, leaving deep pockmarks in the metal shell. He took cover at the front of the vehicle, his breath coming in ragged gasps.

"Don't make this more difficult," Vasili warned. "Accept your fate and die like a man."

"You first."

Cross edged along the front of the SUV until he was directly in front of the headlight. Then he fired blindly in Vasili's direction. The Russians returned fire, shattering the side mirror and taking out the turn signal. That was close. Too close.

Cross stared at the parking lot, freight containers, and warehouses in front of him. A good fifty yards stood between him and the nearest structure. He couldn't escape that way. And just like last night, he was outgunned. But this time, he wasn't alone.

Gunfire erupted behind Vasili, resulting in a surprised scream. Cross didn't understand Russian, but from the gangster's frantic tone, he knew the ambush worked. Vasili's buyers hadn't been pleased by the delay. And they were even less pleased to learn Vasili had lied to them and decided to sell to a competitor for a higher price. The late night exchange and the bag of unidentified powder safely tucked in the back of the Escalade proved it. Vasili had double-crossed them.

The Russian wasn't the only one who could manipulate facts and manufacture evidence. Cross had done the same. Of course, this left him with one big problem. When Vasili's buyers finished dealing with the Russians, they'd want to knock off the competition.

Cross had to get out of here. More shots pinged against his rental, popping the rear tires with a sudden whoosh. Despite the crossfire, Vasili was still determined to kill Cross.

Fuck it, Cross thought. He edged along the front of the vehicle and burst into a run, firing in their direction as he ran for the water. He took two steps onto the rickety wooden pier and dove into the water.

The freezing cold assaulted his senses and cramped his muscles, but he forced his limbs to obey. He swam beneath the pier until he reached the end. Then he surfaced, gripping the wood piling, and waited.

His teeth chattered, and he wondered if he'd freeze to death. His hands and feet instantly went numb. He wouldn't last in the frigid water much longer. But soon, the gunfire abated. He listened, straining to hear over the lapping waves and the blood rushing in his ears.

Finally, he dragged himself onto the pier. Vasili's buyers were gone. The Russians lay dead in the street. The back door of the Escalade remained open. The suitcase gone. Cross snickered, wondering how long it'd take them to figure out they had fifty bricks of flour and cornstarch.

Cross tossed his gun into the water and looked down at Vasili. The large Russian had been struck at least six times. They'd played the same game, but Cross had won.

The sound of sirens grew louder. Someone must have heard the gunfight and called the police. Cross reached into the Russian's breast pocket and removed the ring. The police could clean up the mess. Nothing linked back to Cross. Even the rental car had been procured using a bogus driver's license and prepaid credit card.

He wrapped his arms around his shivering body and set out for the nearest bus stop. From there, he called a cab and went home.

Once he was dry and warm, he made one final call. "I just wanted to make sure you didn't order new letterheads yet."

"Not yet," Justin said.

"Tell Knox he can go home. Vasili won't bother him again."

"Will do."

"Thanks, Justin. Get some sleep. You've earned it."

"A raise would be nice too."

"You already own shares in the company. What more could you possibly want?"

"I'll make a list."

"Fine. Give it to my assistant, and tell him to take care of it."

Justin laughed. "I'll see you tomorrow, boss."

"Actually, reschedule my meetings. I'm taking the day off."

ABOUT THE AUTHOR

Before becoming a writer, G.K. Parks spent some time in law school, only to change paths and earn a Master of Arts in Criminology and Criminal Justice. A few months after graduating, G.K. began writing. *Likely Suspects*, the first book in the Alexis Parker series, was published in 2013. That book went on to launch G.K.'s career as an author.

Since then, G.K. has written over thirty mysteries and thrillers, spanning four different series. G.K. has tackled everything from private investigators to police procedurals to vigilante justice thrillers. Whether the main characters are feisty female detectives or a team of mercenaries, each story contains tons of action, plenty of humor, and a lot of heart. To find out more, visit the author's website:

https://www.alexisparkerseries.com/anthology

RATS

JR POMERANTZ

Ravi's rat problem is about to blow up.

1

I didn't know what else to do—I was hard panicking at this point. So I pulled rubber bands on over my shoes and snapped them around the ankles of my chinos, and then I yanked those rats out of their cages one by one and stuffed them down my goddamned *pants*.

Four minutes.

I looked at the CRISPR for half a second, then scrambled around the edge of my desk, worthless work shoes sliding out from under me, shoving every paper and trace of printed research inside my laptop bag and cramming it shut.

A smell in the lab was my first clue. The smell was the first hint of trouble; a text was the next. It had been six minutes since I got the text on my burner phone, the one my wife didn't know about, the phone that inexplicably came with this assignment.

Boss arrives in 10

Pro tip: if you get assigned a new project at work, and it comes with its own phone, ask a few questions before you accept.

I'd get another CRISPR setup, another transilluminator. Whole new electrophoresis set, a new GelDoc system. Hell, I could get twelve. It was okay if these blew up. Not a problem. I'd have enough money to buy or genetically engineer whatever I wanted by next month.

But my espresso maker? Oh, the *humanity*. My terrorized, rabidly malfunctioning brain fed me half a thought about saving it before I realized I had a kind of distracted madness on the rise, slowing me down, the kind that would get both me and these lab rats killed. The quick wit of survivors always gets top billing after any disaster. Rarely do you hear about all the dumb minutia people think while they're struggling to live.

I guess because those people die. So you don't hear their stories at all.

Right now, if I couldn't fit it down my pants or inside that laptop bag, it wasn't going to survive past the next three minutes and forty seconds.

Thanks to my new super-slim, government-issue computer, I couldn't even fit one rat in there, and get the case closed without compromising rat health.

Can't do that. They're the prize.

The 'boss' arriving, in this case, was an office-sized detonation designed to raze my entire laboratory. The odorous evidence was all around me, acrid in my nostrils, ruining that clean room absence-of-smell I loved.

My other bosses were responsible for this: the smell of explosives, my rush, a sudden decision to level my workplace. And I don't mean the FDA. It's just their building.

Three minutes to make it out of this office alive with four Zucker rats stuffed down my pants.

Yes, Zucker rats. Obesity research rats. Not an easy cargo. And not comfortable, for any of us. Pens, flash drives, sketches, a spare petri dish hidden under my planner...wait, why was I packing pens? Jesus, no, *don't* wait.

I should have put the rats in my pants as the final act, not the first.

Go, go, go.

Here's the other rub: one of those obesity research rats was already sliding out from under the rubber band.

Whoever they are, my bosses, I didn't know they were the kind of people to commit domestic terrorism. Ballsy move, giving your lone employee ten minutes to save his life's work or it gets destroyed forever.

And so does he.

Zucker rats can get to be two pounds plus, and these bad boys felt like it. I'm not much of an exerciser, but if I ever become one, I'm still not going to use rats as ankle weights.

A muffled digital beep went off, the sound of a microwave under a blanket. I jumped like it was the explosion.

One minute to go after the warning beep, they'd instructed. Raspy voice, blocked number. If I didn't start out now, I would be inside-out, and so would the rats.

I grabbed my picture of Pritya and the kids, yanked one escaping rat out from under the cuff of my pants, hurled both into the laptop bag. Hippocrates caught mine with his own red eye. I pressed the case shut as best I could without hurting him, and bolted for the nearest door.

But I couldn't use that door. It faced the cafeteria; everybody would see me flee an 'accidental' explosion.

Forty-two seconds.

I turned the corner, shouldered open the security doors on the interior hallway, shuffle-loped through another set of doors, rats bobbling up and down. I could feel Aristotle's tiny heart thudding against my calf muscle.

It was a rough day for all of us.

Almost to the exterior doors that faced the parking lot, thirty-six seconds to go, three rats secured above the rubber bands, no colleagues in sight, in the home stretch, soon to be out the door, sixteen tortured paces to my *how-does-a-government-employee-afford-that*-911 Turbo, and then on to—

The exterior door opened and Richard waltzed in, whistling.

"Richard!" I must have shouted it, all stress. Luckily Richard didn't pick up on social cues, or vocal inflection, or make eye contact, or even make eye-to-body contact.

I could have had rats taped to the outside of my body, and he might not have noticed. Certainly wouldn't have said anything.

"Oh, um. Hi, Ravi," he said.

"What are you up to?" Thirty-two seconds. My brain was going to explode before this bomb could. I had to get me *and* Richard *and* rats the hell out of here.

"I forgot my coat in the lab."

"You know what? Ji-Sun has it. She's looking for you."

"Really?" His whole face brightened, though still pointed almost directly at the ground, ninety degrees.

"Yeah. I saw her just now. She headed over to the lunchroom. I locked up."

This was a cruel lie under any other circumstances. Richard wanted nothing more in this world than to be thought of by another member of the team. But I was willing to risk his damaged feelings over a corpse squad scraping Richard's once-interesting mind off the floor of my lab.

"Oh, wow. Okay. Thanks." Richard led me and my covert rodentia out, even held the door for us. I peered out for a split second, torn between the indoors threat of a soon-to-explode lab and the outdoors threat of running into a more observant co-worker. Then I followed.

"Sure thing. See you later."

I watched Richard saunter himself out of harm's way. Imagined an investigator getting this information from Richard the day after the blast. Maybe Richard wasn't oblivious. Could he actually see it all: my lumpy chinos, my bug-eyed stress? But the inverse situation: *dead* Richard, even *maimed* Richard, was worse. I'd have to take the hit of potential suspicion. Maybe he would forget all about my bizarre untruth, in light of the destructive excitement to come.

In twelve seconds.

Eleven seconds.

Ten seconds.

2

I strolled at a normal pace to my car, just another guy leaving the office, heading for lunch. About a month ago, I'd already done the most suspicious thing a person could do: buy an overtly flashy car outside his means, beyond the financial reach of mere mortal and salary-capped federal employees.

Senator Fletch had assured me that consulting fees were absolutely normal. He was happy to pay me for my services.

Back then, this study was merely interesting. Didn't reek of future bomb threat. And the Senator's rapt, financially viable interest in it was only vaguely interesting to me, too.

What was it people said nowadays when they messed things up awfully?

'Mistakes were made.'

I swung open the Porsche door and saw yet another one of my mistakes: there was no containment system for four rats in a Porsche. None at all. If I still had the Maxima, I could have fit those suckers in the center console and the glove, two a piece. No problem.

Not this car.

Normally I was a pretty dry guy, but in the last nine minutes and five seconds I had sweat right through my undershirt. I climbed in and shut the door to hide my lumpy legs and guilty face from any passers-by. No foot traffic yet.

I opened the glove, pulled a rat out from the bottom of my right pant leg, and set him in gently. He looked dazed, placid. That was good. Agitated rats would not help the situation. But there was no closing that glove compartment. He was a big boy. I noticed a scrap of paper on my windshield. I got back out of the car and yanked it out from under the wiper.

The note said:

Put a rat in the box in the woods

What? I swiveled my head in all directions. No pedestrians near my car. There would be any second though, once the—

In unison, my phone vibrated, and my lab exploded.

3

I took the stresses of the day out on the gas pedal of my Porsche, the way God intended. Plato vibrated in the cupholder, alert and severely muffin-topped. Hippocrates didn't make a sound in the laptop case, wedged in by paperwork and office debris, and Aristotle was lounging in the glove compartment. I had 30 minutes to get to the Columbia Island Marina parking lot.

Now, Socrates, *he* was in a box in the woods behind the FDA, where I'd been forced to deposit him, running away from a crime scene and into the woods in what may have been my most suspicious display yet. Another one of the day's many surprises. No obvious eye witnesses.

But we'll see about that one, right?

Luckily, studies had shown that eyewitness testimony was never reliable.

Thank God for experiments.

Ha ha.

Little science-versus-faith joke.

I imagined a lawyer in an expensive suit grilling the witness.

"You mean to tell me, that you saw a man, with rubber bands around the ankles of his pants, *and*, you *allege*, (he really draws this part out, my imaginary lawyer) multiple (he shouts it) rat-shaped (he basically screams the word rat) lumps." By this time, whichever one of my colleagues who caught a glimpse from their office window, the side of their eye, a brief glance while heading out to the parking lot, is sobbing, really sobbing. And then my lawyer says, "You drink, don't you, Missus..."

If you ever want to take some years off your life— ironic if you, like me, research the extension of the human lifespan for a living —here's how:

1. Leave three stolen rats in your Porsche, a car you bought with some Senator's shady payments, after your lab was just blown up, possibly by said Senator, you don't really know, and

2. Then respond to a note on your windshield from your boss, which you suspect is from your 'real' boss, to pre-emptively steal a rat from whatever thieves you're about to meet by running into the woods behind your job with a rat in your laptop case mere moments after your office exploded.

The new instructions on my life-ruining phone were: get to the Marina, park way down on the far end, by the LBJ memorial, and wait. They'd find me.

Thirty minutes to get to the Marina, or what? I didn't ask. It seemed obvious: people who will blow up a lab will blow up a person. Right?

I sat and waited. I pet all the rats.

"I'm sorry," I said. "I didn't know it was gonna be like this."

You can't guarantee a lab rat a good life. The bottom line was, the vials they delivered to my lab, that I injected into these guys on the daily, came with very little info. Really, no info. I was studying the effects, sure, but I didn't know what was causing them. At least they were relaxed. I wasn't. I bounced one leg until I couldn't take it anymore, and I got out of the car.

Quiet at the marina. It was unseasonably cold today, clouds rolling in. I checked out the boats and the water, the flag flying above the Pentagon. I shivered even though it was June. Calm, quiet weekday in Washington. I liked to think I was inconspicuous, but there wasn't really anything incognito about a Porsche.

Early midlife crisis, I'd told Pritya. Just sit back and let it happen. And she had. We both were surprised.

Good stock picks and a consulting gig, I told her.

A Toyota Corolla eased its way over to my side of the parking lot. Slightly dented on the front bumper. Older model. Nothing flashy about the rat pickup crew. It parked, left the car idling.

Was I aiding and abetting the theft of federal property? Yes. What was the sentence for that?

Nobody was around to witness it. I headed over, opened my car door.

The guy got out of his. Looked like any other government worker, really. Middle-aged white guy with a paunch and a receding hairline. An unfortunate rosacea situation on his face. I don't know what I was expecting. Somebody who looked edgy, too unemployable for the CIA, I guess.

Somebody with a taste for biotech espionage.

"Hi," I said.

He nodded. He said nothing.

I pulled open the door, dug out the laptop case, and I handed it over to him, reluctantly.

"The others are—" I started.

My red-faced mystery extortionist hauled Hippocrates out of the laptop case, immediately, didn't even wait for me to finish my sentence or gather up the others. He plopped Hippo down on the ground, a meaty plunk of research rodent hitting pavement, and put his dirty sneaker overtop. Wedged little Hippo's head right up against the ground.

I lunged forward. "No!" I shouted without thinking. It was an instinct. Sure, I had been experimenting on them in a potentially deadly way, and with a mystery substance, even, but these were my babies. I had the right not to see Hippo's brains smeared on the pavement. I'd started off all wrong, all wrong that day, for sure. Saving Richard's brains had set a dangerous precedent, one in which I tried to save all creatures. At my own expense.

The thug pulled something out of his pocket—I couldn't see *what*—and shoved it under his shoe. Then he pulled it out, and jabbed fist-with-object into the closer of my calf muscles. And plunged.

Plunged the hypodermic needle. Sticking out of my leg.

"What the fuck!" My voice cracked, and so did I. I staggered back.

The needle drooped at an angle, empty of biological content. "Did you just inject me with rat blood?"

Because the biological content was in my goddamned leg.

"These rats are four percent human," this biotech thug said. "Guess now you're four percent rat." He twitched his shoulders, *just doing my job*. Maybe this guy worked for the government too. He sure had the assumed indifference down.

"Fuck. You." I said. My brain was blank. I pulled the needle out and threw it on the ground. And the guy actually retrieved it, put the safety cap back on, and stuck it in his own pocket. Then plopped Hippocrates into my dangling hand.

"Wait for further instructions," he said. And he got into the car, slammed the door shut, and drove away slowly, with a little wave, even, while I stood there, a rat in my hand, two more in the car, a shot of rat blood in my leg, and who knew what else?

4

I put Hippo back in the laptop case and set him on the floor. I was woozy, maybe from whatever experimental drug I'd been injecting in him for weeks, now in me. He didn't seem in great shape either.

Well, he wasn't. He'd been bred that way. For science.

It was stuffy in here. I felt like I was suffocating, though nothing had changed in the car, and it was so cool and cloudy outside the interior was comfortable.

The car had taken on a musky smell, source confirmed by the puddle under Aristotle in the glove compartment.

I exhaled through my throat, same way I did when the kids destroyed some relevant part of the house.

It was a 3-mil needle, too much blood to remove from a regular-sized rat. I propped open the laptop case.

Hippo was alive, no doubt, eyes open. He was more than double the weight of an average rat and the biggest of the bunch. If any rat could take a hit, it was him.

"Are you okay?" I asked. "You lost some blood."

No response. He was a rat. Response not expected. He was dirty and he'd lost some blood but otherwise doing alright, for a lab rat.

For no real reason I felt a little better, holding the laptop case open, talking to Hippo.

“What the hell was I shooting you up with?” I asked. Hippo just sat there.

What to do now? I’d thought the whole point to coming here was to bring the rats.

Turns out I was only delivering myself, and one needle’s worth of rat blood. Was it fatal? I pressed two fingers against my carotid. Normal for an adult male thirty-something Indian-American father of two who had recently been in an explosion.

Go back to work? It seemed ridiculous, but it made sense. If my story was that I went out to lunch before the blast, I’d have to unwittingly return and discover it, wouldn’t I?

I eased onto the Parkway, a little smarter than I had been on the drive over: With these passenger rats on board, it wasn’t a good time to get stopped by the police, so no breaking any speed records. Even though a Porsche doing the speed limit is borderline tragic. I turned on NPR, thought it might soothe all of us.

It turned to static in the middle of the weather report.

“Ravi, it’s Jane. You’re about to be intercepted. Stay calm.”

“What?” I said out loud. No response, of course. A hacked FM radio only communicated in one direction.

I scanned my rearview. Black SUV coming in fast on my left swerved into me, jack-knifed me off the road. I ran up on a low curb on the shoulder, then on grass. Tires squealing, me screaming, that stuffy feeling back in my head and all around me, making the skin on my neck slick with sweat in places I didn’t even know sweat glands existed. And I’m a biologist. The Suburban ahead of me wobbled onto two wheels and nearly tipped over. But didn’t, settled down hard into its shocks instead.

When I saw the guy who got out, I wished it had tipped over. I thought about running for it. I didn’t even know if I could get this car off the curb.

Plato, bless his pudgy body, was still wedged in the cupholder. Hadn’t budged.

And then my second thug of the day was upon me. This guy was more wiry. And he tore my door open with focused energy, something I’d run out of.

"Where's the rats?" He demanded.

I spread my hands out in the car where there were two visible. Then I tilted open the laptop bag to reveal the third.

"There's supposed to be four," he shouted, and he pulled a gun out of his pocket, leaned way in, shoved its muzzle into the middle of my throat.

"T-there's only three," I stuttered. Was the muzzle warm? Did this guy shoot errant corrupted government employees all over town for a living?

"Show up tomorrow with all four," he said, jabbing me a little deeper in the throat with each word. We were alone on the shoulder. Typical. Plenty of cops on the road when I was testing the limits of my high-speed car, none when there was a gun vivisecting my throat. I was gasping in short panic breaths. "Or we'll visit Pritya."

When he said my wife's name, I stopped breathing altogether.

"I'll send you the address tomorrow," he said. He pocketed the gun and got back in his SUV. My phone—my *legit* phone—played a little song. I hauled it out of my pocket.

It said:

Pick Punam up from daycare

5

I eased my Porsche off the shoulder and aggressively merged back onto the Parkway, because as soon as drivers see a turn signal, they try to kill you with their cars.

"Call Pritya," I said.

The stuffiness in my head had been replaced by a gnawing feeling deep inside. I guess it had been a while since breakfast, and it was true that I'd missed out on lunch, but this hunger was way out of bounds.

As soon as I heard the click of her answer I started my whining procedures.

"But sweetie, I don't have the car seat."

"I dropped it off at the daycare," she said.

"I'm in the Porsche, it doesn't even fit in the backseat."

"I know it doesn't, Mister Indy 500. Just put it backward in the front seat and try not to risk our beloved daughter's life because you caught some American-style showing-off disease."

"I love you."

"I love you too, despite this unbelievably stupid purchase you made."

"You're beautiful and perfect."

"Despite the fact that you are now trying to use that stupid purchase as an excuse not to pick up your own child from daycare."

"See you in a few."

I didn't have time to go to work and pretend to be shocked at my exploded lab. I had to pick my daughter up from daycare.

Then I had to figure out how to steal a fourth rat back from my boss, not the Senator who paid me off to inject rats with God-knows-what and then had my lab blown up, my real boss at the FDA, Jane Foxhall, who made me put one of those rats in a box in the woods for no specified reason, or some goon was going to shoot my beautiful, perfect wife in the face.

6

Punam lifted her arms in the air. "Dada dada dada," she shrieked. I scooped her up.

I swore she was speaking in compound sentences, with clauses and thoughtful pauses back when she used to spend the whole day with Pritya. Since daycare she'd definitely regressed. "Okay, baby. Let's go home."

"She ate her whole snack today," Miss Nicole informed me. She pointed to the car seat in the corner I'd have been lost without.

I didn't know exactly how to interpret the info, but it seemed good. "Great," I said. I tried to look happy or at least not-maniacal while I thought, I may have gotten her mother killed with my stupid side hustle car fund.

"Say bye-bye to Miss Nicole," I said. I always winced at the title-plus-first-name monikers. Seemed demeaning. If anybody came into the lab calling me Mr. Ravi I'd show them the door. Obviously anybody who called offering cash, I just bent over backward, awful sucker that I am. Sacrificed my own life and the lives of my family for some dumb car, hopefully also one iota of intellectual curiosity.

At least that gnawing hunger had gone away.

Miss Nicole hit the automatic door opener, and I carried my whole bundle, Punam in one arm, car seat in one hand, her go-bag on one shoulder. And then I realized I'd left all the rats in the car in full view. That would be big news at home.

Punam may have regressed, but she would still be tough to discredit. I had to hide them from her.

"Hold on, kiddo." I set the car seat down, her in it. On the pavement. An incoming mom judged me with her sour stare-down. I smiled and nodded, waited for her to get inside so she didn't judge me on what I was about to do. I yanked open the driver's door, lifted Plato out of his cup holder and eased Aristotle out of the glove compartment—his urine had dried, but now it was covered in shit, rolled everywhere, which actually made me worry for half an instant about the other two and their digestive health.

I grabbed the laptop with my other hand, hit the trunk button with my pinky, checked on Punam, in my view, with the rats out of hers, sitting happily in her car seat—thank God it was her and not Naveen. He would have rebelled for sure and been in my face in a second with some pointed questions.

With the rats safely tucked in the trunk, I opened the passenger door.

"Up and at'-em, kiddo!" I shouted, with forced cheer. Did kids know when their parents were lying in their tone? Probably depended on the kid. Punam sprang up. I set about cursing and struggling with getting the car seat buckled in the right way, just in time for my judgmental compadre to exit the daycare, kid in tow, pass by too close with her signature glare.

"These carseats," I laughed. She grunted.

"Whole whole whole," Punam chanted. "Whole daddy."

"That's right, sweetie. I'm your dad."

"No," she shouted. "Whole!"

I followed her finger, and there in the front of the passenger seat of my nearly-new Porsche 911 Turbo, I saw what she was saying.

Hole.

An obese rat-sized hole. I stuck my hand in there, and sure enough, it went all the way back. And up.

Hippo wasn't in the laptop case after all. He was deep in my Porsche's upholstery.

The drive home was a living nightmare of imagined scenarios, one in which Hippo went rabid, somehow, and burst out through the center of the passenger seat, and ate off one of my kid's fingers.

But I also had to admit to myself that some part of me felt pretty satisfied, almost happy. And it was a part of my brain that, earlier, when Hippo was squeezed into the laptop case, had felt smothered.

Then hungry.

And I had to wonder if it was the stress that made me somehow, lightly, perceive myself as being connected to Hippocrates.

Or if it was something in our blood.

7

"We need to talk about containment," Jane said.

"Containment," I echoed back, dumb.

"And a ten-piece chicken nuggets," a guy shouted behind me. The parking lot of the McDonalds across from work had seemed like an okay meeting point when Jane had first suggested. Now I wasn't so sure.

She handed me a flimsy, innocuous backpack, heavy in the bottom with a gun-shaped weight.

"What do you expect me to do? Blast my way out of this?"

"Fletch needs you alive."

A wave of desperation surged through me all over again, as fresh as when he'd first uttered Pritya's name. "It's not me he threatened," I said.

I'd do anything to be free of this. I'd do anything for Pritya and the kids.

Jane either read my expression, or she'd also been injecting some mental networking juice in her spare time. "The only way out is through," she said.

"What the hell does that mean?"

"Fletch isn't going to kill you. He needs you. We all need you, to go to Afghanistan, handle the lab work, get this thing out of the ground. Quick."

"Any other scientist not available?" I said, with a sneer. I immediately regretted it. Because if any other scientist could do it, there was no vested interest in keeping me alive.

"You're the only one who's worked on it so far. And you're the only person with it in your veins."

"I didn't sign up for this."

"I know," Jane said. She held my gaze, no apology in her eyes or on her lips. "It's a war, Ravi. None of us signed up. We got conscripted."

"Whose war? Not mine."

"Soon it'll be everybody's," Jane said, with a lifeless chuckle that made me cold all over, made me realize whatever it was she knew, it was a nightmare, a tiny part of which I was living right now.

"Fletch didn't have me injected with rat blood," I leveled with her, "You did."

Her eyes flashed recognition. "I did," she said.

"What is it?" I opened up the car door, threw the backpack and its deadly cargo onto my ruined passenger seat, and slammed it shut again. "What did you have them put in me?"

"Do you know what you're injecting those rats with?"

"No," I admitted. "We get a shipment of it every Monday, serial codes only. I have no idea what's in those vials."

"Fletch didn't tell you?"

"Fletch didn't tell me. He gave me a phone, and a laptop to send the reports. That's it."

"Three of the rats get Mineral X. Future miracle drug. Cures Parkinson's, Alzheimer's, a host of other brain disorders, metabolic dysfunction, reverses aging. You name it, this drug does it. Best thing since marijuana."

I raised my eyebrow. That wasn't federal policy. Jane was really off the record here.

"What's the fourth rat get?"

"There's something else. Located next to Mineral X. And it's a doozy."

"You had me chemically mind-networked with a rat, Jane."

"If there was any other way to get you out of this alive, Ravi—"

I didn't want her to say any more about how deep I was, how near-fatal this whole arrangement had gotten, so fast. How the real test subject here, was *me*. So I interrupted with a logistics question.

"You said go to Afghanistan, quick. *How* quick?"

"Two weeks, tops," she said.

"I can't leave Pritya and the kids. Not with this threat hanging over them."

"The gun isn't for her, Ravi." Jane folded her arms over her blazer, already sick of spelling everything out for me. "It's for you. If you contain this now, nothing will happen. This guy's just doing his job. Fiercely," she said, with a shrug. How much of this was speculation on her part? "If you stop him, Fletch won't send another. We'll get you to Afghanistan."

"Are you sure?" My slow, stress-addled brain couldn't process everything Jane was saying. I was going to Afghanistan. For safety.

"I'm sure. And I can send someone to keep an eye on Pritya while you're gone."

She had perfectly manicured hands, I noticed. Lousy for lab work. I wondered if they'd ever shot a gun. I had no idea if Jane Foxhall was a friend or an enemy.

"Thanks," I said. "But I'm not that kind of person. I'm not a murderer."

"I know," Jane said. "Just keep the bag in case you change your mind." She slid into her BMW and took off without looking back.

8

My problematic biotech thug watched me approach, on foot, east side of the Anacostia River, under the 11th Street bridge. Four in the morning. I held out the bag, four pairs of balled up socks with rolled quarters inside each to simulate four obese rats.

My hands were shaking along with all the rest of my body. Hippo wasn't anywhere near me, so I couldn't pin this one on him. Our delicate mental connection seemed to dissipate from one day to the next anyway. A few milliliters of rat blood mixed with a mystery drug. And still, what I'd felt had been undeniable.

I still had to get him out of the seat. He'd slept there overnight. Or maybe he'd died from eating all that expensive leather and filler.

I hadn't slept at all.

And I was probably about to die, too.

I saw my thug underestimating me, just a skinny little Indian guy, lab rat, no muscle on me. In the bag, his smirk said. In the bag like the rats. He grabbed the sack. No recognition that something could be amiss.

I'm a law abiding citizen, I am. Not a deadly bone in my body, for real. Still, when pushed, you think I'm not gonna put a bullet in one douchebag's head for my wife?

"Senator Fletch sends his—"

Before he could say *regards*, I blurted, "Pritya says *hi*." I held the gun up to his head at a distance and angle whose consequences could lead to only one thing.

And I pulled the trigger.

I was too close. Blowback splattered. Adrenaline coursed through me. Or just fear. And shock, raw shock. Big chunk of frontal lobe lifted out of his shattered skull.

My hands were shaking so hard, I almost dropped the gun.

Worth it, though. Worth it. I repeated it over and over to myself. Worth it, worth it. My breath was ragged. Don't look. Worth it, worth it. I had no other choice. I couldn't leave Pritya and the kids with their imminent murder hanging over my head.

What makes you think they're not going to be murdered anyway?

I had to ignore this very sane voice in my head, and I didn't look at his body where it lay. I pocketed the gun. The bag of quarters in socks was too soiled to retrieve. I walked away.

Jane Foxhall's bullshit adage seemed more and more accurate every day: the only way out of this was to get through it. Problem was, it got harder and harder, and the tasks at hand got worse and worse. Did this murder ensure my family's safety? I had to hope. And next week I had to head to Afghanistan.

9

I stopped at the McDonalds on the way...to where, exactly? I couldn't go to work with blood spattered all over my shirt, and I couldn't go home, either. Not until Pritya left for work.

"Can I get a large fries?" I shouted.

"No fries until 10," the speaker informed me.

"Hash browns," I said.

"Is that all?"

"And a small coffee. Cream. No sugar."

I only rethought our transaction after it had already transpired. How much blood on you is too much to enter a fast food drive-thru in the United States of America and go unnoticed?

A lot, I imagined. More than a smattering of blood flecks on my shirt. I'd wiped down my face and hands, neck. I wasn't a monster.

One murder to protect your family does not a monster make.

I parked the car, not far from where I'd met Jane the day prior. I set the coffee in the cupholder and dumped the hash browns on the passenger side floor.

Then I waited.

Just moments later—not even moments—only a slow inhale's worth, and then Hippocrates poked his head out of the hole he'd chewed, mosied on out, *welcome to breakfast, buddy*; he plopped himself onto the floor mat, and he discovered his hash browns.

He looked as pleased as a lab rat gets.

And I was a little bit happy, too.

ABOUT THE AUTHOR

JR Pomerantz was raised in New Jersey, moved sixteen times, from Albuquerque to Kabul, and now resides in Silver Spring, Maryland. Hobbies include using all the forms of transportation in the world, flamenco guitar, and knitting.

Rats is a companion story to the biomedical espionage thriller, Love in the Time of the Improvised Explosive Device. The author's debut novel, Corporate Torsos Need Not Apply, is a near-future cli-fi action-adventure comedy. All three are standalone but interconnected stories in the New Espionage Series. They can be read in any order.

www.jrpomerantz.com

THE SILENT ONE

JACK PROBYN

Contract killing's hard. Especially when the next name on your list is your father's.

1

THE DYING STAR

Wind whipped and whistled around the building like a steam kettle finishing its boil. Hissing, screeching. Ominous. Like something deadly was about to happen.

Not half wrong.

It brought with it a bitter chill. The kind found in the Arctic. Where intrepid travelers wore dozens of layers to keep their facial hair from freezing over—along with the rest of their body. *The threat of frostbite up here is very real,* he thought.

More real than the Y2K nonsense everyone was talking about. It was everywhere. On the news, on the radio, talk shows, papers. Making people panic and freak out about what was going to happen.

The answer was nothing. Absolutely nothing. Just another conspiracy theory designed to send the world into a frenzy.

But if word spreading on the rumor mill could be trusted, it wasn't nearly as bad as what else was to come. Although that was a political conversation for another time.

And he wasn't about to get into the habit of talking to himself.

Not when there was a job to do.

An important one, no less.

Otherwise, why else would he be alone on the thirtieth floor of the Stoughton Office block, sitting just over several hundred yards from the

—aptly named—Millennium Wheel, buffeted and battered by the blowing wind that was blistering its way through the half-completed construction work, with a gun in his hand? A sniper rifle, to be precise. An Accuracy International AW50, to be even more so.

Earlier in the week, he'd been given the location of where he needed to be. Then, a few days later he'd received the time. Then it was the target's location followed by the precise time they were going to be there.

All the leg work was done for him. The only thing he needed to do was pull the trigger—the way a contract killer was supposed to. Sometimes, when he allowed his mind to think about it, it felt like a robbery charging the prices he did. But at the end of it all, he was the one risking his reputation, his career, his future, his life.

In that order.

Being caught meant going to jail. Going to jail meant having to live with The Memories—having to relive the harrowing and haunting experiences he'd only just managed to wean out of his psyche. And it wasn't long ago that he'd been able to silence the buzzing, the whining that sounded like power saws chopping through plasterboard.

Bzzzzzz.

Bzzzzzz.

Bzzzzzz.

The mobile phone he'd placed beside the AW50's bipod started vibrating. He answered the call.

The voice on the other end was deep, gruff, hidden behind a machine to distort and fragment the sound waves coming through the microphone.

"Are you in position?"

"As instructed," he replied.

"What's the view like?"

He cast his gaze out of the building and scanned his surroundings. London. Big Ben. The River Thames. New Year's Eve. And the skyline was no different to the last time he'd visited, save the addition of the Millennium Dome that had just finished construction a few miles east.

"It's glorious," he lied. It was everything but. Especially the distant sounds of men, women and children cheering from the other side of the embankment, eagerly counting down the time until they left all the shit and baggage in the old millennia and started afresh in the new. He checked his watch. 23:45. "You have the information for me?"

"Thought you'd never ask."

He soon wished he hadn't.

As he observed the bustling and vibrant hubbub of the embankment below, the phone vibrated in his hand. He pulled it away from his face and opened the text message he'd just received.

As part of their one-way method of communication, he was always drip-fed information in the run-up to the hit. And the last piece of information he received—right until the last minute—was the name and identity of the target. The most vital. Like Hansel and Gretel, they were leaving a trail of breadcrumbs for the wicked police to lose their way in the enchanted forest.

He stared blankly at the screen, acutely aware of his employer's impatient breathing coming from the phone's speaker. Looking directly back at him was the face of his next target. A man he'd known for thirty-three years. A man he wished he didn't for the last six. A man who'd made a half-arsed attempt at raising him.

A man who, for most of his life, was known to him as Dad.

"Everything in order?" his employer asked.

Tearing his thoughts away from the image, he said: "How'd they get a capsule? I thought they closed off the entire structure for the display."

"When you're as powerful and corrupt as them, rules don't apply. Thought you'd be the first to know that."

He said nothing, shuddered as he felt the icy breeze roll over him for the first time.

"Don't you want to know why your father's on the list?"

"What difference will it make?"

"There are some things you should know about him. Things you probably already do. Things you have no idea about. And things you probably had a hunch about. But what I think you should know—and this might help you justify killing him—is that he's a slippery man who knows too much. He's a man with many spinning plates, too many eyes and ears watching. Constantly.

"He knows things I'd rather he didn't. And a lot of other people feel the same way. Myself and my investors stand to make a lot of money off the back of this Y2K fiasco, and your father is standing in the way of that. Silence is the winner in all of this." There was a pause; how brief, how long, he didn't know. "We won't have any issues, will we?"

Another pause. His mind trying to process everything he'd discovered in the past thirty seconds. This time, he was aware of it, along with the pain that was forming in the small of his back from where he'd been standing hunched over for too long.

"Of course," he replied. "No issues."

Was he lying? Telling the truth? Was he capable of killing his dad?

"There's a reason they call me The Dying Star," the voice in his ear continued. "Would you like to know why?"

No. But there was no point responding. It was rhetorical, just like all the other questions.

"When a star dies, it sends a shock wave throughout the universe, creating a ripple effect of epic proportion. When I order someone to die, it serves the same purpose. It sends a message: that under no circumstance is anyone to *fuck* with me, otherwise they'll suffer the same fate."

A smirk grew on his face just as another gale of wind flicked his hair and he stifled a chuckle. "Sounds like a fairy tale. A good one, but a fairy tale nonetheless."

"There's a reason they exist. To frighten little children," The Dying Star replied. "You've got five minutes. At exactly 23:58, your dad and some of his associates will step onto that capsule. By the time we roll into the new year, he'll be at the top of Wheel. I'll let you be creative with the minute details. Your money will be transferred once it's done."

The line went dead, and he was grateful to no longer have to hear any more of The Dying Star's incessant egotism.

Because there was something more important to focus on.

Like the five minute countdown that had now turned into four.

Like the group of men dressed in suits that were currently wandering along the embankment toward the Wheel.

Like the fact that he was going to make a hundred grand for shooting one of them in the head.

He opened the address book on his phone, dialled the number at the top, then leant closer toward the window and watched as the man he recognised as his father answered the call.

"Son? Didn't think I'd be hearing from you tonight. You calling to wish me Happy New Year, or do you want to give me an apology? Six years too late for that, don't you think?"

Three minutes and fifty-six seconds.

"Dad, listen to—"

"You think now you get to—"

"Dad, it's important. Your life—"

"Let me guess, it's in danger? Tell me something I don't know. Every day I wake up knowing that I might end up with a bullet in my skull. Your life choices haven't helped diminish that."

He sighed. Pointless. His stubborn arsehole dad wasn't listening. As usual. But there was one thing that was going to make him sit down. Shut up. *And* listen.

"It's about Mum," he said as he watched his father arrive at the base of the Millennium Wheel. The man stood still, surrounded by his entourage of two others and probably a dozen others who were undercover, blending into the background.

Finally. Silence.

And then. "What could you possibly know about your mother? You've not reached out to her in years."

"Dad, it's—"

The line went dead, and the silence it left behind was quickly drowned out by the increasing excitement and furore coming from the other side of the River Thames. Screaming, shouting, cheering. A helicopter somewhere far off in the distance rattled and raved its propellers.

One minute twenty.

His dad and associates had stepped onto the Wheel and were being hauled to the top. Double time, faster than the average citizen. Perks of working for Her Majesty's Secret Service. Getting the best view of the fireworks.

A hundred grand, he told himself.

A lot of money. More than he'd ever earned from a contract before. Now he understood why. Was that how the underworld operated: the closer your relationship with the target, the bigger the bounty—as if the extra cash was supposed to somehow alleviate the mental and physical suffering of killing your own flesh and blood? He didn't think so. He just knew it was The Dying Star's way of securing the hit, making sure the deed was done.

Twenty seconds.

"Well, you can go fuck yourself," he hissed.

And started packing up his things. Beginning with the rifle. Removing the bipod, followed by the magazine. He was just about to put the weapon into its carry case when something distracted him—something innate, a sixth sense, the imaginary clock in his head finally ticking over into the new year.

He glanced out of the window. Scanned the horizons. His dad was at the top of the Millennium Wheel, floating in the air in a small yellow pill. The sky was a canvass of black, interspersed with minute dots of light. And then the fireworks began. An array of colours shot into the air up and down the Thames, hissing and whizzing, exploding as they reached their limit, quickly filling the atmosphere with Sulphur and smog.

Marking the start of a new year.

But he paid it little attention. He was more focused on the man inside the pill. On sending him one more scathing message before he turned away, not knowing when they'd see each other again. Not giving a shit about it either.

The explosions were continuous. Bang. Bang. Bang. They assaulted his senses from every angle. He finally understood why dogs hated it so much.

A flash—unlike any other that was surrounding him—caught his attention. It was only the smallest of movements, but years of experience had taught his brain to acknowledge it, question it, fear it.

He grabbed a pair of binoculars from his bag and honed in on the capsule.

A spider's web of blood was splashed against the other side of the pod, his father's thick, heavyset body slumped to the floor, head tilted to the side, a river of red dribbling from the back of his skull. A quick look at the bullet hole—which was on the bottom left of the capsule—

told him everything he needed to know. After working out the trajectory of the shot, he deciphered where it had most likely come from.

Beside the offices was a hotel. The South Bank Plaza. The same hotel he was staying at.

Someone from inside that building had assassinated his father.

And he was willing to bet the hundred grand he'd just lost that it was someone in his hotel room, preparing to frame him for the murder.

2

THE ANGEL OF DEATH

He'd hired the hotel room using an alias; a tactic he'd learnt early in his career. Stay in the area, scout the target's location, find and arrange a suitable vantage point. Those things took time, and if he could stay in a comfortable hotel room while he did it, then all the more reason. Anything was better than that shithole he'd been living in during the Gulf War.

Bzzzzzz.

Bzzzzzz.

Bzzzzzz.

For a few seconds following the shot, he'd done nothing, his mind devoid of any thought and comprehension of what was going on around him. Then he blinked and eventually came to. In the time that he'd been out of his body, the capsule where his father had been murdered had moved to the bottom of the Wheel, and droves of police cars and ambulances were pulling up to the scene.

Time to get out of there. Fast.

Just as he was about to grab his phone from the windowsill, he caught sight of someone. A figure, dressed in a black gilet, a black jumper beneath and a black backpack to match.

He recognised him at once.

The Angel of Death. Criminal, assassin, contract killer. So named because it was reported that, out of his entire kill list of 97, every one of his victims was shot in the head so that the explosion from their brain created a halo effect over their body. Wanted in thirty different countries for the deaths of dozens of politicians and wealthy, influential people, The Angel of Death could blend into his surroundings at will, unseen, unheard, unnoticed.

Leaving the rifle behind, he grabbed his phone, along with the contents of his backpack and made it to the bottom of the building within thirty seconds, jumping down a flight of stairs at a time, shocking the heels of his feet and joints in his knees. As he breached into the open, he staggered into a wall of bitterness. Dense clouds of vapor expelled from his mouth and disappeared in the air like speech bubbles. Blue and white lights flashed furiously on the other side of the Jubilee Park as dozens of police officers and emergency response teams raced to the crime scene and surrounding area.

The fireworks had stopped.

The celebrations were over.

The new year was underway.

What a start.

The last he'd seen of The Angel of Death, the man was heading north toward London Waterloo. The underground. Bakerloo line. Jubilee. Northern. Where, within a matter of minutes, The Angel would melt into the background of the city.

That was unacceptable.

He gave chase. Jogging down the pavement, weaving his way in and around knots of people, celebrators who were excitable, stumbling sideways as they walked. Inebriated. The worst sort. It was important though for him to look as inconspicuous as possible—another lesson he'd learnt long ago. And yet it was an important part that many newcomers to the industry often overlooked. He'd heard too many stories of young contract killers—of which the pool was only small—getting caught and killed because they'd made stupid mistakes.

Natural selection at its finest.

Over a hundred yards later, he eventually caught up with The Angel of Death. The man was walking confidently, upright, with his right hand clasped over his backpack strap and the other buried deep in his coat pocket. Over the years he'd heard many stories of The Angel of Death—and what he kept inside that coat pocket.

Several stories. Several weapons. Several inanimate objects that could be used as weapons.

He followed The Angel of Death up the steps at Waterloo and into the main terminal. The vast expanse of space bustled with life. Revelers, partygoers—all of them shouting loudly over one another, imbued by the alcohol that was swimming around their veins. He paid them little heed. The Angel was getting away from him, and fighting against the tide of reprobates was slowing him down.

On the right-hand side of the station were half a dozen trains, each preparing to travel on a tentacle out of the city and into the south of England somewhere. He tried to calculate The Angel's movements, but it was too late; The Angel made the first move: a sharp left turn into the Underground.

He followed, keeping his distance at all times.

They descended the escalators, made another left turn and arrived at a set of turnstiles. A row of ticket machines was placed to the left. There they joined the back of the queue at opposite ends.

As he waited in line, his mobile vibrated. He checked the screen, recognised the number and ignored it; it was his turn to purchase a ticket.

After he'd bought a Travel Card that granted him access to unlimited rides on the Underground, he stepped away from the machine.

Froze.

The Angel was gone.

Panic set in. Had he been spotted? Had he been given the slip? Or had he just been slow, seconds behind?

He snapped his neck left and right. And then caught sight of the assassin's backpack at the top of the escalators.

He followed the man to the bottom of the escalators and into the nearest Jubilee Line train. Keeping his back to the assassin, he shuffled his way to the other end of the carriage and found himself a seat. Uncomfortable, but it would do. There was a lingering smell of staleness in the air, and the quality of the air was thick, black, like the smoldering remains of a human carcass burning away beside him in the desert. Next to him was a couple linked in one another's arms, the woman falling asleep on her partner's chest.

He'd had that once—a life of loving, of unconditional adoration, of wanting to share the rest of his life with someone—but it quickly became apparent it wasn't for him.

He looked up at his reflection in the window, at the couple beside him. And then his eyes lingered at the rest of the cabin. Despite the havoc and hubbub of the New Year's celebrations above ground, it was dead quiet. He counted seven or eight other bodies. Too few to conceal his identity for too long.

Shit.

Ten seconds later, the train pulled into Southwark, the next station. He leant forward and glanced out the corner of his eye. The Angel of Death remained where he was, standing with his back toward him, hand still planted in his pocket.

As soon as the carriage doors closed, he eased himself into the seat and kept his profile hidden behind the couple. Allowed himself time to reflect. On what had happened. How his dad was now dead, obliterated. How there were two contract killers on the same train and nobody surrounding them was any the wiser. He compartmentalized the thoughts about his dad and then wondered how the passengers would react if they found out who they were—*what* they were.

Shit themselves, most likely. Panic. He'd have done the same if he didn't know any better.

The train pulled into another station. London Bridge.

This time, The Angel of Death turned seconds before the train had reached a halt and the doors opened. As soon as they did, The Angel exited the carriage and paced toward the escalators.

Something was wrong. The Angel of Death's movements were different. His body seemed tauter, tenser.

He followed, scanned his ticket through the turnstile and exited the station, breaching onto a busy street. Pubs and bars littered the road, and the tenants had spilled out onto the thoroughfare, forming small clusters. Twenty minutes had elapsed since the country had greeted the new millennium with open arms, and the celebrations showed no signs of abating.

But he couldn't dwell on that for much longer. A plan was forming in his head. Right now, he and The Angel were out in the open, seen by hundreds—if not thousands—of people, each of them potential witnesses. They needed to get somewhere quieter. Somewhere discreet. Someplace he could seek revenge.

Fortunately, the opportunity presented itself a few moments later.

Fate was one crazy fucker.

As they neared an abandoned convenience store, The Angel of Death cut right into a narrow road and then a left into an alleyway just behind the store's rear entrance.

Immediately behind, he reached into the small of his back and wrapped his fingers around the small Glock he'd kept as backup.

The alleyway was poorly lit, but there was enough ambient light from the surrounding street lamps to filter through. The Angel of Death came to a step and turned.

Busted.

"You're getting sloppy, James," The Angel said. His accent was European rather than the Russian he'd expected it to be. "I'm surprised you've survived for as long as you have."

"I'll take that as a compliment."

"I wouldn't."

James wrapped his fingers tighter around the hilt of the gun and pulled—

The Angel of Death was too quick. The man removed his hand from his coat pocket and threw a handful of powder in the air, disorienting James. He recognised it immediately. Chili powder. The smell, the taste, and then the burning sensation as it landed in his eyes, filling his vision with salty liquid. He groaned, but it was too late. In the time he'd taken to rub his eyes, The Angel of Death had dropped his bag, tackled him to the ground and was strangling him with a charging cable.

That fucking coat pocket.

The Angel's weight overpowered him, his legs straddling and pinning James to the damp concrete. The cable quickly ate into his flesh and airways. He gasped, choked. His eyes barely able to open. He relied on touch only.

The Angel of Death applied more pressure on his throat, rapidly starving his brain of the oxygen he needed to survive. Like letting the air out of a balloon.

James felt his face swell. With blood, adrenaline, lack of oxygen—he didn't know. But it was beginning to hurt. If he wasn't careful, soon the pain would stop entirely.

'Gr— Bi— Pl—'

Pointless. Speaking only made The Angel of Death press harder on his throat. The killer's expression was plain, devoid of any thought or emotion. Like a psychopath sucking the life out of their next victim. To The Angel it was just business. A means to an end. No emotion. No excitement. No aggression, fear, repulsion for his actions.

James realised he could use that to his advantage.

He shuffled his right hand over the uneven cement to the small of his back. In the fall, he'd landed hard on his Glock, sending shock waves of pain up and down his spine, a pain that he'd quickly forgotten about thanks to the cable around his neck. In his mouth, he collected a load of saliva and prepared himself to launch an assault. A brief moment, that was all he needed. A brief moment of respite for—

He spat. The globule of saliva landed in The Angel's face, and the man flinched. It was only a minor movement, minuscule, but now he had the element of surprise behind him. The time to attack. James grabbed the gun, pulled it from beneath him, and angled it upwards.

He fired.

Twice.

Three times.

The sounds were deafening, and this time there were no fireworks to disguise the noise.

The bullets penetrated The Angel of Death's leg, arse and spine. The killer's body stunted and froze, like he'd been turned into taxidermy at the flick of a button. But there was still that fight between his eyes. The burning ambition to kill. At all costs.

Another gunshot. This time angled a little higher. Straight through the back of the head. Blood and brain matter exploded over James, showering him in a downpour of crimson. The Angel of Death slumped to the concrete, his head and shoulder colliding with the ground heavily. As soon as the killer's weight was free, James gasped for breath as the cable gradually came loose from his neck. He rolled onto his side, choking, air rapidly flooding his lungs. He was alive, but only just. For a while he laid there on his front, his cheeks kissing the ground as he summoned the energy to compose himself.

After the last gunshot, there was a profound silence. He didn't know whether the bullets had been heard, whether the police were on their way, or whether the paranoia was in his head.

Bzzzzzz.

Bzzzzzz.

Bzzzzzz.

Using what was left of his rapidly depleted energy levels, he lumbered to his feet, retrieved his belongings—including the gun—and staggered out of there with his hood pulled over his face.

He made it as far as the other end of the alleyway before his phone started ringing.

This time he answered. With pleasure.

"Have you learnt your lesson?" The Dying Star asked smugly. The bastard was probably sitting in a fancy room somewhere, surrounded by nice amenities, security guards, weapons, women, drugs, alcohol.

A smile grew on James' face. "Would you like to know why they call me The Silent One?"

No response.

James dropped his gaze to The Angel of Death's body. "Just had a little one-to-one with your friend. Nice fella. Shame he didn't stick around for long. I'm sure he had a lot more he wanted to say."

Silence. Utter, profound silence. It was beautiful.

The Dying Star stammered but said nothing cogent.

"I think maybe it's you who's learnt the lesson today." James paused. "You may have underestimated me in the past, but now I hope you've realized that was a mistake."

"I will kill you. I will destroy you."

'You already have. And now it's my turn to return the favor.'

3

THE SILENT ONE

Morning. At least James assumed it was, thanks to the warming sky and the quiet streets. For once, it seemed the city was asleep. Somehow, in the early hours of the morning, he'd found a hiding place inside a car. The little shut-eye that he'd got was uncomfortable, mostly because images of his father's death flashed in his mind, and now his mind and body were feeling groggy.

But there were bigger things to worry about.

His life was now under threat. More than it ever had been. His every movement had to be carefully calculated, considered. Many people thought that this profession was filled with solitude and isolation, that every professional hitman worked alone. But that was wrong. They were businessmen, and just like businesses, they needed clients, contacts, trade professionals.

Fortunately for him, he had several. Most important of all was the one whose car he'd broken into.

The Silent One reached into the footwell, grabbed his backpack and started toward his client's two-million-pound mansion in the north of London. He stepped up to the ten-foot-high wooden door and knocked. Thirty seconds later he was greeted by a sleep-addled man dressed in a gown.

"James? What are you doing here?"

"I have something you might want to hear, Clark."

After a brief explanation, Clark let him into his office—away from his small family—and made a cup of tea. Before James could observe too many of the newspapers on the walls and desk, Clark returned with a mug in his hand.

"You look like you could do with some warming up."

"That reminds me. Your car. I slept in it."

"Fuck off."

"I'll give you the money to get it fixed. I've got some stashed away."

"Why didn't you just knock?" Clark sat and set his mug on the table.

"Thought you guys might have been celebrating." James took a sip of the tea and groaned excitably as the warm liquid descended his throat and heated his entire body.

"Not with the little one. We were up all night trying to get her to bed."

"Everything all right?"

"She's doing fine. Mary's been excellent, so understanding."

"And work?"

Clark's eyes widened. "Well, it promises to be better after what you're about to tell me, I hope."

James turned his attention to his backpack on the floor. It was still a little damp from where it had been lying in a puddle—or was it blood? —but the contents were still safe. "Everything you need is in there. It's my insurance package."

"Insurance package for what?"

Another sip. And then another. Until he finished the drink. Clark asked whether he wanted another. He declined.

"My father was murdered last night," James began. The words didn't pain him to say. They were just normal, like he was asking for a coffee in the morning.

"I heard about that. It's been all over the news. Police haven't got the foggiest idea who did it."

"I was hired to do the hit."

"*You* killed your dad?"

"I couldn't. Someone else was drafted in to account for that eventuality."

"Who?"

"They call him The Angel of Death." James unzipped the top of his coat, revealing the red and black ligature marks around his throat and the blood on his shirt. "At least, they *called* him that. Until he tried to kill me."

Clark eased into his chair, retreating a little. "I don't like this, James. Please, I have a family."

"You're one of the few people who know what I am and what I do. Right now you're the only one I can trust. After our conversation, however, you *will* need to look after them. More than ever. I have contacts and people who can help, but I came to you first."

"Why?"

"Because there are things the world needs to know."

Clark grabbed a pen and paper, a natural reflex of the lifetime journalist.

"No need," James said, reaching into his bag and producing a memory stick. "Use this. There are dozens of recordings already on there. Everything I'm about to tell you, all backed up. Copies of copies. All over the place, just in case."

Clark looked at him in disbelief. James could see the pound signs lighting up behind his friend's eyes.

He began: "The man who hired me to kill my father is called The Dying Star—a moniker he gave himself to fuel his own narcissism. Real name Mikael Karuk. Global tech tycoon. You've probably heard of him."

"The billionaire software developer and telecoms superstar?"

"The very same. Apparently he stood to make a lot of money off the fear of all this Y2K nonsense. How exactly, I don't know. But there are things my father knew that scared Mikael. So he needed him silenced." James placed his backpack on his lap and hugged it. "What I have in here are dossiers and files of all the other clients he's hired throughout the years, as well as the names of those that have been killed by him. Everything you need to know about him is in here."

"Everything?"

"Everything. Photographs. Video recordings. Emails. Texts."

"May I?"

Clark gestured for the bag. James gave it to him.

For the next five minutes, Clark perused through the contents of the files, his eyes glued to every word on the page, every photo and printout attached to the corners of the documents. Like a child reading a new book for the first time.

"This is a lot."

"And you're the man capable of dealing with it."

"But what's going to happen when we do?"

"Back page. The list of contacts I told you about. They'll be able to help protect you."

"And what about you, James?"

James dipped his head and played with his fingernail. "I need you to name me as your source."

"What? No way! Don't be stupid! You'll be killed!"

"It's the only way people will believe it. If you have to get me on TV, then so be it. My days are numbered now, anyway. And it's about time someone brought this fucker down. Time someone took it to him."

"I don't like this, James." Clark set the documents on the table and leant forward, resting his elbows on his knees.

"I can take it elsewhere if you'd like?"

"That's not fair. You know I need this. My bosses don't like me letting my politics get in the way of what I'm writing."

"Journalists have political views?"

"We're only human. But I still don't think we should do this."

"The Dying Star needs to suffer the consequences of his actions, Clark."

Just like we all do.

"And you're sure there's no other way?"

James nodded. His friend let out a deep sigh and turned to the documents.

"How quickly can you turn it around?" James asked.

"Later this evening."

"Should be long enough for me to go somewhere."

"Where?"

"I have an idea in mind."

They continued for the next hour, discussing how they were going to do it, the likelihood of it working, the possibility of getting his face on television and sharing his story. From now on, he would have to spend the rest of his life in constant fear. The Dying Star's net spread far and wide, his tentacles burrowing into every government and industry possible. But they needed to try. Otherwise, his dad's life would have been in vain.

As James stepped out of Clark's office, his wife exited their bedroom, holding their newborn daughter in her arms. They locked eyes with one another, and then hers fell onto the line wrapped around his neck. She said nothing, neither did he. They didn't need to. Instead, he gave her a nod, a smile and then left. He wondered whether she'd ever forgive him for what he'd told her husband, how he'd put their lives in danger: hers, his, their daughter's.

Somehow, he didn't think it likely.

"Take my keys," Clark said as he stepped out of the house. "You're going to need a car to get to wherever you're going."

James looked down at the keys in Clark's hand and smiled. "Thank you."

"You have my details?"

"I'll call you if I need anything. Good luck."

"You too."

"Protect them, OK?" He told Clark. "Both of them. They're beautiful."

4

THE BUZZING

Six months later

And nothing. Six months of fear.

Six months of paranoia.

Six months of looking over his shoulder at every turn.

Six months of second-guessing anyone and everyone he ever came into contact with. And still there was nothing.

No change.

Clark had been true to his word and published the article detailing Mikael Karuk as a murderer and criminal the day after he'd left. And the contact he'd given them was just as quick in making sure that Clark and his family were safe. Within a few days they were moved to a remote part of the country, left to create new lives for themselves under new names, new stories.

James hadn't heard from them since. It was a flop. Mikael Karuk, through his various channels and immeasurable sphere of influence, had squashed any article of libel against him and got it swiftly buried under the carpet. Everything James and Clark published about him was a lie, a revenge attack from someone looking to discredit his name.

James's name had been given to the press, and Mikael had even gone to the extent of saying that James was a disgruntled former employee looking to get some payback. Maybe even a big pay check.

For the past six months, life had been nothing short of hell. He hadn't eaten much; hadn't drunk much either. He was a prisoner in his own house, locked behind the pulled drapes and blinds in every room, barely able to think of anything aside from his father's murder investigation. As expected, it had stagnated and been forgotten about. A cover-up was coming, most likely. And the strange circumstances surrounding the murder of The Dying Star—real identity still unknown—had also remained unsolved.

Just like that, everything had been forgotten about, discarded. Yesterday's memory. The only saving grace was that he was staying in his parent's old holiday home in the Lake District, a few hundred yards from the lake where his father had taught him to master the art of fishing.

He'd spent almost every day looking out at the water from behind the kitchen window, reminiscing about all the wonderful, joyous times he and his family had shared over there. The penalty shootouts with his dad. The real shootouts with the air rifles in the nearby woodland. The fishing trips sitting there on the boat.

The fishing trips.

The boat was still there, although it had rusted and eroded over the years. One day he'd taken it down to the water, to test whether it floated. That was about the only successful thing that happened to him in six months.

And that set the ideas spinning around his head.

Rather, *idea*. One. Singular.

Today the sun was shining. They were just entering the height of summer—his favorite month as a child, his favorite month still now. The leaves were in full bloom. The grass looked healthy, the trees, the surrounding wilderness. There was a vibrancy in the air. That everything was alright in the world. Like there was nothing to worry about.

He'd always found the sun had that effect on him.

It had even stopped the buzzing again.

As he filled his stomach with a coffee—his first in months—he packed his things and prepared himself for a day out on the lake. The excitement was gradual at first, but then as he dragged the boat nearer to the water, his body shook with the excitement of his former fifteen-year-old self. During his father and son bonding time, they'd often spend hours out there, just floating, talking to one another. He'd frequently talk about anything and everything, and his father would listen—sometimes attentively, sometimes not. And then they'd return in the evening with dinner already on the table.

Back when life was good. Back when there was nothing to worry about. Back when they were a happily family.

James reached the water's edge, clambered into the boat and rowed into the middle of the lake. A brilliant white line of light reflected from the water and blinded him as he eased himself to a stop.

He dropped the small anchor into the water and sat upright. Exhaled deeply, letting the crisp air fill his lungs. It was a welcome change to the stale air inside the house he'd grown accustomed to for half a year.

In the distance somewhere, birds were singing, fishes were bobbing their head on the water's surface before diving back down again. It was bliss. At one with nature. Just like he had been all those years ago.

With him, he'd brought his backpack.

He reached inside and pulled it out.

There was no point contemplating it anymore. It was done. There was no going back. He'd failed. His life was over, one way or the other. If Mikael Karuk found him, then he knew it wouldn't be a swift killing. It would be torture, sustained over a period of time. He didn't want that. He wanted it the same way it had happened to his dad. Swift. Easy. One bullet. One shot.

And that was what he had.

One bullet inside his Glock, cleaned and ready for use.

One shot.

As he placed the gun in his mouth and pointed upwards, he realised The Dying Star was right.

That under no circumstances was anyone to fuck with him.

And then he swallowed the bullet.

Fate really was a bizarre fucker.

ABOUT THE AUTHOR

Jack Probyn is the author of the DC Jake Tanner series. He hasn't spent much time on the planet, but he knows what he wants: to entertain and enthral readers across the globe with his stories. Growing up as an only child and never owning a pet - something he reminds his parents of constantly - Jack spent a lot of time reading and writing.

After just about completing an English degree, he decided to turn his passion from a hobby into a career. When he's not writing, he's usually enjoying a sudoku or a true crime drama on Netflix. He lives in Surrey with his partner - who also one day dreams of owning a pet. Preferably a dog.

https://www.jackprobynbooks.com

https://meet.jackprobynbooks.com/theredvipersignup

SUPER SOMETHING

JOHN HINDMARSH

Penny was on a mission of revenge and retribution. Russian agents had similar objectives. She was a super recognizer; one of the Russians was the Poisoner. Penny wanted to win. Mark Midway would be proud.

1

Linda Schöner attempted another sip of coffee and cursed softly when she realized the container was empty. She checked her watch. Seven-thirty, Monday morning. Maeve Donnelly, her boss, would be in her office in an hour. With Schmidt, their Cerberus US CEO, assassinated, Maeve was delegating work so she could take over his management role, which added to Linda's own workload.

Worst of all, she was hours behind with her reviews of new assignments, reports, and workloads. Her analysts would be arriving soon, although most of them worked remotely. Her computer screen wasn't cooperating; it was flashing different colors. Linda frowned. Now that, according to her IT team, was supposed to be impossible. Someone had penetrated her laptop. She stared at her computer screen as if daring it to continue to misbehave. The flashes disappeared and the screen reverted to the login page.

A tiny graphic floated across the screen, bounced off the right-hand side and headed up towards the top, blinking as it moved. She tried to capture the message block with her cursor. It flickered. The graphic bounced again, changed color, and slowly faded. It had done its job, capturing her attention.

Words appeared along the bottom of her screen, disappearing so the text string was behaving like a television Chryon. "Linda. URGENT.

Please visit me in the basement office. Your life is in danger. Leave your office now. URGENT. Penny."

Linda used her pen—she checked the top was on first—to scratch the back of her head. The itch was both illusive and imaginary. She threw the pen down. Penny. Penny? Ah, she realized, Penny was the new contractor from Cerberus UK. What was she? A specialist on contract. Linda hadn't met her and couldn't recall her specialty. She was vaguely aware Schmidt had grabbed Penny for an urgent assignment and when she arrived last week, he had based her in the nether regions of their building. Linda had lost track; she—and her entire team—were still coping with Schmidt's death.

The words stopped scrolling, flashed, and disappeared. The next Chyron simply repeated the word Danger.

Cerberus US and Cerberus UK were two sides of a coin. Both had illegally conducted DNA experiments and enhancements. The results: thousands of enhanced—well, victims, she supposed. Mark Midway and General Archimedes Schmidt had forced abandonment of Cerberus DNA experiments and Schmidt had taken on management of the US organization while Mark now controlled Cerberus UK.

She checked. Yes, she had a note in her diary—Schmidt, before his death, had arranged to brief her this afternoon on Penny and her project.

Linda had no option. She stood and reached for her jacket, lifting it halfway from its hanger.

No. Yes.

She decided she should wear it. The jacket would hide her small .38 Glock; her weapon might be needed if there really was danger. She stepped out of her office. Her PA's office was vacant. He was late.

The elevator stopped at B2. She'd never ventured into these depths, mainly because no one worked down here. At least, not until Schmidt set up whatever he'd set up.

Linda tried to recall the building's floor plans. There were more levels, lower, not serviced by the elevator. This section had, if she recalled correctly, its own rear entrance and separate security system. She headed to the left to the stairs, which led down to another level. And then another. The dim lighting wasn't helping.

Specialty. Her mind jumped. Specialty. Aah. Penny was a super-something. That's it, she was what Scotland Yard called a super recognizer. According to Schmidt, Penny was a super super recognizer. Or what they called a super-squared recognizer. Linda shrugged. Apparently, Penny could identify someone, for example, based on an image of a portion of the person's ear, no matter how long ago she'd seen the image.

Linda opened the door to what she thought was the office. It was in almost total darkness. She felt for her Glock, touching it for reassurance. With her other hand, she reached for a light switch, hopeful there was one on the wall inside the door.

A small hand wrapped over hers and pulled it away from the light switch. Another hand adeptly tugged her Glock from its holster.

A female voice whispered in her ear, "We don't want noise or light in here. Hold Ladder's sleeve. He'll lead you into our working office."

Ladder? thought Linda. *He's another of Schmidt's recruits. Young. A genius software developer—a gun code cutter, Schmidt had called him.*

Whoever was behind her—probably Penny—closed the door. She heard the key turn. She reached for Ladder's arm and followed his lead, occasionally bumping into an item of furniture or something larger than a trash bin. She was intrigued the two of them were working together in this basement. Her escort warned of a doorway. She sensed Penny, following closely. Linda heard her lock the second door they passed through. They crossed what seemed to be another office, larger, and Ladder fumbled to unlock and open another door. Finally, after crossing another office, he tugged her through the doorway and hit a switch.

The burst of light almost blinded her. She turned, her eyes clearing. The person following was a young woman. Penny, she thought, remembering the image Schmidt had sent. She had purple hair, hopefully dyed, and bright blue eyes, and looked to be about sixteen, although reportedly she was twenty-two. She was dressed in torn jeans, boots—Linda recognized them as Doc Martins; she thought they'd gone out of fashion—and a black blouse. She wasn't wearing makeup. Multiple rings hung from her ears. Tattoos decorated most of her visible skin spaces. The final touch were the black silk gloves.

Penny, her eyes closed, said, "Cerberus. Twenty-nine years old. Masters degree with honors from Wharton. Analyst, lead analyst, and now responsible for the team; what, seventy-five of them. One inch scar above your right eye, result of a skiing accident. Little finger on your left hand is slightly bent, same accident. Three freckles immediately below your left eye. Height is five ten. Build is slender, athletic. Classic American office attire." She took a breath. "Navy jacket, white blouse. There's a crease in the collar, right hand side. Modest mid-blue skirt. Hair tied back. Almost blond. A slight touch of makeup. The black Nike runners provide an interesting contrast, though. Here's your weapon back. Nice."

Linda accepted her Glock without comment. She looked down, checking her shoes were clean. She liked to walk to and from work; at least as much as possible, depending on weather and crowds. Weather in Washington in the Fall could be very changeable. She spun around to confront Ladder. He was wearing torn jeans, sneakers, an AC/DC t-shirt, and a black hoodie.

"What the hell is this all about?"

The young man jerked his head back, as though stung. He turned and pointed at the wall and Linda counted. There were twelve over-large monitors, new, expensive, racked in two rows along the wall. Cables were everywhere and she checked under the ex-military steel table currently serving as a makeshift desk. Yes, there were six large computers, presumably each connected to two monitors. Keyboards and two laptops were on the table.

"I maxed out my credit cards," Ladder explained indicting the equipment.

"He's fortunate. He had cards. Schmidt promised me one, and I'm still waiting. It's such a pity he was shot."

"We all miss him. You're Penny, I take it?"

"Yes. And I hope you're Linda."

"Yes, she's Linda Schöner," Ladder confirmed.

"I'm relieved we got that settled," Linda said. "As I asked, what the hell is this all about?"

"Sit here," Penny said, indicating one of the chairs at the table. "That way you'll get a good look at what's happening."

Bemused and still wondering why she was in a sub-sub-basement office—by the look of it, a very temporary office—Linda sat as instructed. Penny dropped into the chair on her left side and Ladder selected—it was the remaining chair—on her right side.

Linda felt slightly hemmed in. She looked around the makeshift office. There were two tables, no desks, no other chairs. A dozen or more dark green steel filing cabinets, battered, obviously surplus to requirements, were stored somewhat haphazardly in the corner nearest Penny. The main focus of the room was the computers with their connected displays.

Penny was examining two monitors positioned in the center of the rows. Internal cameras had picked up two men leaving a stairwell and followed them as they walked along a corridor. Penny turned to Ladder, "Look, I said they'd be here."

"You're right," Ladder said, leaning closer to the monitors. "Steroid Sam and Poisoner Pete."

"Use their proper names," Penny chastised. "Sergey Govorov and Petr Zhukov. It's crucial for accuracy and reliability of identification processes." Her tone had moved the needle to very serious.

Penny looked at Linda and said, "This is live. We've coordinated the cameras to follow intruders. This is from your floor."

For some reason Linda wasn't surprised when the two men found and entered her office. They were strangers; she didn't recognize either man. They both were well-dressed in grey business suits. They spoke Russian.

Penny said, "I can translate?"

"No, I speak Russian." Linda was absorbed.

The conversation was brief. The first man said, "This is her office, I'm sure. Quickly, Petr. Just the mouse and the Enter key."

Petr was wearing what appeared to be surgical gloves. He reached into his briefcase and withdrew a small bottle; it was large enough to contain four or five ounces of liquid. He opened the cap and spilled a drop or two of its contents onto a cloth, which he rubbed onto on her keyboard and mouse. He capped the container and returned it to his briefcase. He opened a plastic bag and used it to store the cloth. He peeled off his gloves, added them to the plastic bag, and sealed it. He closed his briefcase. He had not spoken a word.

The first man instructed, "Good. Let's get out of here. The sooner the better." The cameras continued to follow the intruders as they made their way back along the corridor.

Penny looked at Ladder. "Said so."

"I'm a believer."

"Can either of you tell me what the hell this is all about?"

Penny was silent for a moment and when Ladder was about to speak, she raised her hand. She said, "I have a talent. It's almost unique. I can scan through hundreds, perhaps thousands of images—usually criminals or suspected criminals—and identify them from snippets from other images. Or vice versa. Show me a snip of a portion of someone's face, and I can view thousands of images and link the snip to any related image I've seen. I'm fast, I'm accurate. I'm classed as a super-squared recognizer by Scotland Yard. Your Schmidt persuaded me to come here on a short-term contract. I arrived on Thursday, five days ago. Schmidt had arranged for Ladder to meet me and to set up whatever equipment we needed." Penny didn't mention the task Schmidt had charged her with.

She pointed at the screen. "We've been watching these two all weekend. About an hour ago they hailed a cab and we managed to determine the address they gave the cabbie. It was this building. We debated. I guessed they were after you, because they already had Maeve Donnelly, your boss."

Penny frowned at Linda's attempt to comment. "Let me continue. Early Saturday morning, while I was reviewing videos of Friday's international arrivals at Reagan, I saw a familiar face. Ladder and I immediately went to Defcon whatever, which is why we're being so cautious. The face belonged to Petr Zhukov, aka The Poisoner, the man we just saw in your office. He's wanted by Interpol for murdering people in Germany and England. He's suspected of assassinating ten Russians, people they call enemies of the state. And other people, not Russian.

"Ever since we set up here, we've been raiding cameras everywhere and we've found a lot we could access. And files, lots of files. I also identified Sergey Govorov—he's the second man in your office—and four other Russians. They're working as a team. We saw a video from earlier this morning when we believe they took your Maeve Connolly. She was carried out on a stretcher from her apartment building to a waiting ambulance. We've tracked them and have a video of them taking Maeve into what appears to be a small private hospital. We've tried calling her mobile to confirm; however, there's no answer."

Penny was silent for a handful of seconds. Linda didn't try to comment. Penny continued, "We've traced the team back to their controller using street and business cameras. We've recorded conversations remotely, using their cell phones, thanks to Ladder. Someone close to the president has apparently made an arrangement with a Russian Foreign Intelligence Service team. FIS are trying to take over Cerberus. They have White House support."

"I—I don't know—"

Ladder jumped in. "We have hours of videos, some with voices. Hundreds, no, thousands of still photos. Penny is very good." He looked from Linda to Penny, anxious.

Penny shrugged and used finger quotes. "No, we don't have proof. I'm relying on my abilities, video files, and recorded conversations. Seeing Govorov and Zhukov in your office pulls it all together. You need to make a decision. My suggestion? Contact your Cerberus military team. You're going to need some genetically modified muscle if you want to save your boss. We have the address, and we can help with her rescue. I suspect they've set poison traps here and in other key Cerberus offices. Do something or people will die." Penny pushed back her chair, had a second thought, and pulled herself back to the table. "Ladder, run the exit tape from Maeve's apartment building, this morning."

The image was of a street view, which Linda recognized. She watched silently as two emergency responders wheeled a gurney and patient from the apartment building to a waiting ambulance. The patient's face was partially covered. Ladder froze the video when Penny signaled, and she matched copies of reference images from Interpol files on another display.

"They're team members."

Penny nodded for Ladder to continue and he stopped again at her signal. She added images to the second display.

"The image showing a portion of the face of the person on the gurney matches Maeve's facial images. It's definitely her. As I said, the men are members of the team. Sergey Govorov and Petr Zhukov leave later. They're all Russians, and I've matched them to images I was able to access in Scotland Yard and Interpol. I managed some from Russia, too."

Linda dug her phone out of her pocket and hit a shortcut code. She let the call ring until it went to voice mail. She said, "All right. Maeve's not answering. You've both made me a believer, too. Let me broadcast a Code 33 message to all Cerberus. Ladder, send me copies of Interpol or Scotland Yard wanted notices."

She explained to Penny, "A Code 33 is Schmidt's dispersal instruction for all of Cerberus. He was always worried we could be attacked or taken over. We've had training sessions, in case."

After Linda prepared and broadcast emails and phone messages, she called Helen Chouan, the commander of 145th MP Battalion; they were all Cerberus. Bravo Company provided security for Maeve, and Linda thought it was likely the Russians had eliminated her on-duty protection team.

"Helen?" She put the call on speaker. "Yes. I just sent out Schmidt's Code 33. We suspect a group of Russians, with support from the White House, are trying to take over—"

"You're certain?"

"Almost. Gathering evidence. We've had some Russian visitors and I've watched a video where they set a contact poison trap on my computer. I suspect they've set other contact poison traps here and possibly at some of our other offices. I suggest you put Fort Brewer into total lockdown, in case you have unexpected visitors. Do it now. Even if people arrive with papers signed by the president, keep them out, tell them it's a biological accident, or it's a Cerberus contamination. Use words like pathogens and toxins and hemorrhagic fever viruses. Anything. Just keep them out. Treat this as a critical contamination—have your people wear their MOPP gear." Mission Oriented Protective Posture Gear would add veracity to their lockdown status and should help protect members of the 145th from any attempt of the Russians to use their contact poison. "The Russians are willing to kill anyone. We're all at risk."

Helen said, "Hang on."

The phone was silent for thirty seconds or so.

"I've issued our lockdown signal and the base will be tight as a drum in ninety seconds."

"Good. Let's go to video. I need to share you with two people here. You may like to add your captain—what's her name—Willow. You'll need someone to take charge of investigations and If I recall, she has the skills and experience."

It took less than a minute to establish encrypted video connections. Helen Chouan introduced Captain Jen Willow and one of her lieutenants, and Linda introduced Penny and Ladder, each at a computer.

Linda continued, "We know Maeve's been taken, I've seen the video. We don't know the state of your protection detail."

"Are you certain about Maeve?" The questioner was Captain Willow.

"Ladder, share your screen and run the relevant portion of the video where Maeve is moved from her building to the ambulance. Penny, describe your identification process."

When Penny finished, and after watching the video clip, the captain nodded. The lieutenant took notes.

Linda continued, "Helen, we need your involvement, your MPs. Maeve's rescue is top of our action list. We know where she's being held. You need to find out what's happened to your team. The 145th can go all out to help us deal with these Russians and whoever's backing them—we'll provide more details for you. Finally, we'd like a small team to help with security for us, here at the research center."

"How safe are you?" Helen asked.

"There should be no one else in our building, assuming they've received and reacted to the Code 33 message. Anyone who ignored it is at risk—I can't do much about them. We're in a part of the lower basement, somewhat hidden, I hope, at least from casual searches. We only have one weapon." Ladder raised his hand. Linda corrected, "Two weapons."

"You're exposed. I have resources—whoever's available from Maeve's protection detail and a standby squad—in Washington. I'll deploy them to your location—they should be at your office within twenty or so minutes. I'll send men to check what's happened to Maeve's duty detail. Reinforcements from here, MPs and medics, will be in the air inside thirty minutes. Add an hour or more to reach Washington. I'll be aboard. We'll protect you, any other Cerberus people who might be at risk, and rescue Maeve."

"Good. Send me contact details for your local squad. I'll brief them. I'm not sure it's safe for them to enter our building."

"Sent. Once I have additional details, we'll talk further. Otherwise, let's liaise every hour or whenever something hits the fan. Okay?

"Works for me." Linda gave a thumbs up and closed the video link. She turned to Penny and Ladder. "It looks like you're my current team. I'll talk with—" she checked the details messaged by Major Chouan "—Sergeant Tom Fielder. Let me do that first."

"Tom Fielder?" She had her phone on speaker. "This is Linda. Your CO should have contacted you?"

"Yes, ma'am. I've just sent some of my men to check on the duty team. We haven't been able to raise them."

"Tell your team to wear protective gloves. They shouldn't use their bare hands to touch anything or anyone."

"Yes, ma'am. I'll be at your location soonest."

"Call me when you arrive. Do not try to enter the building; doors and other access points are likely to be booby trapped with contact poison. We're dealing with an FIS operation, or else some Russians have gone rogue." The sergeant acknowledged Linda's instructions and disconnected.

Linda turned to Penny and Ladder. "Show me where Maeve's being held."

Penny pushed her chair away from the table, giving Ladder the task of presenting the sequence of video files tracking the ambulance as it moved through Washington DC. She had a task to complete—authorized by Schmidt; however, not something she could share with Linda. She had also decided Cerberus US was one weird organization and her driving desire was to stay alive so she could return to London, preferably on an early flight.

She moved her chair to the end of the table and disconnected her laptop from one of the large monitors. She was going to continue searching.

Her eyes-closed description of Linda Schöner when she first entered their makeshift office had triggered a molecule of thought. Or should it be a neuron? A synapse? There was something—she'd find the answer.

She had to expand her search routines. There were records, she recalled viewing, from Linda's high school days. Her skiing accident had happened halfway through her final senior year, about ten years ago. Penny's task was to find photos from her senior year. Yearbook. Any form of public record. Perhaps a driver's license. She did a mental riff through her memories. Ah, yes. Linda had obtained her pilot's license in her final year.

Penny adjusted her searches. It was akin to re-building a cascade of data gathering algorithms. First find an on-line copy of the yearbook, search for the photographer, follow-up with a search to find his current business—or personal—address, find his computer, find images for the yearbook. What flight training schools were in business near Linda's school ten years ago? Could she penetrate their records, assuming they were computer-based? FAA records. The hospital—they'd have a report, probably computerized, if she was lucky, of the skiing accident.

When they first met, last week, Ladder had checked her collection of software programs and added new ones from his work. Penny had presented him with some of her more complex routines and in turn, updated portions of his work. The resulting swapfest of code had occupied almost a day, an easy task once they had relaxed in each other's company. He had even told her why he was called Ladder. She smiled to herself. It had been an interesting lowering of personal shields. And almost the full story. The omissions were critical.

Ladder had also introduced her to his penetration of the Cerberus server cloud where a copy of her main search programs now resided.

Hidden, of course, from any but the most diligent experienced searcher. Penny clicked the run command. She'd get a message when her search process completed.

The tension built as the morning passed and switched over to afternoon with no contact from any member of the 145th. Penny watched Linda as the senior Cerberus analyst began to display minor yet definite signs of concern.

"Give the sergeant another call," she suggested.

"Sergeant Fielder's a lost cause. I've called him five times in the last half hour." Linda shook her phone. "Even Helen is offline."

Penny said, "We can fight back. Just because they're Russians doesn't mean they're invincible."

Linda sighed. "There's only two of us with weapons."

Penny realized she hadn't responded when Linda had asked who was carrying and decided to not correct the count. It was embarrassing. She had a plastic 3D weapon—the barrel was metal, and she had a pack of frangible bullets, both acquired locally. The magazine, eight bullets, was loaded. Under the right circumstances, enough to severely deter an attacker. She hoped.

She turned to Ladder. "Do you have any current videos that might show where everyone is?"

"I checked Fort Brewer cameras five minutes ago. The streets and paths are deserted. There's no one on duty at the main entrance. There's nothing. The cameras are watching over a deserted military base."

"Any trace of Fielder?"

"I can't find him on any camera. You don't think he'll come to help us?"

Penny detected a quaver of fear in his voice. She poured another three coffees; hot, black, no milk. They didn't have a refrigerator. She handed out the mugs and returned to the end of the table where she'd placed her laptop and watched as the computer completed shuffling through its search algorithms. Its search had concluded. She had the data she sought.

She had confirmation of Schmidt's suspicions.

Her other searches had already backtracked Ladder as far as she needed—he was not the innocent he was made out to be. A task for later.

The sudden blackout was the only signal indicating they were in immediate danger. Ladder felt a vibration as a generator kicked in, powering the servers and monitors. Penny had helped him test the back-up equipment and they'd checked it had enough diesel for their possible needs. However, it wasn't connected to either lights or internal cameras. He switched off all except the two closer monitors, which left the room dimly lit. He grabbed his backpack and checked for his pistol; it was an old—very old—Luger, and he enjoyed using it for target shooting whenever he visited a range. It had an eight-shot magazine and fired 9mm rounds. His elderly uncle had given it to him when he had turned twenty-one, three years ago. It was supposed to be a WW II souvenir. He placed it next to his keyboard.

Ladder looked in Linda's direction; her face was softly illuminated by the light from the monitors. She was biting her bottom lip and had sat lower in her chair. He interpreted her body language to mean the 145th wasn't about to ride to their rescue; they'd been waylaid somehow, somewhere. He checked the exterior cameras; he hadn't realized at least three were being fed power by the generator. One camera showed two men standing outside the front lobby. A second camera displayed another two men in the rear lane near the general delivery door. Their positioning implied there were other men, out of scope of the cameras. Unfortunately, the cameras didn't move. The third camera was disabled before he could assess its images. Destruction of the other two followed immediately.

Penny said, "Russians."

Linda straightened in her chair, looked up at the blank monitors, and said, "I suggest we prepare for enemy infiltration. Soon. I assume Penny's two friends—Sergey Govorov and Petr Zhukov—with some of their team—are inside the building."

"Can we call for help?" Ladder wondered aloud.

"Sergeant Fielder's a lost cause. The Russians will be done and gone by the time police respond."

Ladder tried to soften Linda's pessimism. "We can fight them?"

"I told you. We'll be outnumbered and out-gunned," Linda snapped

"We could be lucky?" Ladder was trying.

Linda sighed. Her voice was slightly above a hoarse whisper. "Look, Ladder. We're going to be attacked by at least two Russians. I can't see any of us surviving the resulting firefight. I don't think they'd want to keep us alive. They probably don't know about Penny—she might escape, although I don't see how. You're a junior member of our organization; you're toast. I'm well and truly Cerberus; however, they won't want to keep me around—I'd be too much trouble. I've no leverage for them and they can rebuild my research team without much of a struggle."

Ladder was shocked at Linda's pessimism; it was as though she'd already surrendered. He couldn't think of a suitable response. He tried to appear calm as he sipped the coffee Penny had delivered. His other hand tightly gripped the Luger, imprinting the pistol's handle design on his palm. He raised the mug in a belated thank you to Penny. She nodded. He thought she'd become very quiet. Perhaps it was her way of coping with the apprehension they all felt. No. He had to be honest. It was fear.

He had nothing to do except wait.

Doors, somewhere between their office and the stairwell, crashed as they were forced open. It was a gradual heralding of the approach of possible death. He shuddered.

Pistol shots and an automatic weapon response punctuated by shouts, in Russian and English, filled the air.

"That's Fielder's voice," Linda said. Her voice contained a touch of optimism.

The Russian comments following a second burst of automatic weapons fire indicated the sergeant's attempt at a rescue had failed.

"The Russians lost men." Penny said.

"We lost Fielder. I recognized his voice." Another door was beaten down. "The Russians are coming." Linda held her weapon, aimed generally at the door into the office.

Ladder looked around. Penny was missing. Linda had moved off to one side of the room and was laying on the ground, apparently to present a low profile. He decided to shift to the other side, near the filing cabinets, and took up a prone position, the Luger aimed at the doorway. He was about to comment when someone smashed into their door. While it was locked, it was unlikely to survive a vigorous attempt to beat it down. Two more blows were enough. Someone pushed the shattered door and it fell into the office. Another someone had a flashlight and flicked its beam around the room.

Ladder held his breath.

An intruder jumped through the doorway firing short bursts into the room, shattering monitors and computers. Linda fired back. A single shot. The Russian—at least Ladder assumed he was Russian—collapsed to the floor, moaning. His weapon clattered as it fell away from his body. While Ladder didn't understand Russian, he assumed the shouts from outside were intended for the now dead intruder. At least Ladder hoped he was dead. The voices outside stopped.

Ladder was tempted to fire at the intruder's body, in case it still held life. The thought quickly disappeared when further bursts of automatic weapon fire shattered the silence. This time the attacker didn't enter the room; instead, he held the weapon around the side of the door and fired. There was enough light from whoever was holding the flashlight to outline the weapon and part of an arm. Ladder, to his surprise his nerves were steady, trusted to his training with the Luger, aimed and fired. The shooter yelled and dropped his weapon. There was another burst of Russian shouting. Ladder grinned to himself. His ears were ringing, and he shook his head. The remedy was unsuccessful. He had been almost deafened by the weapon fire in the enclosed office space.

He heard movement from Linda and barely understood her whisper. "Ladder, I'm hit. Take care." She coughed and fell silent.

Ladder weighed his Luger and cursed softly. Linda, he assumed, was dead. He had no idea of where Penny was. Somehow, she had disappeared. Perhaps—. He wondered at his thought of heroic effort. Him, a hero. In a way it could be a form of redemption. He needed forgiveness, something which he knew couldn't be achieved. He listened to the voices. There were, he thought, two or three people in the area just outside the office door.

His decision made, he leapt to his feet and, Luger at the ready, charged through the doorway, targeting and firing at each Russian. Two men fell to floor. The third one returned fire and Ladder fired two more shots at the man, not knowing if his bullets struck home. Blackness and pain melded together and forced him to drop to his knees. He released the Luger as he fell. He did not feel his face hit the floor. Nor did he realize Penny was behind him, a strange weapon in her hand.

Penny fired at the surviving Russian. Surviving might be an overstatement; at least, he was standing, with blood running from a bullet crease along the side of his head. She raised her weapon. The two frangible rounds, although small caliber, were enough. A head shot, twice, between the eyes. The Russian screamed and he dropped to the floor. Silence followed; Penny relaxed. The man was dead.

She checked the other Russians. She recognized Sergey Govorov and Petr Zhukov; Ladder's foolhardy stunt had won some benefits. Each man had been shot twice. Zhukov—the Poisoner—was still breathing. She stood on the man's wounded leg. He struggled, screamed, and tried to open his eyes. He was struggling for breath with blood flavoring each gasp. Penny suspected the second shot had penetrated his lungs.

"Petr. At last."

"Who—who are you?"

"Your nemesis. You murdered my sister. Bristol. Last December."

Zhukov groaned and more blood flowed. Penny debated. If she left him, he might survive. She raised the plastic pistol and fired again. The weapon completed its task as the bullet pierced his eye and fragmented into the Russian's brain. She dropped the makeshift pistol. There were other weapons if she needed them. She checked. The man was dead.

A soft groan startled her. Ladder. She'd almost forgotten.

"Ladder." Penny stood over him, his Luger in her hand. Ladder moaned. He had a chest wound, a bullet through his shoulder, and a furrow across his temple. She thought, based on the blood flow, he also had been shot in his leg. He'd probably survive. She searched for the Glock and found it a foot or so from Linda's outstretched hand. She left the Luger with Linda's body.

Penny returned to Ladder and knelt down; the small handgun held carelessly. She smoothed Ladder's hair back from his forehead.

"Ladder."

He opened his eyes.

"I want to know something. Do you remember Esmerelda Cortez? She lived in New York State. It was about two years ago."

Ladder struggled, as though willing his body to sit or stand. Penny leaned on his shoulder, pinning him to the ground. Ladder almost screamed with pain.

She continued, "Poor girl was raped and murdered. Very messy. No one has been charged with the crime."

"How did—"

"It's what I do. The perp—that was you?"

Ladder frowned. His eyes flicked away and back. His lips were closed as though to prevent words from escaping.

Penny reached over and pressed down on Ladder's chest wound. He moaned. She eased her weight off his chest.

"No, don't. I helped here—I shot the Russ—." He faded and again, when he opened his eyes, he attempted to sit. One of his hands struggled and reached to where his Luger had been.

Penny said, "Tell me the truth. You were there. At the party. You offered to drive her home because her boyfriend was too drunk. Instead, you took her to a desolate area—some kind of run down industrial area. You threatened her." Penny was ad libbing. She had points of reference and was constructing the details.

"No—no."

"The authorities have DNA. They can match it with yours." The body had been cleaned; however, the perpetrator had made mistakes. "You didn't clean up as well as you should have."

Ladder's face had grown paler. He was losing blood. He shook his head.

"You stole her stockings and garter belt. That's what you wore the following week to the fancy dress party. That's why everyone called you Ladder—you laddered them when you got dressed."

"Not—Ladder."

"The name stayed. You adopted it. Proud of your crime?"

"No—" Ladder was moaning.

Penny ignored the tears.

"Tell me. Did you rape and murder Esmerelda? Redemption, Ladder—confession is good for you when you're about to die." Penny was pressing all the buttons she could think of. Time was running out. Police could be here any minute.

Ladder was gasping for breath. "I'm going to die?"

"Yes. That chest wound requires immediate surgery. Answer me, damn it."

Ladder groaned. "Yes, it was me." In between gasps he added, "I'm sorry, I didn't mean to do it." Another gasp. "She struggled and hit her head."

He faded out of consciousness and back again. "I'm so sorry."

Penny stood. She lifted the Glock and fired. Ladder stilled.

She messed with the weapons, wiping and adding fingerprints from the various bodies. When she finished, she headed to the barricade of filing cabinets and recovered her laptop and backpack. Her presence would not be obvious. Now, she thought, she needed to leave as quickly as possible.

She had to remember she was no longer Penny. Charlie—her real name, at least for now. Charlie, not Penny. Charlie Mercer. She'd washed the color out of her hair, scrubbed off the temporary tattoos, dumped the torn jeans and Doc Martins in convenient waste bins and now wore soft and comfortable designer travel clothes—a tailored jacket and pants for comfort, a cream blouse, and soft runners, expensive, major departures from her Penny persona. She joined a very short line at the entrance desk to the first class lounge. Her flight to Heathrow wasn't departing for at least an hour, and she was looking forward to relaxing before boarding. The person in front of her headed into the lounge and Charlie moved up to the desk and handed over her boarding pass and passport.

The lounge attendant returned her travel documents and said, "Oh, I have a note for you. There's a gentleman in the lounge who asked me to let you know he's here. He's in the first alcove on the left. A Mr. Thomas Robbins." She smiled.

Charlie smiled back, accepted her documents and headed into the lounge, cursing under her breath. She had a good idea who was waiting, and his name was not Robbins. She stopped for a moment and looked around the lounge, tempted to ignore the waiting Mr. Robbins. She hid her surprise when she recognized two CIA agents seated in separate locations. She looked over to the alcove—Robbins was also CIA. Very senior. And she was correct—his name wasn't Robbins.

Bracing herself she headed towards the alcove. Robbins stood and held out his hand.

"Charlie. It's a pleasure."

They shook hands.

He continued, "I'm Thomas Robbins. My friends call me Tom."

"You look more like someone who would be called Richard. I could even place a surname next to the first name," Charlie said.

Robbins partially hid a grin. "Please don't. This is my—ah—more commercial identity."

"You wanted to meet me?"

"Of course. I wanted to thank you for the Russians. To that extent, I persuaded Management to agree we'd pay you the reward for the Poisoner." He handed across his card. "Send me an email with banking details and I'll ensure your account is credited within the week."

Charlie stared at the CIA officer. "You what?"

"I'm serious. We were far behind you in tracking him down. I don't want to be in your debt. Nor does the Director. Besides, we may want your assistance in the future."

"Thank you. I'll provide the details." She tucked the card into her jacket pocket.

"You'll be pleased to hear the 145th rescued Maeve Donnelly. It took them a while to organize themselves."

Charlie nodded her head. "I checked."

There was silence for a long moment, broken by the senior CIA agent.

"I wonder if you'd satisfy my curiosity?"

Charlie shrugged. "Go ahead."

"Schöner was shot in the back. Your work?"

"She was unconscious, alive; well, until I made sure otherwise. She was a Russian plant. They arranged a substitute when the real Linda visited Russia during her sabbatical before commencing her university studies. There must have been some very slick planning to get it all together. As far as I know, they killed that Linda. The substitute Linda turned against her Russian masters, as far as I can tell, and was supporting a Chinese group. Of course, that was a disaster. The Chinese halted their genetic program when it began to produce some extreme genetic variations. I think Mark Midway altered a large number of Cerberus research papers, copies of which ended up in China. The Chinese team couldn't determine what was going wrong."

"Ah. Good to know. Did Schmidt know about Schöner?"

"He had suspicions. He also told me he'd picked up a rumor the Russians were closing in on Cerberus although he hadn't realized they intended a full takeover. He hired me to do—things."

"Hmm. You certainly did—things. And Ladder?"

"Oh, he was a nice enough lad; however, I sensed something awry in his life story and I decided to backtrack. There was a surprising coincidence—he was in the same place and time as a young woman who was raped and killed. No one had been caught for the crime. I questioned him after he was shot. He confessed. The local police in Massachusetts should be able to match DNA." Charlie didn't mention Ladder had been shot more than once and she'd fired the last shot.

"They'll be appreciative."

"Is that all?"

"There is one thing."

"Yes?"

"While I admire your abilities, neither I nor my director wish to ever see you back in the US."

He paused.

Charlie frowned.

"Unless, of course, we invite you." Robbins stood and offered his hand. "Charlie, it's been a pleasure. Enjoy your flight."

They shook hands.

"Thank you. By the way—your man who's sitting against the wall?"

"Yes?"

"He's an inserted Russian agent. He arrived in the US eight years ago. His name is Viktor Repnin. Enjoy." Charlie stood, nodded her head in farewell to Robbins and turned away. She wanted to find a quieter corner.

Robbins, after a moment of shocked silence, signaled his two agents to follow him and headed out of the lounge.

He didn't look back.

ABOUT THE AUTHOR

John Hindmarsh enlisted in the Royal Navy and saw action on the Bellerophon. He was recognized by Nelson when John was promoted to lieutenant in 1803. He was the first governor of South Australia, appointed in 1836. Note: we have reasons to doubt his veracity—well, he does write creative fiction.

In 2014 John published the first book of his thriller series recounting the adventures of Mark Midway. Mark was genetically engineered, and his driving ambition is to discover his true parents. Murder and mayhem follow Mark throughout the four-book series aptly and creatively titled Mark One, Mark Two, Mark Three, and Mark Four. You can follow John on Amazon: https://www.amazon.com/John-Hindmarsh/e/B005309ASK.

John has written fourteen books and promises there are more to come. To keep up, visit his website: https://JohnHindmarsh.com/

John and his wife Cathy moved to Southern California in 2019. John has lived in ten countries—it's time he settled down.

GETTING THE WIND

STEPHEN COUCH

A man delivering meals to shut-ins finds himself, and his elderly client, caught in a drug war.

1

Kurtis hoped the cops wouldn't come. He was in the sweet spot between monthly drug tests, and had decided to have a little toke while driving his delivery route today.

But then, why wouldn't they come? There was every chance the old guy inside the condo was dead.

So Kurtis leaned against his beat-up car, smoking a regular cigarette now, and waited for help to arrive even as the rest of the food from Senior Meals sat in his back seat, cooling and undelivered. The wind wouldn't pick up no matter how hard he wished, and even he could smell how much he reeked of pot.

He wondered if he should go back to Orson's door and knock one more time -- just one more, and maybe that would be all it took. Orson would open the door, greet him with his usual oversized-dentures smile, and Kurtis could call Senior Meals again and let them know it was a false alarm.

Everything was fine. No need for paramedics. Definitely no need for cops.

Kurtis finished his cigarette, ground it out against the sole of his boot, and lit another one.

Man...why did it have to be Orson? When Kurtis started his community service at Senior Meals, they'd warned him about this. You deal with the elderly, you deal with death. Sooner or later, you would go to drop off someone's daily bread, and find they had passed away.

And now, it seemed to have happened to the coolest old dude Kurtis knew. He still remembered the first time he entered Orson's condo and saw a bong by the leather recliner, wisps of smoke still rising from it. Orson noticed Kurtis noticing it, and tipped him a wink.

"Glaucoma," he laughed.

Since then, Kurtis always stayed a little bit longer, visited a bit more in-depth, with Orson. Kurtis didn't have many friends -- doing data-processing gigs didn't put him in contact with people much. His weed dealer wasn't a hang-out kind of guy; neither was the dealer's security, a gym bro built like a silverback with a spiderweb tattoo over half his face.

His dealer's pad was, suffice to say, a get-in-get-out kind of place.

A siren in the distance made Kurtis cringe, then sniff his clothes with a grimace. He tried to think positive: ambulance, not police.

Not that either option was very positive for Orso --

-- noise and motion drew his attention to the other side of the small parking lot. Orson's front door swung open, and Kurtis felt a burst of happiness. He was alive!

Alive...and being manhandled by two big, burly guys. They frog-marched Orson towards a waiting SUV, and instinct -- or paranoia -- made Kurtis duck down behind his car as they got close.

Even from a distance, he saw the black tape over the old man's mouth.

Even from a distance, he saw the face of one of the kidnappers, and the spiderweb tattoo on it.

The SUV's doors thudded shut, and it pulled out of the parking lot seconds later. Kurtis straightened from his crouch, knees popping, just in time to see them turn into traffic, heading west. Kurtis's eye connected with an incongruous hot-pink bumper sticker on the SUV, then the big vehicle was out of sight.

He had nothing on his side whenever the cops would show. No Orson, no kidnappers, no SUV, nada. Just his word, his public urination charge from two weeks ago, and the stench of pot in his clothes and car.

They'd run him in for filing a false report and possession without a medical-marijuana card...then where would Orson be?

Kurtis slumped against his car and groaned. The kidnappers had gotten further and further away while he'd been here with a thumb up his butt. No way of finding them. He couldn't flee the scene -- the police would just track him down. He'd let his friend down, and now --

-- Kurtis blinked.

Where would Orson be? he'd asked himself.

The answer was obvious.

Kurtis stumbled, running around to get in his car. The worn-out engine caught on the third crank, and he was out of the condo parking and turning west, fired up and ready to give chase.

He was so intent on his goal, he didn't even see the pickup as he made his turn. But he definitely felt it as it smashed into his rear bumper.

Kurtis cussed a streak as his car swung a full ninety, winding up perpendicular to traffic, cars and motorcycles and soccer-mom vans all skidding to a halt as he blocked both lanes. He could hear more crunches of metal and plastic as the pile-up grew.

Kurtis saw the woman who'd hit him get out of her fancy pickup -- power suit, mussed hair, and a small trickle of blood oozing from her nose. She looked at the dented front of her truck, steam rising from its grill, then stalked towards him, jabbing viciously at her smart phone.

The truck's license plate read MS LAWYR.

He cranked the ignition, but the car wasn't cooperating. Traffic on the other side of the street had slowed down, with plenty of rubber-neckers getting a good look at him and his car. Drivers on his side of the road were getting out of their vehicles, shouting and pointing.

And 'Ms. Lawyr' was almost to his window.

"Oh, come on, come on!" he yelled at his car, turning the key again and again, expecting to hear the tell-tale sound of a flooded engine at any moment.

A rap at his window from a fist with expensively-manicured nails. "Hey, asshole!"

He glanced up, panicked to see all those people slowing down to gawk, all of them on their phones, doing their duty as upright citizens.

Just like Kurtis was trying to do, wanting to help an old man who'd never hurt anybody.

Over the shouts and honks and the pounding of fight-or-flight in his temples, he almost didn't hear the car start. But he felt that familiar rumbling spread up through the floorboards to his seat, and he pumped the air with his free hand even as the woman at his door gave a yell of protest.

Kurtis turned the car back west with a frantic, spinning grip, stomping the gas pedal, the wheels bouncing as they mounted then dismounted the thin concrete strip in the middle of the street. He saw a few flashes from the opposite lanes as people snapped pictures with their phones, and heard hollered threats from the woman, but he was free and clear now, roaring down the street, blasting through the next two lights as they turned yellow.

He glanced back as he made his getaway, and saw alarming clouds of black smoke spilling out in his wake.

He thought the car might die any second as he made the turn to head to the lower west side, following the familiar route to his dealer's house.

The car might die? Hell...he might die.

Far away from the accident, Kurtis took stock.

It was obvious where the kidnappers were going. One of them was his dealer's bodyguard. Where else could they be headed?

The problem now was what he'd do once he got there.

Sheepskin, his weed guy, was not the most stable person. And if he was abducting old folks out of their homes, it seemed he was further gone than Kurtis had imagined.

So what were his options? Go in, guns blazing? That required Kurtis to own a gun, which didn't really mesh with the lazy pothead lifestyle. Maybe if he'd taken up coke or meth, he'd be armed for bear, but that wasn't the case.

He glanced down at the debris in his passenger seat. Offer them a half-eaten stick of jerky in exchange for Orson? Smack them on the nose with a rolled-up Legion of Super-Heroes comic?

His phone buzzed in his jacket pocket, and he checked it. Senior Meals. With a pained sigh, he ignored the call. The meal trays in his back seat had to be cold and on their way to spoilage by this point.

The car hit a bump and gave a shimmy that took a couple of blocks to smooth out. He'd given up on looking in the rear-view mirror: the smoke hadn't abated.

He just needed to get there, period. He'd figure out what to do if he could just get his junkheap within walking distance.

He rounded the corner into Sheepskin's neighborhood: bars on every house's windows and BEWARE OF DOG signs on every fence. Kurtis felt himself more aware than ever of the roughness of his surroundings. The threat to Orson, and the imminent demise of his getaway vehicle, left him vulnerable in a way he hadn't imagined he could be.

And at the end of the street, he saw something that made him feel downright helpless.

A half-dozen cars and trucks sat outside Sheepskin's place, and a steady stream of guys hustled back and forth from house to vehicles.

Some of them carried long, heavy duffle bags. Some of them carried armloads of guns without the need for baggage.

Kurtis pulled over two blocks away, killed the ignition, and watched the heavily-armed hive of activity, his guts churning. Was Orson in the middle of this chaos? Had they brought him here, killed him, and were cleaning out the house to relocate?

He couldn't see the SUV he was looking for among the collection of vehicles, and a little ember of renewed hope sparked inside him. Maybe they hadn't brought him here after all. Maybe this was something unrelated.

Maybe they were taking a day trip to Afghanistan.

He looked down at the pitiful, weaponless contents of his passenger seat, and considered what might happen if he just blithely walked up to the front door and knocked, strolling past all the gun-toting flunkies without a care.

No. Bartering the beef jerky was a better strategy than that.

Activity slowed, with some guys hanging around the van talking and gesturing, while others had gone back inside and stayed there.

Kurtis closed his eyes and scratched at an eyebrow. The mellowness of his earlier smoke-out had been burned away by the acid of adrenaline, and he felt twitchy and at odds with himself. He had to do something, right? The cops were looking for him, guaranteed, either from the ambulance call at Orson's, or the car crash, or his community service violation from not reporting back to Senior Meals.

He had to see this through and find his friend. He thought about poor old Orson, scared and at the mercy of these guys. (Or dead, said a voice in his head he tried to ignore).

No more visits. No more magic tricks (Kurtis still couldn't figure out how Orson had made that ping-pong ball disappear). No more funny voices (Orson could imitate just about any cartoon character, and claimed to have worked for Hanna-Barbera back in the day). No more chats about good strains of weed, no more games of checkers after Kurtis had finished his deliveries, no more...

If Orson was still around, Kurtis had to track him down. If he wasn't still around, Kurtis had to --

A knock at his window, and Kurtis jolted, opening his eyes.

Sheepskin stood at the passenger window, grinning.

"Man, did you pick a bad time to stop by!"

The air in the house hung heavy with cigarette smoke, the smell of menthols and Swishers everywhere. Kurtis sat on the same red-leather love seat he usually perched on when picking up a baggie from Sheepskin. The dealer sat opposite him in a fancy recliner, shouting at someone on the phone. Thugs stood around, picking at their nails, shifting duffels and boxes here and there, or staring at Kurtis with dead eyes. Even the throw pillows on the love seat seemed tense.

Sheepskin finished his phone call with a grunt. "Ain't that some shit." He shook his head then turned his attention to Kurtis. "...So what can I get you, my man? The usual?"

"Um, sure. Yes. Please."

Sheepskin looked at him, then around the room. "Don't worry about all this bullshit, Kurtis. We've just got some business to take care of." He snapped his fingers and one of the thugs stepped up. "Get this man a nickel of Jade Monkey," he ordered. and the guy silently left the room.

Kurtis stared at the far wall, where the dealer's twelve framed diplomas hung in a neat grid. He'd never taken the time to look at them to see where they were from.

"So how's things?" Sheepskin asked, as though he and his crew weren't gathering enough armament to start their own banana republic. "You still feeding the old folks?"

"Yeah, yeah, it's, um, it's good work. A good thing, y'know."

Sheepskin pursed his lips and nodded. "I've been meaning to ask you, how do you sign up for that shit? My gran, she's in a wheelchair and whatnot. Hard for her to feed herself sometimes, and --"

A muffled bang sounded from outside, and everyone stiffened. Kurtis felt an urge to fold in on himself.

"For God's sake," Sheepskin spat. He stood, waving a hand in Kurtis's vague direction. "Be right back." He pointed at a couple of the larger thugs, and the three of them headed outside, Sheepskin pulling a pistol out of the back of his waistband.

The other guys in the living room were fixated on what might be happening outside, and the dude who'd been sent to fetch the nickel bag hadn't returned. Kurtis wondered if he could slip away and search the place for Orson. He stood, but a couple of guys snapped eyes onto him, scowling. Kurtis made as if to stretch his arms, then sat back down. Everyone went back to ignoring him.

Things in the house were so still, Kurtis wondered if he concentrated, could he maybe hear Orson crying out from another room? He closed his eyes and tried to focus his hearing.

Something smacked him in the face and dropped to his lap. He looked down to see the little baggie of weed. The man who'd gotten it stood there like a monolith from Stonehenge.

"...Thanks," Kurtis said, his mouth dry. "Do, um, I pay you, or wait for...?"

The guy just stood there.

The front door swung open, and Sheepskin came back in, tucking away his pistol. "False alarm," he called out, and his crew got back to work. He strode back to his chair and plopped down, smiling at Kurtis with a bit more impatience. "All good, man? Up to your rigorous standards?" Sheepskin chuckled.

"Yeah, man, good as gold, thanks. Let me," and Kurtis fished out his wallet. He opened it to find zero cash. "Ohhh. Oh, shit."

"Man, come on," Sheepskin said. "I'm all about making a sale, but I got shit to do." He snapped his fingers at another thug, who stomped over and pulled out a smart phone with a little debit-card reader plugged in the top. Meekly, Kurtis swiped his bank card. The thug studied his phone's screen for a moment, then gave a thumbs-up to Sheepskin.

"You're good to go," said the dealer. "So go." Kurtis stood, feeling soreness in his thighs and back. He started to walk out, but turned back to Sheepskin with a sudden flash of inspiration.

"Hey, where's..." and he went blank for a second, realizing he didn't remember the man's name. Kurtis reached up a hand and mimed spiders crawling over half his face. "Is he okay?"

Sheepskin grunted. "That numbnuts? Who knows? I haven't seen him all day."

"Oh!" Kurtis said, then to cover his surprise, got out his wallet and retrieved a business card for Senior Meals. "For your grandma."

Sheepskin waved him away. "Give it to Leon. He's my admin. Now go on, Kurtis, get your ass on out of here."

Kurtis had no idea who Leon was, so he laid the card on a little table by the door as he walked out. Past the guys outside who were stepping up their activity again, past another house until he got to his car, his back tight in anticipation of a bullet that never came.

As he opened the driver's door, he saw something like a huge used condom hanging from the front of the steering wheel.

His car had finally realized it had been in a wreck and deployed its airbag.

Kurtis drove around the block and parked in front of another house, this one with a big crucifix hanging from the front door. He figured living in a neighborhood with a drug dealer had gotten people used to strange cars and too cowed to call the police about it. The thought gave him a little pang; that he was exploiting peoples' fear to facilitate his stakeout.

Following Sheepskin and company to whatever this 'business' of theirs was felt like the right next step. Orson was with web-face, web-face was connected to the drug dealer, so wherever Sheepskin went, the lambs were sure to go. Or something along those lines. What it amounted to was, Kurtis was otherwise out of clues and desperate.

He pondered on the whole situation. All this because he'd tried to do the right thing and walk home from the bar one night instead of driving while buzzed, only to get caught short halfway home by an overflowing bladder.

All this because he desperately had to pee. No community service, no Senior Meals, no Orson...

From where he sat, he could see, through a catty-corner gap in some fences, one of the pickups in front of Sheepskin's crib. He kept an eye on it, ready to move when it did.

Ready to continue letting dumb luck be his guide, since it had worked out for him so far. He considered that he should have asked Sheepskin if they'd had a spare gun for sale, and almost laughed.

In an eyeblink, the truck he was watching pulled away from the curb. Kurtis gave a ten-count, then started the car and headed off after them.

Time for a day trip to Afghanistan.

The car had stopped puking black smoke, but the shimmy came back, twice as bad as before. Kurtis clenched his teeth against the car's vibration.

The caravan of a half-dozen vehicles meandered through the neighborhood like a funeral procession for someone not particularly well-liked, onto and north along a major street. Kurtis hung back, accelerating if a light threatened to turn red on him, but otherwise keeping his distance. The cars were easy to keep track of, and not aware of his presence...he hoped.

They passed a burned out shopping center that jogged Kurtis's memory. Rumor had it a pot dispensary was supposed to open there, but the place had burned down before it opened. Someone must have been smoking on the job, he imagined.

It was a shame, because how nice would it have been to go to a clean, friendly, well-lit store to buy weed? True, he'd have to find some way to finagle a medical-necessity card, but that sounded like the easiest thing in the world compared to buying his weed from a place perennially filled with piss-eyed, trigger-happy gangbangers.

The chain of vehicles took the on-ramp to the highway. As they drove along, Kurtis got more and more confused. The only things in the direction they headed were richer and ritzier neighborhoods. Fancy condo towers rose in the distance, far nicer than the mid-scale place where Orson lived. Past the big, new football stadium Kurtis's taxes would be funding for the rest of his life, past the huge open-air mall. When Sheepskin's group exited, they did so into a section of town that screamed 'old money.'

Even more than in his dealer's part of town, Kurtis felt self-conscious here, what with his bashed-up car and thrift-store clothes. He wondered if he should get his annual gross income tattooed on his forehead to complete the ensemble.

They passed a couple of cop cars here and there, Kurtis flinching every time. Was there a BOLO out for him? How many calls had the cops gotten? How many smart phone pics of him and his car had been emailed to the police by citizens helpfully wanting to play Big Brother?

Considering how screwed he'd be when all this was over, he at least wanted a living, breathing Orson to come out of the situation.

Past the big Methodist university, past another huge collection of shops that looked more like an amusement park than a mall. Eye-watering property taxes as far as one could see. At last, the lead vehicle turned into a large, circular drive, the others lining up behind it as it stopped at a call box mounted on a shiny steel post in front of an ornate sliding gate. Kurtis had no choice but to get in line behind them, and he tried to duck behind his steering wheel in case someone in the rear-most car was looking back. But they had to notice him: six shiny, well-maintained cars and trucks, and bringing up the rear, a beater that looked like a peeled-off scab. One of these things was not like the others.

He heard a loud beep from ahead, and saw the community gate trundle open. The cars filed through, and he, giving up on the pretense of stealthy pursuit, followed along. When they turned right, he went left, though, trying find somewhere he could park unnoticed. Nothing presented itself until, at the far end of the sreet, sat what looked like a gardener's shed, with a pickup outside whose bed overflowed with sacks of mulch. Kurtis pulled up beside it and got out, shielding his eyes against the sun as he watched Sheepskin's crew go all the way to the other end of the street to one of the biggest houses in the community.

He set out at a jog, until a cough settled into his lungs after a block. Kurtis walked the rest of the way, wondering when he could expect a rent-a-cop golf cart to whiz up and detain him.

"Orson, dude," he whispered as he closed in on the McMansion ahead, "please be there. Please be all right."

He stopped short, a half-block away, as he saw most of Sheepskin's men loitering outside, all leaning against their vehicles, looking menacing. None had guns out yet, but he could feel that need for action, for explosion, for blood, radiating off of the whole scene. At the front door stood more brick-wall types, arms crossed, looking like bouncers with Master's degrees in Advanced Homicide.

Kurtis crouched and mimed tying a shoe as he continued checking out the front of the huge house. He spotted the SUV with its hot-pink bumper sticker, and felt a thrill of success. He was at the right place.

If only there were some way to get in alive.

Kurtis stood back up and cast his eyes fruitlessly up and down the street. Perfectly trimmed lawns and shrubs, immaculate homes, expensive vehicles sitting idle in front of each one. These were the houses of doctors, politicians, investment bankers, and...well, whatever Sheepskin's buddy at the end of the lane did. Doubtful it was anything good, not with that kind of security.

He looked the other way, back to where he'd left his car, and the realization struck him like a pool cue jabbed between his eyes.

The house he needed to get into was locked down tight. But there was a building here in the development with considerably less security.

Maybe one held the means to solve the other.

No one noticed him as he walked back up the street wearing baggy coveralls, giving the occasional topiary or rosebush a squirt from the metal wand he held. The tank of chemicals on his back sloshed as he moved, and he wasn't certain if he dosed out weed killer or insecticide to the plants as he strolled along. The canister in the gardener's shed hadn't been labeled. The coveralls had -- their sewn-on name patch read ESTACADO, and Kurtis hoped that person didn't show up for work and raise an alarm on finding their work outfit had been swiped.

He reached up and pulled down the brim of the baseball cap he'd likewise stolen, shading his eyes. Not much further to go before he'd find out if his plan was a winner or not.

He crossed the curb and stepped onto the property where Orson was being held. Some of the thugs looked him over, and he tipped them a brisk wave as he gave a hedgerow a healthy series of sprays. A few feet more, and he was out of sight of the house's front and making his way to the rear, keeping up the pretense. Kurtis idly wondered if, tomorrow, the community would wake to an epidemic of brown, withered hedges and greenery. Hopefully Mr. Estacado wouldn't get the blame.

At the back of the house, no guards stood. There was a set of double patio doors and, as he watched, a young red-headed woman in a frilly maid outfit walked outside and emptied a litter box into a nearby flower bed, dust from the dumped litter rising in a billowing cloud. Kurtis quickly raised his wand from where he'd been spritzing a small lemon tree and waved at the maid.

"Hey," he said, "Somebody called the exterminator?"

She looked at him and seemed satisfied with his appearance. "Wasn't me, but go on in," she said, and gestured to the open patio doors. "But, uh, don't do the upstairs right now, okay? Just stick to the ground floor."

Kurtis thanked her and entered the house, feeling a chill from the roaring central air. He looked around a home so spotless he couldn't imagine a single bug ever living there. Ahead was a large hallway that opened up on a wide foyer, from which rose two curving staircases.

No one guarded the stairways, and the maid was still outside tending to something, so up the steps Kurtis went. At the top, he reached a corridor with a partial balcony overlooking the grand foyer below. At each end of the hallway stood doors, but only the one to the left had guards posted.

Kurtis took a deep breath and went to say hi to the two men.

He gave a baseboard here and there a spray as he approached the guards, ten feet, eight, seven... "Hey," he said, holding up his empty hand. "Exterminator. Mind if I...?"

"Come back later," said the shorter of the guards. His face was impassive, his eyes unreadable behind sunglasses.

"I, well, okay, but we..." Kurtis's wheels spun for a moment. "We had a report of Afghanistan Biting Roaches. I really should get in there and give it a once-over. They spread disease, y'know."

"Are you deaf?" asked the taller guard. "Come back later." Both guards shifted their crossed arms so that one hand reached under a lapel.

Kurtis nodded and said, "Okay." Neither guard seemed to notice how much weight, how much fatalism, was in that one word.

Kurtis brought the wand up and hosed down both their faces.

The canister may not have been labeled with what product it contained, but there was a big, bright sticker warning you not to get whatever it was in your eyes or mouth.

Both guards dropped to their knees with minimal noise, silently retching and clawing at their faces, rolling over and going into shivering, weeping fetal positions.

Kurtis looked away, sickened. He stepped over them, avoiding a palsied hand that sought to grab his ankle, and opened the door.

Men crowded the room, standing in clumps on opposite sides. Some he recognized from Sheepskin's place. The dealer himself turned from where he sat, on the other side of a huge, expensive desk from another man: tanned, white-haired, and dressed in a way that clearly marked him as the man of the house. Beside him stood web-face, who looked up from where he'd been glaring at Sheepskin.

And off to one side, tied to a chair, sat Orson, his mouth gaped in astonishment.

"Exterminator?" Kurtis said, and he could see the eyes of everyone in the room slip past him to take in the two guards squirming in agony outside the door.

"Kurtis?" Orson and Sheepskin asked as one.

And also as one, every thug in the room pulled their guns and pointed them at Kurtis.

After they'd secured him to his own chair, Kurtis took in the room fully. As well as he could, that is: the rest of the men from outside and elsewhere in the house had all been brought inside, and the meeting room was standing room only.

The tan, rich guy stalked the room, everyone making way wherever he walked. Sheepskin sat, frowning. And Orson looked like he wanted to talk to Kurtis if only a dozen killers weren't standing nearby.

A thug walked into the room, wiping wet hands on his pants. "How are the Deodato boys?" the tan guy asked him.

"A lot better, Mr. Burr. We called Poison Control. Turns out we had to wash their faces with a mixture of milk, lemon juice, baking so--"

"I asked how they were, not for your grandma's cookie recipe," the tan guy shot back. He turned to survey the room. "What," he said, "the shit is going on, Sheepy? I thought we had a gentleman's agreement. You take care of the ass of this town, and I run the heart."

"That's how it is, Mr. Burr," Sheepskin began, but Burr cut him off.

"So why all this?" he shouted. "I get a call from my guy," and he pointed at web-face, "that you're thinking of encroaching on my territory. Then I get word from you that this fossil," and he pointed at Orson, "is the one trying to move in on me. But after that you," and finally he pointed at Sheepskin, "bring your army of buttplugs over, armed like they just came from the gun show."

Kurtis turned to Orson, eyebrows raised. His best guess had been Orson was being called to the carpet for not paying a weed debt to Sheepskin. But he was a player in the local trade?

Orson met his gaze after making sure no one was looking, and shook his head, which only left Kurtis more confused.

Sheepskin protested. "Mr. Burr, I don't even know this old fart. And I did not call you about him."

Likewise, web-face: "I didn't call you either, sir. Sheepskin is still staying in his territory, like I always report to you."

"You fucking Judas," Sheepskin said to his supposed bodyguard. "What did he offer you to spy on me?"

"He promised me he wouldn't sit around all day bragging about his goddamn diplomas," said web-face. "By the way, bitch, you know online college doesn't really count, right?"

"Fuck you, you G.E.D.-having motherf --"

"Enough!" Burr roared. He spun to stare at Kurtis, so angry he could barely get the words out. "And -- and -- and who is this dipshit? Does he work for you, or the old guy, or...?"

Sheepskin looked at Kurtis with hard eyes. "I've never seen him in my life."

"You said his name when he came in," Burr said, teeth clenched. "How many more lies you got in you, Sheepskin?" He reached into his jacket and pulled out a pistol. "If he's not your guy, then you won't mind if I do this." He cocked the gun and pressed it to Kurtis's forehead.

Kurtis squeezed his eyes shut, and had the most meaningless last thought he could conceive of: he remembered that web-face's real name was Antoine.

"Mr. Burr," Orson said in the overwhelming silence, "I believe I can clear all this up."

The cold ring of the muzzle stayed against Kurtis's head a moment longer, then went away. He opened his eyes to see Burr had trained the gun on Orson instead. Kurtis struggled against his bonds, the wooden chair rocking.

"Talk, gramps," Burr ordered.

Orson straightened up as well as his restraints allowed. "My name is Philip Woodhead. I'm an agent with the DEA, investigating you and," he nodded at Sheepskin, "Mr. Skinner here."

Kurtis reeled. None of this made any sense. And the weirdest thing was, it wasn't even Orson's real voice. It was one of the voices he did when he was doing his party-trick imitations; a character from some old TV show called "Dragnet," or some such.

"I'll get to the point," Orson said. "We're willing to cut you a deal. We want Mr. Skinner's supplier, and can offer you immunity in exchange for that info." Sheepskin's eyes grew wide at this, and some of his men tensed, hands drifting ever so slightly in the direction of their holsters.

"Or," Orson said, "we can offer you the same, Mr. Skinner. No charges in exchange for flipping on Burr." At that, Burr's men shifted positions, keeping their eyes on Sheepskin's guys.

Burr looked at Antoine, Sheepskin, and finally back to Orson, never dropping his arm. "Or," Burr said, "we can kill you and...whoever the hell this other guy is, take you to one of the funeral parlors I own, and wipe out every trace of you in the crematorium." He shook his head. "You're about ten years past mandatory retirement, gramps. No way you work for anybody except as a greeter at the department store." He walked over to Sheepskin and pointed the gun at him. The tension of the two opposing groups of thugs grew, bouncing back and forth between them like a feedback loop.

"Last chance, Sheepskin," Burr said. "You lie and tell me this guy is competition; he lies and tells me he's DEA; you say you don't know the exterminator, but you clearly do...and the most confusing thing is you're too stupid to hatch any kind of plan because you don't even know your number one guy is in my pocket. So tell me the real story, and tell me now."

Kurtis turned to look at Orson as he heard the old man take a deep breath. Then, with a bellowing voice not his own, but every bit a perfect imitation of Antoine, Orson shouted, "Fuck you, Burr, I quit!"

And as Burr jerked his head up to look at Antoine, Orson switched voices again, flawlessly duplicating Burr. "Gun! Motherfucker's got a g--"

Asking who fired the first shot was academic. The ultimate point was, once one person fired, everyone fired.

Kurtis jerked to the side, tipping his chair over so it struck and tipped over Orson's as well. The two went down below the level of the hailstorm of bullets. Kurtis screwed his eyes shut and prayed his heart out as deafening bangs and roars flooded the room, overwhelming the attendant screams of pain and death.

It took only seconds. The ringing in Kurtis's ears, and his fear of opening his eyes again, took a bit longer to go away.

"Hold still," Orson said, as he undid Kurtis's ropes. "Took me a minute to get loose. Luckily, that crappy chair busted up when you pushed me over."

Kurtis looked around the room from his sideways angle, the stink of gunpowder and blood filing his nose. The room was heaped with dead bodies; it looked as though he and Orson would be the only ones walking out.

"Up you get," Orson said, and helped Kurtis to his shaky feet. "We need to get out of here. You have your car?"

"I can't," Kurtis said. He felt like he was going to puke. "I...they're looking for me."

"Who?"

"The cops, because..." and it spilled out in messy chunks of info: seeing Orson getting kidnapped and trying to rescue him, and the all the complications in between.

"I see," Orson said. "Well, we should wait for the police, then. Better now than later."

Kurtis leaned against him. "Can't you just call the DEA?"

Orson looked at him for a second, eyebrows raised, then laughed. "Oh, Kurtis...you didn't actually believe any of that, did you?"

As they left the room, Kurtis noticed a bullet hole in the wall right beside where they'd leaned his tank of chemicals, right next to the side of the tank with another safety decal: FLAMMABLE. DO NOT PUNCTURE.

He felt like puking again.

Outside, they sat on the steps and counted the minutes before the cops arrived. Nearby, the redhead and two other maids consoled each other.

"You arranged all this," Kurtis said. "Why?"

"It was for my granddaughter," Orson said. "She was going to open up a pot dispensary here in town, but one of these lowlifes burned it down before she could even get started. Cost her entire life savings." He shook his head. "I thought I'd turn them against each other. It took a while, getting names and contacts, but in the end it was simple. They all use burner phones, you know, so no one knew if it was a real or imitation person calling them. But I knew there was no way I could get out alive. So I set her up as the beneficiary of my life insurance and will. That way, she could pursue her dream after..." He teared up, but waved away Kurtis, fishing a tissue from his pocket.

"You saved me," Orson said after blowing his nose. "You gave me a chance to see her succeed. I'll give her money from my investments. And now, she has a fair shot at making her dream work." He glanced over at Kurtis. "You don't look very happy to be alive, son."

Kurtis stared at the perfectly cut lawn. "The cops are gonna skin me alive. That lady lawyer I ran into? She's gonna sue me to pieces."

"Ridiculous," Orson said. "Your entire part of the story is true. You saw me getting abducted, and came to my rescue. You may get in a little trouble, but not much once I tell my side of the story."

Kurtis boggled. "You're going to tell them what happened?"

"Of course," Orson said, and Kurtis could see that slight change in his expression that meant he was about to put on a performance. Orson's eyes glistened with fresh tears. "I was trying to get some of that marijuana to help with my glaucoma, and these vicious gangsters said I owed them when I know I paid them, and they came and kidnapped me, and if not for that brave boy that delivers my meals, I would have..." Orson snapped out of his weepy reverie and flashed Kurtis a grin of big dentures. "Or something along those lines."

Kurtis wanted to laugh, but kept thinking back to what lay in that meeting room upstairs. He settled for giving Orson a pat on the back. "Thanks, dude."

"You're more than welcome. Although I do wish we had time to give you a shower before the police get here. " Orson wrinkled his nose. "Frankly, you reek of pot."

ABOUT THE AUTHOR

Stephen Couch is a computer programmer, a karaoke fiend, and a lifelong Texan. His short fiction has appeared in such venues as Cemetery Dance, The Best of Talebones, and Edgar Allan Poe's Snifter of Terror.

https://stephencouch.wordpress.com

STRAIGHT FLIGHT

ARLEIGH JACOBS

When a girl is kidnapped, Colt has one path: Get her back.

1

Talia "Colt" Levin counted herself amongst the millions of Americans who didn't like flying. Not that she thought air travel was unsafe. No, she just preferred to do the flying herself. Economy class had more elbow room than her Super Hornet, but the view was restricted, and if anything went wrong, she was helpless. Justin called it control issues. She called it playing to her strengths. She pulled a book out of her bag, prepared to spend the flight with the memoir of Britain's first female fast-jet pilot. Halfway through the book, and Colt had never related to anyone so much.

A man and a little girl pressed up against her row. Wearing jeans, a black T-shirt and a brown leather jacket, he was a direct contrast to the dainty fairy princess with him. He nudged the girl into the center seat, then ignored her as he settled in, plugging in his earphones and closing his eyes.

Colt did her best to tune them out, but the little girl leaned on the arm between them, distancing herself from the man. Colt downgraded him from indulgent dad to estranged father who didn't know how to interact with his daughter. Her thoughts on him descended more when the plane taxied, and the little girl nearly slid out of her seat. A glance at the man showed his eyes were still shut, hands clenching the arms of his chair. Colt reached over and buckled the girl's seat belt as the plane lifted off.

"My ears hurt," the tiny fairy whimpered, clinging to a battered brown teddy bear.

"Suck your thumb," Colt suggested.

The fairy's eyes opened wide. "Daddy says that's bad for my teeth."

"I'm sure he'll forgive you this once."

The fairy settled back in her seat, teddy clutched against her, one thumb firmly in her mouth. Colt returned to her book, wondering why the girl hadn't even looked at the man beside her when mentioning her father.

Once at altitude, the man woke long enough to find paper and crayons for the girl before dozing off again. Colt returned to her book, keeping one eye on the girl. As the flight descended, Colt helped the girl stow her drawings and prepare for landing. The man's snores competed with the engines as they went into reverse thrust. Colt considered choking him for poor parenting.

As soon as the seat belt light went out, the man sprang from his seat, bag in hand. Dragging the little girl behind him, he was the first to head for the exit.

Colt waited for the aisles to clear, in no hurry to battle the crowds until she noticed the abandoned bear beside her. Grabbing the bear and her backpack, Colt forced her way toward the front. The man was at the exit. Once he reached the jet bridge, she'd never catch him. She shouted, waving the bear. Another passenger tapped the man's shoulder and pointed.

"Your daughter left this," Colt called, holding up the bear. She waited for the chagrined look, the exasperated eye roll of "not again," the pantomime of negotiating a return of the bear.

None of that happened. He stared at her, his face blank, the only indication that he heard her a tightening of his jaw. Then he turned with a jerk and ducked out of the plane.

Bear in one hand, phone in the other, Colt followed the procession of passengers up the bridge and into the Scranton airport. The flight from DC had only taken two hours, but there was still the sense of reentering the world. Once she'd cleared the tunnel, she hit the call button and tucked the phone into her pocket. Justin's voice greeted her over her earbuds.

"Hawk, the kid next to me on the flight left her bear behind. The dad knew, could have waited for me to get it to him, but he didn't. Is that weird?"

Justin "Hawk" Halversen had five sisters. If anyone knew the outcome of a girl separated from her bear, it would be him.

"Very weird. My dad would have risked missing the next flight rather than have one of my sisters crying the whole time because she didn't have her bear."

"That's what I thought. How soon can you get here?" She stared at the bear.

"I thought you had your motorbike there?"

"I do. But something's not right."

"On my way. What are you going to do?"

"Call the number on the bear's butt."

The worn patch said the bear belonged to "L. Harris." Colt dialed the number stitched under the name.

"Simon Harris." The voice was clipped, nervous.

"Mr. Harris? I have your daughter's teddy bear."

She wasn't prepared for the blubbering panic that poured through the phone. "Is she okay? Where is my daughter? I'm doing everything you asked! What more do you want? I want to speak to her!"

The knot in her stomach jumped from a standard reef knot to a monkey ball. "Mr. Harris, is your daughter in danger?"

"Of course she is! You have her!"

"I don't. But I did just spend two hours sitting next to her on a flight to Pennsylvania."

The only sound over the line was a hitch in his breath.

"I can help." The words slipped out before she could stop them. When she thought of the tiny girl sliding off her seat, Colt had no question that she would do whatever she could to save her.

"No! The police can't be involved—no one can. They said they'd kill her!"

"I promise not to endanger your daughter, but I'm going after her." They were still in the airport. She had a narrow window to catch them before they disappeared.

"No!"

"Do you want your daughter back?"

"Yes! Of course. You don't understand! She's only four!"

"Let me guess. They've threatened to hurt your daughter if you don't meet their demands. So you're going to do two things. One. Do anything they ask. Two. Call this number and tell him everything." She gave him Hawk's number. While she chased down the man and the little girl, Hawk could figure out the details.

"But—"

"Stop arguing. Call him. I'm going after your daughter."

Colt ended the call. With one hand, she stuffed the bear into her backpack next to her book and with the other, she texted Hawk. "We need Kendra."

With her brown hair, gray eyes, and average height, Colt did not stand out in the small airport. The man in jeans and brown jacket blended in equally well. A glittery pink fairy princess on the other hand shone against the drab walls and muted colors around her.

Colt caught a flash of the little girl's dress by the escalators and took off through the airport. Another flight had landed while she was on the phone, slowing her down. Scranton was the end of the line, so no one was in a rush to get to their next gate. It was one of the reasons she chose to fly in and out of that airport, but today she could have used a little less lethargy.

The escalator was crowded, so she skipped it for the stairs. By the time she made it to the ground floor, her quarry was outside next to a dark-colored SUV. The girl was pulling back, crying. As Colt watched, the man gave up fighting and grabbed the girl. He bundled her into the back seat, climbing in after her. The SUV pulled away from the curb as Colt burst out the door. Her eyes went immediately to the license plate, searing it into her memory.

The road looped around the parking lot, and the SUV would have to maintain a slow pace until it reached the main road. Colt yanked on her backpack straps to tighten it against her body and took off at right angles to the disappearing SUV, not caring that she jumped in front of oncoming traffic. A car slammed on its brakes to avoid hitting her, but she didn't have time to respond. She reached full stride by the time she was across the street, and her pace increased as she darted through the tunnel into the covered parking. Her footsteps echoed off the cement walls.

The SUV rounded the far turn, entering the back stretch as Colt reemerged into the sunlight. She ducked her head, pulling air into her lungs, forcing her legs to move faster. She concentrated on landing on the balls of her feet, searching for steady footing. Even if her genetic condition precluded her from feeling pain, a twisted ankle now would slow her down too much. The rows of cars disappeared behind her, but the SUV was closing the distance faster than she was.

She was still two rows away from the end of the lot when the SUV reached the intersection. Her plan to throw herself in front of it at the stop sign was thwarted when it barely slowed. It continued straight through without stopping. She gave up her futile chase, coming to a halt, lungs heaving, keeping the vehicle in sight.

Why were they going to the cell phone lot? Surely they weren't sticking around for someone else. No, they turned off. A large green sign pointed the way. General Aviation.

They were heading for a charter flight.

2

Colt changed her trajectory, glad she had parked her motorbike at the back of the lot. While she waited for the Ducati's 821cc motor to warm up, she unlocked her helmet and synced her phone to the built-in headset. She had a missed call from Kendra.

She redialed, then pulled on her fingerless gloves. Hawk had bought her a pair shortly after they had met, to protect her hands against damage she couldn't feel, and now she rarely went anywhere without them. Commercial airlines frowned on anything unusual, so she had opted to leave them off during the flight.

"Special Agent Kendra Mitchell."

"Kendra, it's me." She put the bike in first and headed for the toll booth.

"Colt. Hawk said you needed my help."

"I'm currently chasing a kidnapped four-year-old. Sat beside her on a flight out of DC. Father is Simon Harris. Adamant the police not be involved."

"And yet you called me." There was no amusement in Kendra's voice, only a business-like desire for all the details.

"I promised not to call the police. I didn't say anything about the FBI." Colt scanned her credit card at the machine and waited for the boom to lift.

"Where are you now?"

"At the Scranton Airport. In pursuit of a black SUV, probably a domestic model. License number KWK-9509"

She could hear Kendra tapping keys.

"Colt, hold up."

"Why?" She stopped at the intersection, waiting for other vehicles to go ahead of her.

"I just ran a check on the girl's father. He works at the courthouse in DC as a guard. Right now, Liam Sykes is on trial for multiple counts of homicide. Psychological evaluations have all flagged him as having clear markers for psychopathy."

"And his friends have a little girl." Colt clenched her hand, inadvertently making the Ducati's engine rev. "Tell Hawk I'm heading to General Aviation. Call you later."

"No, wait—"

Colt cut the call as she rounded the main office building. The gate was open, so she carried on through. Several small charter planes sat on the apron. No one was around. Even the SUV had vanished.

She chalked up the silence to the lunch hour; nonetheless, it was disconcerting. She sped along the apron, checking inside each of the hangars. Most were empty of people. A couple of guys in greasy coveralls sat on camp chairs inside one, enjoying their lunch.

The last two structures sat apart from the others. She slowed, the knot in her stomach tightening. She flicked on her dashcam, angling it toward the hangars. Starting up again, she maintained a steady pace, her head focused on the far end of the runway. Movement inside the hangar called her attention, but she forced herself not to look. Still, there was a restless energy that she could sense. And out of the corner of her eye, a flash of pink.

The final hangar was closed, with no sign of life. Colt passed a row of fuel trucks and de-icing equipment as she circled around behind. She dropped the bike into neutral and pulled out her phone. Opening the dashcam app, she saved the most recent footage to her cloud and sent a link to Kendra.

A familiar brown pick-up came to a stop on the road outside the fence. The gate at this end was closed, but she spotted a keypad mounted on a pole a few yards back from the gate. She stared at the buttons a moment, wondering if she could extrapolate the code from the most worn numbers. She dismissed the idea. It would take too long to go through the various permutations. Leaning over, she punched in the tail number of one of the planes she had seen on the apron. After a moment, a motor whirred and the gate slid open.

"So original, guys," she murmured, nevertheless grateful they used the same system most small airfields used.

She parked her bike behind Hawk's truck and joined him in the cab. Together they reviewed the footage.

"That her?" Hawk asked, pointing at the splotch of pink in the far corner of the hangar.

"Yeah." She wanted to add something, but what more was there to say?

"We need to get her out of there."

"I know." She was glad Hawk was on board with her plan. He was the rule-follower and had gotten her out of heaps of scrapes during their time in the Navy. This was one argument she hadn't planned on losing. She was just relieved she didn't have to make it.

"No, we *really* need to get her out of there." Something in his voice made her pause the replay and give him her full attention.

"Talk to me."

Hawk pulled out his phone to check his notes. "The demands are for Mr. Harris to slip a handcuff key to a prisoner, Liam Sykes, on the way into the courthouse this morning. He did that. At the end of the day, he's to escort the prisoner to the bathroom, then leave him alone. Mr. Harris checked. The bathroom window has already been loosened, just not enough to set off the censors."

"This thing is well planned. How long do we have until the escape?"

"Based on the last few days, they'll likely recess around four."

"So we've got less than three hours."

Hawk sucked in his breath. "Liam isn't the problem."

"He's not?"

"No. Liam is on trial for raping and murdering women. His brother... has much younger tastes."

The monkey ball in her stomach reappeared. "And the brother is in the hangar."

Hawk tapped the screen, indicating one of the men in the center, facing off with Colt's fellow passenger. "Greg Sykes."

Colt's phone rang, interrupting the silence in the truck. Colt accepted the call, putting Kendra on speaker.

"I watched the video," the FBI agent said. "We've got a problem."

"I know. Hawk told me."

"I have a Hostage Rescue Team on their way. We have enough time to resolve this situation prior to the end of the court day. A second team will deal with Liam Sykes as he tries to escape later."

"How long until HRT gets here?" It was a solid plan. Wait for the guys with guns and armor.

"It will be an hour until they reach you. I should pull in local law enforcement, but with a child involved and so many moving pieces, we decided it was better not to."

"That's too long."

"The team is not able to arrive any sooner."

"I'm not leaving that little girl with those guys any longer than absolutely necessary."

It wasn't a great plan, but it was a plan. They reviewed it twice, looking for holes. Well, more holes than the ones they already knew about. Their goal was simple: break in, find the little girl, get out. The HRT could deal with the men. Colt was confident they could pull it off with a little destruction of property and some lockpicking.

"We're assuming the girl is still in the same spot," Hawk cautioned.

"We're assuming a lot of things," Colt agreed.

They had relocated to the far end of the cell phone lot. They had a good line of sight on the hangar, one they hoped wouldn't draw attention from its occupants. Colt leaned under her seat and unlocked the hidden storage locker. Hawk had brought along her Beretta M9, her pancake holster, and a spare magazine. While she checked the weapon over and clipped the holster onto her belt, Hawk climbed out to dig through his tool box.

She joined him at the back of the truck where he laid out a row of tools on the tailgate. She skipped over the hammer and duct tape, instead picking up a small mirror on a long metal handle.

"You steal this from your dentist?"

"No. It's got a telescopic handle."

She dodged his attempts to reclaim it. "I like it. Might come in handy." A pair of pliers joined it in her pocket, along with her lock-picking set.

The last piece of equipment was the most important. Colt retrieved the teddy bear from her backpack. The blue cover of the memoir she had been reading caught her eye. The book would have to wait, as much as she regretted losing her peaceful afternoon. *Later,* she promised herself.

"What's the girl's name? It just says 'L' on the tag."

Hawk watched her a moment. "Lauren. They call her Lolly."

"Lolly." Colt's hand tightened on the bear. Tiny fairies named Lolly did not deserve to be around scum like the Sykes brothers and their associates. "Let's go get her back."

3

It was a short walk from where they had parked to the end of the cell phone lot and the stairs to the service road above. From what she had seen, there were no cameras on the backs of the hangars. Colt jogged up the steps, Hawk's voice in her ear. He was on overwatch until she was past the fence, then he'd pull the truck around closer.

She felt the world retreating, her mind hyper-focused on the task at hand. It was a familiar feeling, one honed from her years as a fighter pilot. The tunnel-like effect of the covered stairs helped with the mission-brain transition. The plexiglass sides were scratched and murky, inhibiting her view, and sounds came to her weirdly muffled. As she emerged at the top, the midday sun reflected off the fender of a new Dodge pickup driving by. The lunch hour was ending, and traffic would soon pick up as people returned to work.

Tucking her hands into her pockets, she crossed the street. Her hand wrapped around the pliers. She'd have no trouble climbing the fence, but expecting to get the little girl over with the barbed wire in place was a bit much.

"Car coming at you from the south," Hawk said.

"South-west," she countered. She kept her head down, one hand raised to ostensibly brush hair out of her face. After it passed without a glance from the driver, she lifted her head, scanning the surrounding area again. Even up close, she could see no evidence of security cameras. "Five yards out. How we looking?"

"No traffic. You're clear to go."

The fence between the two hangars stretched from one wall to the other, a few yards from the end. She slipped around the corner, glad for the slight cover. A fire hose hookup protruded from the side of the building, protected by a pair of bright yellow bollards. She climbed up, balancing with one foot on the rounded top of the bollard, the other toed into the fence. Four quick clips from the pliers, and the barbed wire hung down from the center pole. Back on the ground, she secured the strands to keep them out of the way upon her return.

"Wire's cut. I'm going over," she said.

"Roger. Moving up to secondary position."

She heard the truck starting up. Knowing Hawk would alert her if anything changed, she took a deep breath and hopped the fence. The fingerless leather gloves she wore to protect her hands absorbed the stabs from the wire at the top of the fence. She landed with ease and turned to the door.

It was a standard thirty-six inches wide. Metal, painted brown. The lock was the bigger concern, but on first inspection it didn't offer any extra challenges. She checked the door for signs of an alarm. The contacts would be on the inside, if there were any. Trusting that the system was all linked together and the alarm turned off when the main doors were open, she tested the handle. No point in picking the lock if it was already open. No such luck.

She fished out her lockpicking set. She closed her eyes, focusing on the feel and sound of the pins as her fingers navigated the lock.

The final pin clicked into place. Replacing the picks in her pocket, she tugged the teddy bear out of her jacket. But she couldn't hold the bear, her Beretta, and open the door at the same time. After a moment's deliberation, she opted for the gun. She set the bear on the ground beside her within easy reach.

"Door's unlocked," she told Hawk.

"I'm stopped about 100 yards back," he said. "I'll move up shortly."

She stayed in a crouch, back against the wall. Reaching up with her right hand, she turned the handle. It caught for a moment before releasing with a pop. She held it steady, counting off seconds in her head in case anyone had heard the noise. The metal door was heavy and reluctant to open after a long period of unuse. The angle was awkward, but after a moment she was able to open it a few inches.

Her field of vision was limited, showing only a few yards of the back wall. Junk was piled on metal shelves, paperwork sliding out a cabinet that wouldn't stay closed. An old wooden desk, the kind that needed a forklift to move, held court to the left. A black leather executive chair sat beside the desk, its stuffing coming out in places. Tied to the chair was the fairy princess.

Her hair was still up in the two pigtails, although one was looking a bit droopy. Her pink dress was crumpled, hitched up around her knees in layers of crinoline and satin. The fairy wings were tossed on the desk, one broken tie hanging over the edge. The girl was frowning at her shoe, picking at a blue gem stuck to the side.

Colt shifted her hands, using a small piece of broken pavement to keep the door from closing. Time for Hawk's telescopic mirror. She stretched it out to half its length, then angled it through the crack. It took a moment for her to adjust it to be able to see anything. Its range of visibility offered little in the way of a broader image. She was able to determine that no one was nearby and that just inside the door, another row of shelves blocked the view from the rest of the space. Distant voices reached her, too far to make out what they were saying. The usual hum of a large building helped wipe out individual sounds. A motor was running somewhere, adding to the background noise.

She returned the mirror to her pocket and picked up the bear. "Alright, buddy. Show time."

"You say something?" Hawk asked.

She'd forgotten about him. "No visual on bogeys near the target. Moving in."

Opting for speed over stealth, she got to her feet. She eased the door open just enough to admit her and slid around the frame. Held the door until it stopped against the rock again and sank to her haunches. No one was shouting or screaming, so that was a win so far.

Someone had seen her, however. Lolly was staring with eyes big and round. Colt waved with the bear while pressing a finger to her lips.

Lolly looked ready to squeal, quickly stopping herself. Colt smiled and nodded, encouraging the little girl to be calm.

"Why are you here? Are you waiting for your mommy too?" Lolly asked, face serious.

Colt shook her head, then looked over her shoulder. She couldn't see anything through the shelves. "Are they close?" she asked, barely above a whisper.

Lolly pursed her lips, and little frown lines formed between her eyes. She looked around, sitting up tall in her chair. "No, they're far away."

"Okay, good. We're going to be super quiet, okay?"

Lolly nodded. Colt slipped to the end of the shelves and peered out. Lolly was right, no one was close by. However, two men she didn't recognize were seated at a card table with a clear line of sight to Lolly. The younger Sykes brother, Greg, was pacing near the front of the hangar, phone pressed to his ear. The man from the airplane was tinkering with something at a workbench. None were close enough to hear her talking to Lolly. Still, she wouldn't be able to reach the little girl without being spotted.

She slipped back into hiding. Lolly was only a few yards away. A few yards of open space that she couldn't cross. And Lolly was tied to the chair, so she couldn't move either. The girl watched Colt, kicking her feet. It made the chair rock back and forth on its wheels.

"Lolly, have you ever pushed yourself around in a chair like that?" Was she too small?

"Yeah! Daddy and me play in the rolly chair all the time!"

"Okay. Do you think you can roll over here to me and Bear?" She held up the bear, making him dance.

"Why?" She continued to bounce, making the chair shift farther away.

"So you and Bear and I can go home."

"The man said Mommy was coming here to see me."

Where was Hawk when she needed him? He was better with children. How was she going to convince Lolly it was a bad idea to wait? "Isn't your mommy usually at home with you and your daddy?"

Lolly stopped bouncing, sagging into the giant seat. "She used to be.

Then she went away. Daddy said we're never going to see her again, but the nice man told me he knows where Mommy is."

Her mother was dead. Why had no one told Colt?

"Hey, what's the kid doing?" a voice called from across the hangar.

Colt froze, lifting her finger to her lips again. Lolly nodded, her eyes going wide again.

"She's just playing in the chair." The second voice sounded bored.

"Looks like she's talking to someone." This voice had a nasally whine.

Colt grabbed the bear's legs, making him dance. Lolly giggled. "Your turn," Colt mouthed.

Lolly raised her arms, waving them over her head and kicking her feet.

"See, she's just playing. Kid must be bored."

"I could help with that," the whining voice said. Colt shuddered. If the man came over, she'd have no compunction over killing him to keep him away from Lolly.

"Don't even think about it." This voice Colt recognized. He had only said a few words in her hearing on the plane, but it had a deep, raspy element that stood out. "We had an agreement, and you're going to stick to it, or I'm walking."

Colt turned back to Lolly. She needed to get her out of there while the men were arguing. "Lolly, we need to leave now. Can you do that? Mr. Bear really wants to give you a hug."

Lolly looked at the men, then back at Colt. Her little mouth pinched as she concentrated. "Okay. Do I need to bring the chair?"

"No, but I can't come to you to untie you. How are you going to get out?"

Before she could finish, Lolly solved the issue by raising her arms over her head and sliding out from under the strap that was holding her to the chair. She ran the few steps to Colt and fell on her. "Bear and me really want to go home."

"Good idea." Colt pressed the button on her ear piece to wake it up. She hadn't heard from Hawk in a while and wondered if the call had dropped. It rang once in her ear before he picked up.

"Colt, get out of there."

"We're coming now."

"Good. We've got a problem."

Colt moved to the door, staying low. They'd slip out, she'd shut the door properly, and they'd have a few moments to scale the fence before the men noticed Lolly was missing.

"Okay, out you go," she whispered, pressing the door open.

Nothing happened. No little pink fairy ducked around her legs. Colt glanced down. No little pink fairy beside her. She turned. The little pink fairy sat on the floor, cuddling her teddy.

"Lolly! We have to go," Colt hissed.

Lolly ignored her. Colt eased the door against the rock again and tiptoed back. "Come on," she said, forcing her voice to be cheerful. She had images of having to carry a screaming, flailing child out.

"Where are we going? Can we get ice cream?" Lolly looked up at her as if it didn't matter if they got ice cream or stayed right there.

"We need to go find Daddy. And yes, we can get ice cream along the way."

Lolly considered the offer. "Okay. I like ice cream." She stood deliberately, brushing down her dress and adjusting the skirt. Colt tamped down the urge to pick her up and run. She ushered her to the door, not giving Lolly the option to veer off-path. The little girl chattered to the bear, reciting her favorite ice cream flavors.

"Hey! Where's the girl?" A shout rang out behind them.

Colt scooped Lolly into her arms as she shoved the door open. Wrapping around the door, she ran the few steps to the fence. Hawk was there, waiting, the truck doors open and ready. A crack sounded from the hangar, followed by a punch to the door as a bullet shot through the metal.

Not stopping, Colt grabbed Lolly around the waist with both hands. The girl weighed far less than she had expected. She tossed the girl as high as she could. For an instant, it looked as though the pink bundle of satin wouldn't make it over, then Hawk was stepping forward, and Lolly landed safely in his arms.

"GO!" Colt cried, flinging herself up the fence.

"Bear!" Lolly screamed, halfway to the truck with Hawk.

The bear was on the ground. Colt snagged it with one hand and jumped at the fence. Clinging to the wire, she threw the bear toward Hawk. He stooped long enough to grab it, then bundled girl and bear into the truck.

"Colt!" he shouted in warning.

She looked behind her as the door flung open. Her foot slipped, sending her back to the ground. No time to climb the fence again.

Trusting Hawk to take Lolly and leave, Colt spun around to the man attacking her. She sprang forward, her direct attack making him pause. Right before reaching him, she leaped into the air, crashing down on his chest, sending him to the ground. His gun went off, the bullet hitting the other hangar. He struggled to sit up, his right arm pinned under Colt's knee, the rest of her weight on his chest. She punched him once, twice, his head bouncing on the pavement.

When his eyes rolled back in his head, she sprang up, grabbing his weapon. She shot a look at the fence. The door handle rattled. She was out of time. Had Hawk had enough of a head start to get Lolly out of there? She didn't know and wasn't about to risk leading the kidnappers straight to the little girl.

She sprinted down the alley. Shouts echoed from inside the hangar, and a motor rumbled to life. A gun fired behind her, and a bullet pinged off the ground by her feet. Bad shot or not wanting to kill her? She wasn't going to wait to find out. Twenty feet to the end of the alley. Then what? Turn left, into the waiting arms of the other kidnappers? Or right, and hope the closed hangar wasn't locked so she could slip inside? There was no shelter, nothing to hide behind. Anything was better than staying in the alley. The guy behind her might improve his aim at any second.

As if to prove her point, another shot rang out. She didn't see where it hit this time. Twisting to her right, she hugged the corner, staying as close to the building as she could. A personnel door stood a few feet away. She slowed enough to test the handle. Locked. A bullet slammed through metal siding above her head. She still had the first assailant's weapon in her hand, so she fired a couple of rounds to discourage her pursuer. She ran toward the far end, a dark figure silhouetted against the beige hangar. Keeping her head down, she put everything she had into running for the second time that day. A few more yards and then—

Smack!

Colt bounced off the chain-link fence and landed on her back. The fence ran at an angle away from the corner of the hangar. Colt stared up at it from her position on the ground. With her head down, she hadn't noticed it. She flipped over, checking if it was safe to get up.

The man from the plane was standing on the apron, a long hunting rifle in his hands. Nope, there was no way she was waiting around to see what he could do with that. Twisting to her feet, she ran for the nearest cover—the de-icing machinery. A round pierced the boxy tanker. She hunkered down behind the oversized tire and peered out.

The man wasn't aiming at her. He fired twice more, at each of the other two de-icers before turning and shooting his last two shots at a fuel truck that was parked at an angle. She stayed down. He was too far away for her to have any hope of hitting him. After his last shell casing ejected out the side of his rifle, he turned and walked back into the hangar. Colt slumped down against the tire, trying to catch her breath. She pulled out her phone to check on Hawk. What had he said? Something about bigger problems?

4

Shouts from the men rang out. Colt could only identify three voices, pairing them to the brief glimpses she had of them as they moved in and out of her view. As far as she could tell, the man she had knocked out in the alley way was still out of commission. Even if he had regained consciousness, he'd be too woozy to be much of a problem.

"Where are you?" Hawk asked.

"Oh, you know, hanging out. Where's Lolly?"

"We're at the clinic across the street. A nurse just took Lolly to find a popsicle. Her dad's on his way with the FBI."

"Good."

"Get out of there. Liam Sykes tried to escape and was captured by the FBI. These guys are going to bolt any second."

"Fun times," she said, barely registering what he said. The SUV had made a reappearance, towing a plane out of the hangar. The Beechcraft B55 Baron still had its original red and white paint scheme.

"Colt, you need to leave. These guys don't mess around."

"Can't."

"Are you trapped?" Hawk's voice immediately went deeper. She pictured him running to the truck.

"No, I'm fine." She paused to sniff the air. There was a smell, one she couldn't quite identify yet. "However, they've just pulled a Beechcraft Baron from the hangar. It's got more than enough seats for all of them and plenty of range to reach Canada or even Bermuda."

"And you don't want to let them leave."

"There's no way I'm letting them leave." *Not after they kidnapped Lolly.*

"Can you wait? The FBI will be here soon enough."

"I can disable the plane. If we let them take off, who knows where they'll disappear."

"Do what you can without getting close, okay? I'll see if I can get through to the tower. I'll be there in five."

"Roger." Colt ended the call and looked around. The sweet smell was getting stronger. Maple syrup. That's what it was. She looked down. Her boots were planted in a growing puddle. The de-icing trucks weren't empty. Who leaves trucks full of flammable liquid sitting around? She darted to the next one, hoping it wasn't leaking to the same extent. Pale yellow liquid poured from holes on either side of the tank. The environmental cleanup was going to be a pain. She reached the last one and paused.

The men were unhitching the SUV from the Beechcraft. She doubted they'd get approval from the control tower, but the airport wasn't that busy. They could easily find a window and take off without clearance. The fourth man, one who had been watching Lolly, was doing a visual check, clipboard in hand. The guy from the flight climbed into the SUV and drove back into the hangar. Greg Sykes moved around in jerky circles. If he was trying to patrol, it was an ineffective method.

The stink of maple syrup made her cough and her eyes dry. The only other cover was the fuel trunk. To get to it, she would need to cross ten feet of open space. The two holes punched in its side were higher up, and the fuel had already escaped below the marks. A dark puddle slowly stretched toward the one she was standing in. At least the smell of the fuel would be less intense. Bracing herself to stay low, Colt waited until Sykes was facing the other way and bolted across the void.

She almost made it before a shout told her she had been spotted. The pop of Sykes' handgun quickly followed. The fact they were willing to continue to fire openly in daylight told her all she needed to know about the chance of help coming from any of the nearby hangars. She was on her own. And that was fine with her.

The bark of the rifle replaced the handgun. Colt positioned herself behind the tires, keeping her head down. She didn't dare shoot back. Even if she had been close enough, the fumes from the ethylene glycol in the de-icer were strong enough that firing her gun might set it alight. She wasn't concerned about incoming rounds doing the same. Despite what the movies showed, bullets couldn't actually create enough heat to ignite fumes.

Either way, she couldn't stay where she was for long. The fumes were making her eyes water and couldn't be good for her lungs either. She checked the gun she still held. A Kel-Tec PII. The guy she'd taken it from chose a budget option. She knew it worked—he had fired at her, and she had used it to rattle the men chasing her. But working and accurate aren't the same. She stuffed it into her pocket and pulled out her Beretta. With this one, she knew she could hit the center of a target ten times out of ten at fifty yards. The Beechcraft was half that distance again, but the engine wasn't a small target.

A deep breath sent her into a fit of coughing. She checked on the men as she recovered in case they decided to sneak up on her. The pilot was testing the vertical stabilizers. Sykes held the rifle, muzzle pointed over his shoulder. The whining of a small engine accompanied an annoying rattling as the main hangar door lowered. They were gearing up to leave. If she was going to act, she had to do it now.

She stepped out from behind the tanker and aimed for the windscreen of the plane. Movement behind the glass warned her someone was inside. As much as she wasn't overly concerned about the well-being of these men, she didn't feel like killing one of them. She lowered the muzzle until her sights lined up with the plane's engine cowling and emptied her magazine.

The pilot reacted faster than she would have thought. He leaned out of the cockpit, pistol in hand. The curving arc of light gave her a two-second warning of what was coming.

She didn't think. She ran forward. The flare hit the pool of de-icer mixed with gasoline. Colt threw her arms over her head as the world around her disappeared in a flash of light.

Seventeen seconds.

She was being overly optimistic. The pools of fuel and de-icer were already on fire.

Fifteen seconds.

There was no way she could reach the hangar in time. The tank of jet fuel would explode long before those fifteen seconds were up.

Thirteen seconds.

Through the roiling smoke, she saw the door open. Thank goodness. Hawk had made it through. She sprinted faster, heat dogging her every step.

Ten seconds.

A man stood in the doorway, features obscured. As his arm lifted toward her, she noted he was too short to be Hawk. Something slammed into her leg, making her stumble. She caught herself and pressed on.

Seven seconds.

The door slammed shut. No! She felt the air shift and sizzle around her.

Five seconds.

No time to fight the door. She flung herself against the hangar, pressing her body into the corner where building met pavement.

Three seconds.

Boom!

Debris rained down around her. Colt waited until the worst was over, then pushed herself to her feet. The Beechcraft had been flung around to face the other way. No sign of the pilot. She bent down to retrieve her Beretta. There was a good chance of debris in the muzzle, so she tucked it back into her pancake holster. Her jacket was torn, shreds of leather hanging off her right arm. A red stain leeched across her jeans. She narrowed her eyes. The small calibre round didn't appear to have done much damage. Flexing her leg, she decided she could deal with it later. Thankfully she couldn't feel the pain, so the injury wasn't going to hold her back.

Pulling the Kel-Tec out of her pocket, she reached for the door handle. She wasn't about to back down now. Not after they'd tried to blow her up. And shot her. Wary of the heat the handle might have absorbed, she used a strip of her torn jacket to protect her fingers. Yanking the door open, she marched in, gun raised.

Sykes stood a few feet away, near the hangar door control. Her passenger buddy was helping the fourth man to the SUV.

"I shot you," Sykes said, hands scrambling for the bulge in his coat pocket.

"Yeah. Not a fan." Colt closed the distance between them in two steps, slamming the gun into the side of his head. He crumpled to the ground, and she turned toward the other two.

One. The injured fellow waved weakly from where he was leaning against the hood of the SUV. Weapon raised, Colt spun around to see the other man swinging a knife at her.

She jerked back, out of range. His arm hit hers, knocking her gun to the ground. She responded with a swift kick to his kidneys, but he recovered quickly. Blocking the next attack with her forearm, she stepped inside his swinging range and hit him in the face with a solid right. They parried, him attacking with the knife, her staying just out of reach. The few blows she landed weren't enough to bother him much. She watched for an opening.

He came at her with a wide swing, holding the knife in his fist. She blocked the blow with one hand, stepping forward into the movement. Her elbow collided with the side of his head, and she followed up with a knee to his stomach. He stumbled backward, dropping the knife. A roundhouse kick to the side of his head sent him to the floor.

"Stop!"

Colt froze. The injured man was holding the gun she had dropped, aiming at her head. While she wasn't convinced he'd be able to aim straight the way he was weaving about, he was close enough not to miss by much. She grabbed the knife off the floor and flung it at him. He staggered back with a cry, grasping at his shoulder where the knife was buried.

She stood, pushing her hair off her face.

The rear door of the hangar blew open. Men in tactical gear poured in, shouting.

"FBI! Everyone on the floor!"

Colt brushed herself off. "About time. I've got a book to finish."

ABOUT THE AUTHOR

Arleigh Jacobs first saw the TV show *JAG* when she was twelve years old, and she promptly fell in love. F-14 Tomcats became her obsession, and her dream was to become a fighter pilot. Her biggest heartbreak was learning that the Royal Australian Air Force fleet did not include the Tomcat. Her second heartbreak came when she discovered she didn't have the stomach for excessive gravitational forces. She now writes about fighter pilots instead of being one, although she still dreams of one day flying in an F-14.

You can find more Colt stories, including a free novella, at https://arleighjacobs.com/straightflight/

THE PACKAGE

N GRAY

All I had to do was hand over the package. What could *go wrong?*

1

I glimpsed at the entrance then at my watch. He was thirty minutes late. This wasn't something I did—ever. Donnie would divorce me and take the boys if he ever found out I was here and doing this. I doubted I looked ladylike, sipping nervously on my whiskey, but I couldn't help downing the heavenly liquid. The sting of alcohol eased my nerves and deadened my senses, if only for a second or two. I couldn't wait any longer and collected my bag to leave, but the door opened and slammed shut. Without looking, I knew it was him. I felt his presence, like ants on my skin.

I flinched when my cellphone vibrated in my pocket.

I felt the man's dark gaze as he approached.

I checked my phone; it was only Donnie. I exhaled sharply and sent Donnie a thumbs-up emoji at his request for me to buy milk on the way home. I quickly pocketed my phone.

June ... June ... June ... I chanted the fake name so I didn't forget.

"Jane?" the man asked. His voice was husky, like he'd smoked a pack of cigarettes every day.

"Yes, that's me." I glanced up and swallowed hard.

He surveyed his surroundings then sat beside me, dismissing the bartender who'd approached us.

I tucked loose strands of hair behind my ear and shifted uncomfortably in my seat. I pulled my jacket tighter around my body.

The other patrons paid us no attention as they continued with their own conversations.

The man smirked.

My heart fluttered, and disappointment engulfed me. I knew he sensed how nervous I was. I needed to relax, to pretend we were just friends meeting for a drink. I studied his tanned face, the deep crescent scar near his left temple and smiling eyes with years of experience. The tension between my shoulders eased, and I exhaled slowly.

He cleared his throat. "You have the package?"

I refocused on my mission and unzipped my handbag. "Yes." I removed the package and handed it to him.

"I assume everything's in order?" He retrieved an envelope from his tailored suit's breast pocket and placed it gently in my palm.

My eyes widened when I saw the gun peeking from his jacket. I'd seen guns before but not one like that. "Uh-huh." I plastered on a smile. This experience was terrifying yet exciting—one I'd never forget.

The man stood but hesitated. He studied me and opened his mouth to say something as the entrance door flung open.

Men wearing black entered with guns drawn and yelled at everyone to get down.

My pulse thundered in my ears.

The man beside me grabbed my hand and pulled me from my seat and barked, "Let's go."

I hesitated; I wanted to pull my hand free of his, but I couldn't. A cold sensation enveloped me as the numbness prevented me from escaping this man.

"If you want to get out alive, come with me." He pulled me along a dark corridor and away from the chaos.

I didn't know this man and didn't know if I was safe with him. My job was to wait for him, hand over the package, and that was it. Now ... I was running for my life, with him dragging me along. If I went back into the bar, I'd have to face men with guns, and I didn't know if they were cops or FBI or someone equally as dangerous as the man tugging my hand. What was my alternative? To face Donnie and explain my actions. He thought I was at a book club.

Shouting continued behind us as the men in black ordered everyone to the ground with that familiar sound of guns cocking. I'd been with Donnie to the shooting range and had fired his personal pistol many times, so I recognized that sound. I didn't know if these men wanted what we had exchanged or for another reason. If they were there for us. How did they know where to find us?

My chest ached from the sudden exertion. My thoughts wildly reviewed what had just transpired. There wasn't anything they could arrest me for, apart from the envelope safely tucked inside my handbag. If these men were the police, Donnie would find out. They would call him after they had arrested me, and they'd tell him what I'd done and where I was—a singles bar in a hotel. He would divorce me and take the boys. I couldn't let that happen. I had to follow this stranger and hope he'd get me home. I had no option but to trust him. I prayed he would only do that—help me and not hurt me the moment we were behind closed doors.

"I don't even know your name." I asked, out of breath and trying to keep up.

"Kade," he said in a grunt and pulled my arm.

"Ow, not so hard." I moaned as I glanced over my shoulder, unable to see anything behind us but I heard as more men entered the bar.

We ran down the dark passage, passed the bathrooms and stopped outside a door at the far end. Kade kicked open the door, and we entered the stairwell. We rushed down two flights, then Kade pushed me against the wall. I felt his hot breath against the side of my neck as he listened, but all I heard was my pulse in my ears.

"They're coming up," he whispered, opened the door for the fifth floor and pushed me through.

"Is it the police?"

"No."

"Who are they?"

Kade stopped to respond.

An uneasiness settled within me and cowered under his gaze.

"They are after the package, Jane." His tone was deep and hollow. "If they find either of us, we're dead. Do you understand?"

I nodded, my jaw slacken as I processed what he'd said. "Do they know who I am?"

"They've seen your face, but they don't have your actual name."

"Do you?"

He turned to me again, and his silence answered my question. "Let's get out of here. I know a way."

I squealed when he grabbed my hand again, making me flinch.

We ran around the corner to see a man reading a newspaper approaching us in the elevator's direction. He hadn't seen us yet when he stopped by the elevator doors. The bell chimed, and doors screeched open.

A hand holding a weapon raised and fired, striking the unbeknownst man.

He smashed into the wall and crumpled to the ground, unmoving.

I gasped and hid behind Kade as he tried the nearest door.

The hand and the weapon disappeared.

Kade grabbed the trolley packed with linen and found something. He pushed against the door again, and the light clicked green. He opened the door as I saw a man in black assess the corpse slumped against the wall on the floor.

My chest rose and fell as I sucked in deep breaths. A man was dead because of me—because of us. "He's dead, isn't he?" I knew the answer but asked anyway and entered the unoccupied room.

Kade closed the door so slowly I barely heard the lock click shut. "Would you prefer to be the one lying there?" He stepped from the door and approached with purpose.

I backed up. Something in his hand caught my eye—the keycard he'd snatched from the trolley outside the room. My heel collided with the bed. I whimpered from the impact and bounced on the soft mattress.

"Well, Jane, do you want to die?"

"No, but—"

"There can be no buts, Jane. You signed up for this, remember. You knew the risks, and you did it anyway," he said in a raspy whisper, making all the hair on my body stand on end.

I nodded; Kade was right. Melissa had warned me. She had asked me twice if I was sure. I was sure, and I had understood what it meant. I had wanted to do this but hadn't fully comprehended the risks and that civilians might be killed. I wanted some excitement in my life, and I had made extra cash, but that didn't stop the rogue tear from falling. They would've killed us if that man wasn't there, affording us the time to escape inside this room.

"You're right." I wiped my face with the back of my hand. I had to take control of my situation and my emotions. I couldn't allow myself to fall to pieces. Donnie had trained me to think on my feet. Even though I was a civilian, I could handle this. "They're on every floor, and they're looking for us. How do we get out?"

"I said I had a plan." His grin brightened his dark demeaner.

"You enjoy this too much," I mumbled as he passed me and headed toward the window.

"I love it! The adrenaline rush and the excitement. You can't tell me you're not enjoying it a little."

I didn't admit it out loud, but I did. "What are you looking at?" I asked, curious why he was standing by the window.

"We need to get over there." He pointed at a window on the far side of the hotel.

"What's over there?" I squinted.

"A way out. This hotel is old, with rooms that lead straight to the basement. And that one"—he pointed—"is our way out."

That sounded easy enough. We still had five floors to go before we could escape. If that room held the key to getting out quickly, I'd take it. But ... "How? We're here and don't know how many are out there or on this floor."

Kade headed for the door and stopped before he opened it. "If it looks like I won't win the fight, run. Don't wait for me. Don't see if I'm okay, just run. You got that?"

I stared dumbfounded as he unlocked the door and slowly opened it.

He stuck out his head and glanced both ways. With his right hand, he motioned for me to join him.

I didn't like the idea of going out there without knowing who we were up against. I scanned both sides of the passage, and it was devoid of men wearing black—or of anyone. We passed the elevator, and the man I'd seen gunned down had already been removed, but red stains remained on the carpet. I noticed my reflection as we passed the elevator; I was pale and wide eyed yet stoically calm—that could just be me in shock and having found a way of dealing with my situation.

We were halfway when footsteps quickened in our direction. We rounded the corner as someone ran into Kade.

An elbow connected with Kade's jaw, followed by crunching sounds.

I thought Kade would go down, but he didn't. He rocked from one foot to the other. He ducked, missing the punch from the attacker's other fist, and rammed his fist into his diaphragm.

The attacker doubled over.

Kade hit him in the face, and, as he came to kick him, the attacker pushed away his leg.

Dark, stormy eyes glanced in my direction, and I shuddered. The man in black licked his lips and blocked Kade's punch, advancing with his own to Kade's stomach.

It was Kade's turn to clutch at his waist.

I backed away from the fight, wanting to scream for help, but without more men joining in. Instead, I cupped my hand over my mouth. Thankful Kade had been with me; there was no way I could defend myself against this guy. If I was honest with myself, I was an easy target. I desperately needed to rectify that.

The men punched, kicked, and pushed each other, each taking turns nursing a wound, then retaliated. They were spent.

Kade glanced at me, smirked then refocused on his opponent. He inhaled sharply, ran for the attacker and kicked up his body, hitting him once in his sternum and once in the neck.

It sounded like a bone snapped, and the attacker crashed to the ground with a loud thump, followed by a moan.

Kade grabbed my hand again, and I carefully stepped over the unmoving body.

I didn't know if he was dead, and I didn't want to hang around either. I followed Kade to the end of the corridor.

Kade kicked open the door and entered the dank room that reminded me of our basement.

I hugged my body and pulled the jacket tighter. "This is a strange, little room."

They filled the room with broken tables and chairs and shelves packed with linen. The walls hadn't seen paint in years, and water damage marked the ceiling in the corners. If any guests came back here, the conditions would appal them, and to think the staff worked here.

"That's our way out." Kade pointed at the laundry chute. "Before they turned this into a hotel, it used to be an apartment block. Residents would drop off their marked laundry bag, which they collected in the basement and cleaned then returned. Each floor has a room similar to this one housekeeping still used for laundry. It's a bit of straight drop, but I'm confident there's something to catch us at the bottom."

"Are you serious? You know how crazy that sounds? What if we hit concrete?"

"Trust me." He switched on his flashlight to illuminate our only exit then handed me the flashlight.

"I'm not climbing in there." The crawlspace was tiny, although it was bigger than the usual laundry chutes I'd seen.

As big as Kade was, he could fit in it, albeit a little squashed. "There are ways to get out of the building, but this is the only one close enough where you can get out unharmed."

I stopped to face him and shone the light in his face.

He cowered behind his hand, shielding his eyes.

"How do you know all this? You were barely in that bar for five minutes, and you're telling me you know a way out?" I may be inexperienced, but I wasn't stupid. It was oddly convenient Kade knew the history of this hotel. I'd lived in Chicago all my life and never knew about it.

Kade stepped out of the light, and I lowered the flashlight, highlighting the carpet instead.

"Thanks." He exhaled audibly and wiped his brows with the back of his hand. "I'm good at what I do, Jane. I need to know everything about the building I'm entering: where the exits are, the layout of the venue—you know, all those types of things. And those men who stormed the bar are not your typical government agency but our competition. Agencies would announce who they were; these guys didn't."

"What?" I asked as a sense of dread fell upon me, and I sank against the cool wall.

"They want the package." He patted lightly over his breast pocket. "If they had found you with the envelope, you wouldn't be going home tonight."

I closed my mouth as I comprehended the weight of his words.

"They want this information and don't play well. They asked me to hand you the envelope, and you were going to give it to your handler?"

I didn't trust my voice at the moment and nodded as I exhaled a ragged breath.

"The only reason I'm doing this is because I know this area very well and could protect the person I was supposed to do the exchange with. We suspected they would come tonight, but we weren't sure. That's why we had two drops instead of just the one. It was a test to see whether we had a mole. Now I'm giving you more information than I need to, but you must understand your predicament."

I swallowed, and the back of my throat hurt. I coughed into my hand. "Am I in danger?"

"I will make sure you get home safe and sound. Luckily, these guys don't know who you are, so you have that going for you. But, if they'd caught you, all that would've changed."

"But nobody knows my proper name."

"If they caught you, they could get your fingerprints and pull any information on you—that includes your credit cards, your home address, and your spouse."

His words sent a chill throughout my body I'd never experienced before and tried not to break down. I was in over my head and so stupid to think I could do this. I couldn't ask Donnie to fetch me, and certainly no one in my or his family. I was not tough enough to get out on my own, so I had to keep it together. And my only way out was standing in front of me. "And I can trust you?"

"Yes. I will ensure you get home safely, and they will never know who you truly are."

I nodded and felt a little better. If Kade meant what he'd said, it was possible for me to get out, fetch milk and get home, all in one piece.

"It's either that or it's them." He thumbed the closed door behind him. "Choose wisely."

"No," I grumbled, not wanting to take my chances with the men out there. I glanced at the small space again and sighed. "Fine." I twisted the flashlight nervously in my hands and climbed into the crawlspace. I crawled into the chute but pressed my hands and knees to the sides to keep from falling.

"Don't think about it. Just let go."

I stared down the dark space where the light couldn't touch, closed my eyes and let go.

Kade climbed in after me, and I heard the metal of the lid scrape closed. His voice echoed behind me.

My stomach dropped to my feet as I fell, hopefully not to my death. If there was nothing to cushion my fall, it would be too late for me to do anything anyway.

"Don't touch the sides," Kade yelled from higher up. "Brace yourself. We're almost there."

"Just don't land on me," I yelled back.

A light swallowed me as I fell with a thump onto soft sheets.

The laundry cart moved forward, and Kade dropped into the one behind me.

We moved freely but still joined at the base of the carts.

"Get out." Kade climbed out his cart and, in a crouched position, stealthily moved behind the industrial washing machines.

I fumbled with the linen and froze when a door opened.

Two people entered, laughing at a joke they'd shared.

Kade motioned for me to join him.

I waved him away, fell quietly into the laundry cart as the two people passed me and headed for the break room on the far side of the laundry room. When the area was clear, I climbed out. My foot caught on the edge, and I crashed to the floor.

Hands curled around my upper arms, helping me to my feet. I felt his breath against my neck. “Stop messing around. We need to get out of here,” he said near the shell of my ear.

“I didn’t do this on purpose.” I righted my jacket.

“Come.” He ran to the washing machines, checked then dashed to the exit on the opposite end. He tried the door, but it was bolted shut. He slammed his palm into the wall and cursed. He surveyed the area and pointed. “Let’s go that way.”

We entered the staff change room, but all the lockers were locked, with a few uniforms on hangers waiting for the next shift.

“Here.” Kade handed me a maid’s outfit.

“You’re kidding?” I held up the gray attire.

“Does it look like I’m joking?” he said and undressed.

“Wait, turn around if you’re going to do that.” I felt my cheeks flush.

Kade sighed and turned around. He removed his holster, jacket, and T-shirt without caring whether I was watching him.

I saw scars on his back; some were circles, while others were long. I guessed by the sizes someone had shot, cut, or lashed him. I turned around and removed my jacket. The maid’s dress was two sizes bigger and could fit over my clothing. And besides, I could never go home wearing someone else’s clothing, let alone a uniform. Donnie would be suspicious immediately. The gray dress with white frills matched my jeans and sneakers. Admittedly, I hadn’t worn the appropriate clothing to a bar either; I was meant to be at a book club where most of the women wore casual clothing. And Donnie had dropped me off on the corner of the restaurant they had scheduled us to meet. I couldn’t fit another outfit in my bag, dress, redress and everything else; it was just too complicated for me. Plus, I was afraid I would forget. If the lie was closer to the truth, I did well at remembering what to say—hence the top and jacket with jeans and sneakers. It was casual, yet with the jacket a little more formal. If anyone asked why I smelled of alcohol, I could tell them I was at a restaurant, which was technically true.

“Remove your pants, put them in your bag and take these shoes.” Kade handed me a pair of black slip-on loafers.

"Do I have to?"

He arched an eyebrow.

"Fine." I yanked the shoes out his hands and lifted the dress, undid the button and unzipped. I kicked off my shoes and removed my jeans. Once the loafers were on, I spied Kade dressed like a concierge with a gun impatiently waiting for me.

"Are you ready?"

"Yes." I smiled sweetly.

He grabbed my hand and pulled me to my feet.

I stuffed my jeans and sneakers into my bag and exited the locker room. I walked behind him toward the service elevator.

We heard a commotion and raised our heads when the elevator stopped on the floor above us.

Shouting erupted after the doors opened.

I flinched at a pop sound, followed by someone falling.

"Stairs," Kade said in a grunt and reached for my hand.

We ran toward the stairs.

The elevator stopped on our floor. The familiar sound of the bell chimed. The doors opened. Men spoke. Men ran on the carpet toward us.

We exited the floor, but instead of going down to the employee parking area, Kade took us up the stairs. When we reached the second floor, he stopped, pushed me against the wall, and we waited.

My chest heaved as I tried in vain to steady my breathing.

The door below us opened and closed as men ran down the stairs.

"Come," he said, and we ran down the stairs again.

My heart hammered in my chest, and it felt as though I was hyperventilating. The adrenaline coursed through my veins at such a rate I was sure I could fly to the next building. I'd never felt so alive in my entire life. I should've been scared, but I wasn't.

I'd felt something similar when Donnie had taken me to the shooting range, and I'd fired three different weapons that day. It had been such an exciting experience, one I hadn't had in a long time. Being a full-time mother and helping my father-in-law with his financial business had taken its toll on my mind. My body was okay, but I was bored. I felt like a human zombie. I'd wake in the mornings and get the boys ready. Once they were at school, I would go to my father-in-law's company and do his bookkeeping. At one o'clock, I'd fetched our youngest from school, then the middle child at two, then the eldest at three. I'd take them to chess, football practice, or karate. I did this day in, day out. I was a mother and a wife. I'd get home from a long day to make dinner and ensure the boys were fed and in bed. When Donnie got home, I made sure I fed him too. I did this every day and never complained because I loved them. They were my family, and I wouldn't trade being a mother and a wife for the world, but I had wanted more. I had wanted this. I had wanted something to get my blood boiling. I'd always known there had to be something more out there for me and not just the mundane activity of being a mother.

When I had first met Melissa and she had hinted at her extracurricular activity, I had to know more. She had confided in me, and when her handler had said he had two jobs on the same night, she asked if I wanted to take the other, and I had jumped at the chance. *Why not? What could go wrong?* I'm so glad I did it. I felt wonderful. I felt free and exhilarated by this experience. I felt like *a Jane*—someone who could do anything and become anybody. I didn't have to worry about feeding anyone. I didn't worry about getting anyone to bed. This was my time. This was my book club time, and even though the job was dangerous, I loved it.

***

We rounded the corner, entered the ground floor and exited by the service entrance. I stood straighter and neatened my uniform as I walked beside Kade.

He surveyed the lobby while I tried to do the same, but my vision was blurry. Still holding my hand, he pulled me behind the pillar and away from the front desk.

From what I could see, men sat in large chairs, reading newspapers. One of the front desk receptionists helped a man check in. A server offered a couple drinks. The bellhop pulled the empty luggage cart toward a new arrival. It was like a normal hotel lobby. So far, there were no men with guns.

The butterflies had stopped as I tasted freedom. We were right by the exit, and I could finally go home.

A man burst through the door we'd just used and spotted us. He casually approached, fixing his black top and righting his weapon that stuck out the front of his pants, not worried who saw him.

Kade pushed me beside him and away from the man. Slowly, we walked toward the exit.

As the man followed us, he eyed his surroundings then us, careful not to collide with any guests or staff.

The bellhop entered the lobby again, pushing his luggage cart now full of suitcases and garment bags between us and the man.

Kade shoved me out the entrance door and was right behind me as I glanced over my shoulder at the man in black fighting the bellhop to get out his way. We took a sharp left once we exited, and Kade pulled me down a dark path. We bolted through the small garden until we reached a side gate. Kade flicked open the latch and pushed me through.

The man hadn't seen us and continued straight.

Kade closed the door and latch quietly.

We walked casually down the alley and turned as headlights illuminated our path in the once dark alley.

Kade unholstered his weapon and pointed it at the vehicle.

They revved the engine.

Kade fired a few rounds.

The car jerked toward us as they smashed the gas.

Kade and I ran.

The car neared.

We were close to the end of the alley. As we reached the road, Kade fell into me.

The car zipped past us and into the busy road; horns blared, and people screamed.

Kade pulled me to my feet. "Take off your clothes."

"What?"

"The gray uniform, take it off," he said as he removed the concierge uniform but kept on the white shirt.

I removed the uniform and pulled on my jeans without bothering to notice if he was watching; I suspected we had more important things to worry about than whether my underwear matched or that I wore cotton. I pulled on my sneakers and threw the uniform into the heap of trash.

"Come."

We casually traversed the sidewalk as if nothing had just happened.

I sucked in the cool air and swallowed. My throat felt raw, my muscles ached, and a strange strangling sound came from the base of my throat; it wasn't quite a whimper but something similar. Relieved to be out of that hotel, I glanced over my shoulder and didn't see anyone following us. A smile flirted across my face.

Tires screeched on the road.

Kade and I turned toward the sound's direction.

The same car that had almost knocked us over swerved across the road, narrowly missing another vehicle. It parked in the first open space, and someone climbed out then slammed the door.

I could faintly decipher the person's features—bulky, black clothing and a shaved head.

He reached for something.

Kade grabbed me again, and we entered the nearest diner. "We have to get to my car," Kade whispered. "If he follows us in here, you need to run out the back, pass the tow truck shop until you reach a BMW." He handed me a set of car keys. "It's the only one in the parking lot." He glanced over his shoulder as we rushed toward the kitchen area.

Nobody bothered us. It was as if we weren't even there, but that was short lived. The chef yelled when he saw us, pointing a cleaver in our direction.

The swinging door opened behind Kade, knocking him into me. He pushed me out of the way and yelled, "Run!" He turned around and smashed his elbow into the assailant's face.

I wanted to watch, but I knew I had to get out. I shoved the chef out of my way and ran out the back. I passed the refuse, jumped over black bags and slammed my palms against the wooden gate, but instead of it opening, it bounced back and hit me in the face, and I crashed to the ground. I climbed to my feet and pushed slowly against the gate this time around. The opening was large enough for me to squeeze through; I scraped my palms on the ground as I crawled out. I glanced left and right and didn't see anyone approach. I had no idea where I was. It was dark, not as busy, and the area was the industrial part of town I'd never seen before. Up ahead, under dim lights was the shop Kade had alluded to. I carefully crossed the street at a brisk walk. I righted my bag, now slung over my shoulder, and walked with purpose —to get the hell outta here.

The BMW sat alone in the parking area. I pressed the fob, and the doors unlocked. I was about to climb in when a hand came from behind me and pushed it closed. I squealed and spun around. Then I did the only thing I thought of; I hit him with my bag.

He doubled over, and I brought my knee to his nose, followed by the sound of bone crunching. I opened the car door wide, hitting his shoulder and head, and he fell to the ground.

"Alright, you've made him pay. The guy is down for the count," Kade said through a light-hearted chuckle.

Blood caked near the scar, and his eye had swollen.

Kade grabbed the man's wrists and pulled him out of the way. "You ready?"

I nodded. "Definitely."

"Let's get you home."

Kade stopped a block from my house and left the car idling. Sweat peppered his face along with specks of dry blood. He did as he had promised; he'd saved me from being taken, killed one or two bad guys, and got me home safely. I would gladly trust him again with my life. He had protected me, didn't hurt me, and considered my feelings—as pathetic as it sounded—and I was grateful. It was strange to think those thoughts for a trained killer, but he had guided me throughout my entire experience. He had literally held my hand every step of the way.

I said goodnight.

He responded with a curt nod while one side of his mouth curled upward.

I closed his car door and traversed the path leading to our home as he drove away. The air was cool and crisp with the smell of rain. A mist dusted my face, making me flinch. I removed the compact from my bag and glanced at myself in the tiny mirror. I quickly wiped the perspiration off my face, dusted my cheeks and forehead with the face powder and spritzed perfume near my neck. Hopefully, I didn't smell too much like cigarettes, sweat, and lies.

When our house came into view, I smiled. Ignoring the fact I could've died tonight, I had thoroughly enjoyed myself. It was exciting and something I might do again, but only with someone like Kade. But next time, I wanted to be better prepared. I could join Donnie at the shooting range and take a self-defence class. Donnie had always suggested them to me, but I never had the urgency, until now. Then, when I was ready, I could do this on my own—if it was okay with Melissa's handler, of course. Thoughts of a more exciting future sent a flurry of butterflies loose within my stomach.

The porch and our bedroom lights were still on. Donnie was most likely waiting up for me. Feelings I hadn't felt since our honeymoon stirred within my core, and I couldn't wait to get home, shower and lie beside him. What I had done tonight helped with the monotony of my life—a lot. It filled me with excitement and adrenaline along with relief; I had a wonderful home to come to and someone who loved me.

I climbed the steps. My enthusiasm grew as I unlocked the front door and opened it. The interior light was on, and my heart dropped to my feet.

Donnie stopped on the last step with a chocolate bar in his mouth and a mischievous smile. I'd caught him red-handed when he was on a diet; chocolates were his kryptonite. "Babe, you're home"—he glanced at his watch—"early." He quickly stuffed the empty wrapper into his pocket and enveloped me in his arms while I clung to his waist, not wanting to let go even when he did. He realized I wasn't letting go and held me again, and we stood like that for a few minutes. "Is everything okay ...? Did something happen at your book club?"

"Nothing happened. Everything is fine. Actually, it's perfect," I said into his chest as I breathed him in—a little woody with hints of musk, as well as the chocolate he'd just eaten. Somehow, during our years together, I'd forgotten what he smelled like. We'd been intimate, and sometimes it felt robotic, but as I stood there and he held me, I remembered what it was like in our earlier years, and I wanted us to go back to those days. "Did the kids behave?" I managed to say in our embrace.

"When I'm around, they always do. All I had to do was threaten them with the handcuffs, and they scurried away in silence." He chuckled and kissed the top of my head. "You sure you're okay?" He moved, and I sensed he was staring down at me.

"Uh-huh." I glanced up as he tilted his chin toward me.

Our eyes locked, and his compassionate smile brightened his winsome face; an expression I loved and always reached within my core, lighting it on fire. My heart raced in my ears. I could no longer control myself and rocked onto my toes, wrapped my arms around his neck and kissed him. I pushed him against the wall as our tongues tangled and our hands fought to touch every inch of each other. My heart fluttered as he held my head with a hand while the other roamed under my shirt.

When I finally pulled away, he stared wide eyed, not quite believing what had just happened. "Wow." He grinned. "I mean, it's a good wow." He licked his lips. "See you upstairs?" He winked wickedly and smacked my ass.

"Put this in the fridge." I handed him the milk. "I'm just going to shower, then I'll see you under the covers." I darted upstairs while he switched off the lights.

Donnie opened the back door, traversed down the steps and opened the trash bin to throw the black bag inside. Leaves crunched, and he spun around with his weapon aimed at the figure emerging from the shadows.

"Easy there, tiger." Kade stepped forward with his hands raised and a smirk on his face.

"I could've killed you," Donnie whispered and closed the gap as he holstered his weapon. "How was it? You look a bit beaten up. I listened in when I could but didn't get everything."

"I'm good. It's just a scratch." He raised both thumbs. "It went really well. You should be proud. She's such a trooper." He slapped Donnie's shoulder.

Donnie couldn't contain his smile as he remembered the kiss they'd shared—a kiss he'd forgotten since their honeymoon.

"I think she might be up for another drop."

"Really? You think so?"

"Oh, yeah."

"But so soon. This was only her first time."

"Boss, she revelled in the chaos and excitement." Kade's voice raised.

"Shh."

"She did everything I asked and perfectly. I suspect she might want to start some class so she can fight for herself."

"Good. I've been telling her to attend one for years, and she never wanted to." Donnie nodded to himself as he pondered it. "If she enjoyed it so much, maybe we can do another round next month?"

"We could," Kade said, deep in thought. "Maybe a speedboat chase or something?"

"Do you think the guys want to do it again?"

Kade nodded. "Oh, hell yeah. They had just as much fun as *Jane*." He grinned knowingly.

"Let me think about it." He needed to be sure it's what she wanted to do. He didn't want Maddie doing anything like this again if she felt unsafe.

"I thought maybe we can turn this into a thing, you know, like an event where others paid for it."

"Okay, maybe. It sounds like a plan."

"And you owe me a hundred for the cleaning materials and tips we had to pay up front."

"Sure." Donnie shook Kade's hand. "Good job. I owe you bigtime, and tell the guys drinks are on me Friday."

"You got it." Kade turned in the same direction he had come from and waved over his head as he blended with the shadows.

Donnie entered the house, switched off the lights and ran up the stairs two at a time. He was pleased the night had ended in success.

Donnie had noticed a change in Maddie the last couple of months and had become concerned. She'd stopped smiling and didn't want to meet up with any of her friends. Then, when she had said she didn't want to go for Sunday lunch at his parent's house—which they did every week—it was the last straw. He knew he had to do something, and quickly. He wasn't a psychologist, but he knew Maddie; they'd been together since high school, and he loved her with every inch of his heart. She was the mother to their boys and his soulmate. And when Kade kept badgering him about what was wrong, he confided in him. It was Kade who had suggested she might need a little *action* in her life.

"Just try it once, and, if it doesn't work, then you'll know," Kade had said over beers a month ago. *"Leave it up to me. I'll get a few guys I trust to help me out, and you'll see. She'll bounce right back,"* he had said with a wink.

Donnie smiled to himself as he closed their bedroom door. He raked his eyes over Maddie's naked body as she stepped out the shower, not bothering with a towel.

She stared at him with the similar look from years ago, and he knew everything that had happened tonight was worth it. His Maddie was back.

ABOUT THE AUTHOR

N Gray lives in Cape Town, South Africa with her hubby, daughter, and two fur babies. During the day she's an analyst and provider profiler for a medical insurance company. At night, she types on her curved keyboard creating fictional characters some may love, and others you want to kill yourself.

She writes in three genres: thriller, urban fantasy, and horror, with a series available in each.

Keep in touch with N Gray via the web: https://www.ngray-books.com/

TEMPTRESS

FALLON RAYNES

When local bars become the hot target for thieves, Detective Reyes is reminded that temptation comes in many forms.

1

A vision in a red dress and spiky, black heels fluttered into the bar. Her short, flared skirt danced at her long legs from the rush of the evening breeze coming through the open door. She brushed a strand of flame-red hair behind her ear. The door closed, darkening the room. The lady in red stood there at the entrance as she searched the dimly lit surroundings. Behind the bar was Frank, the owner of the outdated bar called Lucky's. He stood frozen with his gaze on the woman, his mouth agape.

Grady smirked, thinking the guy's sad old eyes had probably never seen the likes of this gal. His gal, in fact, and aptly nicknamed "Red," her favorite color.

Finally, she found what she was searching for—or more accurately, *whom*. Grady grinned and made a "tipping of the hat" motion. Red's full lips turned up in a smile as she sashayed over to him. He held out his arms, and she threw herself into his embrace. Her skirt twirled up as he swung her around a few times before setting her down for a kiss. He sucked in a deep breath of air and tasted her sweet perfume. He looked around, noticing the patrons at the bar and pool table were just as enthralled with them as he had hoped they would be.

She pulled herself away and blushed demurely. *Ah, she's good,* Grady thought. He steadied her and offered the chair next to the pool table.

The sharp smacking of the balls resumed. He smirked, winked, and then headed to the bar to get her a drink and refill his whiskey.

When he returned, he gave her another quick wink as he set an icy mug of beer in front of her. She took a quick sip and seductively licked the foam off her lips. He had to admit, Red was hard to ignore. And that was exactly what they wanted.

Her grand entrance had actually worked. No one had seen Kent come in and slip to the back office. Their plan was in motion. When her knees started to bounce slightly—a hint that she was getting anxious—Grady pushed down on them gently. He took his thumb and started tracing circles on the fair skin of her inner thigh.

He nodded slightly toward the bar, and she casually turned to look in that direction. The bartender's eyes locked with hers, and she ran her tongue along her top lip while Grady's hand wandered up her skirt. She was definitely the main attraction this evening. Grady continued the play, stroking the inside of her leg with his rough hand. His phone buzzed in his pocket—once, then two more times.

That was the signal. *Show time.* Grady slid Red's chair closer to him, put his arm around her back, hand on her shoulder. He lightly squeezed three times to relay the message. Red stiffened, and he looked directly into those green eyes and gave her a smile of assurance. *Everything will be fine.*

She picked up her mug and sucked in a small amount of the foam. Looking over the rim of the glass, she batted her lashes at Frank. She slowly lowered the mug. Gave a provocative smile, one eyebrow raised. She had all the moves.

Grady glared at the bartender and stood up, knocking his chair to the floor. He hollered at Frank, "Get your eyes off my lady!"

Red grabbed for Grady's arm and pleaded for him to sit down. Grady pulled his arm out of her hold, and stalked over to Frank. Leaning across the bar top, sticking his finger in the bartender's face, he said through gritted teeth, "You've been ogling her since she walked in. Keep your eyes to yourself, old man!"

Frank had backed up against the liquor bottles, which clanked and teetered dangerously. Somehow, none fell to the floor. Fear was etched across his face. He threw his hands up and said, "Don't want no trouble, man. I don't want your girl."

One of the two patrons sitting at the bar hopped out of the way, taking his drink with him. The other man sat there and slurred, "Don't both-errr F-Frank, man."

Grady whipped around to stab his finger into the drunk's chest. "Shut it," Grady growled.

The guy swayed and fell off his stool to the dusty floor. His buddy tried to pick him up but promptly fell over when his legs gave out—clearly inebriated as well. Grady wanted to laugh at their mayhem but refrained, turning his gaze back on Frank, who had moved farther down the bar.

Two pool players headed in their direction, pool sticks in hand, ready to intervene. Red threw her hands out to stop them. The tall, skinny one grabbed her by the arm and shoved her out of the way, causing a yelp to escape her lips. Upon hearing this, Grady spun around just in time to see Red lose her balance and fall to the floor.

He lost his cool, face reddening, eyes narrowing, throwing a barstool out of his way as he stalked over to the guy, whose emaciated body could barely hold up his filthy jeans. Grady's fist connected nicely with the man's ugly face.

Grady had been counting on just this sort of scuffle to keep the attention on them—at least for now. He also thoroughly enjoyed this part of the con.

Kent was holed up just out of sight in the dark hallway. He heard Red's yelp. He sneaked a peek around the corner and saw Grady land a fist into the gangly dude's face. All eyes were on the chaos, and that was his cue. He left out the side door he had used just moments earlier. Grady and Red would be coming out shortly, and he would be waiting with the car running at the front door.

Kent was quick with small, old safes. He had been cracking those since his alcoholic, abusive father had taught him, way back when.

The front door of the bar slammed opened, interrupting his trip down memory lane. Grady had a smile on his face, and Red was flushed as they raced to the car. Kent was driving off before the doors were closed.

"How much did the old geezer have?" Grady asked as they headed toward the expressway.

"About six grand, give or take." Kent checked the rearview mirror to glance at Red. "How are you doin', girl?"

"I'm okay. That skinny bastard didn't have much in him, but I made it look good." She smirked at Kent in the mirror, who chortled at her reply.

He then turned to look at Grady in the passenger seat. "How'd you do, buddy?" When Grady turned to face him, a scowl on his lips, Kent jerked his head back as he saw the shiner for the first time. He winced at the sight. "Damn."

Grady gently touched his eye. "Yeah, I was doin' just fine till the one guy knocked me from behind. Cheap shot. But the black eye didn't come from him—I hit the corner of the table. Asshole. But I laid him out. All's well that ends well, and all that crap," he said with a Cheshire-cat grin.

Kent chuckled. "Sounds like you had fun."

Grady said, "Yeah, just get us to the motel in one piece, will ya?"

2

Wednesday Morning

Detective Reyes answered the phone at his desk early at the Midland Law Enforcement Center Wednesday morning. He listened, grunted a few times as a response, then wrote down the information he was given. Hanging up the phone without saying goodbye, he eyeballed his partner, who sat at a desk across from him.

Detective Hannah merely stared at him, waited. They'd known each other a long time, and sometimes words were not necessary.

Finally, Reyes spoke. "A break-in over at Lucky's—ya know, Frank's place. Someone stole money out of his safe."

"Something you can handle alone?" Hannah motioned to the paperwork on his desk. "I can certainly keep busy here."

Reyes nodded. "Yeah, I've got this covered. Sounds like I'm getting the better deal anyway. I'll leave you to it." He smiled wide as he grabbed his coffee and headed for the door.

He hit every single red light while heading to Lucky's. What normally should have taken ten minutes was doubled. That pissed him off—traffic.

Everyone knew Frank at Lucky's, but the man served fewer and fewer patrons over the years. Since craft beer had become more sought after in Michigan, bars like this were feeling the hit. Frank was hanging in there, though. Sometimes even the younger crowd showed up and raised some hell at the old bar. Reyes knew that always made Frank's cash register a little fuller. But mostly the bar catered to the regulars during the week. So this robbery surprised Reyes, as this was not a hot place for money, to put it mildly. And that made him curious. Very curious, indeed. The thief wasn't looking for a lot of money, it appeared. Small-time crook. Or maybe he had been disappointed in the haul from Lucky's. Still, it was strange.

Reyes slipped his gloves on, walked in, and saw Frank sitting at the bar. He looked broken. The detective spoke in a soft voice, "Hey, Frank. Sorry to meet under these conditions."

Frank turned. "Hey, Ricky. Me too. Me too." He saw the gloves on the detective's hands, and his shoulders sunk a little more.

Reyes caught the change. "So, tell me what happened, as much as you know."

Frank took in a deep breath, let it out. "I came in this morning, counted the till. When I went to put the money in the safe, the damn thing was empty. Open and empty." He dropped his head into his hands. "It's all gone, Ricky. Gone! I don't understand. Everything was locked when I came in."

"Can you show me around?" Reyes said. "I'd like to take a look at everything."

Frank looked up and nodded, slid off the stool. "Follow me."

Reyes eyeballed the surroundings as the men headed toward the office. He'd already noted that the front door did not appear to have been tampered with. The long, skinny, horizontal windows at the top of the bar were the typical style that didn't open. Each was still intact. Reyes stopped beside the alley door and noted the wood frame was untouched. He pulled the door open with gloved hands and examined the lock. Nothing looked like it had been jimmied. He followed Frank into the office and saw the open safe behind the old wooden desk.

Kneeling down Reyes saw no signs of forced entry on the safe, which had an old-style combination lock. Nothing fancy.

Reyes straightened with his eyes on the solitary window in the office—also one that did not open. The frame was untouched. He walked around the office looking for anything the thief may have left behind, but nothing caught his attention. He hadn't really expected that, but hey... a guy can dream.

"Frank, did you find anything else missing?"

"No, my gun goes upstairs with me at night, and as I mentioned, the money was still in the till. I didn't put it away last night. I was a bit frazzled after the fight."

Reyes's ears perked up. "Fight? You didn't mention that. Did you call it in?"

"Yeah. Your guys showed up and took my complaint. The troublemaker had left with a drop-dead gorgeous redhead by the time they got here." Frank paused, chewed on his lip. "You know, that dame was part of the problem, actually."

"Yeah? How so?" Reyes's interest was piqued.

Frank ran through the events that had taken place the night before, starting with when the lady had entered the establishment. Reyes jotted it down in his notepad, all the while forming a mini movie of the evening his mind. With the lack of evidence for a straight-up break-in, he put his attention on this bar fight. It might have been a diversion. The thief could have stolen the money while the fight was taking place.

It was the oldest trick in the book. Magicians used it. And so did con men. While every eye was focused on the diversion, no one ever noticed the quarter disappear, so to speak. Maybe, just maybe, he had his first clue.

He questioned Frank some more about the patrons and how well he knew them. The only newbies were the man and woman. Reyes was really liking this couple for the ruse. He looked around the bar and asked, "Did you ever install any cameras in here?"

"No. I don't know anything about them, and I wouldn't know what to do with them anyway. You know I don't use that new technology."

Reyes nodded, knowing Frank didn't even have a cell phone. The bar owner was a simple man.

The detective excused himself, went out to his car, and grabbed the fingerprinting kit he kept in his glove box. Then he went to work dusting for prints.

The old safe was dimpled and wouldn't pull any clean prints, but he did it anyway. For Frank's benefit, mostly. To reassure the old guy that everything was being done to uncover the robber, or robbers.

Reyes then dusted doorknobs, door frames, and any surface he thought the thief may have laid his hands on. He snapped photos and, last, took Frank's prints.

"Thanks, Ricky. I appreciate you doing this." Frank's brows furrowed at the dusty mess all over the office. "Can I clean up now that you're done? Or does this need to look like a crime scene for a while?"

"Nah, go ahead and clean, get things in order, Frank, I have everything I need. Sorry to make such a mess, but maybe we'll find something helpful." Reyes gave a tight-lipped smile, trying to convey encouragement he didn't feel. Frank was of the generation where you helped people in need. To see him get taken like this was heartbreaking. He knew Frank didn't have a lot to survive on. Reyes vowed to do his damnedest to get that money back for his old friend.

They said their goodbyes, and Reyes stepped outside. He looked around the parking lot, at the building itself, and then at the surrounding buildings. No visible surveillance cameras anywhere.

Frank had mentioned that when he and his customers were interviewed by the cops last night, no one had seen the vehicle the couple had left in. Reyes had been hoping for a video to shed some light on the getaway car. He hopped in his truck and drove around the area, looking for security cameras. Or any other inspiration.

3

Thursday Morning

Detective Reyes was in the LEC the next morning looking over the reports that had come through for the fingerprints. Most of the prints were smudged, and the only clean set of prints matched Frank's. He'd had no luck with security cameras, either. Frank had given him a detailed description of the couple who had been at the bar that night. Reyes had a strong feeling they were in on the heist. But where to start when there were no leads?

Yet.

He raked his hand through his brown hair, determined to find focus and get justice for Frank.

"You look like you could use this." Hannah set a cup of coffee down in front of Reyes as he passed his desk.

"I've already had three, but thanks." Reyes picked up the cup.

"Any leads from those prints?"

"No. Frank's were the only match. The rest were unusable. I'm going to hazard a guess and say the thief was wearing gloves. The safe didn't pull up much. It was an old safe, lots of dimples. No cameras in the area to pinpoint a getaway vehicle. Our only chance is they hit again—and screw up." Reyes frowned, setting his cup down. "At least that's how it seems right now."

“Well, Frank has always been good with faces, so maybe that will help.”

“Yes, the details he gave were perfect.”

Hannah nodded and looked down at his desk. He picked up the piece of paper lying next to his phone. It was a new lead for a case that had come in while Reyes was out yesterday. “Well, perhaps this will interest you.” He tossed the paper over to his partner’s desk. “There was a stolen car called in yesterday. A connection with the robbery?” He shrugged. “Maybe, huh? They found the car near the edge of town. Let’s go check it out.”

“Let’s,” Reyes said without hesitation. He’d take any lead he could get.

4

Kent and Grady had each taken a few hundred for themselves the minute they'd arrived at the motel. The rest they stashed in a vent in their motel room. Red was out on a food run. When she returned, they would discuss their next steps over a few hamburgers. They wanted to make two more hits, if they could. Then they'd lie low for a while. The two old friends had grown up in the Tri-Cities. Bay City, Midland, and Saginaw were easy to access from their cheap hideout near the US-10 exit.

Red was the newest to the team. She was a hot looker who had been seeing a guy Grady had worked a job with before. She had run into Grady the night she and the guy broke up. Cried on Grady's shoulder, she did. And that was that. She was "in." Kent suspected she'd get bored with him soon enough, though. Red came across like she was destined for more than hanging around two common thieves. She wore nice things. Expensive things. Things Grady couldn't afford; he liked to fight and couldn't hold down a job.

A car door slammed shut, and Grady went to the window, pulled the curtain aside, and peeked out. It was Red, juggling some McDonald's bags and a drink tray.

Grady opened the door with a love-sick grin on his face. Red glided in wearing red shorts and matching tank top and kissed his cheek.

"Food's up, guys," she said as she dropped the fast food on the small table. The smell had Kent's stomach growling, and he realized it had been a long time since he'd last eaten. He shoved some fries in his mouth just as Red was heading back out the door. "Be right back," she said with a wave of her finger. Upon returning, she carried a few other shopping bags. Red sure was on fire to spend the dough.

The group settled in around the little table with Red on Grady's lap—there were only two chairs in the room. Grady was feeding Red fries as she giggled. Kent just shook his head. The two were nuts for each other; that much was clear. The display they made last night had been part of the plan, but he knew Grady was falling hard for this little minx. He hoped she didn't break his heart. Grady was like the brother Kent never had.

The trio finished their feast and cleared the table. Kent grabbed the drawings of the two locations they could possibly rob tonight. Ray's Tavern in particular was preferred. If the parking lot wasn't too busy, they would hit there first. Kent and Grady had already been to all the area bars quite a few times over the past few weeks. They'd gone in separately so as not to draw suspicion. It made a job easier when they'd familiarized themselves with the layout of the establishments and the movements of the staff.

Grady had not been able to get into the office at Jackson's Watering Hole; the door had been locked. And he was almost caught trying to pick the lock. So Ray's was better to try tonight. It had a safe in the office closet that was a combination lock—Kent was a wiz at those. They knew it would be a quick in-and-out. In fact, the bar was similar to Lucky's.

Grady nodded at Kent. "Easy peasy."

"Should be," Kent agreed, rubbing his chin.

They had been left alone to work out these plans, as Red had run off to the bathroom with her bags. She seemed to care less about preparation and more about the spending of the loot. But she was good at her game, and they were happy to oblige her nonchalance.

"What do you boys think?" she said, exiting the bathroom.

Grady gave a low wolf whistle in appreciation.

Kent beamed from ear to ear. "Sexy mama!"

In a blond wig that came down just past her shoulders, Red twirled around in a white, flouncy skirt with red polka dots on it. The red peasant blouse was pulled down low on her shoulders—she was braless, to boot. Red always picked out the flared skirts so they would fly up when Grady twirled her, giving the voyeurs a quick peek at her panties. She was a temptress with a capital T.

"What time are we leaving?" Red asked as she sauntered over to the table. Just as Kent started to respond, she said, "Ooo," and gently caressed the shiner on Grady's face. "We need to cover that up first." She grabbed her bag and pulled out her makeup case. After choosing a tube of skin-colored goo, she applied it around Grady's eye. When she stepped back to admire her work, Kent was surprised to see the black eye was no longer visible. *Impressive. Girl's got skills,* Kent thought.

Grady said, "Feels funny," and raised his hand to touch the area.

Red quickly smacked his hand away. "No touchy. You'll mess it up."

Kent laughed at Grady's expense. "Okay, ten minutes till we head out. Are you guys ready?" He established eye contact with each of them as they simultaneously responded with, "Yep."

Kent rubbed his hands together, then stood. He was more than ready to test their lucky streak, especially with the next bar being such a sure thing. "Okay, then. Gather your stuff, and let's make some scratch."

5

Thursday Evening

Grady held Red's hand as he led her into Ray's Tavern with its low lights and loud music rushing from the jukebox. The place had a dance floor with room for a band and a few pool tables. Muffled conversation filled the air while they made their way to the tables near the dance floor. There was one waitress working, and the bartender was behind the bar. The waitress was new, at least to Grady. He hadn't noticed her before; it had only been the bartender whenever he'd scouted the joint. This could be tricky.

Grady glanced around the room as they grabbed a seat. There were a few couples stretched across the bar, keeping to themselves. Not many at the tables. One man sitting at the end of the bar was talking to the bartender. A couple of single guys were standing around the pool table at the back of the room. One of them was racking the balls for the next game. It was a small, quiet crowd. Grady hoped it stayed that way.

"What'll it be, folks?" the petite, dark-haired waitress asked.

"We'll have a couple of drafts, please." Grady smiled, handing her a ten.

She plucked the bill from his fingers. "Comin' right up."

Grady made his way over to the jukebox and saw that there was no song scheduled to play next. He dropped a bunch of quarters in and loaded some tunes to set the mood. They had a few more minutes before it would be dark enough in the alley. Then Kent could slip in the side door from the dark alley without anyone noticing. The fourth song Grady selected was with purpose. He wanted to grab the attention of everyone in the room when it started playing. He and Red had practiced earlier that day behind the motel. She was a quick study. All eyes would be on them in no time.

The barmaid was dropping off their drinks when he sauntered back to their table. He gave her a quick cowboy nod and took his seat at the table, next to Red. They both took long draws of their drafts. Red had already caught the eye of one of the pool players. She licked the froth off her lips as the guy watched. Grady held in a chuckle. The girl was something else. He couldn't wait to start the show.

Grady and Red flirted with each other while they waited for their cue. The second song came on, and the barmaid headed to the back. Grady watched for her to return while keeping up his end of the flirting. When the third song started to play, Grady could feel the knots forming in his stomach. Red's knee started to bounce—her nervous twitch, so to speak. He slid his hand onto her thigh to gently reassure her, like he had the other night at Lucky's. The waitress still had not returned from the back.

Red raised an eyebrow at Grady, who shrugged. Maybe this wasn't going to work out after all. About the time he had decided to go ahead and text Kent the Code Red signal—effectively nixing the operation—the waitress walked back into view, drying her hands on her apron. Grady and Red visibly relaxed, taking long swigs of their beers. Grady looked around and verified that everyone else was still accounted for. The song stopped. The fourth song came on, and Grady stood up. This song was long, flirty, and contagious. He grinned from ear to ear as he reached for Red's hand, all gentleman-like. "Would you care to dance, ma'am?"

"Why, yes, I would love to, kind sir." Red blushed and giggled as she placed her hand in his like a princess.

Grady sent Red spinning onto the dance floor. She squealed as she twirled, her skirt flying up and out. Her red panties made their debut, and gauging by the crowd's full attention, the peepshow was a hit.

Red took her stance as Grady had taught her. He danced toward her, a routine he knew well. The chicks loved it, and, man, he loved the chicks. Especially this one. Red was his "Baby," and he was excited to play the part of Johnny tonight.

The people started cheering them on as they played out the scene from *Dirty Dancing*. The famous part was coming up. Grady felt the tension from the onlookers as they anticipated it.

Red took off and floated through the air. He caught her. Perfection.

Cheers and whistles erupted from the crowd as he brought her back down and kissed her hard on the lips. Red couldn't wipe the smile off her face as the song ended and the next track Grady had queued started to play.

Everyone went back to what they were doing. Grady's phone buzzed the signal from Kent. It was done. They only had to finish their beers and leave. Grady dropped a five on the table for a tip, then gave Red a passionate kiss, indicating to anyone who was watching that they were ready to leave the bar and light up another room—like a bedroom.

They stood. She wrapped one arm around his middle and didn't take her eyes off his face as he escorted her from the bar.

He couldn't tell if she was still acting or if she was falling for him.

6

Kent waited at the curb a few spaces down from the front of the bar, trying to control his accelerated heart rate. *What a rush!* He loved the thrill. He'd sent the code message off to Grady while the car idled, and upon seeing his partners exiting the bar, he let loose a long sigh of relief. It was now 10:30 p.m. and he didn't think they would have enough time to hit the second bar on their list. Besides, that one was a little iffy anyway, as Grady had never been able to put his eyes on the office. The team had figured out these bars picked up on Thursday nights around this area.

Grady let Red slide in the front seat between him and Kent. She was glowing. The bar was pretty soundproof, but Kent could hear the music at the door. When the fourth song had started, he had let a few seconds pass and then entered. He caught part of their act as he casually made his way to the back. The office was unlocked. He was quick and efficient. He saw Red take flight. A heart-stopping sight.

Grady looked around Red at Kent. "I wish you could have seen us. We knocked it out of the park! Red, you were sensational." Grady squeezed her shoulder as he put his arm around her.

"Oh my God! I can't sit still. I want to go back and do it again!" Red bounced in her seat with delight. "That was so much fun!"

"Well, some night when we're all caught up, you'll have to do a repeat for me." Kent laughed as he pulled onto the street, heading to the expressway. With both of them worked up, he knew for sure there was no way they could pull off another heist tonight. "We're headed to our motel home, kids. That's enough for tonight."

"Sounds good to me," Grady murmured as he pulled Red into his chest. She planted a big, wet kiss on his lips.

Here we go with these two, Kent thought with a small grin. *But a damn good team.* In no time, they were on the expressway. They'd be back to the motel and counting their haul in ten minutes.

"When you wanna hit Jackson's?" Grady asked after coming up for air.

Ken said, "Let's see how things go. Maybe tomorrow, hit it at eight-ish before it gets busy. This time, remember, we'll all go in together."

"Tomorrow is Friday. You think it's safe to do? Maybe we should hold off until next week when the place won't be too busy," Red suggested.

"I think it'll be fine." Kent shook it off with a smile at Red, then looked back at the road.

"Yeah, Baby, we've got it covered," Grady said, using her nickname from the routine they had completed.

Still grinning, Kent glanced at the two of them. "Yeah, *Baby*."

Red shrugged and let it go, but Kent noticed that her smile had faded as she looked out the windshield. Kent turned his focus back to the road.

The trio went silent the rest of the way to the motel. The parking lot held a few more cars in it since they had left. Kent pulled the bag from the trunk. They all went inside. He dropped the bag onto the table and pulled on the zipper. The money was askew in the bottom of the bag; a few of the rubber bands had broken.

Red kept walking to the bathroom and shut the door. Kent looked at Grady and whispered, "You think she's good?"

"Yeah, yeah. I'm sure the high wore off on the way back." Grady glanced back at the bathroom door as if to reassure himself she wasn't listening.

“Because if not, we can take tomorrow on by ourselves. We’ve done it before.” Kent kept his voice low.

“Nah, dude, she’s good.” Grady nodded his head at the bag. “Let’s get this counted so we can relax the rest of the night.” They both reached in and grabbed handfuls of money until the bag was empty.

7

Reyes drove by the Backdoor Bar on his way home. It was similar to Frank's. He decided to stop in and see what Chief was up to. Maybe do a little scouting to see if he had cameras, in case his place was next. The stolen car had been a bust. There were witnesses that saw a couple of teenagers crash the car and run. He pulled into the alley, parked, and turned off the engine.

He immediately noticed the side door of the bar wasn't lit up like it normally was. He got out of his unmarked car and flipped his cell phone's flashlight on. Looking around, he didn't see anything out of the ordinary.

He continued into the bar and saw a handful of people gathered at the pool tables and a few patrons talking to Chief at the bar. There was a couple necking in the back corner booth. Everything seemed normal, and not too many heads turned to look his way when he entered.

Chief looked up and waved him over. The detective smiled at his tall, burly friend as he made his way over.

"Hey, Chief. How goes it?" He nodded when Chief held up the whiskey bottle with Reyes's favorite label on it. "That sounds good tonight."

Chief poured the whiskey, neat, and brought it over to him. The customers he'd been talking to wandered over to a table near the jukebox. Reyes had Chief to himself for a few minutes. "Pretty quiet tonight for a Thursday, isn't it?"

"Yes and no. It's been pretty steady lately. Tomorrow night, it will be a bigger crowd." The big guy smiled. "How have you been? I haven't seen you in a few weeks. Wife keeping you busy, or is it the mistress?" He winked at the detective.

"The mistress, for sure." Reyes chuckled at Chief's label for his job that keeps him away from his family. "There's a case I'm working on. Mostly the reason I made time to stop in tonight."

"Oh? Why would that involve me? There haven't been any fights in here since last summer."

"I know. There's a case I'm working, like I said. I think they're hitting places like yours. Oh, that reminds me... Did you know your bulb is burnt out in the alley?"

"Weird. I just replaced that thing the other night." Chief scratched his head. "You mind watching the bar while I go grab another bulb and put it in?"

Reyes sipped on his whiskey and nodded. "Go for it."

"Thanks. When I get back, I want to hear more about this case of yours."

Reyes surveyed the room, looking for little red blinking lights to indicate a camera was in use. He didn't see any, or at least they weren't visible to him. He finished his whiskey just as Chief returned wearing a puzzled look on his face and carrying a package of light bulbs.

"That bulb wasn't burnt out. It was loose. Almost loose enough to fall out on someone." Chief rubbed the back of his neck, "I know darn well that I tightened that bulb when I replaced it. And it worked."

"Do you have video cameras? I was glancing around, and I'm not seeing any."

"Not in the alley. I have a few hidden cameras in here and my office. The kind that fit into small spaces. The footage gets loaded to the cloud. My daughter Lucy put them in for me last year after the last fight at the bar."

"Good. Do you think you could get a few put up on the outside tomorrow?"

"Yeah, I'm sure she can do that. Question is, why?"

"Like I mentioned earlier, a few bars like yours are getting hit. Play it safe."

Chief shrugged. "I hear ya. Will do."

Reyes pulled his wallet out and flipped Chief a ten spot. "About that light bulb… I think you might want to check your cloud footage."

"Doubt I'll see anything. I looked at the lock. It wasn't jimmied, and nothing has been touched in here."

"Yeah, maybe they didn't make it inside this time, but that bulb didn't loosen itself, Chief. Call me if you find anything." He pulled his card out and handed it to the bar owner, who agreed to do just that.

Reyes flipped him a wave as he left the bar. If he were a betting man, he'd put money on that call tomorrow. And Reyes *was* a betting man. He slowly pulled out of the alley and made his way around the block, looking for more cameras set up on the few businesses in this area of town.

For whatever reason, he felt it in his gut: the Backdoor Bar was on the hit list. He decided to swing back around to watch the bar for another hour before he went home.

8

Friday Morning

Reyes arrived early at the office the next morning. His impromptu stakeout had been unsuccessful. But when he found a message waiting on his desk, he cursed out loud. The thugs had hit again. He was pissed. Ray at Ray's Tavern had noticed his safe was empty at the end of the night. Ray had called the station a little after two that morning. Another detective had taken the call. It appeared he had already done the legwork for him.

The copy of the report was with the message. Reyes sat down at his desk and finished reviewing it. He logged into his computer and brought up the local dive bars on the map. Ray's Tavern was on the other side of town. He grabbed his coffee and headed out, planning to scout the area for video footage. The other detective had mentioned there were no cameras in the establishment. More work to be done. Most likely the prints would be nonexistent, like with Frank's place.

There were only two more bars in town that fit the description. Places that were easier to hit—no visible cameras. He needed to get to Jackson's Watering Hole when it opened at noon. He would grab some lunch, give them a heads-up. He would set up surveillance at Jackson's tonight. He knew time was running out before the thieves moved on to another town. Or worse, someone got hurt trying to be a hero. So far, no one had caught them in the act. And no weapons had yet to be involved. He didn't even want to think about the list of things that could go wrong. Either way, he wanted vindication, and most importantly, to return the money stolen from Frank—a true friend; in fact, more like a father to him than he'd ever had.

He could not fail.

9

Reyes's phone buzzed on his way back from Jackson's Watering Hole, and he punched up the call. "Reyes here."

"It's Chief. Can you stop by?" The bar owner sounded antsy, speaking at a fast clip.

"I'm not far from you now. I'll be there in five."

He made it there in four minutes and rushed through the door, anxious to hear what Chief had discovered.

"Thanks for coming so quickly." Chief and his daughter Lucy were standing at the door when Reyes walked in.

"No problem. You seem stressed. What did you find?"

"Lucy has the camera footage on my computer."

As they walked to the tall bar top, Lucy filled him in on setting up the other security cameras outside. Reyes said a small prayer of thanks for the woman's skills.

She motioned for Reyes to have a seat. "Check it out. This is what we saw when I brought up the footage from last week." She clicked to play the video. "As you can see, this is the camera for the back office here. I also have more footage of this guy from other cameras. I saved it all on this thumb drive for you." She dropped the drive into his open palm.

Reyes watched as the video depicted the office door opening. The intruder searched the room and then, *bingo*, a camera shot of this fool's face, up close and personal, as he eyeballed the safe.

"Thanks, Lucy. This is great!"

"There's more footage on that thumb drive, shows him on the other cameras and his other visits here." She slid a piece of paper to Reyes. "Here is a printed picture of his face. It's the best one I could find from all his visits."

Reyes was beyond impressed. "Lucy, this will help me break this case, I can just feel it."

Chief beamed and put his arm around his daughter's shoulders.

Reyes held the thumb drive up, then pocketed it. "Thank you both. This is a hot lead. I need to get back and get this sorted. Do not go near this guy and his accomplices if they come in here. Let us do our job. We'll be here tonight, watching." Reyes gave Chief a stern look.

Chief threw up his hands. "No problem. We'll stay out of the way."

"Thank you." He could barely contain his enthusiasm as he headed back to his car.

10

Friday Night

Grady, Kent, and Red walked into the latest soon-to-be victim's bar, where a jukebox was playing a slow song and two couples were glued together on the dance floor. The trio had a different plan to play out tonight. They were here to get in and out quickly, so they could pillage one other place too. Tomorrow, they'd move on.

Red looked at Kent with her pouty lips and held her hand out for some quarters. He dipped into his pocket and handed her a wad. The waitress dropped by the table after Red got up to select her songs. They ordered drafts for themselves and one for Red. She came back and sat down. She leaned into Kent's ear and whispered something. Kent smiled. Grady pulled Red into his lap. He held his arm around her possessively, glaring at Kent.

The barmaid brought the beers back to the table. Kent flipped her some cash to cover the drinks and a tip. They wouldn't be here much longer. They all took a few sips of their beers and made small talk. Red's song came on, and she pulled Grady to his feet and dragged him over to the dance floor. At the same time, Kent got up to make his way to the back office. He was intent on getting the job done and hitting the road. Red wiggled her fingers at Kent as he walked past them.

Grady turned red in the face and stopped dancing. "What the fuck was that about?"

"What was what?" Red asked incredulously.

Grady wiggled his fingers, duplicating her wave to Kent. "That!" he growled. "Do you want him or me, because you can't have us both!"

Red raised her chin defiantly. "I don't know what you're talking about. I was just waving at him. Get over yourself."

"Well, quit flirting with him. You're with me. Don't be a tease!"

"Wh-what did you just call me?" Her eyes widened, and her nostrils flared with anger.

And just like that, all eyes were on them.

"You heard me. You do this every time we go out!" Grady took it up a notch and lightly shoved Red's shoulders. She stepped back a few paces.

"Don't you do that!" she shouted and put some power behind that exclamation by kicking her booted foot at Grady. He stepped out of the way just in time. He grabbed her around the waist and dropped her over his shoulder. "That's enough! You've caused enough of a scene already, little missy!" With that, he hauled her off the dance floor, despite her kicking and screaming.

Everyone moved out of the way as he made his way to the door. Kent came out of the back, pretending to dry his hands on his pants. He looked up and saw Red's panties bouncing in view beneath her short skirt. He shook his head and then caught the waitress's attention as he was about to walk past her. "I'm so sorry! These two do this all the time!"

"Oh, that's okay." She laughed nervously.

Kent winked at her, and she blushed. He made his exit. He was whistling as he made his way over to his partners in crime. They were aglow with the adventure—Red especially, as she jumped up and down with glee. "We did it again, boys!" They slid into the front seat to the sound of her giggles.

Kent went to open the driver's-side door. "Yes, we di—" But his words were halted by the piercing light that was suddenly cast upon them. "What the...?"

He turned and saw guns pointed at them. Someone yelled, "You're under arrest! Get your hands up!"

He was slammed against the car.

Grady and Red were being pulled from the car on the opposite side.

Kent was kicking himself. He knew they should have left this town sooner. He didn't utter a word as his homemade waist money bag was dropped onto the car hood.

11

Saturday evening

Reyes couldn't have been prouder of his team. They'd executed the plan without anyone getting hurt. As it turned out, this band of thieves were unarmed. Brian Jackson thanked them for busting them outside his place. Reyes had called the other team off Chief's bar—the criminals had been apprehended. Chief was grateful they hadn't hit his place. A motel key had been found on them, allowing law enforcement to find the motel it belonged to. After securing a search warrant, Reyes found their pile of money neatly stashed in the bathroom vent.

The case was wrapped up, and the thieves were behind bars, pending their day in court. Reyes pulled up in front of Lucky's on Saturday night shortly before closing. Frank was busy behind the bar, which made Reyes happy. It allowed Reyes to slip back to the office without Frank seeing him.

Opening the middle desk drawer, he saw the bank deposit bag. He took the envelope of cash out of his waist band. Put the cash inside the bag, then closed the drawer. He tucked the empty envelope back in his jacket and walked out of the office, locking the door on his way out. It had not been locked when he'd entered. *Frank, you're still too trusting.*

With a smile on his face, he went up front and sat at the bar. He was going to celebrate. He smiled at Frank and ordered his drink. He knew Frank had already turned in the claim to his insurance company. This was just icing on the cake. He'd made sure that the portion he'd stuff inside the bank bag had not been included in the evidence count. Reyes was happy that he'd given in to the temptation to handle things this way. After all, Frank deserved a little more for his trouble.

ABOUT THE AUTHOR

Fallon Raynes is a paper pusher by day, writer by night. Writing has been in Fallon's blood for as long as she can remember. Short stories and poems kept her mind at ease earlier on. Life's adventures have swirled in her mind to create some exaggerated stories that she's excited to put to paper and share with the world. To relax, Fallon enjoys watching the ID, Lifetime, and Hallmark channels, reading, and the outdoors.

Fallon resides in lower Michigan with her husband and fur-baby.

https://www.fallonraynes.com/books

LANE DEPARTURE

TOM FOWLER

John Tyler thought he stumbled into a robbery. If only it were so simple...

1

John Tyler thought it was a robbery at first.

The guy standing at the door provided the first clue. His hand clenched and unclenched like it was eager to disappear into his long black coat and pull out a weapon. Instead of one other man, however, Tyler saw four in identical clothing milling around the front of the supermarket. The place closed in under a half-hour. Few customers walked the aisles, and the complement of employees matched their smaller number.

Way too many guys for a simple cash grab.

Tyler turned and reached toward the back of his jacket. "Shit," he whispered when he realized he'd left his pistol in the car. Two of the trench coat crew fanned out, one in each direction. They stopped at every aisle.

Were they looking for someone?

Tyler fished his phone out of his pocket. No signal. He was in a remote part of Maryland, but there should have been coverage here. Whoever these guys were, they were jamming the comms. Tyler hoofed it down the aisle and grabbed a slender stock boy by the arm. Before the young man could object, he said, "Something bad is about to happen. Do you have any landline phones?"

"Uh." The kid blinked a bunch of times. "There might be . . . in the manager's office."

"Good. Listen . . . five armed guys in long black coats are in your store. I don't know what they're up to yet, but I don't think it'll end well."

"Jesus." The stock boy's eyes widened, and his mouth hung open.

"Where's the manager's office?" Tyler asked.

"Um . . . up front."

"No good. What about your receiving area?"

"Yeah . . . sure." Despite the news Tyler dumped on him, the kid held up pretty well. He led the way through two swinging doors into the back portion of the store. Wooden pallets dominated much of the floor space. Plastic shipping containers lined the walls. Tyler spotted a phone sitting atop a desk. An old-fashioned cord connected the handset to the base.

"Call the cops first," Tyler said. "Then, page whoever's in charge back here." He padded to the entrance, standing to the side of the door and peeking through one of the clear plastic panes. It offered a very limited view of the sales floor, but nothing looked amiss.

"Police are at least ten minutes out," the kid said. Tyler frowned. A lot of bad shit could happen in ten minutes. Even if the cops beat their estimate, they wouldn't rush into a probable hostage situation. They'd set up a perimeter and a command post. Try to establish contact. Negotiate. Tyler understood—their strategy was to save innocent lives. It all took time, though and the assholes in long coats could murder a bunch of people while the local LEOs ticked the boxes in the playbook. He used his own playbook honed from his experiences in Afghanistan. The strategy was the same, but the tactics diverged sharply.

A pudgy man with a ruddy complexion walked in a moment later. His white button-down shirt strained to cover his stomach. "What's going on? Who are you?"

"You have five men in your store," Tyler said. "I don't know exactly why they're here, but it can't be for a good reason." He looked around the area again. "Can you move some of these by the doors to control entry?"

"I think so," the kid said.

The manager, however, frowned at Tyler. "Listen here—"

"You listen," Tyler said. "If these assholes start shooting, you'll be glad you took my advice." He moved toward the entrance.

"You're going out there?" the stock boy asked with wide eyes.

"I am. Try to get some of those pallets lined up. We want to make it hard for anyone else to storm back here." Tyler pushed one of the swinging doors open and started checking nearby aisles. A slender fellow in an expensive suit browsed canned goods. From the other end, one of the black-cloaked men scowled and headed toward him. "Shit," Tyler muttered as he glanced around for a weapon.

A selection of cooking pans hung from slender metal pegs a few feet away in the next lane. Tyler grabbed a durable-looking ten-inch model and hurried toward the guy giving the vegetables a once-over. The asshole in the coat reached him first. The suited man took a step back. "Either of you tell me anything about these?" Tyler asked as he closed to within a few feet.

"Buzz off, pal," Dark Coat said right before Tyler drew the skillet back and clobbered him in the face. The metal clang was louder than Tyler wanted. The assailant dropped to the linoleum. The man in the suit cowered against the shelf. "I don't know who you are, but I think it's best if you leave the store."

"Y . . . yeah," he said.

"Let's go." Tyler was about to step over the fallen guy when two more rounded the corner. The smaller one carried a pistol in his hand. In a panic, the well-dressed man ran toward the shooter. Tyler ducked and scampered toward the far end as bullets slammed into the shelves near him. The larger one grabbed the mousy man's arms and led him toward the exit despite his protests. The other kept Tyler covered with his gun as he helped his woozy comrade to his feet.

Once the shooter left, Tyler stayed low and worked his way toward the front of the store. The few cashiers and customers all crouched in the checkout area. In the parking lot, two men shoved another into the back of a van. A third armed with a shotgun kept watch. Tyler waited for them all to pile in and zoom away before he bolted through the doors.

He fired up his Oldsmobile 442. The throaty V8 growled as he put the car in drive and gave chase. The store lay in a remote area. It and a McDonald's were the only signs of civilization. The van made a left with screeching tires. Tyler followed at a reasonable distance. A full moon shone through the trees lining the two-lane road. Tyler killed his headlights and relied on the vehicle ahead of him to lead the way.

The driver kept going. He didn't stop. No evasive maneuvers. No one leaned out a window with a handgun. Tyler's car was a beautiful dark green. The headlights would've been a giveaway. Without them, the guys in the van seemed not to notice they'd picked up a tail. A sharp right led to another street looking just like the previous one. Tyler kept the van in sight but made sure not to get too close. Distance helped maintain his cover in the darkness.

The old car bounced down the road. Tyler maintained the Olds himself, and he'd made improvements over the way it rolled off the assembly line in 1972, but he might need to soften the suspension the next time he crawled under it. Long drives or trips down bumpy roads proved too harsh. The large van's brake lights came on, and it made a left past a mailbox. Tyler slowed his approach. He didn't want to follow too closely even with his beams off. As he rolled up to the shopworn driveway, a shabby mailbox displayed the name McVay.

When the red lights disappeared around a corner to the right, Tyler made the turn. He maintained a slow pace to avoid the 442's engine giving him away. The battered stones of the driveway soon faded to a dirt path. It made a ninety-degree right just ahead. Tyler stayed straight, driving on the grass and heading in the general direction of the trail. He steered near a small outbuilding and killed the engine when he saw the van stop outside a large, dilapidated barn.

Arnold McVay felt someone followed them. He climbed out of his van and scanned the property. No vehicle came in behind them. He couldn't see anyone or hear an engine running. Eugene Byrd sidled up next to him. "What's goin' on?"

"I checked a few times for somebody behind us," McVay said. "You think the guy from the store could have picked us up?"

"I dunno." Byrd rubbed his face. A nice bruise already started. "I kinda hope he does. Son of a bitch."

"You all right? Seems like he rung your bell pretty good there."

"I'm fine," Byrd said.

McVay stared at him. There was no give in his friend's gaze. "All right. You keep an eye on the exterior. If anyone did follow us, you take care of it."

"I will."

"Get this asshole in the barn!" McVay pulled the sliding door open. Three of his friends pushed the frightened lawyer out. His feet missed the running board, and he landed face-down in the grass. McVay put the toes of his boot under Duncan Richardson's chin and lifted his head. "You got some answering to do."

"Please, I don't know what you want!"

"It'll be clear soon enough." He jerked his head, and three sets of hands led Richardson roughly toward the barn. McVay scanned the area again. The moon combined with the lights mounted on buildings to provide plenty of illumination. All looked clear. McVay stomped after his friends. He pointed toward his eyes as he passed Byrd, who offered a solemn nod in reply.

Tyler held his M11 pistol on his lap. The van's driver seemed like a cautious man. Four walked with their captive toward a large dark structure. It was one of two barns on the property; a newer model stood about a hundred yards past this one. One man remained outside. A sentry. Maybe the driver got spooked. Maybe they always took these precautions on a kidnapping run. Regardless, Tyler would need to be careful. He wanted to learn more about what he might be wading into, so he grabbed his phone and called his daughter.

"You're late, Dad," Lexi said.

"I know."

"Let me guess . . . something happened."

"Yeah," Tyler said. "Five men abducted someone in a van. I followed them. They just took him into a barn."

"Jesus. Are you going to call the police?"

"Do I ever? I want you to get my old work laptop. There are a few searches I'd like you to run for me."

"All right." Tyler heard Lexi pad downstairs. A moment later, she said, "It's on. What do you need?"

The laptop belonged to a company called Patriot Security, Tyler's employer after he retired from the army. When he left the private security gig, he didn't bother returning the hardware, and they hadn't come calling for it. Some red team guys developed it, and it did things Tyler couldn't understand. Lexi proved to be a lot better with the computer stuff than he ever imagined. She'd recently begun her freshman year at the University of Maryland, and if she wanted to study technology, Tyler knew she had the brains for it. "Let's start with a plate. Maryland . . . Romeo Bravo three eight eight five Delta."

Keystrokes clattered on the line. "It's a van," Lexi said. "Fourteen years old. Registered to a Francis McVay of Saint Mary's County."

"Which is where I am," Tyler said. It matched the name on the mailbox. Who used their own vehicle for a snatch and grab? "Any info on the nice Mister McVay?"

"He's dead, for starters. Died last year."

"He drives pretty well for a corpse, then."

"Hang on, I'm looking deeper." She typed some more. "His closest surviving relative was a brother who lives out of state. He has a nephew named Arnold who lives in the same county."

Using a dead relative's van wouldn't be a smart play, either. These guys weren't professionals. The lone guard outside the barn made the point obvious enough. They'd done pretty well in the grocery store, all things considered, but this was an amateur crew. It made them unpredictable. Tyler didn't like unpredictable. "Can you tell me anything about this Arnold?" he asked.

"Already on it," Lexi said. "The laptop is scraping his social media." She fell silent for a few seconds while they waited for results. "Looks like's he's only on Facebook. Not a lot of friends. He makes a lot of posts about family farms and Big Ag."

Tyler frowned. "Weird." What the hell was going on? "Thanks, kiddo. I'm going to check some things out here."

"Be careful, Dad."

"Always," Tyler said. "Don't wait up. Love you."

"Love you, too." Tyler hung up. He opened the door as quietly as possible, moved to the rear of the 442, and eased the trunk lid up enough to grab a bullet-resistant vest and knife. Tyler strapped it on, holstered the M11 at his left side, and the blade at his right. He buttoned the 442 up, crouched, and used the outbuilding for cover as he took in the old barn.

"Mister Robinson," Arnold McVay said once the lawyer was lashed to a chair, "you have a lot to answer for."

"Please, I don't know any of you."

McVay got in his face. He could smell the cowardice on the man's breath. "You didn't know any of our families. It didn't stop you, did it?"

Robinson narrowed his eyes. "What are you talking about?"

"I know who you work for!" McVay shouted. He grabbed a clump of Robinson's hair and bent his head back. "You like being a lobbyist for a company taking people's property?"

"It's a law," Robinson said. "Your legislators voted for it."

"I wonder who gave them the idea." McVay released Robinson's hair and punched him in the face. The lawyer's head snapped to the side, and he wore a pained grimace for nearly a minute.

"I was just doing my job," Robinson said.

McVay glanced at Stan Cooley, who stayed behind while the rest of the crew hit the store. Cooley offered a curt nod. "We looked into you, Mister Robinson." McVay paced a ten-foot area in front of the prisoner.

"We may not have the fancy investigators your firm might hire, but we did all right for a bunch of country folk. Learned where you live, where you go in your spare time, and where and when you shop. You're predictable." Robinson didn't respond. Cooley pulled large blanket back. The lawyer's eyes widened as saw what had been behind it.

McVay stared at it. Bags of fertilizer. Good wiring. A detonator and a timer. Plus a few components he didn't recognize, but he trusted Stan Cooley's handiwork. He jerked his thumb toward the bomb. "Know what this is?"

Robinson nodded and swallowed hard. "Yes."

"This is an old barn. My uncle stood up a new one a few years ago. I helped. He kept this one, though, for storage. His granddaddy built it by hand years ago. It ain't so pretty anymore. My uncle thought about knocking it down, but he could never bring himself to do it." McVay shrugged. "I ain't attached to it like he was. If it blows up with some asshole lawyer inside it, well . . . that'd be a shame, but there's a new one."

Color drained from Robinson's face. "What do you want from me?" His voice trembled and sounded like a man who understood his time was short.

"I think you know."

"Do you think I can just snap my fingers and undo everything?"

McVay gently patted the top of the timer. "I think it's in your best interests to try."

Tyler studied the guard. He'd fetched a double-barreled shotgun from the van once everyone else herded their captive into the run-down barn. The guy carried it over his shoulder like he was posing for a photo. Not the best grip for bringing it to bear quickly. Another mark in the amateur column. The guy looked around regularly, and he turned a slow 360 every minute.

When he pivoted away, Tyler moved around the outbuilding to the other side. Trees were thicker to his left. He imagined someone cut a bunch of them down and used the wood to make the old barn many decades ago. Tyler searched the ground and found a stick large enough to throw and make noise. When the guard turned his back, Tyler padded into the forest. He crouched behind a large oak and waited for the opening. When the sentry completed his circuit, Tyler tossed the branch toward some smaller trees about five yards away.

It produced the desired effect. The guard swung the shotgun from his shoulder, letting it drop too far before steadying it with his other hand. He moved toward the noise. Tyler kept his back to the tree, inching around as the other man stalked toward the sound. "Anybody there?" he said in a harsh whisper. Interesting. He didn't call anyone or try to make noise. Whatever happened in the barn took priority. The sentry stood with his back to Tyler. It made sneaking up on him easy.

Tyler pushed the muzzle of his M11 into the guard's neck. He stood at a full arm's length. Too far for a headbutt or quick back kick . . . if this guy even had such moves in his arsenal. "Drop the shotgun." The other man didn't respond or react. Tyler repeated his command.

"Or what?" the guy said.

"Or a couple of your vertebrae will leave your body via your throat. Put it down." The man raised his other hand and set the shotgun on the ground. "Three steps to your left." He complied. Tyler backed off one pace. "Turn around." The man he'd whacked with the skillet glared at him. "What the hell are you all doing here?"

"You wouldn't understand." The accent gave him away as being born and bred in southern Maryland.

"I've never kidnapped someone in a grocery store before," Tyler said. "I suppose I wouldn't. Why don't you try to explain it to me?"

"You ain't the cops." The other guy sneered. "You're some jackass who likes to hit people while they ain't expecting it. Why don't you throw your gun down and see what happens?" This guy was taller, younger, and broader than Tyler. Not a good combination on the surface, but experience tilted the scales. Still, Tyler didn't want to get into a fight in a random patch of trees in St. Mary's County. This guy was stalling. If he couldn't stop Tyler, he wanted to keep him from interrupting whatever happened about two hundred feet away.

"Maybe some other time." Tyler stepped forward and clobbered the guy in the head again, this time with the butt of the pistol. He was out cold before he hit the ground. Tyler saw a length of rope hanging from the guy's belt. He dragged him to a tree, turned him face down, and put his legs around the large trunk. Tyler tied the rope around the unconscious man's ankles. Even if he came to, he wouldn't be able to free himself. He could yell, however, and Tyler realized he had nothing to put over the guy's mouth. He'd deal with it if and when it happened.

Tyler inspected the discarded shotgun. It was loaded and looked to be in good repair. Two shots. Plenty of stopping power. He could take out a pair of kidnappers quickly before switching to his pistol. Tyler carried it close to his body as he padded through the trees and closed in on the barn.

Tyler put his back against the wood. Up close, he could tell the barn missed a lot of upkeep over the years. He crouched beside a window near the rear corner. The remote county location meant background noise wouldn't be a factor.

For years, Tyler had valued being quiet and listening in situations like this. In Afghanistan, he met a lot of young soldiers who wanted to storm a building and empty the magazine. Tyler tried to teach them a smarter way. No matter what you learned from intel reports and drones, listening to your targets always paid off.

"We can't just stop it!" a desperate voice said. The captive. At least he was still alive. It changed the breach plans running through Tyler's head. "It doesn't work the way you want it to."

"You made sure of it, didn't you?" another voice said. This one was angrier. Younger. Accented like the guy tethered to the tree. "You lawyers are always good for tricks."

"It's no trick. It's what the statute says, and it's how the process plays out." Tyler recalled what Lexi told him. Arnold McVay posted about family farms and Big Agriculture. If those two ever appeared in the same sentence, it never turned out well for the home team.

The unmistakable sound of someone getting punched pierced the silence. "Maybe you can figure out some other way for the process to go. They paid you to do it a certain way. Don't it mean there are other options?"

Tyler couldn't fault the fellow's reasoning, but he also couldn't continue to stand here and listen to the debate play out. The captive was badly outnumbered, to say nothing of any weapons his abductors might have. Tyler was about to move when a simple question made him stop. "Do you really need a bomb?"

The other guy confirmed he did a moment later with glee in his voice. "Shit," Tyler whispered to the darkness. Explosives were the great equalizer. He'd seen plenty of good soldiers maimed or killed by IEDs. Simple operations which should have gone without a hitch turned into bloodbaths. It wouldn't take much to knock this barn down, and even a small charge would be enough to kill the poor guy held captive inside.

Tyler thought about walking away. This wasn't his fight. Short of braining someone with a skillet and tying him to a tree, he'd stayed out of whatever the conflict was. No one knew him down here. He could drive the two hours home, say goodnight to his daughter, and get on with the rest of his life. The hostage inside stared down terrible odds, however, and the bomb only made them worse. If Tyler left, the man trapped inside was dead.

He cursed his conscience and risked a glance through the grimy window. Someone sat strapped to a chair, his back to Tyler. Five other men stood near him. The one doing the talking was the voice he'd been hearing. "Does it make you think about what you've done?" he said as he leaned closer to the other man.

"I have a family," the captive wailed in protest.

"We all had families. Didn't stop you and your rich friends from ruining everything."

Tyler ducked under the window and skulked down the length of the barn. He peeked around the front corner. The coast was clear. One of the doors remained open wide enough for someone to slip out. Or in. "I need a smoke," a new voice called, and a man squeezed through the opening a moment later. He fumbled with a pack of cigarettes as he headed in the opposite direction from where Tyler kept watch. This left four inside.

If these guys were going to give him an opportunity to reduce the odds, Tyler meant to take it. He moved around the corner, saw no windows along the front of the barn, and kept going. A single step took him past the opening, and he kept going when no one shouted an alarm. The smoker lit up a hundred feet away, about halfway to the newer barn. Lights mounted on its walls lifted the blackness. Tyler crouched and stalked closer. The guy drew in a lungful and blew out a plume of smoke. He turned a little to his right, so Tyler fanned out toward the left.

Fifty feet.

Tyler smelled the smoke as he drew closer. He'd never acquired the habit despite sharing barracks with a bunch of people who lit up. Memories of his grandfather smelling like a stale chimney were enough. Twenty feet. The guy looked at his watch and pivoted a quarter turn to his right. Tyler stepped to the left, but the smoker's head followed him.

Time for a change in tactics. Tyler sprinted the remaining three steps. As he ran, he pulled the double-barreled shotgun back. Before the Marlboro Man could alert his friends, Tyler smashed him in the face with the stock. He grunted as he dropped to the grass. The lights were still on, so Tyler whacked him again. They were in the open, so there were no trees to tie this one to. With the bomb being a factor, Tyler didn't want to waste the time it would take, anyway. He patted the prone man down and found no weapons.

Then, he moved toward the old barn.

"Set the timer."

Arnold McVay issued the command, and Stan Cooley followed it. He pushed a few buttons, and the digital display showed 10:00 in bright red numerals. One additional press would begin the countdown. Cooley's finger hovered over the small switch.

"You're going to kill us all," Robinson said.

"Just you." McVay jabbed a finger at him to emphasize the point.

"What will it accomplish? You kill me, and nothing changes. No one's going to listen to you with blood on your hands. You'll go to jail and lose your properties anyway."

McVay saw Harry Black frown. Was he considering the lobbyist's words? Nothing a bigshot lawyer said could be true; they were incapable of it. Something would still happen. Something would change. Even if he went to jail, McVay would keep all their farms out of the hands of some faceless corporation. "I'm willing to take my chances," McVay said. "We're screwed if we don't do anything. You and your asshole friends have guaranteed it. Might as well take our shot."

"Robby's been outside a while," Cooley said.

"He's smoking," McVay said without removing his eyes from the frightened lawyer. Robinson squirming in the chair made him smile, and they hadn't even started the countdown yet.

"Don't take this long."

"You worry too much."

Cooley stepped away from the bomb and started toward the barn door. "I'm gonna check on him." He stopped after taking a single step. McVay followed his friend's gaze.

A stranger walked in, and he leveled Byrd's double-barreled shotgun at them.

Everyone froze when Tyler walked in. He moved away from the door, keeping it to his right side as he covered everyone with the scattergun. The man bound to the chair was the one abducted from the grocery store. Four others all dressed in faded jeans and shirts surrounded him. They must have doffed their black coats in the van.

Tyler noticed the crude bomb right away. It sat atop a battered table. The prisoner was about five feet away. If it worked, there wouldn't be enough left of him to bury in a bucket when it went off. The timer displayed ten minutes, but the crew didn't start the countdown. "I'm going to offer you an easy solution. Walk away. Get back in your van and leave."

"And if we don't?" one of them said. The same voice doing the talking before. Probably McVay.

Tyler pointed the shotgun directly at him. "Then I guess your friends will save about two hundred pounds on the escape run. Might make the van a little faster."

The fellow closest to the explosive inched toward it. "Don't move." Tyler swung the gun toward him. A long stride would get him there. Tyler's finger curled around the trigger.

"Do it, Stan," McVay said as he stared at Tyler. "He ain't gonna shoot."

"I can assure you I will," Tyler said.

"This don't concern you, old man. You don't understand what's going on."

"Enlighten me." Tyler never took his eyes from the guy who'd moved toward the bomb. Stan, McVay called him.

"These men are crazy," the hostage said. "You need to stop them."

"Shut up!" McVay punched the seated man again. Stan took it as his opportunity to lunge for the bomb. Tyler fired as soon as he registered the movement. The slug took the guy in the chest. He was dead before he landed on the dirty barn floor. His desperate effort paid off, though.

The countdown was on.

Tyler swung the shotgun back toward McVay. If he were smart, he would've stood behind the captive. It would take the shotgun out of the equation. Instead, he remained in the open. The other two covered their mouths. "You only got one left," he said. "Still three of us."

"I have an M11 on my hip," Tyler said. He wondered if the second man he'd knocked out would join the fray at some point. If the bomb went off, he was a good hundred feet from the rundown barn. He'd probably be fine. The one in the woods was closer, but the cluster of trees would protect him. "I was a marksman twenty years running. I like my chances."

"Stay in your lane. You don't understand what's going on here."

"A bunch of you snatched this guy from a supermarket. You brought him here and rigged a bomb. The plan is either to scare him or blow him up. I'm pretty sure you've achieved the first one." The captive nodded in confirmation. "What's your name, hostage?"

"Duncan Robinson," he said. "I'm a lawyer.'

"Nobody likes lawyers," Tyler said. "You might want to leave it out the next time you get kidnapped."

"I think Mister Robinson should explain it to you," McVay said. His two friends paced behind him. They didn't possess his level of calm. Tyler figured they would bolt before the timer got anywhere near all zeroes. Only a true believer would see it through to the end, and these guys didn't cut it. "Just so you know what we're dealing with here."

"I . . . I represent a large agricultural company," he said. "We've been looking to expand out of the southern states. There are a lot of old farms around here which have fallen on tough times. We petitioned the county to acquire them through eminent domain, and they agreed. The process is—"

"I understand how eminent domain works," Tyler broke in. "Sounds like you snatched up a bunch of farms which had been in families for generations." He glanced at the red numbers. Seven and a half minutes remained.

"The families got paid," Robinson said. "The county got paid. The company is slated to get the land we need. Everyone wins."

"A bunch of us lost!" McVay bent down to get in Robinson's face. "It ain't just land to us like it is to you." Robinson fell silent.

"What are you trying to accomplish?" Tyler said. "Even if you scare this guy shitless, I don't think he can undo the entire process."

"He can try."

Tyler looked at the lawyer, who shrugged as much as his restraints would allow. "I might be able to get a little more money," he said after a moment, "though I think everyone has been fairly compensated."

"You go to hell," McVay said. His two remaining compatriots continued to pace behind him. The shorter one kept looking at the bomb.

"I'll be honest," Tyler said, "I'm tempted to lock this place up and let you all sort it out. If you can't come to an arrangement, I think the world will keep spinning."

"I don't wanna die," one of the men behind McVay offered.

McVay glared and turned around. "For Christ's sake, Jimmy."

"I don't. This was supposed to be easy. Grab this guy and get him to change his mind. Then, Cooley wanted to make a bomb, you went along with it, and I think we got off the rails somewhere."

"Your friend is the smart one of the bunch," Tyler said. "It's damning with faint praise, but you should listen to him." He glanced at the clock again. Six minutes.

"I'm going to press charges," Robinson said. "I've been kidnapped, threatened, assaulted, and—"

"Shut up," everyone else said in unison.

Tyler continued, "You're not the sympathetic figure I thought you were in the store. Still, you don't deserve to get blown up. Here's what we're going to do."

"Why should we listen to you?" McVay said.

"Ask your friend on the ground how independent thought turned out." He pointed at Jimmy. "You're going to untie the lawyer. We're going to collect your friend outside and walk to the new barn. Once this place blows up, we call the sheriff's office, and I leave."

"What's to stop us from bolting?" McVay asked.

Tyler's only reply was a smile.

Once Robinson had been untied, Tyler held the shotgun out toward him. "I don't know how to use this," he said, looking at the weapon as if it were a rotten fish on his plate.

"It's not hard." Tyler gripped the gun until Robinson frowned and took it. "Point and shoot. Just like an old camera."

"Doesn't it only have one shot left?"

Tyler drew the M11 from the holster on his hip. "I can handle the rest. Let's march."

They all trudged to the new barn. McVay and Jimmy helped their friend shake off the cobwebs and get back to his feet. Once everyone was inside, Tyler told Robinson to shut the door, which he did. He then handed the lawyer a length of rope. "I'm sure you'll find a knife or scissors around here somewhere. Tie their ankles together."

"Where's Byrd?" McVay said as he glowered at Tyler. "You kill him?"

"He's tied to a tree," Tyler said. "He's far enough away to be fine."

"What if he ain't?" Tyler shrugged in response, and McVay scowled anew. A couple minutes later, Robinson finished turning the tables on his captors. A little over two minutes remained by Tyler's count.

"Thanks, mister," Robinson said. He held his hand out. "I don't even know your name."

Tyler stared at the hand until the lawyer withdrew it. "It doesn't matter. What's important is what you're going to do after this."

"What do you mean?"

"These men shouldn't have kidnapped you, but you seem to work for a pack of assholes. You're going to do what you can to make things right for all the families whose farms got scooped up."

"And if I don't?" Robinson asked.

"I'll be keeping an eye on the news," Tyler said. "Remember I know your name but not the other way around."

Robinson swallowed hard and nodded. "All right. I'll do what I can."

"Good." Tyler figured only a few seconds remained on the countdown. Right on cue, the old barn blew up.

Robinson called 9-1-1 a couple minutes later. Tyler found him another slug for the shotgun if he needed it, but he didn't think it would matter. He got back into the 442 and headed away from the McVay farm as quickly as he could. About a mile down the road, a trio of police cars sped toward him, sirens howling and lights flashing red and blue in the darkness. Tyler was happy to pull over and wait for them to pass.

Once he drove past the border of St. Mary's County, he called Lexi again. "I'm on my way," he said when she picked up.

"How did your situation go?"

"Fine. In the end, though, I'm relying on a lawyer to do the right thing."

"Doesn't sound like a good place to be," Lexi said.

"The sheriff and his deputies will do the heavy lifting. I just need to follow the news out of this county."

"Which means you want me to do it."

"I knew you got a scholarship for a reason," Tyler said.

Lexi yawned. "How far away are you?"

"Depends how fast I want to drive. You don't need to wait up, though."

"All right," she said. "Love you, Dad."

"Love you, too." Tyler looked at the speedometer. Sixty-eight. A county road sign showed a speed limit of sixty.

He felt like driving a little faster, and 442 was happy to oblige.

ABOUT THE AUTHOR

Tom Fowler was born and raised in Baltimore and still lives in Maryland. All his stories are set in his home city and state.

At about age seven, young Tom wrote a "murder mystery" story. Being a polite lad, he was far too nice to kill anyone (and, in fact, everyone recovered quite well in the hospital). This and many other awful stories in his youth started a lifelong love of writing.

He's since gotten over the aversion to killing characters.

Tom is the author of the ongoing C.T. Ferguson mysteries, and his new series is the John Tyler thrillers. Both feature action, snark, and flawed heroes. Tom lives in Silver Spring, Maryland with his wife and daughter.

www.tomfowlerwrites.com

https://bit.ly/midnitedrive

HUNTING DARKNESS

A. K. HUGHEY

Death waits for those who dare to stop the traffickers.

1

"I don't see nothin'," a man shouted over the barking of three unhappy dogs chained in the yard. He stood on the shaky wooden steps of the single-wide trailer, his eyes scanning the garbage piles and rusted-out cars that surrounded him. "Shut up already!"

Lucia hid behind one of the long-dead vehicles, confident he wouldn't see her. She and Shelby had approached the property from the west, through the national forest. The blinding rays of sunset through the pines had aided their concealment from the men in the trailer.

The man on the steps grumbled something inaudible before returning inside and slamming the door behind him.

Turning, Lucia met her partner's dark eyes and nodded.

Shelby nodded back, her tawny brown skin aglow with the sunset's last remaining light. After shrugging a small hiking pack off her shoulders, she pulled a bottle of rubbing alcohol and a black rag from it. She uncapped the alcohol bottle, then shoved the rag into its mouth.

Lucia peered around the trunk of the car to study the trailer's rag-covered windows. To her relief, no one stared back. "Do it," she said softly, training her unblinking eyes on the windows. It was a reflexive habit. Always anticipate what might go wrong.

Shelby launched the bottle overhead, the rag tail aflame. It landed in the seat of an ATV parked in front of the trailer. Lucia retreated behind the car only a second before the bottle exploded, spitting liquid flame in all directions. The barking from the dogs intensified, and one of them yelped.

A new man was the first one out the door. "Shit!" He raced down the steps toward the fire.

Two more men followed him, but only one had sense enough to turn on the hose. While they were distracted with the ATV, Shelby unclipped her gray compound bow from her shoulder sling and kept a lookout. Lucia slipped into the hoard of rusted-out vehicles, adrenaline coursing through her veins. The property owners had so closely packed the old cars and trash together that she easily made it to the back of the trailer without losing cover.

When she reached the back door, she pulled her Sig Sauer from her leg holster and twisted the doorknob. She leaned forward to push it open and let it swing inward, then leaned back and raised her pistol to methodically clear the room beyond. All she could hear were the frantic voices of the men in front as they tried to put out the fire.

Just as she stepped across the threshold, a pale face appeared from a hallway adjacent to the dismal living room. Tangled, dirty blonde hair hung loosely around the woman's bony shoulders.

"Miranda?" Lucia recalled the picture from the woman's missing poster. Her stomach tightened as she compared that image with the person before her now.

The skeletal woman's green eyes were dim and glassy, but she reached out a trembling hand. "Help me," she said hoarsely.

Lucia put a finger to her lips and nodded. She reached for Miranda's hand, but the woman hesitated, stopping to point downward. Lucia followed her finger, then clenched her jaw against the rage that boiled in her core.

The men had padlocked a heavy-duty dog chain around one of Miranda's ankles.

"Damnit," Lucia cursed. They had planned for this possibility, but she still didn't like it. "Can you lock the door?" She pointed to the front.

"I can't reach," the woman replied, shaking her head. Tears welled in her eyes as she glanced at the chain. Her ankle was chafed and raw.

Despite the November weather, the woman wore nothing but shorts and a tank top, and the lack of clothing revealed the extent of her abuse and starvation.

Lucia reached down to the radio clipped to her belt and tapped the push-to-talk button three times. Several seconds later, another small pop resounded outside. The dogs' yelping pitched again, and the men's shouts faded as they moved toward a new fire and farther away from the trailer. She glanced at her watch.

5:03 pm.

Dropping her pack off her shoulder, Lucia pulled a handheld, cordless Dremel tool from the front pocket. She knelt beside Miranda and gestured for her to sit. The tool came to life with a quiet buzz when she pressed the switch, and she carefully brought it to the half-inch thick shank of the padlock.

When she pressed the spinning cut-off wheel to the hardened steel, sparks showered Miranda's ankle and the buzz turned to a high-pitched whine. Lucia couldn't tell if the sparks hurt Miranda, because the woman said nothing. But her furtive glances between the door and the padlock told Lucia everything she needed to know.

The blade had only made it halfway through the shank when they heard two pops in quick succession. Lucia gritted her teeth against a curse, heart thundering in her chest. Shelby was ruthless, but she was also outnumbered, and they needed to get out of this clean and in one piece. If these men caught them, they would likely disappear forever.

"Faster," Miranda cried, her voice barely audible over the whining of the Dremel.

"Almost there," Lucia murmured. She needed to focus, and they needed to get out before Shelby got too creative. Seconds felt like hours as she watched the blade slowly eat away at the steel. Finally, the wheel surged through the shank.

Lucia turned off the Dremel and twisted the padlock, releasing the chain links. After shoving the Dremel back into the front pocket of her bag, she took a pair of size eight running shoes from the main pocket and handed them to Miranda.

The woman slipped them on and tied them in thirty seconds flat.

Lucia studied Miranda as she rose on shaky legs. Sometimes

victims were too drugged-up to try to escape, or were too lost in the mire to believe they could ever be free. But Miranda, Lucia was surprised to see, was ready. Eager, even.

The shouts of the men had faded away into the forest as Lucia led her out the back door she had come in through. As their feet left the rickety wooden steps and touched the leaf-covered earth, Shelby silently appeared from behind a tree.

"This way," Lucia whispered, starting down the path they had mapped and planned for over the past two weeks. But a hand grabbed her arm and pulled, stopping her. When Lucia looked back, Miranda's sunken eyes filled with tears and she shook her head.

"I can't leave without my baby."

2

Lucia glanced at Shelby, who returned her confused look, before turning back to Miranda. The woman's mother, Ginger, had mentioned nothing about a baby. Then again, Miranda had been missing for a little over a year now.

"What baby?" Shelby asked, stepping closer to Miranda.

The woman nodded before pointing east, the opposite direction of their intended extraction. "In another trailer, just a little ways down. I've been there a few times. They said if I behaved, they wouldn't hurt her."

An uncontrollable chill ran through Lucia's body. She knew what people like this did to children, and infants were no exception.

"Let's hurry!" Shelby hissed impatiently.

"We didn't plan for this," Lucia argued. "We don't know what we're walking into, and—"

"You're kidding, right?" Shelby raised an eyebrow and propped a fist on one hip, her bow dangling from the chest harness. The daylight was all but gone, and in the shadows of the forest, Lucia could barely make out the details on her friend's face.

"We have a plan," she insisted.

"They…" Miranda choked on her words before continuing, voice shaking. “They’ll sell her when they realize I’m gone.” In a flash, the dam broke and a flood of tears overcame her.

“It’s not even a question, Luce,” Shelby said through gritted teeth.

“Damnit.” Lucia knew her friend was right, and she knew in her heart they couldn’t leave without the child. On-the-spot changes to a solid plan filled her mind with sordid and macabre possibilities, but she would fight every last one of her fears for the chance to save a child. “Are you sure you know the way?”

Miranda nodded through her tears and pointed again. “They walk me there a few times each week to feed her since taking her from me. They wanted me to behave without the drugs. I love her, and I’ve been praying for a miracle to save us.” Her hands trembled as she wiped her cheeks.

“Let’s go, now!” Shelby insisted, unsnapping an arrow from her hip quiver and readying it against her bow.

“Lead the way,” Lucia agreed, grinding her teeth against the drastic change in plans. It was hard enough to get Shelby to stick to a course of action without any added complications.

Miranda moved quickly down the path despite the darkness, and Lucia was convinced the woman had memorized it. Light and noise were their enemies now, but they moved more quietly than she had expected. Acres of dominant pine gradually gave way to deciduous trees. Through their leafless branches, a full moon shone in the cloudless sky. The ambient light helped them move fluidly along the narrow trail.

Shelby walked directly behind Miranda, ready to burst forward and defend the woman if needed, while Lucia guarded their six. The well-worn path curved through the trees, taking them farther eastward, away from safety and escape. When they finally spotted the well-lit exterior of an old double-wide trailer, they could no longer hear the barking of the dogs behind them.

Miranda paused and pressed herself against the rough bark of a towering oak tree. “I don’t know who’s in there.”

Lucia leaned in close to her while studying the trailer. Although it was in better condition than the other, it was still surrounded by a hoard of garbage. There was a deck and sliding glass door on the back of the trailer. At least she couldn't see any sign of dogs this time. "How many are normally in there?"

"A woman, I don't know her name. She's evil," Miranda spat. "She's the reason I'm here."

"What?" Lucia returned her gaze to the woman.

"She tricked me into backing her car out of a parking space at the grocery store. I got in to help her, and that's when they took me."

The discount grocery store's parking lot was the last place Miranda had been seen, but she had walked into an area that wasn't covered by cameras. She hadn't been spotted getting into a vehicle.

"Who else?" Shelby asked, her eyes still glued to the trailer.

"Sometimes a man. He's quiet but big. He..." Miranda trailed off and looked away. It was the look of a woman remembering the awful things that had been done to her.

Lucia chewed her bottom lip as she tried to work out a new plan in her head.

"The other three will be back to the first trailer soon. I bet they'll come here first. They know she'll come for the baby," Shelby reminded Lucia, nodding at Miranda. "We don't have time for this."

"If we go in guns blazing, we could get killed or captured—"

"What's that thing your mom always says?" Shelby interrupted. "The thing about torpedoes?"

Lucia rolled her eyes, but she knew Shelby was right. They couldn't leave without the baby, and the longer they waited, the better their chances of having three more scumbag enemies to deal with.

"Get your mask on," she ordered her friend as she slipped a black ski mask from the cargo pocket of her pants. She pulled it over her head and adjusted it to fit her face. "Remember, we don't kill unless we have to."

"Why not?" Miranda asked. Lucia recognized the protest in her voice.

"They aren't going to call the cops here about a stolen woman and baby. But if someone dies, there's a much higher chance of the police getting involved. And then we're running from the law. Trust me, some prosecutors don't care if a victim gets fried."

"These people don't deserve to live," Miranda declared through gritted teeth.

"Just stay here and let us handle this. Be ready to run, and keep an eye out for the other guys. Shelby, let's go."

Shelby moved without a word, silently making her way around the trailer, deliberately avoiding the back deck and the wedge of light cast through the white curtains beyond the sliding glass doors. Lucia stepped to the nearest window, lifting herself onto a rusted freezer chest so she could see inside. Peeking through the sheer curtains, she found a nightlight on in a small bathroom and a dark hallway just beyond. The hallway's shadows were broken by the ambient light of what she guessed was the open living room to the left.

Stepping down from the freezer, Lucia silently made her way around the right side of the trailer. She climbed onto a group of blue plastic barrels to look in another window. This window on the end of the trailer was larger than the others. Her eyes adjusted and she surveyed a darkened bedroom beyond the shabby curtains. The bedroom door was partially open, allowing a cone of soft light to shine in. A woman sprawled motionless, face-up and naked on the bed. Only a slip of a white sheet lay over one leg. Her body was so still Lucia couldn't tell if she was even breathing.

Once more, Lucia stepped down and moved right. When she peeked around the corner, she found Shelby's face waiting for her at the opposite side of the trailer. Her chest tightened as she studied her unlikely friend's calm, cold gaze. A chill crawled down Lucia's spine, but she fought the sensation. There was no one more loyal than Shelby, no one more dedicated to their mission. Nervously, she pulled her desert-tan tactical gloves tighter over her fingers.

A single, orange porch light illuminated the front steps, and all was quiet. Lucia's breath fogged in the frigid air that had fallen with darkness as she surveyed the property. A white Impala sat in the short driveway next to a green, crew-cab Sierra. More of the area's signature towering pines lined the dark and silent dirt road beyond. The probability of passersby tonight was slim to nil.

Before Lucia could make a move, Shelby walked to the Impala and uncapped the stem valve on one of the tires. Lucia followed her lead and went to the truck. While Lucia was great at planning and executing, Shelby excelled at improvisation.

Grabbing a short screwdriver from her pack, Lucia pressed it to the pin in the center of the valve stem and began letting the air out. She had finished the two left tires of the Sierra when she heard the front door of the trailer open. The sound sent her scrambling behind the truck and out of the line of sight of the porch.

"Who's there?" a man's voice boomed. "I saw you by my truck. Tommy, if you're trying to steal dope again, I swear it won't be a slap on the hand this time." The man spoke with the malformed redneck accent of poor country folk from the state's rural areas. Whatever humble beginning he had come from, he wasn't quite as poor anymore, and he had made his way through the vilest of means.

Gravel crunched under heavy boots as he stepped off the porch and walked toward the truck. She was more worried about what Shelby would do than the man approaching her position. That woman had a bone to pick with traffickers after having been taken herself and barely escaping. She was altogether bereft of mercy and had no qualms about spilling their blood.

Although Lucia also enjoyed the idea of eliminating people like this after nearly being kidnapped and murdered the summer before, she was desperate to avoid leaving a trail for law enforcement. The law and its officers didn't believe others should try to do the work the legal system often failed to do: protect communities and rescue victims from the darkest souls walking the earth. The system had already failed Lucia, succumbing to the money and political pressure of the wealthy, well-connected family of the man who had tried to have her kidnapped and assassinated.

"I'm gonna beat you within an inch of your life this time," the man growled as he rounded the truck.

3

Lucia spun around the opposite corner of the tailgate and unholstered her Sig as she rose to her feet. She pointed it at the man's head and propped her forearms on the back of the truck. The man froze mid-step, his face stiffening as his gaze locked on the gun pointed at his face. Heavy shadows obscured the details she wouldn't want to remember later. It would be easy now, while she couldn't make out the fear in his eyes, but she still hesitated.

"Hands behind your back, big guy," Shelby's soft voice sailed smooth and clear through the evening air. She had crept up behind him in a crouch, only standing once she was behind him, the muzzle of her pistol angled upward at the base of his skull. Ever aware of what was on the other side of the target, Shelby and Lucia had trained to avoid accidentally shooting each other–or covering each other in a target's DNA.

"You don't want to do this," he insisted, shaking his head.

"What I want is to scatter your brains all over your flashy truck. But I'll settle for a little bondage." The contradiction between her airy, nonchalant tone and the gravity of her words was blood-chilling.

Lucia said nothing. She wouldn't argue with Shelby in front of an enemy.

The man hesitated briefly, then returned his focus to Lucia as he moved his wrists behind his back. Shelby removed a pair of handcuffs from the left cargo pocket of her tactical pants while her right hand steadily kept the pistol pointed at her target. Lucia watched the man's face twitch and opened her mouth to shout a warning to Shelby, but it was too late.

He whirled and grabbed each of Shelby's wrists. A mountain of a man, he towered over her. Lucia's first instinct was to shoot, but she hesitated. She worried about missing and striking her only real friend in the world.

"Stop now or I'll shoot," she commanded instead, keeping her voice low so she wouldn't alert whoever was inside the trailer.

"I can't believe your boss sent women," the man taunted without taking his eyes off Shelby.

It almost amused Lucia that he thought some rival had sent them. She moved around his side so Shelby would be out of her line of fire.

The man leaned in close, grinning as his beastly hands crushed Shelby's wrists. Others might have faltered under the pain, but Shelby shot back a toothy smile before pulling her head back and then slamming it into his nose. He cried out in pain and released her, dropping to his knees on the frozen earth. Before he could make another move, Shelby raised her pistol to his head and squeezed the trigger. Brain matter blew out the back of his head and sprayed the area where Lucia had previously been standing.

All was silent as they considered the metaphorical doorway they had just passed through. Lucia fought the nausea that rolled in her stomach and turned her eyes away from the mess that used to be a person. Looking to Shelby, she found her friend staring at it, eyes unyielding. Lucia opened her mouth to speak, but Shelby raised a hand to stop her.

"Kill or be killed. Kill these bastards, and we get to save the people they treat like livestock. The ones that'll murder their victims for fun or for the right price. They would do it to us, too." She grasped a flashlight clipped to her bow harness and flashed it over the ground until she found the spent casing. Stooping, she plucked it from the ground and put it in a cargo pocket before returning her gaze to the corpse.

"I know," Lucia choked out. The man she had shot in self-defense over the summer had survived, unfortunately. This was the first kill in the name of the mission, for the sake of the voiceless and defenseless. She had to get over it; this wouldn't be the last. Not even for the night, the way things were going.

"Don't you dare throw up–" Shelby started, but she was interrupted when the door to the trailer opened. A middle-aged blonde woman in a jarringly festive red sweater and gray flannel pajama pants stood on the steps with the door open behind her.

"Don? Was that you?"

Lucia looked to Shelby and shook her head. They both raised their pistols and rounded the truck so the woman could see them.

"Hands up! Police!" Shelby shouted the lie.

Lucia shook her head again. That was yet another thing that hadn't been part of the plan.

The woman froze, then ducked back inside and slammed the door shut. Lucia heard the locks click into place even as she sprinted toward the door.

"Shit!"

"Get away from the door!" Shelby grabbed Lucia by the arm and yanked her away from the porch. "You think she doesn't have guns in there?"

She was right, as usual. Lucia held her tongue against more curses, and they moved left around the trailer toward where they had come in on the trail. She wanted to check on Miranda before they worked on the woman inside.

To her dismay, Miranda was not by the tree where they had left her.

"Hurry!" Shelby shouted. Lucia turned and watched her sprint between the trash piles toward the deck and the sliding glass doors. The door was open, and she thought she heard a cry from inside.

She sprinted for the door, skipping every other step up the deck and barely stopping before bowling into Shelby. Her friend stood stock-still in the doorway, her gaze on something in the open living room. Lucia pushed past her and through the open door, then saw what had shocked her friend.

Miranda was near the door with her back turned to them. She sat on top of the woman in the sweater and pajama pants, whose face was now pressed into the dirty green carpet. Her limbs were still and limp.

Lucia moved slowly toward Miranda, and Shelby followed her lead after closing the sliding glass door behind them. "Miranda."

The young woman looked up, tears filling her eyes. "She helped beat me, helped hold me down for them. She helped them drug me." Her white-knuckled fingers held either side of a thin leather belt, and she was still pulling even though the woman appeared to be dead.

"I think she's gone now," Shelby observed. "She can't hurt you anymore."

"We need to make sure," Miranda sobbed. "So she can't do it to anyone else ever again."

"We will, honey," Lucia assured her. "Get up."

Miranda finally uncoiled her fingers from the belt and struggled to her feet. Shelby rushed to her side to hold her up. The traumatized woman stared intently at the corpse.

"Help me look for the baby," Shelby directed calmly.

"My little girl," Miranda whispered through her sobs and finally tore her gaze away from the corpse. She turned and pointed down the hallway. "Please tell me she's still here."

"I'll go look," Shelby said before pulling her gun and sweeping the hallway and the bathroom quickly. She ducked into a side bedroom while Lucia checked the body of the woman on the floor.

Placing her gloved fingers against her carotid artery, Lucia held her breath and counted the seconds. After a minute had passed and she had felt nothing, she was sure the woman in the red sweater was dead. The crushed fragments of dry leaves on the carpet beneath her face did not move.

"She's dead," Lucia confirmed, looking up at Miranda. The trembling woman nodded firmly and swiped at her tears with her fingers. Two people were now dead, and the chances of them getting out of the woods before the other men tracked them down were disintegrating by the second.

"We have a problem," Shelby announced, poking her head out of the small bedroom she had disappeared into.

4

Lucia clenched her fists and strode toward Shelby, keeping her frustration to herself. Before she could reach the side bedroom, a gunshot thundered from the deck and the sliding glass door shattered behind Miranda. Lucia dove into the hallway and Miranda went the opposite way, scrambling behind the counter in the open kitchen.

"Little mouse," a younger man's voice called out from the deck. "Where do you think you're running to?"

Lucia didn't know if he had seen only Miranda or both of them but decided to play as if he hadn't seen her, too. Surprise would be an advantage if they had it. Only, there were two more men out there somewhere, and they had an advantage as well.

Glass crunched underfoot as the man walked over the threshold. Lucia maintained a prone position and, as quietly as possible, slid her Sig free from the holster. Once it was out, she aimed it at the edge of the hallway and waited for her target to stroll into her line of fire.

"I saw old Donny out there," the man said as he took two more slow steps over the broken glass. He wasn't in her line of sight yet, but as soon as he was, she'd have him. "You know you were his favorite? I'm not sure how you got the gun, but you need to give it up now. I can't promise you won't be punished, but it'll be worse if you don't stop now."

Finally, he sauntered into sight. Long, sandy hair topped a thin, pale face, and one hand held a silver pistol down at his side. He tapped it impatiently against his thigh as he focused on the kitchen. Unwittingly, he had turned his back on Lucia in the hallway. Just as he reached his free hand toward the counter Miranda hid behind, Lucia flicked off the safety and squeezed her trigger once, twice, three times. The pistol rocked in her hands, and the explosive sound of the shots reverberated in the narrow hall, but her impact earplugs helped dampen some of the noise and concussion.

All three shots landed center mass in the man's back. There was no blood spray to indicate an exit wound, but he crumpled to the floor all the same, with only a single grunt uttered as he fell. The scent of gunpowder filled her nostrils, reminding her of her range training and reinforcing her courage and resolve. She breathed deeply, savoring the reminder of how many hundreds of hours she had spent preparing for this.

Only a few seconds elapsed before more footsteps could be heard running up the deck's stairs. Glass crunched as another person entered out of Lucia's view.

"You're dead, Mousey!" a man roared as he rushed into view. Unlike the first man, this one looked both ways and spotted Lucia immediately. His light brown face belied his surprise, and before he could say anything to alert the third man, she squeezed the trigger twice. Both shots hit him in the chest, and he staggered back until he bumped into the counter. His knees softened and he moaned, sputtering blood as he slid down to the floor next to his buddy.

Lucia's heart thudded in her chest as she held the dying man's gaze. His arms slumped to his sides as he choked and wheezed through shallow breaths. Nausea rose in her throat again, but she fought it, turning her focus to the counter beyond the two bodies. All was quiet for a moment, but she didn't dare move. Miranda peeked around the counter and met Lucia's gaze. Lucia simply shook her head and held up her hand to indicate to the woman she should stay put. As her ears stopped ringing, a new sound carried through the trailer: the high-pitched cry of an infant.

Something needed to happen, and fast. The longer they stayed, the greater the risk of backup arriving or someone calling the police. That thought alone spurred her into action, and she rose to a crouch and made her way to the bedroom Shelby had disappeared into. When she poked her head in, she immediately saw the problem Shelby had tried to warn her about.

Instead of one crib as they had expected, there were two. Two babies were here, in a house quickly filling with dead traffickers. There's no way they could take one child and leave the other.

"Shit," she whispered.

Shelby nodded, and Lucia looked to her friend, who already had two car seats ready with blankets. A diaper bag was nearby. Shelby pointed a thumb toward one crib, then headed to the other to get the baby in the car seat. Both infants were dressed in girls' clothes. One child had a pale pink complexion and blue eyes, while the other had a light brown complexion and bright blue eyes. Both were awake, their little limbs wiggling, but their crying had stopped. Lucia gently picked up one child and buckled her into one of the car seats before covering her with a soft green blanket.

Bright, innocent eyes looked up at her, and the girl cried a little when Lucia moved away. She grabbed the diaper bag and dug until she found her prize: a pink pacifier. After giving it to the baby, she found Shelby had done the same, and both infants were calmed and ready. Lucia and Shelby knelt beside the car seats, keeping their profiles low until they were ready to make a plan and move again.

"Wait here," Lucia whispered. "Stay low. There's still one more out there. We have to flush him out so we can get the hell–"

Shelby stiffened and looked up into the doorway behind Lucia.

Lucia's blood ran cold.

5

"Well, well. What do we have he—"

Before he could finish, Shelby ripped her pistol from its holster and fired over Lucia's right shoulder. Lucia ducked to the left but the explosive concussion still blasted too close to her right ear. She cried out as she hit the floor and the second shot rang out. Even her special earplugs weren't enough protection when the first shot had been fired so close to her head.

Shelby's first shot angled upward and hit the final man in the gut, and the second in the chest. He was so close she would have blown apart his head if she'd had more than a split second to draw, aim, and fire.

The dark-haired man fell backward into the hallway, groaning and clutching his stomach. A silver revolver slipped from his fingers and thudded onto the carpet. His deep groan was overwhelmed by the infants' tiny screams, which sounded tinny and far away to Lucia's damaged ears.

Although everything could have gone wrong, Shelby's impulsive and effective shooting had saved them. Lucia couldn't be more grateful or proud, even as all the alternate scenarios of how it could have played out vied for space in her head.

Miranda appeared in the doorway and fell to her knees in front of the little brown girl, kissing the baby's cheeks to comfort her.

Shelby re-holstered her Sig before kneeling next to Lucia. "Are you okay?" she asked.

Lucia could barely hear her. "We need to leave." She reached out her hand and Shelby took it, pulling Lucia to her feet.

Shelby grabbed the second car seat by the handle and gestured for Lucia to head out first. "You'll have to run point now," Shelby said.

Lucia nodded, still dizzy from the ringing in her ears. She patted the Sig in her holster for reassurance it was still there. Only two shots remained in the magazine. As they exited the room, she paused in the hallway over the final man's body.

Something was missing from her mental picture of the situation. Looking left, she saw the bedroom at the end of the hall, its door cracked open. Flashes of the woman lying naked on the bed filled in the gaps. Lucia wondered if she was a victim too, and the mother of the second child.

"Do you know about another woman?" Lucia asked Miranda.

She shook her head. "They bring a lot of girls here. They'd have the babies here because that bitch was a nurse." She nodded toward the body of the woman in the red sweater. "This is where they'd keep the babies until they... auctioned them off." Her voice trembled, and she barely finished her sentence.

Lucia crept toward the bedroom and pushed the door all the way open. As the door swung inward, light from the living room spilled onto the bed and the naked body of the woman. Lucia's stomach tightened as she inspected her. After all the gunshots and screaming of babies, this woman hadn't moved at all since Lucia had first spotted her.

She reached forward and placed a gloved hand on the woman's left foot, then wiggled it. It was stiff and cold; there was no give in the muscles. Lucia leaned in closer, carefully examining the body. Puncture sores and bruises covered the woman's arms. They were tracks, Lucia realized.

There was no blood, no marks around her neck, no other obvious signs of physical trauma, so Lucia guessed the woman had overdosed. She wished they could have arrived a few days earlier. Maybe then they could have rescued this woman, too.

Pushing down the heaviness of regret for a life they were too late to save, she headed back into the hallway and made a beeline for the broken sliding glass door.

"Wait," Shelby said. Lucia stopped and watched as Shelby knelt over the man in the hallway, placing her fingers against the side of his throat.

Miranda set the carrier down and gently comforted her frightened baby, stroking her smooth face and playfully kissing her tiny fingers, while Shelby made sure the last man was dead. They couldn't afford for any of the traffickers to be left as witnesses, either for the police or for those ruthless individuals higher up the chain.

Finally, Shelby dropped her hand and picked up the car seat again. The whimpering baby inside quieted as the seat swung with Shelby's stride.

They made their way through the woods as silently as possible, moving only as slowly as needed to be safe. In thirty minutes, they reached the trailhead in a copse of tall pines. There were no lampposts or lights in this rustic parking area, only a dark brown sign with yellow lettering that read, "Manistee National Forest."

The tops of the pine trees wavered, their needles rustling, in the growing breeze, as clouds began to obscure the moon. Lucia paused and looked up at the sky. They had been so lucky on this night. The weather and the sky had been ideal, and they were able to save two more innocent people than they had intended. A change in plans hadn't meant failure; it had offered greater opportunity, albeit with a steeper price.

"A rival dealer and his boys murdered your captors," Lucia explained as they loaded the car seats into the back of her crew-cab pickup truck. "They let you live because they don't deal in flesh. You don't know why they let you take the babies and go, but you didn't bother questioning them."

Lucia let Shelby drive as her ears were still hurting. Once they were on the road, she continued her instructions for Miranda. "We have a contact. She's part of the cause, and she'll take you to the hospital."

"But th-that woman back there, she worked for the hospital."

"It's going to be okay," Shelby reassured her. "I escaped. I was terrified. I didn't trust anyone, but I went to the cops anyway and they helped me. There are enough good people out there to outweigh the bad ones. Once you're there, you'll be safe."

"And we'll still be watching," Lucia added. "We're not going to let you disappear again."

Miranda was silent a moment before breaking down into sobs.

"The cops are going to ask for details." Lucia's body ached as they drove away from the trailhead, but she couldn't rest yet. "Tell them as much as you can about the location so they can find it, but stick to the script. You're scared and malnourished, and you've been abused and trafficked. It's okay to not remember all the details of your escape."

"It already feels like a blur," Miranda admitted wearily.

"And that's okay," Lucia reassured her. "They're going to press you, but just stick to that... otherwise, we'll fry for helping you and the babies, and we won't be able to help anyone else. There are drugs in those trailers, right?"

"All over the place," she confirmed.

"Good. So a rival dealer came to take out the competition," Lucia restated. "They let you take the babies and run. Lisa was driving home from her brother's place when she saw you trying to walk down the road with two car seats. That's all you need to say, nothing more. Nothing about the two of us."

"I can do that," Miranda agreed, her voice steadier this time.

"And as soon as you're in the hospital, insist they call your mother immediately. She still has the pub, and she's working tonight–"

"You know my mother?" Miranda interrupted.

"Yes, we do," Shelby interjected. "We're here because of her."

"Thank you, God," Miranda cried. "Thank you both."

Lucia reached her hand behind the seat and held it out. The survivor grabbed it and squeezed hard, and Lucia knew she'd be okay. With her mother's help, she could recover, grow, and beat her trauma. She could raise her little girl in a safe and loving home, free of fear and exploitation.

The darkness would never sink its claws into Miranda or her daughter ever again.

ABOUT THE AUTHOR

A. K. Hughey is a thriller author hailing from West Michigan. When she's not writing, working, or spending time with her family, she's researching issues surrounding human trafficking in North America and working to raise money for organizations that help survivors build new lives. Learn more and join the newsletter for updates about events and upcoming releases at bit.ly/akhughey.

THE FIRST HIT

CRAIG MARTELLE

They say the first is the hardest.

1

They say the first is the hardest. It wasn't. They were shooting at my squad. It seemed only natural that we shoot back, or we'd get ripped a new one by the platoon sergeant. Fear was a motivator, but not the fear of getting killed.

We were young and invincible.

That was a long time ago. A different life, and I was a different person.

My name is Ian Bragg now, and I'm an operator, I reminded myself for the hundredth time.

The contract was clear: take out a drug dealer plying his trade on the streets of Los Angeles. What made him different from other dealers? I had no idea, and it didn't matter. The Peace Archive had put out the contract, and the faceless people at the top had chosen me.

Why weren't we taking out all the dealers? It wasn't my place to question.

My employer was the Peace Archive, but I wasn't going to get a tax document from them. I was a subcontractor with all finances funneled through a bank in the Caymans, where the information was protected from prying government eyes. That's what I was told, anyway.

I had bid fifty grand above the minimum. This would earn me a cool six hundred and fifty thousand dollars. Somebody was paying a hefty sum to remove that guy.

In the brief for the winning bidder, this street corner was listed as one of a few where he worked his deals. I hadn't been in town for more than a day, and this was the first corner I staked out. Like it was meant to be, he appeared. I hoped all my gigs would be this easy.

The first half of the total sum was already in my bank account. That gave me a sense of relief like I'd never had before. Financial independence had never been in sight. I was your average working stiff. *Was.*

Still, money wasn't everything. This was my first contract hit.

It felt different from my time in the Marines.

I eased onto the street corner, dressed in ragged clothes I had picked up at a second-hand store. I had bought a beater car for cash and a promise to register it later. It was parked two blocks away. I carried a single key without a keychain in my pocket. I also had some bills but no wallet.

Paranoia kept me from taking him out right then.

There he was. I could walk across the street, act like I wanted to make a deal, and crush his throat or break his neck. But could I get away afterward? Did the camera dome over the intersection include him? If it did, why weren't the police stopping him, since they had all the evidence they needed?

But taking him out? I expected that would be frowned upon while selling drugs was acceptable. I didn't understand, and I would never know, just like I didn't need to know who had submitted this hit to the Archive to be turned into a contract. I only needed to act, and they were paying me well to take care of it. They weren't paying me to ask questions.

I had a month to execute the contract, but the adrenaline had already begun to flow. What a rush! My muscles ached, begging to be unleashed and deliver a maximum amount of violence on a parasite like Guillaume Bandeau.

Once I discovered that I had been awarded the contract, I decided the target was no longer a human being. He deserved a nickname to represent his new status as a soon-to-be corpse. "Gum Band." That worked.

A car pulled up to his corner. Suburban trash, but they shook hands like old friends. An exchange was made, the buyers left, and Gummy looked for the next customer. A pedestrian strolled by, stopping when she reached Gum Band. They quipped and joked, had a laugh before she continued. Not a customer.

A friend. How bad could someone with friends be? Gum Band struck me as a happy guy, enjoying life, not hurting anyone. But he was bad, or there would not have been a contract. I had faith in the system that said he deserved death.

I sneered at the world from under my dirty ball cap. A woman walking with her small son steered well clear of me. I flopped down on the sidewalk and tossed my cap on the ground in front of me, open to donations while I watched the world go by. All the while, Gum Band plied his trade without a care in the world.

My five o'clock shadow hid most of my face. My hair was ruffled from having gone a couple days without getting washed. No one coughed up a dollar bill for me. I had to up my game. I staggered around until I found the obligatory square of cardboard. An oil puddle in the corner from a car with a heavy leak gave me my ink. I used my finger to write "PLZ HLP" in the biggest letters that would fit, moved directly across the street from Gum Band, and flopped down again with the sign balanced across my lap.

Given a drug dealer's margins, I expected Gummy Boy could throw me a nickel or two, but he dutifully ignored me.

Which was exactly what I wanted. I made it through the next half-hour before two big men appeared, wearing less-than-congenial expressions. They crossed their arms and stood in front of me, attempting to intimidate me.

"You're blocking the sun!" I shouted in my best crotchety voice, waving at them to move out of the way.

"You're chasing away the customers, so we're here to chase you away."

"That's discrimination," I grumbled, letting my head flop sideways. The man-mountain twins were starting to draw attention. "Fine. Fine. Deny a man a decent living, you scallywags."

"What?" The men looked at each other, unsure of what that meant.

It was time to make myself scarce. I pulled myself up the wall and carried my sign as I staggered away at a faster pace than one who was as drunk as I was making myself out to be could move. The two didn't follow.

When I reached the street corner, I crossed to the same side as my target. I staggered halfway down and set up shop, dropping my hat to add to the allure. I wouldn't turn down any lunch money that came my way.

Two men walked past, kicking my hat away from me until they sent it into the street. I kept my head down and lamented my misfortune. I didn't want to tangle with these guys since they looked to be making a beeline for my target. Gum Band lost his smile, straightened, and became all business. In an instant, a pistol appeared in his hand.

I didn't see where it came from, his motion was that quick. He focused one hundred percent of his attention on the two men. I hoped they'd pull their guns, everyone would kill everyone else, and I could get the second half of my contract fee.

That was a revelation I hadn't previously contemplated. I only had to see that he died. I was not compelled to kill him myself. The cleanest of all kills were the ones that couldn't be tied to the operator. I jumped up and yelled, "He said screw you guys, this is his turf!"

All three looked at me.

I ran with a tottering gait feeling there was no need to get away since they wouldn't chase me. I hit the corner and waited for the light. I glanced back to find that I was already forgotten. They were close together, each posturing in his own way. I couldn't see Gum Band's hand. I wanted to know where the pistol had come from so I could figure out a way to defeat it. Gum Band's small-caliber pistol changed the dynamic. Dirty Harry carried the .44 magnum, a veritable hand-cannon, but real assassins made do with a .22 fired at point-blank range.

Noise was a problem when one desired to live to fight another day, so a well-armed enemy changed how a hit would go down.

I needed something that could reach out and touch my target. In the Marine Corps, that meant an M14 firing the stalwart NATO 7.62 x 51mm round. I had neither of those, which made this job even more compelling than the justice of getting paid to kill bad guys with no questions asked.

In the Marines, I'd fancied myself one who could make do with anything at hand—the improvisation king.

I tossed my cardboard sign down and stopped, leaning against a wall with my hands in my pockets. I glanced in all directions to look psychotic enough that no one would stop to ask me any questions. Anonymity was my friend.

I chastised myself for my ham-fisted attempt to start a fight between my target and his rivals. It was almost like I was an amateur.

I wanted to win, and that meant killing the target and getting away without a trace. I was in competition with the machine. With bureaucracy. I hated bureaucrats, and too often, the reason scumbags like Gum Band were on the street was because of pencil-pushing bureaucrats who weren't forced to live with the consequences of their decisions. They'd wash their hands of them, leaving the locals to deal with their messes.

Or me, after someone with money decided enough was enough. Law and order, but outside the justice system. That was for the regular people, not individuals like Gum Band or whoever had paid to have him killed.

The altercation was settled as fast as it had started. Gum Band and his rivals shook hands. The pistol had disappeared. Gum Band strolled across the street, seemingly without a care in the world, and set up shop on the opposite corner. The other two assumed his former place, leaning against the fence of the abandoned lot behind them.

Now was not the time to engage. I had time, but the contract weighed on me. I didn't know enough to be confident I could complete it.

I was worried that I would lose, and that wasn't the right frame of mind. I staggered off to the car to get changed and stake out Gummy's home.

His greatest vulnerability would be traveling between his home and where he worked. I needed more information if I wanted to do this right, especially since I didn't know where he lived. That hadn't been in the brief.

I drove my beater car away before stopping in the Walmart parking lot to change clothes so I could go inside and buy a couple of things, like a computer and a burner smartphone.

It had cost me a great deal, the entirety of my life savings, to get a fake ID that would pass muster at both the state and federal levels. Once I had that, other things became possible.

From my secret bank account, I'd made wire transfers via Western Union to my newly adopted persona, Ian Bragg. I sent money in five-thousand-dollar increments and made a transfer every few days until I had enough cash to do the job. I had no credit cards. I didn't need those to tie me to the scene of the crime. Cash was king. Cash was untraceable.

The idea that what I was going to do was illegal grated on my soul. I had been in the Marines, and I'd earned my honorable discharge. Justice and honor still meant something to me.

I'd been recruited for this job by my old platoon sergeant and my company commander. They said I had the right skills: improv, fearless but cautious, and a keen shot. We hadn't had a sniper unit to support us in the desert war, so I had filled the role. I could shoot straight under the stress of combat.

The ability to perform under a great deal of pressure was what counted the most. They didn't care if I used a gun or a bomb or poison or a push over a railing. The perfect hit was a dead victim of a crime that would go unsolved. They only cared that nothing led back to the Archive or me. They didn't want to lose an operator.

We were few and far between.

I was now a member of an exclusive club, although they'd told me I'd never find out how exclusive.

In my mind, there were a lot of bad guys who needed to take a dirt nap. But how many successful people were willing to pay more than a million each to make it happen?

That was the hierarchy's dilemma. My challenge was helping Gum Band cross the rainbow bridge. Using my burner smartphone as a hotspot, I brought up the computer and downloaded the software I'd need, a VPN and a dark-web browser. I wanted to access the information that wasn't available on the front end. Sometimes it didn't cost anything, and other times it did.

The VPN made it look like I was browsing from somewhere else. I chose a different country each time to keep the watchers from seeing a pattern. Those were bad. My anti-terrorism training in the Corps had taught me that.

To pay those who roamed the chaotic and ever-shifting landscape of the dark web, I used a pre-paid credit card I'd bought with cash.

Cash made it much easier to hide, especially when I had bought the credit cards at a store two states away. I couldn't have a direct trail leading to me.

I got online and navigated into the turbulent waters of the dark web from the front seat of my car. I turned the music down so I could concentrate but didn't turn it off. Rush had been my constant companion. They'd help me through this first contract, too. I stopped, thumbed the player to *Earthrise,* and got back to work.

Gum Band didn't spend a lot of time online, and he did very little once there. He took the greatest care not to reveal anything about himself, but two things that stood out were his electric and water bills. Hidden deep within a recently compromised local utility, I found what I was looking for.

I pulled up an internet map with my VPN, which suggested the search was coming from Liechtenstein, and entered the address. It was right on the edge of the high-rent district, well away from where Gum Band plied his trade.

"Good," I said, trying to convince myself it was a good thing. "I won't look out of place." That was more hope than confidence. An axiom I lived by was "Hope is a lousy plan." With the directions in hand, I turned up the music.

After a dinner consisting of a fried chicken sandwich with extra white sauce, I was ready for a long-term stakeout. Gum Band's home stood a block from where I was parked. I had a clear view of it through the windshield. No matter which direction he came from, I'd see him arrive. I had parked directly under a streetlight so no light shone into the car, keeping it dark inside.

I didn't know if he had a car, used public transport, or rode in taxis everywhere. Maybe he bummed rides from people—a dealer living within his means.

The house with his name paying the utility bills was an upper-scale two-story on a corner lot. It didn't have a garage since it was a little older, but there was a matching carport next to a side entrance that probably led to a kitchen. It wasn't where I would have expected to find a hard-core drug dealer.

Ours is not to question why, I thought, *although it would be nice to know where my contract came from to help me gauge how to shape the hit.*

The clock ticked away the hours, and I let the car idle for so long that I burned a quarter-tank of gas. I didn't want to run out, so I shut it off. I didn't trust the battery, so I didn't play any music either. I cranked down the window and reclined a touch, sucking in the heavily polluted Los Angeles air. If only an ocean breeze would crop up.

Afternoon turned to evening turned to night. I wondered if Gum Band lived there. Who knew what his hours were? I didn't care. This was my current lead, and I was following it.

This was my job. I'd stay here until morning if I had to. Patience would give me the edge.

As midnight approached, I found I had a hard time staying awake. I got out of the car to stretch my legs, keeping to the shadows as much as possible. A Mercedes S600 with blackened windows and custom wheels rolled by. It was better than a Cadillac Fleetwood with chandeliers on the front fenders, but not by much.

It screamed "drug dealer" to me, but I didn't spend much time in LA. I had no idea what the two-hundred-grand custom-car market represented. A Mercedes-Maybach special edition was something different, though, not for your average day-worker.

Why would Gum Band drive something like that?

Or was this his supplier?

I crouched behind the car, not wanting to have the dome light pop on when I opened the door. I reminded myself to shut that off whenever I could get back in the car. It was almost like I'd never done this before.

I glanced around to make sure I was alone. To anyone behind me, I had to look suspicious. This wasn't optimal. Why did this jagoff arrive during the two minutes I was outside my car?

The Mercedes slow-rolled up the driveway and parked. Two dark blobs got out. Neither looked like Gummy. They beat on the door loudly enough that I could hear it a block away.

They walked around the house and then got back into their car. Ten seconds later, they were cruising slowly down the road.

I hurried into the driver's seat and closed the door. I started the engine, thankful it ran, and turned on Rush. *2112* was playing. I back-tracked to the beginning of the album and started it again.

I was taking serious hits, falling asleep every minute or two. It had been a long day, and I resigned myself to the fact that Gum Band didn't live there. I turned on the lights and put the car in gear. I drove toward the house I'd been watching and turned down the side street it abutted. A car came from that direction, turn signal on as it closed. I slowed without hitting the brake.

The driver's outline was clear as he passed.

Guillaume Bandeau.

I drove to the next corner and turned, then stopped and parked far enough down that he wouldn't see me. I shut off the car and jumped out. I hunched my shoulders and bowed my head while walking with my hands in my pockets. Gum Band didn't believe in low-profile, like his buddies in the Maybach.

He drove a Cadillac CT5-V Blackwing. I wouldn't be able to run him off the road with my two-thousand-dollar side-of-the-highway car.

A light came on inside the house. I slowed my approach even though I kept walking so as not to alarm the neighbors. The shades were down, and I couldn't see inside. I needed different equipment to scope the house as it was. An infrared camera. A whisper-quiet drone. Listening devices I could attach to the windows.

I had none of that and wasn't about to buy it in this area. If I made the hit and police started looking, they'd connect the dots, and even with my best efforts, they'd get a security-camera image of my face. I couldn't have that. It was my first contract. I needed to establish credibility with the Archive. Earn more contracts. Be the best. My competitive nature thrived even though I had no idea who I was competing against besides myself. Be better. It was a constant struggle when sometimes I couldn't see what "better" looked like.

It wasn't about the money. It was the game. It was seeing the risks and eliminating them until a clear path to the target remained, along with a clear egress. The exit strategy was more important than the hit itself. There was no value in getting caught or killed.

Not to me, anyway.

But I had learned something valuable: Gum Band lived alone. There was no space for a second car. No one waited for him inside. No wonder he hadn't been in a hurry to get home.

The lights flicked off. I continued walking. A light came on upstairs. I turned the corner, studying the house out the corner of my eye, not turning my head to avoid appearing like I was watching. Curtains were drawn, but not the blinds. A shadow passed the window, but he didn't pull the shades aside to look out. He wouldn't be able to see into the darkness anyway. The only benefit of looking out would be to spot someone who wanted to kill him.

That someone was out here, although I couldn't take the shot since I didn't have a firearm. I should have rolled another dealer on a different corner. Being armed in this part of the world appeared to be critical. Thugs don't drive a Maybach. So who was pounding on Gummy's door at midnight?

It wasn't safe to be out here.

I laughed at the irony. What if I was the most dangerous person? I hoped I was, but hoping didn't make it so. I needed more training in a gym, in a dojo, and on a combat range—a little bit of everything. I was strong but could be stronger. I was fast and my moves were smooth, but I could be faster. Sparring sharpened the eye and shortened my response time. I could shoot. Range time would reinforce what I already knew while keeping me at the top of my game. I didn't feel I could improve there.

I loved to shoot. There was a lot to be said for pulling a trigger to deliver a projectile exactly where intended, no matter the distance. That was the art of the shot. I was very good.

Now I was doing a job where I wasn't carrying a firearm.

Next time, I'd rectify that. I'd help myself to some delinquent's piece at the beginning of the setup. It needed to be an option. Probably not the first option, but one in a hitman's toolbox nonetheless.

Not every problem was a nail that required a hammer, but when it *was* a nail, it helped to have a hammer in hand.

The house went dark and I continued down the road, turning at the corner and then once more to get back to my car. I crawled into the backseat and threw a blanket over myself, then set the alarm on the burner phone for six, giving me four hours. Gum Band wouldn't be up then, so I'd put myself in a position to follow him.

I had no other plan besides that. Follow him, look for a pattern, find the vulnerability.

And exploit it.

I woke up as refreshed as one could be after sleeping contorted in the back seat. I threw off the blanket and sat up, trying to collect my wits. I got out to climb into the driver's seat, being too big and too old to crawl over the center console.

The car turned over instantly and came to life without a backfire. I put it in gear and headed for the nearest gas station to fill up and get a cup of coffee. I was back where I'd started the evening before by six-fifteen. Gum Band's car remained in the driveway.

I choked down a microwaved gas-station sausage biscuit and sipped my coffee, appropriately doctored with four designer creamers to a twenty-ounce cup. It was what I liked, and I wouldn't apologize to anyone for it.

For having had a minimal amount of bad sleep, I felt sufficiently rested. My beard kept growing. It itched, and I couldn't wait to shave it off. As soon as the hit was made, I'd change how I looked on my way out of town on a path I hadn't determined yet.

I didn't have enough information to form a plan.

It was noon before Gum Band strolled to his Blackwing, the most expensive vehicle in the Caddy line. It came in at well over a hundred thousand dollars.

Then there was the Maybach driver. Drug dealers didn't seem to have a problem flaunting their wealth.

How were they not in jail for tax crimes? That was what had brought John Dillinger down. Bureaucrats had much more influence over law-abiding citizens, who quaked with fear when the tax police came calling. The dealers probably put out hits on tax collectors' families—the power of violence.

Just like I was going to employ.

Gum Band rolled easily out of the neighborhood until he hit the highway. He accelerated up the on-ramp until he was out of sight. I did my best, but the poor four-door didn't have the guts. I hit the top of the ramp almost at the speed limit and kept the pedal floored to accelerate into traffic and cross to the fast lane, where I joined a line of vehicles trying to set new land-speed records. On a bend ahead, I saw Gummy's Caddy slowing for a traffic jam.

I slalomed my way forward, getting honked at and given the finger until I was four cars behind him. That was close enough.

Such anger. I never understood why people lived in big cities just so they could be unhappy.

I turned up Rush's *Mystic Rhythms*. I cranked the window down and hung my arm out to feel the heat boiling off the pavement. Traffic crawled along for the next mile, then things broke free past where everyone felt obliged to gawk at an accident. I would never understand big cities.

Gum Band dodged hard to the right toward the upcoming exit. I signaled and dove into an opening that was smaller than my car, happy the driver behind backed off rather than get hit. I was amazed that I didn't get into an accident. It was refreshing to turn onto the exit ramp and follow the Caddy down. He took a right at the bottom and continued toward a mall. He rolled twice around the parking lot and was breaking the anti-cruising law when he finally pulled into the last spot in a long row.

He got out, leaned against the light pole in front of his car, and waited.

I headed to the end of the outside lot and parked where he couldn't see me. I got out, staying low, and maneuvered to a place where I could watch him from between two trucks and over the hood of a car without standing out.

Cars rolled up and stopped for a quick chat. I couldn't see if anything changed hands. I assumed it did.

Which meant Gummy kept the drugs in his house or on him. Was that what the late night was about, restocking the merchandise?

A plan started to form.

An hour after Gum Band's parking lot drug-sales emporium opened for business, a police cruiser approached. He smiled and waved, fearless. It made me wonder what kind of backup he had and how the Archive could put out a contract on that guy, the next one up the food chain.

But that wasn't my job.

The police stopped and didn't bother getting out. Gummy talked to them briefly before they continued on their way. Gum Band got back into his car and drove away. He left the parking lot, caught the light, and was long gone.

I had lost him.

But I knew what I needed to do.

I returned to my hotel room for the first time since yesterday. I caught a shower and hit the rack for a long nap. When the clock struck eight, I got up, took another shower, got dressed, and headed for the high-rent district.

I was going to get something good to eat because I had no intention of making a hit on an empty stomach. That was why the platoon sergeant and the captain wanted me. Pragmatic at all times.

After eating, I'd go back to Gum Band's house. We had a date.

Despite my best efforts to find a sit-down restaurant, I ended up at the drive-through for In-N-Out Burger, where I picked up a double-

double animal style and fries. I didn't get a shake since I knew it would sit heavily in my stomach when added to the fries.

With burger trash in the passenger-side footwell, I parked a block away and on a different street from the previous two times I had been in Gummy's neighborhood. I pulled my hoodie over my head to cover my face, jammed my hands in the pouch, and strolled down the sidewalk. I walked past the front side of Gum Band's dark house and around the corner to the side entrance. As soon as I reached his driveway, I darted into it.

Although Gum Band had floodlights, they weren't set to automatic. I'd seen that when he arrived the previous night. I imagined the neighbors complaining about random blinding rays throughout the night as a nearby bush, blown by the wind, kept activating the floods.

At the far end of the driveway sat a roller garbage can, one of the big ones that could be picked up by a sanitation truck. Workers didn't even have to get out to empty those. I looked inside—two bags of foul-smelling kitchen trash. I removed them and tucked them behind the stairs.

I found climbing into the upright can problematic. I needed a step stool, something I didn't have. The can was on the opposite side of the driveway from the short stairs that led into the house. I tipped the can over and climbed in, and with a push-off and a wild gyration, I managed to get it to stand upright.

I then practiced getting out.

"I'm going to get killed," I mumbled to myself.

I ended up dumping the can on its side, making way too much noise. I crawled out and listened to make sure the neighbors weren't alarmed, but if they were, I'd find out when the police showed up. Isn't that what alarmed neighbors do? Call the police.

I put the garbage bags back inside the can, wiped down anything I had touched, and maneuvered the can a couple of feet closer to the neighbor's fence. I made myself as small as possible behind it and sat facing the street with the can between me and it. That gave me room to adjust when Gummy's headlights cast shadows when he pulled in. I had to stay out of the driver's line of sight.

Then I waited. I rocked to my feet with each passing car. Ten became midnight before headlights turned in.

I slid my feet under me and stayed crouched, ready to spring into action.

My heart jumped.

It was the Maybach. Two men hopped out and repeated their performance from the night before. These were men who were bigger than me. As soon as they turned away from the house, they'd see me. I had to act.

I ran toward them while one pounded on the door and the other stood ready to burst in. His hand remained in a pocket, where I expected he had a gun.

I dodged to the side as I passed, tripping the man on the first step and pulling him backward until I was sure he'd fall. I grabbed the man at the top of the steps and slammed him into the closed door before pulling him back to toss him on the first man, who had hit his head on the concrete but only hard enough to make him mad. The second man landed on him.

When they started to rise, I jumped off the top step and delivered a two-legged kick into the middle of the top man's back. I pushed off after impact, but it went awry. I hit and rolled, coming to my feet quicker than my opponents. I still didn't know who they were, but this had gone sideways and was now out of control. The only thing I wanted to do was get out of there.

That was no longer an option. The garbage can blocked one side, the car the middle, and the two-man mini-pile the other. I closed to disarm the first man, but the second was in the way.

I'd replay this debacle in my mind as long as I lived, which I hoped was longer than tonight.

The first man pushed the second off him and pulled a .357 magnum out of his pocket. He tried to roll toward me to take aim. I lunged forward and dipped to launch a roundhouse kick past his face and into his forearm, sending the pistol flying from numb fingers.

I jumped away and scrambled toward the pistol, only to find I had company. I tried a side kick, but the man was upright and dodged to let it slide ineffectively past his hip. He grabbed my hand. I twisted to hit him with a left jab, but it was weak, and he shook it off. He hammered me above the belt with an uppercut that drove the breath out of me. He pushed me away, but I got my feet under me and surged into him, body-blocking him into the steps.

His friend was struggling to his feet. I could hear his breath rasping and gurgling—broken ribs and a punctured lung from my first kick. He'd only be a threat if he was armed.

I wrenched my hand free and punched the side of my opponent's neck. He staggered, and I followed with a kick to the groin that struck home. While he stumbled back, I dropped to grab the magnum and raised it, only to find myself facing a Glock 19.

"That's about enough," the man said with a heavy wheeze. "Are you here for us or for Bandeau?"

"Bandeau. I thought you were friends."

"Bandy owes me fifty large." He coughed and nearly doubled over from the pain, almost dropping the pistol. I didn't charge into him, a wounded animal being dangerous and all that. The other man lay on the steps, groaning.

"Do you want him to pay, or do you want him dead?"

"Pay and then dead. There won't be any more chances for him." The two men were mostly incapacitated. I had won the fight, except they still had a pistol. But they weren't the target. I wasn't being paid to kill them, and I had no beef with them except that they had blown my plan.

"Move your car down there." I pointed to where I had been the first night. "And we'll wait for him right here. All of us. He doesn't owe me any money, but he got my little sister hooked. She committed suicide because of what drugs did to her, so it's time for him to die."

"Touching." He didn't sound like he was impressed, but he was in no condition to be impressed by anything. "Why should we work with you? We can handle this."

"You were here last night, too," I started, but that would go nowhere. "You don't look too good. Need me to call an ambulance?"

"Hell, no!" He leaned against the railing to support himself. The man on the steps straightened with a grunt before putting his hands on his knees.

"Why in the nuts?" he grumbled.

"I didn't want to get shot. Still don't. I only want Bandeau to die. Tonight. I'm tired of waiting and watching."

"Move the car," the wheezer ordered.

The other glared at me as he limped past, but he continued to the car, fired it up, and backed into the street. He drove it down the road to where he could turn around and park it where I had been yesterday.

I wondered if he was going to call for backup, then dismissed the idea. The wheezer had a gun and could have shot me. The second man was hired muscle. He did as told. If he came back with a gun and flashed it at me, I'd end them both.

"Nice ride," I told the wheezer.

"What's your name?" he asked.

"No. You don't want to know my name any more than I want to know yours. We're going to do this thing, and then we'll be on our merry way." It was time to play my cards. "I know what you're thinking. Hit Gummy and then make it look like he and I killed each other in a shootout. I'm thinking the same thing because I don't want to go to jail, just like you don't. Ain't no prisoners driving a Maybach in the Gray-Bar Motel."

"You recognize my car. That's worth something. You are right. I'm trying to think of a way to kill you both, dump the guns, and walk away. After I get my money, of course."

"Of course." My mind raced through a hundred scenarios, and I died in too many of them. "You stand up here with your boy, and I'll wait down by the road to block Gummy in as soon as he starts up his driveway. You know he has a gun."

"No kidding. There's no one around here who doesn't pack." He watched me as his mind worked. I could see it behind his eyes. When the other man walked up, he sent him down the sidewalk to wait. "He'll block him in while you and I wait right here."

"Just stay in front of me. Don't take this the wrong way, but I don't trust you."

He laughed until he coughed but didn't reply. We had an understanding. One of us was going to die that night. We waited. The man by me grew paler and paler. I wondered if he was going to die before Gummy returned home.

By one-thirty, he looked like he was going to fall over. "I think you should have your boy take you to the hospital. I'll take care of this. You can count on it, but I'm not going to look for your money. Sorry."

"Despite your kind offer, I'll have to pass. I'm not leaving here without my cash."

"Have it your way." I threw my hands up in resignation. I didn't throw them too hard since I still held the .357. I liked the way it felt in my hand.

Lights shone on the street. They cautiously turned in and started up the driveway until they saw us. I took aim, as did the wheezer, but his hand shook to the point that the safest place to be was where he was aiming.

The other man ran up behind Gum Band's car and hammered his hands on the trunk, but he was unarmed. Gummy jacked the Cadillac into reverse and floored it.

I hammered the wheezer in the side of the head with the butt of my pistol. He fell like a load of bricks. I ran down the driveway as Gummy bounced over the man who had thought to stop him with his body or by force of will. Neither had worked.

I skidded to a stop and dropped to a knee. Gummy put the car in drive. In that brief moment, the car was perfectly still in the dead space between backing up and driving forward down the street. I fired twice.

A double-tap. He was dead with the first round, which exploded his head across the inside of the car. I charged while the car idled forward toward the corner intersection with a dead driver behind its wheel. I wiped the .357 and stuffed it into the hand of the freshly run-over man. I didn't bother to check if he was alive. That didn't matter. Neither of those men could recognize me.

I bolted through Gummy's yard to come out on the other street as the Cadillac slow-rolled into a curb and ground to a halt.

I pulled my hood up and walked quickly down the block and around the corner. I started my car and drove out the far end of the residential area. My heart pounded.

Three druggies for the price of one.

I headed onto the highway, where traffic was fairly light. I couldn't be seen in the car since it had just left a crime scene. The gunfire should have woke the neighbors since there aren't many things louder than a .357 banging away in the open air.

LAX. A massive airport.

I pulled into short-term parking, where I casually wiped the car down, securing my burger trash, and taking my music with me on the way to get my bag out of the trunk. I had kept my small bag with me because I never knew when I wouldn't be able to return to the hotel. It held my computer and the burner phone, although neither had any information stored on them.

I kept my hood up as I strolled toward the terminal. I stopped at the first bathroom, changed clothes, ditched the trash, and shaved. Between massive amounts of hand sanitizer and scrubbing my hands until my skin was translucent, I figured I had removed any gunpowder residue. I didn't need security crawling up my butt because I made their machine buzz. I then used my smartphone to find the next flight to Denver. It left in two hours. I couldn't make reservations since I didn't have a credit card with enough on it, but there were seats available. I headed to the airline counter, paid cash for my ticket, got the third degree at the checkpoint because of the cash ticket purchase, but was cleared.

Breakfast sounded good. I looked for a sit-down place.

I deserved an omelet, and I'd buy headphones so I could listen to Rush. *Roll the Bones* would help me relax after the dog's breakfast I had made of my first contract. No one would have to know, but I would never forget.

They say the first one is the hardest. But it was done, and soon enough, I'd be out of California. My old beater would get towed after a few days, and in a week, no one would remember it had ever existed.

Just like me.

ABOUT THE AUTHOR

Craig Martelle is a science fiction and thriller author with over a hundred titles to his name. He is a retired Marine and a retired lawyer who lives in Alaska and writes full-time. Ian Bragg is his newest series. Hopefully you found the character compelling. You can find all of Craig's books at https://craigmartelle.com including the Ian Bragg thriller series, now three novels and growing.

LOATHSOME JUSTICE

M A COMLEY

This story is in written in British English – there are no typos in here.
The game is up!

1

"Shit! We've got another one. I had a feeling this bastard would strike again soon."

"Feeling? As in, your water?" Pete chuckled.

Lorne narrowed her weary eyes and glared at him. "You can be such a jerk at times, partner."

"Yeah, but I brighten the dreariest of days for you, right?"

Lorne punched him in the arm and whizzed past him. At the door to the incident room, she turned back to face the team. "You all know what to do in our absence. AJ, trawl through the CCTV footage. See if this fucker had an accomplice waiting for him or if he's truly causing all this mischief and mayhem alone. Either way, I want a concerted effort from everyone today. Push yourselves to the max if necessary, so we can get this shithead off the streets and behind bars where he belongs."

Pete followed her down the stairs and out to the car. He belched loudly once he was seated beside her which gained him another glare and thump on the thigh.

"You're such a vile pig at times. What the hell did I do to have the misfortune of choosing you as my damn partner?"

He grinned and smiled. "Because I'm such a catch, and they say opposites attract."

Lorne burst out laughing, she couldn't help herself. "Er...I think you'll find that response can only be used when a couple are dating. Thank Christ that isn't the case with you and me. I swear I would have throttled you years ago if we'd been romantically involved. Oh God, just the thought of it." She mock-heaved. "Bugger, I nearly brought up my tuna baguette then." She started the engine and flicked on the siren, drowning out any response he had to offer.

No matter how much they ribbed each other during the day, they had a solid partnership which achieved phenomenal results within the Met Police.

Lorne groaned. "Damn, I was hoping we wouldn't run into him again so soon." She pointed at Jacques Arnaud, the new pathologist in the area.

The guy was French and had an eye for the ladies, at least that's how she perceived it. All the female officers back at the station had all gone gooey-eyed over him—not her, though. His type didn't interest her in the slightest. Even if her own marriage was fraught at times, she could never stray, not with the likes of him. He was far too arrogant for a start.

A twinkle sparkled in Jacques' eyes the second he spotted her and Pete walking towards him.

"Stay calm. I'm sure he does it to wind you up," Pete said out of the corner of his mouth.

"I know. Bugs the hell out of me how he manages to do it, too. You know me, I never usually let cretins like that get to me."

"Ignore him. Want me to take the lead on this one?"

She winked and smiled at him. "If I did that, he'd be rubbing his hands, thinking he'd won."

"Just be yourself. I'll have a chat with him for you, if you want."

"Nah, let him play his churlish games. I'll continue to be the ultimate professional like always."

Pete chuckled, earning him a dig in the ribs. "Ouch!"

"Ah, the mighty Lorne Simpkins has arrived at last. It's kind of you to grace us with your presence, Inspector."

"Cut the crap, Jacques. Just tell me what we've got."

"Such a way with words." He laughed and pointed at his van. "You two need to get suited and booted first. I refuse to let you near my crime scene until then."

Tutting, Lorne and Pete raced over to the van and sourced a couple of protective suits. Pete had a job finding one to fit his stout figure, as usual. He squeezed into one a size smaller, and Lorne laughed at the way he waddled back to the crime scene.

"Stop it! You can be so cruel, and there was me about to put my honour on the line for you not five minutes ago."

"I know. Wicked boss, ain't I?"

Jacques was organising his team of forensic technicians, who then darted off in different directions, allowing Pete and Lorne access to the corpse.

"Jesus, not again!" Lorne said.

She observed the body of a male around thirty. His eyes had been removed and placed on his chest, just like the other three victims they'd discovered over the past two weeks. The killer had inserted rubies in the eye sockets. The other victims all had different precious stones left behind. The first emeralds, the second diamonds, and the third sapphires. All the stones had been stolen from jewellers throughout the London area. Some of the staff had been killed in the robberies. What Lorne hadn't managed to figure out yet was why the killer/thief was choosing these particular men as his victims and decorating them with the jewels. None of it made any sense, at least it hadn't up until now.

"Any DNA, clues, fingerprints?" Lorne asked, more out of hope than expectation.

Jacque's gaze met hers, and he nodded. "You're in luck. He slipped up this time. We have a possible footprint alongside the body and a potential fingerprint on one of the rubies."

"Wow, let's hope they're good enough to bring this fucker down."

"Leave it with me. I'll do my best, you know that."

And she did. In spite of what she thought about the man on a personal level, he was exceptional at his job. Professional to the point of being anal. "What else have you got for us?"

He shook his head in disgust. "Always wanting more from me, never satisfied with what I offer."

Lorne rolled her eyes. "You know that's not true. You're also aware, the more we have on the killer, the easier it's going to be to haul his arse into court."

He crossed his arms and tapped his foot. "Do you really have to state the obvious every time we meet, Inspector?"

"Not every time, no." She flashed her pearly whites at him.

"Enough of this. I need to get on with my examination now. Will you be attending the post-mortem later?"

Pete heaved beside her. He had a dodgy tummy where sliced up bodies were concerned.

"I think we'll give this one a miss," she replied.

"As you wish."

They hung around for another fifteen minutes while Arnaud examined the body and his photographer took the pictures which would be used for evidence when the case went to court, if it ever did.

Soon after, Lorne received a call from the station. She and Pete had left the scene and were in the car.

She put the phone on speaker. "Hi, AJ, what have you got for us?"

"Exciting news, boss, he slipped up. The bastard knocked out the cameras in the jeweller's and sprayed a couple of cameras on the neighbouring shops, but I took a chance on one of the shops opposite having footage and hit the jackpot."

"Well done, you. That's excellent news. Tell me you were successful picking up the suspect."

"Let's just say the camera caught him in all his finery and he had an accomplice waiting for him in a getaway car."

"Tell me you picked up the plate number, AJ?"

"Not yet. I'm working on it though, guv."

"Good man. We're on our way back to base now. Hopefully, you'll have it all sorted by the time we get there."

He chuckled. "No pressure then. We've been working the case for a couple of weeks and—"

"I know. I'm expecting miracles, but if we don't catch these guys soon...well, I don't have to fill in the blanks for you, do I?"

"You don't. That's why I'm busting a gut to get the images for you, boss."

"Do your best, that's all we can do in the circumstances, AJ. See you soon." She ended the call and continued on the journey. "Are you all right, you seem a bit quiet?"

"I'm fine. Reflective, I suppose you'd call it. So, it could be good news, you know, him having an accomplice."

"In what way?"

"Doing the research. It's always better looking for two crims rather than just one."

"If you say so. Let's hope we can pick the pair of them up soon."

"Every chance that'll happen if they're in the system. Why take the eyes out?"

Lorne blew out a breath. "You tell me?"

"All right, let me put it another way. Why take the eyes out, leave them at the scene, and replace them with expensive jewels?"

"Correction, expensive *stolen* jewels, you mean."

"Yeah, that as well."

"If nothing else, this tells me that it's not about the money. These guys have an agenda. What we need to find out is one, what that agenda is, and two, how the victims are linked."

"Do they have to be linked? Couldn't these shits have just targeted strangers?"

"That's a possibility, of course it is, however, I'm inclined to think it's the former."

AJ was bouncing off the walls like an excited puppy who'd overdosed on the choc drops he'd discovered in a cupboard after nosing around where he shouldn't be.

Lorne motioned with her hands. "Hey, calm down. What's going on?"

"We've got a match. Two brothers, Jimmy and Alan Bell."

"Those names ring a bell," Pete quipped.

Lorne groaned and gestured for AJ to continue. "What's their background?"

"They're in the system for petty burglary."

"So they've upped their game considerably. I wonder why?"

"I reckon they got put in the nick and learned a trick or two inside from the other cons, thought they'd try their luck when they came out," Pete offered.

"Hmm...maybe. Tell me you've got an address for them, AJ."

The young detective, relatively new to the team, waved a sheet of paper at her. "I have. Two addresses. Although they're within spitting distance of each other."

"Okay, let's get everything prepared. I want them caught without a bloody hitch. There's been too many of them lately with this case. Find out who their friends are, get their addresses, if at all possible. I want to know what cars they drive and if they're both seeing anyone, just in case they go on the run."

"On it now, boss," AJ shouted enthusiastically.

"I want the whole team on it, not just you, AJ. Pete, I could do with a coffee, and it's your turn to buy. I'll be in my office, I need to inform Roberts of what's going on."

"I'm right here." DCI Roberts scared the crap out of Lorne.

She spun around and clutched at her heart. "Blimey, you almost caused me a have a heart attack, sir. Pete was just getting the drinks in. Care to join me in the office, and I'll run through the case with you."

"That's kind of you, Pete. Two sugars and white for me."

Pete smiled awkwardly. Lorne knew what was running through his mind: the thought of forking out for three coffees, he was the type whose arse squeaked when he walked, he was that tight.

Once they were settled in the office and Pete had deposited the coffee on the desk and left the room, Lorne went through the cases that had blighted her life for the past two weeks. DCI Roberts steepled his fingers and tapped them against his chin, listening intently to her account.

"And you say you know the two who are responsible now?"

"That's right. AJ has just located their names in the database. Ex-petty burglars who appeared to have upped their game considerably since doing a spell behind bars."

"Bugger. How many times does that happen?"

"More times than I care to think about. Once a crim, always a crim in my book."

"Don't let the higher-ups hear you say that. What about the rehabilitation aspect?"

"Counts for nothing these days, not for some folks anyway."

Sean sighed. "Okay, let's put that aside for now. I want in on this."

There, I knew he'd utter those five sodding words sooner or later. "Of course, if that's what you truly want, sir."

"I do. It's not that I don't trust you, it's more about me keeping my hand in. I'm fed up of sitting behind a desk all day, not being involved in the action."

"I get that. Does this mean you'll be in charge, sir?"

"No. I'll just tag along for the ride. You'll still be giving the orders as usual."

"That's magnanimous of you, Sean."

"I know." He laughed.

They'd been partners once upon a time, in and out of bed. When he'd shown up six months ago as her superior, she thought he'd make her life hell. Sometimes he had but mostly he'd trusted her abilities. He'd returned to her life a better man than he'd left it, that was for sure.

"What's the plan then?" he asked eagerly.

"The team are doing the necessary research. We can't make a move without those facts, it'll be too risky."

"Right. I'll get back to the office then. Ring me when you're ready to make your move. Will it be soon?" He glanced at his watch. "It's almost three now."

"Clock-watching? We don't tend to do a lot of that around here. I'll holler when we're about to leave."

"Do that." He left the room, taking his drink with him.

After a few moments had passed, giving Sean the time to leave the outer office, she bellowed for Pete to join her.

He plonked into the chair without waiting to be invited. "What's up? Making your life hell, is he? Only asking because it tends to come down the line when he does."

"Bollocks, Pete Childs. I never take my bad moods out on you and the rest of the team."

His eyes widened. "If you say so."

"Anyway, ignoring your insults for the time being, he wants in."

Pete tipped his head back. "Damn. I take it you did your best to try to dissuade him."

"That goes without saying. We need to play things by the book on this one, not that we don't usually."

"I'll let the team know."

"How are things progressing out there?"

"It's all coming together well. We should be able to make a move soon."

"This evening?" she asked hopefully.

"Could well be. Will the chief be okay with that?"

"He'll have to be. If he wants in on this then he'll have to go with the flow."

"Any chance we can get some scran first?"

"Always thinking of that damn stomach of yours, Pete. You're a bloody nightmare."

"I know. It takes a lot of calories to sustain this physique, you know."

"Whatever. How you manage to pass a medical every year is beyond me, unless you give the examiner a backhander, which wouldn't surprise me."

"Cheeky mare. I sail through them."

"Go, bugger off. I have paperwork to do. Give me a shout when things slot together enough for us to get on the road."

He stood. It was an effort and was accompanied by a groan. "I'll come and get you."

Lorne had managed to tackle half the paperwork messing up her desk by the time she received the call from Pete. She immediately requested DCI Roberts join them in the incident room. Once Sean had arrived, the rest of the team issued the information they had successfully gathered in the last few hours. Adrenaline rushed through Lorne's veins. She could see the end in sight and would hopefully catch the bastards before they swooped and plucked out the eyes of yet another victim.

"All right. Let's get out there. Karen, you remain here to man the phones and the computers, just in case we need you to check anything for us."

"Rightio, guv."

"The rest of you, let's go catch ourselves some killers."

Outside in the car park, Sean insisted that Lorne and Pete should join him in his car.

"Are you sure? Is it equipped with a siren?" she asked, bemused by his offer.

"Yes, of course."

Pete hopped in the back, and Lorne sat in the front, next to Sean. He drove to the address they had on record for Jimmy Bell. His car was outside the property. The three of them exited the vehicle and approached the house.

"Pete, there's an alley there. Go round the back in case he tries to make a run for it," Lorne said.

Pete set off, trotting down the alley. Lorne gave it a few seconds and then knocked on the front door.

"Don't expect him to welcome us with open arms, will you?" she warned Sean.

"I'm well aware how these things have gone down in the past, Inspector. I'm not that green."

The door remained unanswered. Instinctively, Lorne left Sean at the front door, and she darted around the back. She found Pete lying on the floor. "Pete, Pete, are you okay?"

"The bastard head butted me in the gut, knocked the wind out of my sails, that's all. I'm fine, you need to get after him, he's getting away."

"Not until I help you on your feet first."

Chief Roberts rounded the corner. "Hey, are you all right, Pete?"

Pete dusted himself off. "Injured pride, that's all."

"Okay, we need to call this in. Make the others aware, he could show up at any number of the addresses we've got for them."

"My take is he'll head for his brother's gaff," Pete added. He took a comb out of his top pocket and fixed his messed-up hair.

"We're wasting time," Sean announced.

Lorne stared and shook her head at him for stating the obvious. "Let's get over to his brother's place, it's just around the corner."

Pete snorted. "And you think they're going to still be there?"

"I doubt it, but stranger things have happened. Keep the faith, Pete," Lorne replied. She legged it up the alley back to Sean's car, her two colleagues close behind her.

Upon their arrival at Alan Bell's house, they were horrified to see there had been a shootout and two uniformed officers were down.

Sean immediately got on the phone to request an Armed Response Team.

Lorne tapped him on the shoulder and whispered, "Maybe we should ask the helicopter to attend, too."

"Good idea," Pete mumbled from the back seat.

Lorne got out of the car to assist her team and the paramedics who had just drawn up. "What are we looking at, AJ?"

"Two shot, one seriously, and the other got away with just a flesh wound. I've insisted they both get checked out at hospital, though."

"As they should. Do we know what happened?"

"Jimmy arrived. He was the one who shot the two officers. Before either of our teams could respond, he drove off again. I placed the call; we've got teams out there chasing them. It's the best I could do, guv, in the circumstances."

"Hey, no recriminations from me. We'll catch the bastards." Lorne left her colleague and made her way over to the ambulance.

Both officers were awake. The female officer who was injured the worst tried to sit up to greet her.

Lorne gestured for the PC to stay where she was. "I'm sorry you got involved in this shit. Can you tell me what went down?"

"We'd just arrived, didn't know what hit us. We'd been asked to assist by the desk sergeant. All of a sudden, this car approached the house. The driver took pot shots at us, all of us. We were the closest, there was no way we could avoid getting hit. Then another man ran out of the house. He shouted at the driver to cease firing, but he carried on. Seconds later, they drove away. We were all too numb to react."

"No one is blaming any of you for this. I've been campaigning for armed police on the streets for years. Maybe now head office will start listening to me. I'm sorry you and your partner got injured. Check in with me later, if you would?" Lorne gave her a card.

"We'll be fine, ma'am. Sam here is a pretty resilient kind of bloke."

"Glad to hear it. Take care." She sprinted back to Sean's car and listened to the chatter coming over the police radio. "I know that place. It's not far from here, down on the bank of the River Thames."

"We'll get over there now." Sean reversed the car.

"Is that wise?" Pete asked. "They're armed and dangerous and, well..."

"There's three of us and two of them," Sean replied, disregarding his concerns.

Lorne smiled at Sean and shook her head while Pete tutted. "You'd better hope the ART show up soon because without them we're not going to be able to pin these guys down."

Sean shook his head. "Ah, I didn't have you down as a defeatist, Lorne."

"I'm not. I generally work in facts, boss. And the facts are these shits have already taken out two officers. If anything, I'm being uber cautious."

"Duly noted." Sean pressed his foot down on the accelerator, and the car surged forward. "Let's get them," he shouted with all the enthusiasm of a cowboy on his way to round up wild horses.

At the location, Lorne pointed at the abandoned car. "Why would they leave their vehicle like that?"

"Maybe they ran out of petrol," Pete quipped.

Lorne rolled her eyes at Sean, and the three of them exited the vehicle. Lorne peered into the car and looked at the gauge. *Shit! He was right, I'll never live it down!*

She joined the others and mumbled, "You were right."

"It doesn't matter," Sean said. "What we need to decide now, is which way they went."

Lorne glanced up and down the bank of the river. "Two choices from what I can see. How do you want to play this, boss?"

"You and Pete stick together. I'll go this way. You've got my mobile number, ring me if you discover where they are."

"Right," Lorne responded, anxious to get on with things.

She and Pete tore along the footpath, through one tunnel, and were about to approach the second when something rolled along the path towards them.

"It's a bloody grenade," Lorne yelled and dived for cover on the grass verge.

Pete froze for a split second as if contemplating what to do next. The grenade had stopped a couple of feet ahead of him. A few long strides later, and he was standing over it.

Lorne watched on, her heart in her mouth. "Pete, get out of there."

It was too late. He bent down and tossed the grenade in the water beside him then threw himself next to Lorne.

The grenade went off. The water swelled and erupted fifty feet into the air, and a huge wave covered them.

"That was a close one. Idiot, don't ever do that again, you hear me?" Lorne swiped her partner's arm and got to her feet.

Pete joined her and brushed himself down. They both resembled a couple of drowned sewer rats.

"Geesh, if that's the thanks I get for saving your life, remind me not to bother in the future," he said.

Lorne pecked him on the cheek and he blushed. "I appreciate your effort, I truly do. Come on, we have a job to finish."

"Yeah, let me get my hands on the bastards now."

They chased after the two men, their attempt to gain any speed hampered by the dousing they'd received.

"There." Lorne pointed at one of the men up ahead.

"Where's the other one? Wait, it could be a trap, Lorne," Pete hollered as she raced ahead. It was unusual for him to use her name instead of calling her boss or guv.

"Don't worry about me, I'll get him," she called over her shoulder.

Her partner pulled up and placed his hands on his knees, gasping for breath. Now she found herself in a dilemma. Did she continue or turn back? Against her better judgement, she decided she had to forge ahead. Upping her pace, she reached the end of the alley and peered into it. There were several doorways and the alley was littered with various commercial-sized bins, easy places for him to hide. She withdrew her Taser and proceeded to enter the narrow confines between the buildings.

A noise sounded off to her right, and a skinny dog bared its teeth at her. She ignored it, gave it a wide berth, and continued. Suddenly, perhaps sensing she was near, Jimmy Bell emerged from his hiding place and ran the length of the alley into the darkness. Lorne didn't think twice about her own safety, she needed to get this fucker, once and for all. Aware he could be loaded down with more grenades, she advanced with caution.

Jimmy cursed and lashed out at something. She peered through the darkness, her eyes adjusting to the glimpse of light available from the window of a nearby building. Jimmy was trapped. A wire fence blocked his path.

"Give yourself up, man. There's no point in putting up a fight." Overhead, the noise of the helicopter sounded. "We're here in force. There's no way you're going to get out of here now."

He yelled and charged at her. She pressed herself up against the wall, letting him pass and then gave chase again.

Fishing out her mobile, she rang DCI Roberts while she ran. "I've got one of them, sir."

"I'm on my way. Stay safe."

She tucked her phone away again and sprinted after the criminal. The silhouettes of two men were ahead of her. One of them was unmistakably Pete's. He stood his ground, resembling the size of a fifty-year-old redwood. Jimmy yelled for him to get out of the way.

Pete remained still and raised his hand. The next second, Jimmy was writhing on the ground at his feet.

"Take that, moron. That'll teach you! Attempt to kill us at your peril, arsehole!" Pete said.

Lorne placed a hand over Pete's. "All right, turn it off."

Sean appeared and took charge. He cuffed Jimmy and yanked him to his feet.

Lorne stepped towards him. "Where's your brother?"

Jimmy spat in her face, earning himself a thump to the stomach from Pete. Jimmy yelled out and doubled over.

Sean pulled him upright. "The lady asked you a question. Where's Alan?"

"On his way to kill someone else." He laughed.

Pete clenched his fist and raised it.

Lorne grabbed his arm. "He's not worth it, Pete."

Sirens sounded, and a couple of uniformed officers appeared within seconds. They whisked Jimmy away.

"What now?" Pete asked.

Lorne shrugged. "You tell me. We haven't got a clue who he's after."

"Let's face it, he can't go far, not if he's on foot. Are you two up to continue the chase?"

"Soggy, but we're up for it, aren't we, partner?" Lorne asked.

Pete grumbled his agreement.

"All we can hope is the helicopter can locate him," Sean said.

The three of them marched out into the open and surveyed the sky. The chopper *thwap-thwarped* in the distance. "Should we go after it on foot?"

"Why not. Let's go," Sean said, already setting off.

The helicopter hovered above a warehouse at the end of the street.

Sean contacted the pilot. "We're at the end of the road. Is the criminal inside the warehouse?"

"Yes, we tracked him to the location. He hasn't exited the building. We'll remain on site until you get here. Backup is on the way."

"Thanks, I have an ART on standby, I'll ring them now." Sean ended the call and immediately rang the commander of the ART.

Lorne listened in as Sean actioned the team to take over. The three of them made their way down the busy street, willing the pedestrians out of the way, knowing that if they warned them what was going on, panic would ensue.

They reached the building and lingered by the entrance for the next five minutes until the ART arrived. The commanding officer organised his team, and they entered the building. Sean persuaded the officer in charge to allow the three of them to go inside to watch. He wasn't happy about it but relented in the end.

Observing the team go about their business, Lorne was impressed by how swiftly they captured Alan Bell. They surrounded him, their weapons pointed, ready to fire if called upon. Alan conceded and came out of his hidey-hole with his arms raised.

Lorne, Pete, and Sean all high-fived each other and they got back in the car.

Sean eyed Lorne and Pete up and down once they arrived at the station. "What about a change of clothes?"

"I've got a pair of jeans and a T-shirt in the back of my car. What about you, Pete?" Lorne said.

"Ditto, somewhere amongst all the takeaway cartons."

Sean nodded. "Get changed. I'll oversee proceedings until you get back."

"Do you want to be in on the interviews?" Lorne asked.

"Nope, I'll leave those in your capable hands."

He left them to it. Lorne and Pete changed out of their wet clothes and began the first interview. Alan Bell went down the 'no comment' route right the way through, much to everyone's annoyance, including his solicitor.

Lorne had to be cagey with his brother. She knew she'd have to tell a few white lies in order for him to reveal why they had killed their victims.

Once Jimmy was cuffed to the table, Lorne said the usual verbiage for the tape and got the interview underway. "I have to tell you, Jimmy, your brother was very obliging during his interview."

"Like I believe you. What kind of fool do you take me for, Simpkins?"

She shrugged. "Who's the fool? Remind me, who's the one sitting in a police station modelling the latest designer handcuffs?"

"You've got a smart mouth," Jimmy snarled.

Lorne tapped at her temple. "I've got a smart brain as well. Smarter than yours anyway. So, are you going to tell us why you killed those people?"

He grinned and bared his tobacco-stained teeth. "Because we wanted to."

"Why? Why rob the jewellers and leave the jewels on the bodies?"

"You mean *in* the bodies, don't you?"

"A minor inaccuracy on my part. Why? Who were these people to you?"

"People who have stood in our way over the years."

Lorne recalled the occupations of the first three victims: a headmaster, a solicitor, and a bank manager. "Is that it? Your sole reason for killing them was because they'd stood in your way?"

"Yep. Over the years they've cost us a lot of money in one way or another."

"So your brother said," she replied, keeping up her pretence. "What about the jewels? Why rob the jewellers?"

"Why not? It added a bit of spice to the proceedings, kept us entertained and you lot on your toes."

"Is that it? Not very inventive, were you? Of all the criminals I've arrested over the years that must be the feeblest excuse I've heard for taking someone's life and going to the extremes you and your brother have gone to. It doesn't make sense."

"Life doesn't make sense. We upped the ante, stuck a few robberies in there, and used the jewels to gain some notoriety in the press."

"Ah, I see. So all this was part of the plan. All you were aiming for was to go down in history as a 'notorious killer', or killers, in the media's eyes."

"Good pun there, Inspector." He laughed.

Infuriated, Lorne slammed her hand on the desk. "This is all a big joke to you, isn't it? Three men have lost their lives, their families destroyed, all because you wanted to get your kicks."

"Sounds about right. It worked though, didn't it? The press called us The Jewel Killer."

"You're warped. Let's see if you're still laughing about this when you're charged and convicted of all the murders. You won't see the light of day again, Bell, I'll make sure of that."

"You think? I have money, I can afford the best barristers around."

"Under the Proceeds of Crime Act 2002, we're going to strip you and your brother of all your assets, including your properties. Still laughing, are you?"

He wasn't. He launched at her across the table. Pete was quickest to react. He stuck a hand on the man's chest and forced him back into his seat.

Lorne brought the interview to a halt and smugly rose from her chair. "See you in court, loser."

Three months later, Jimmy and Alan Bell had their day in court. The jury heard all the evidence and returned a unanimous decision. The female judge handed down six life sentences to each of the brothers.

Lorne and Pete walked away from the court feeling jubilant, knowing that as Lorne had predicted, the Bell brothers would never see the light of day again, ever.

ABOUT THE AUTHOR

M A Comley is a KINDLE UNLIMITED ALL-STAR author as well as being a New York Times, USA Today, Amazon Top 20 bestselling author. She has topped the book charts on iBooks as a top 5 bestselling and reached #2 bestselling author on Barnes and Noble. Over two and a half million copies sold worldwide. She's a British author who moved to France in 2002, and that's when she turned her hobby into a career.

When she's not writing crime novels as well as caring for her elderly mother, she's either reading or going on long walks with her rescue pup Labrador, Dex.

https://www.amazon.com/M-A-Comley/e/B0045YOB9I

AUTHOR NOTES - CRAIG MARTELLE

Written February 28, 2021

You are still reading! Thank you for staying on board until now. It doesn't get much better than that. I hope you found new authors to follow, new stories to spark your imagination, and characters that you want to hang out with.

I want to thank all the contributing authors for taking the time to generate such great stories and putting them in here for the world's first look at them. Every story is unique and published here for the first time. Thank you for trusting me to publish these. But the thanks is best in the hands of readers like you, just like the anthology.

Thank you for buying this anthology and thank you for those reading it with your Kindle Unlimited subscription. It goes to a good cause – an even split of the royalties between all the contributing authors. I hope a few of you have gone through and found these stories to be worthy of further exploration into that author's books. That's all I can ask for. Find one. Follow them on Amazon or sign up for their newsletter. There is some incredible thriller fiction out there and a lot of it is by authors you haven't heard of.

I am happy to be a part of this set, and selfishly, I hope the fans of Ian and Jenny Bragg were gratified to read about Ian's first hit.

It's 2021 which means we've been through a lot. I live where people wanted to be during the worst of the pandemic in 2020. I'm isolated in an area with a population density of one person per square mile. Wearing a mask outside is ridiculous because there are very few other humans here. Life didn't change for us besides all our planned travel was canceled. That's not a bad consolation prize. It allows us to do more at home. We cleaned up our garage and started reducing our ridiculous amount of stuff that serves no useful purpose.

I wish you all the best to keep on keeping on.

Peace, fellow humans.

Please join my Newsletter (https://craigmartelle.com/newsletter) – please, please, please sign up!), or you can follow me on Facebook since you'll get the same opportunity to find books when they first publish or when they go on sale.

If you liked this story, you might like some of my other books. Drop by my website **https://craigmartelle.com** or if you have any comments, shoot me a note at craig@craigmartelle.com. I am always happy to hear from people who've read my work. I try to answer every email I receive.

If you liked the story, please write a short review for me on Amazon. I greatly appreciate any kind words, even one or two sentences go a long way. The number of reviews an ebook receives greatly improves how well an ebook does on Amazon.

Amazon – www.amazon.com/author/craigmartelle

BookBub – https://www.bookbub.com/authors/craig-martelle

Facebook – www.facebook.com/authorcraigmartelle

My web page – https://craigmartelle.com

Made in the USA
Middletown, DE
06 March 2021

34950460R00320